This wasn ~~pupils wer~~ ***sweating.***

He was under the influence. Of what? I would have to restrain him to find out. But he hadn't done this to himself.

He raised the perforator. "I have to drill it out." He turned to Juan's limp, tube-infested body and approached with slow, determined steps.

I took three careful steps closer. "Let me help you, Matt. Give me the burr."

He kept going. Lucia screamed. I shouted too, a desperate last resort. *"Matt.* Turn that burr off. And step away from Juan. *Now,* Matt!"

"Take him down." Ayesha's voice. The tug of her cold hand opening my spastic fist, pressing cold steel there. One of my special dart guns, loaded with a tranquilizer. There was no telling what Matt was high on—I could do him irreversible damage.

Matt touched the perforator to Juan's head. I raised the dart gun, pointed it straight at Matt's carotid.

Dear Reader,

As twenty-first-century citizens of the world, we don't pass a day without hearing news about chemical and biological weapons. With the nuclear variety being too catastrophic to use beyond their deterrent capacity, chemical and biological weapons have become the preemptive weapons of choice.

Luckily, till now, these weapons have had too many shortcomings. Their delivery methods remain deficient, and their degradation during dispersal limits their damage. But the race to rectify their limitations is unrelenting.

In this book, my villain reaches the breakthrough. Combining existing nanotechnology theories and experiments for intelligent drug delivery systems, he manufactures the perfect chemical/biological weapon. Silent, pervasive and impervious. Unstoppable and untreatable.

Until Calista and Damian step in.

I hope that if the same situation comes to pass in the real world, there will be real-life Calistas and Damians to save the affected, find the cure and destroy the weapons and their makers. I hope you enjoy their new adventure. Thank you for reading!

Sincerely,

Olivia Gates

RADICAL
CURE
OLIVIA GATES

Published by Silhouette Books
America's Publisher of Contemporary Romance

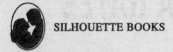

SILHOUETTE BOOKS

ISBN 0-373-51394-1

RADICAL CURE

www.SilhouetteBombshell.com

Printed in U.S.A.

OLIVIA GATES

has followed many dreams in her life. But there was only one she was able to pursue single-mindedly, even though it seemed the most impossible of them all: to write romance novels. The fairy-tale realization of her dreams came after years of constantly learning, writing and sub-mitting her manuscripts, when Harlequin Mills & Boon bought her first Medical Romance book. It was a dream come true, combining her passion for writing, with her vocation—medicine—in one magnificent whole. Now living with her husband and daughter and their cat, she knows dreams are impish little things. They let you catch them only if you pursue them long and hard enough....

To my husband and my mother.
No thanks are enough for helping me live my dream.

Chapter 1

The downpour battering our van became a barrage.

It took me a second. Then I realized.

It wasn't a downpour anymore. It was a side-pour. A rear-pour. And it was no longer water. It was steel. Bullets.

We hadn't been quick enough.

No, no, dammit! We *had* been. But the damn torrential rain had washed down our smoke bombs, cleared our enemies' path.

Those who'd survived.

Made me regret we hadn't made sure no one had.

Okay, Calista St. James. Reality check here. There'd been too many of them. Dozens. And only three of us. As odds went, I should be grateful there still were three, and that we'd gotten out two of the six people we'd smashed into that mini war zone to save.

Grateful was something I rarely was. Never much to be grateful about when we were on one of our regular and too-frequent against-all-odds rescues from grisly situations. This time we were caught in the middle of a white-slavery auction turned gang turf war.

We'd lost more than we'd saved. There'd just been far more gang members than our worst projections. All we'd known, barging in to answer Juan's distress call, had been his choppy and aborted report.

And we hadn't actually saved anyone yet. We'd just reached our van, hadn't even fully secured our two casualties.

Had to change that. Like in the next twenty seconds. Who knew just how armored our van was. Sure sounded like it was getting the ultimate endurance test.

Only bright spot was, the gang filth out there were frothing mad, spewing typical and so-far ineffectual violence, shooting at our bulletproof body rather than going for the sure, fatal shot, our tires.

Couldn't count on their idiocy much longer.

Muffled curses kept tempo with my movements as they sped up, blurred. Every muscle burned, mainly with the effort of blocking out the pain signals. Those were shooting from too many sources and had congealed into a jumbled distress transmission. My lungs sheared against my ribs with exertion, almost a distraction from the rod of agony that ran the length of my vertebral column, pooling in my lumbar area. Almost.

Was it any wonder, after nearly half a mile of forging through solid sheets of pounding water and wading in calf-deep slime and garbage with a comatose woman bleeding all over my back?

I snapped the last harness buckle and glanced at my comrade-in-arms, Lucia. She'd secured the injured Juan. I opened my mouth to yell for her to grab hold before telling Matt to floor it.

I didn't have time to do either. Matt did floor it. And us.

Brutal acceleration interrupted my frantic grab for an anchor, hurled me into Lucia. Her chin and my cheekbone made violent acquaintance. Bright pain burst along with the usual ludicrously inappropriate internal commentary, *There we go—a matching set of black eyes. Make that two sets.*

I twisted in mid-pitch, avoided landing on our female casualty for the price of another bruise on my left hip bone before I took Lucia's taller, heavier body on top and we both crashed to the floor. My lungs deflated. Her weight on me kept them that way. Already taxed, my lungs burned with oxygen deprivation. I still clamped my legs around her body, kept her from falling off me. Moving while Matt was executing that manic getaway-car routine would only buy us more bruises.

Next second the van launched over a huge bump and sailed in the air for what felt like a whole minute. Then it crash-landed, spooling Lucia off me, and we did plenty of the tossing about I'd tried to avoid as the van exploded out of the derelict area, engine howling like a banshee, wheels churning slimy mud.

The gunfire storm had abated, but Matt poured on the speed. A yell gurgled out of my pinned-by-G-force body. "*Matt!* You'll get us killed. Or give us new casualties. Or both!"

I guess he didn't hear my news flash. He yanked the metal behemoth into a hairpin turn, sending Lucia, who still hadn't managed to grab on to something, catapulting over me and into the secondary stretcher's steel support. She cried out. Blood spattered, a hot, sickening fizz on my frozen cheek. Damn!

Her hand lashed out to her head in protective exploration. "Scalp wound…" She gasped her diagnosis, her hand lurching away to grab an anchor. Blood-slick, it slipped.

Damn. *Dammit.* The stretchers and equipment were welded to the floor or harnessed, diminishing chances of further injury to our strapped-down casualties, but all bets were off for our own free-floating bodies.

I snapped open one of the cabinets lining the van's wall, snatched a sterile pressure pad out, tossed it to Lucia. She missed it. Blood was seeping into her eye, and both went into instinctive spasm. I lunged before the pad fell into our muddy tracks, caught it, pressed it into her hand. I helped her into the paramedic seat, then staggered to the driver's compartment.

At the threshold, the part of my mind that was on perpetual macabre and out-of-place-humor duty went, *oh-oh*.

Matt had his huge body hunched over the steering wheel like an overeager kid at the controls of a gory video game. The weeping night outside was filled with fuzzy beacons—on a collision course with us.

He was going against the stream. On the highway.

I stared, lost in that surreal realm of momentary disbelief. Then horror hit, head-on.

Incoming blares yawned to deafening crescendos, dwindled abruptly as headlights veered away in last-microsecond desperation, like moths scared at the advance of a berserk swatter. I screamed that he should get us on the right side of the road. He heard me this time.

Next second made me wish he had ignored me. It'd never been a problem for him to do so and come up with a usually better way of handling matters. I'd said get us on the right side of the road and he just—did. And how. My mouth opened again to shout, but it was too late as he launched over the dividing island, slamming my teeth down on my tongue. Electric blue pain forked straight to my brain.

Couldn't squander any focus on the pain. All my reserves poured into a total-body clamp on the passenger seat, into riding the momentum of the huge arc of screeching cars he passed before he joined the stream. But he wasn't finished spreading mayhem. He accelerated through the cars ahead, his intention seeming to be to ram them if they didn't swerve out of his way fast enough.

I screamed again, *"Matt!"*

His only answer was a rumbled "They're on our tail."

I lurched, peered into the side mirror. So they were.

Then he literally got them there. He slammed his foot down full force on the brakes.

Everything compressed in my heart's next beat. The van

skidding in imploding deceleration. Burning-rubber stench polluting my lungs. Screeching brakes slitting my eardrums. Every cell in my body fast-forwarding to the moment of collision, panic flooding in from all sides…

Then the impact. A brutal jolt from behind, enough to dislodge my very life force one cell at a time. A-hundred-miles-per-hour worth of crashing mass and unspent momentum almost too forceful to feel, too thunderous to hear. It mushroomed through me in a chain reaction. I held on, held together, somehow. The impact went to my only unrestrained part—my brain, floating in its fluids. It didn't stop with the rest of me, tried to ram an exit through my skull.

Existence blinked on and off on the pros and cons of a hard head. On how much the abused organ could stand before it vegetated. And how my last act as a being with any volition had to be filleting Matt alive!

To snatch people in critical condition out of a gang war zone only to kill them in a car crash? Can we say stupidity punishable by death by spitting squad? He was giving reckless driving a suicidal redefinition. Even among stunt drivers. Hell, even among drunk ones. We might as well have stayed and seen the war through. At least we would have died doing something worthwhile.

Darkness receded, crimson fury flooding in its wake. "What's gotten into you, you lunatic?" I snarled.

Matt just put the car in shrieking gear and blasted forward again. My stomach remained half a mile behind. He wiped a soggy dark blond lock from his rugged forehead, shot me a blank glance.

"I got rid of our tail, didn't I?"

He sure had. I doubted anyone would walk out alive from the receding wreck I now barely saw in the side mirror. I could only hope other cars weren't piled up behind them.

"And look who's talking," he added.

Oh, no. He wasn't bringing up my leap-first-and-don't-bother-looking-later affliction. It was he who was jeopardizing everyone now. "If you don't like being called a lunatic, stop earning the name," I snapped. "So you got rid of our tail—and the van's. Yay for you. Now stop trying to get rid of everyone on the road—and your passengers—if you haven't already. That crash could've finished our casualties for all I know."

His bodybuilder's shoulders rose in a distracted gesture and he pressed his foot harder on the gas pedal. I hit him on said dismissive shoulder. "Hey!"

"What?" he grumbled. "I'm under the speed limit!"

"Yeah, for escape velocity! Take the next exit and pull over before Highway Patrol forces us to. I'm driving."

"You mean I'll handle our patients instead?"

Put that way—no. Didn't matter that he was the better trauma surgeon and emergency doctor. He'd just finished letting loose on his biggest ever rampage. The setting, the thugs—this had been too reminiscent of how he'd lost his wife. Best scenario here was he was finding it hard to come down. Worst one was his resident rage was eating through him, a damage potential comparable to a high explosive's. If I had a hard time trusting him with the wheel in his volatile state, I didn't want him anywhere near our casualties. Without immediate intervention, they wouldn't last the hour back. And though his driving didn't stand out so much in the collective lunacy on the highway, we had to get off the busy road, get home through back alleys. A safer but far longer route.

What I had was a load of shitty choices. As usual.

Enough, St. James. Call it.

A breath scraped my spastic bronchi. "Keep driving, Matt. And get us off the highway."

No response. It was only when I poked him that he seemed to register what I'd said. Then he mumbled, "It's the quickest way."

Frustration, hot and stinging, surged, augmenting my whole-body distress. "Yeah, to get arrested. You did notice we're riding a bullet-riddled, smashed-up van fleeing the scene of a massive accident and chock-full of unlicensed medical personnel and critically injured people, didn't you? Get us arrested now and you'll bring our whole operation down."

"Yeah, and I really needed that lecture," he growled, screeched into the next exit. "I got us away, we're in one piece. I'm keeping it that way."

I waited for my stomach to fit back roughly in the space it usually occupied, hissed when I was no longer gagging on it. "No bets on the latter part of your statement. Take it easier, okay?"

I was talking to his absent profile. What *was* this?

This, whatever it was, didn't matter now. *Snap to it, St. James!*

I gave the cars scattering out of the van's path, and my friend—precariously designated so at the moment—one last exasperated glance and let go of my anchor.

"Matt's done trying to kill us?" Lucia burst out the moment I staggered into the back compartment.

"Yeah—I guess. Let's move it."

She snapped off her seat belt, exploded to her feet. We snatched open cabinets, hauled out equipment. I hooked up the suctioning device as she dragged out syringes, saline bags, giving sets and gloves. I caught the pair she tossed me, snapped them on, turned to our patients.

"Clear airways." I made way for her to suction their throats, swooped for the drugs needed for intubation. It wouldn't do for them to regain consciousness or gag while I was doing it.

I kept my eyes off our casualties' faces. Off Juan's. Yeah, I knew him. Well. At least I knew the gregarious, fizzing-with-vitality Juan, not this pulpy, motionless mess.

Stop it. Couldn't afford to let blind emotion into the mix now.

Neither I nor Lucia. She wouldn't allow it. She was a pro. She'd handle it. She had to.

I loaded two syringes, snatched up Juan's arm, struggled for balance and to hit a collapsed vein. I missed three times, heard growls. Mine. Vocal, murderous frustration.

Once I connected, I dumped the load in one pump. With a head injury, IV lidocaine served a dual purpose—anesthesia, and minimizing a rise in intracranial pressure. For the girl, with her gunshot chest injury, an anesthetic wasn't on. Succinylcholine for her, a muscle relaxant instead. At least I could administer that intramuscularly.

"What was that about?" Lucia's wobbly voice filtered through the gargling of heavy secretions shooting up the suctioning tubes.

"Matt's high on an adrenaline overdose. He's over it—" I pumped the SC just as the van launched and crash-landed again. Damn. The needle could have broken in her flesh. "I guess."

Lucia finished suctioning and turned to recording pulse and pressure. "Sure is a sound decision letting our resident berserker drive!" Her voice was fractured with tension and anxiety.

I laid out the intubation gear, assembled the laryngoscope, took my place at the girl's head. "Would you rather have him back here, Lucci?"

Her startled glare said it all. No, she wouldn't. And Matt's berserkerdom wasn't why. She had an overblown view of my skills. To her I was the best.

Living up to her expectations was a pain. I didn't fancy being anyone's role model—or idol. In fact, I hated it. Couldn't figure out how I'd ended up being hers. Foolish girl. A little crazy even. She'd joined my team, hadn't she?

Yeah. Crazy. But what else could each member of my team be? All were medical people who'd relinquished positions, normality and safety to join me in this mad life, forming what I euphemistically called an "extralegal medical task force," our humanitarian aid/vigilante outfit that didn't just reach out to the sick, injured and downtrodden, but defied the system, went after the criminals and oppressors and exacted punishment. Not to mention relieved them of their considerable earnings, using the money to finance our Sanctuaries, where we offered comprehensive medical and many other services to all who needed help and couldn't get or afford it.

Lucia was the youngest of our "core eight"—me and the first seven to believe in my cause and make it a reality. She was developing into a hell of a fighter and the best trauma and surgical nurse this side of Ayesha. She was giving me textbook assistance with everything working against her. Unasked, she released our casualties' heads, managing to hold them in optimal position to protect against cervical injury, providing the best in-line stabilization for me to slip my laryngoscope between their vocal cords and slide the endotracheal tubes down their throats. On first trial each.

First chance I got, I was treating her to that girls' night out on the town I'd once promised her.

Yeah, sure. Like she'd want it now. Should have done it the moment the urge formed. Shouldn't have postponed it to a phantom "later." In our line of work, later meant *probably never.*

I secured the endotracheal tubes, started delivering one hundred percent O2 into lungs that could no longer do their job unaided. Lucia gave me more dismal news: plummeting pulse and pressure.

Had to pump fluids into them, up their blood volume. Putting cannulas in their veins would be a nightmare right now. Wouldn't be the first time—or the hundredth. Our grisly and regular practice over the past four years had been handling emergencies in against-all-odds conditions, in record times.

I snapped a glance at Lucia, found her forehead scrunched in distress, her cheeks shuddering with suppressed anguish. God, how I wished I could spare her help. Spare *her.* This wasn't hitting close to home for her. This was right inside it.

This was Juan, her little brother, lying there dying.

Had to distract her the best I could. "Get me central venous access on the girl. And two wide-bore peripherals. Ringers. Open lines wide. And hook to cardiac monitor and oximeter. BP and O2 sats every five minutes. I'll take Juan."

Didn't think this would minimize her suffering. Had nothing more to offer her. She went to work, silent tears forming pale paths down her smeared cheeks.

It had been Juan's distress call we'd answered at 2:00 a.m. He and a few friends, all but Juan illegal immigrants, had landed themselves in the middle of the white-slavery auction. Their girl-friends had been kidnapped for the sale. They'd been trying to get the women out when another gang crashed the scene, started eliminating the "merchandise" to drive their displeasure home—and the turf war had exploded.

Amid a backdrop of rabid violence, Juan had panted a picture of the macabre scene. Just. We'd had first-row audio seats to his bludgeoning. Even with Lucia's ear pressed to the phone I'd heard the gut-heaving sounds. Bone and tissue squishing under force.

Matt, Lucia and I had been manning the crisis post, as always. We three didn't have much of a life outside our business to lure us away. Ironic really. Of the core eight, we'd probably be the three voted most attractive to the opposite sex. And yet, all we did was scare, alienate or get our potential lovers killed.

I was in a league of my own, though. I scared men off on auto, was doing my damnedest to alienate the one man I could love. And I hadn't gotten the one who'd loved me killed. I'd killed him myself.

Anyway, we'd had no time to lose. The others had arrived too late to do anything but wait for our field report and get primed to receive the injured. Or to retrieve our bodies.

Once we'd located the victims, Matt and Lucia had covered me and blasted away attackers. I'd still had only seconds to examine Juan and the others. Three had already been cold. Three, including Juan, had been EVS, exhibiting vital signs as we called it. I'd had enough experience with the gutted and gored to know that every trick in the book might not get them back to the Sanctuary with any life left to work with. One of the three, a girl, beautiful, damaged, had been by far the worst.

And I'd done the impossible. I'd sacrificed her. Left her behind to expire under the feet of those warring wastes of tissue, while we rescued Juan and the woman with us now.

Lord, I *abhorred* triage! Being forced to prioritize those who stood a better chance—it polluted my soul.

I wondered how many times I'd made the wrong decision, how many I'd sentenced to death this way…. *No time to ponder your crimes of omission. Save those you prioritized!*

"Her name is Mercedes—" Lucia suddenly choked.

Mercy. As if I needed to know that now.

Knowing a casualty's name always rocketed my aggression–oppression levels to exponential heights. And with *her* name… A wave of vicious glee rolled inside me. Lovely to look back and remember I'd shown her would-be murderers none.

If my measures failed now, I'd be back for those I missed. I'd be back anyway.

It was what I did.

"You think this'll do any good?" Lucia's hands deftly cleaned Juan's face and blood-, gravel- and mud-matted black hair, her whisper a tear-soaked tremolo.

God only knows why we whispered around comatose casualties. Guess we believed they'd hear us, freak out, give up, if we divulged our pessimism.

I palpated his depressed fracture among the coagulating mess, felt a permanent furrow cleaving into my forehead. Did I think anything we did would make a difference? Did I ever? I didn't have an answer for Lucia. Never would.

So don't answer. Take this away from dread and drowning in morbidity. Get down to business. "Call ahead. Have the team prepare OR—two stations and twenty units of O-neg. Get me Al and Savannah. I need them to handle one of these two."

Juan? Her bloody gloved hand clamped mine. The furrow pleated all the way down to my heart. I did what I would have given anything not to do. I shook my head. *Not Juan.*

She wrenched free, her eyes gushing her agony and relief. *Sheesh.* I really had to dispel her mythical opinion of my surgical prowess.

But though I'd just promised to handle Juan myself, Mercedes was more critical now.

I turned to her, pressed my stethoscope around the single bullet entry wound marring the perfection of her firm, young flesh, right beside the nipple of her left breast. Her smothered heartbeats, plummeting blood pressure and nonexistent breath sounds made the diagnosis for me.

I murmured it to Lucia. "Tension hemopneumothorax." Air and blood leaking out of one lung, collapsing it, pressuring the other and the heart, stopping their function. Rapidly fatal.

"Thoracostomy needle." It materialized in Lucia's hand, moved to mine, was between Mercedes's ribs in seconds. The characteristic rush of air hissed over the shrieking of the engine. Comparative tension leaked out of my spastic, screaming muscles. Air down—or should I say out? Now the blood. "Recline the stretcher up, sixty degrees. Scalpel and thoracostomy tube."

She carried out my orders. "Local anesthesia?"

"No time." I sliced between the lower ribs, extended the opening through her muscles and pleura with my finger, inserted the tube, hooked it to an underwater-seal drainage bottle. Blood gushed into it. Her lungs should expand. Her heart, too, should start to beat again. *Should.* But what was as it should be here?

Time expanded, warped. I no longer heard the rumbling of the engine or felt the heaving of the van. My eyes were glued to the monitors. They looked static, locked into their dismal-news patterns. My gaze dropped to my wristwatch. Had its damn hands frozen, too? Could it be just ten minutes since we'd returned to the van? And less than a minute since Mercedes's thoracostomy?

Had to do something before my nuts and bolts started loosening. We'd taken care of the ABCs—airway, breathing and circulation. I turned to D, checking for disability, and E, exposure, searching for injuries other than the obvious ones.

Juan and Mercedes had a Glasgow Coma Score of six and seven respectively. The panel for assessing neurological status, scoring eye opening, verbal and motor responses was my only way of assessing theirs now. Less than eight was bad news. Real bad.

But in Mercedes's case her circulatory collapse explained her depressed consciousness. Juan's condition could be anything from severe reversible brain edema to irreversible brain damage. Couldn't begin to guess which without CTs.

I found no more injuries on either. That was something at least. Something that felt like less than nothing.

"Mannitol bolus in Juan's central line, Lucci," I hissed as I catheterized him. That should bring down brain edema, lower intracranial pressure. Had to raise his blood pressure, too. Had to keep his positive pressure ventilation going. Everything to improve blood and oxygen delivery to his brain, guard against secondary brain damage. I hoped.

Nothing more to do until they responded. Nothing but wait.

I had issues with waiting. With standing aside, helpless.

Issues? *There* was a gross euphemism for what ranged from simmering rage to explosive violence. And one temporary-insanity episode, more than six years ago.

I'd been Preemptive Anti-Terrorist Squad's Global Crisis Alliance combat-doctor tagalong on a rescue-evac mission in Darfur. When mercenaries had attacked the villagers we were trying to help, my mission leader, Damian De Luna, had ordered me to leave the sickest to their fate. I could still close my eyes and vibrate with the eruption of madness, burn with the suicidal intentions that had ended in me saving my patients but causing the death of two of Damian's men. And Melissa. His lover.

Damian had banded with PATS's head honchos and my bosses and gotten me kicked out of GCA. Even Sir Ashton, GCA's director then, hadn't been able to defend me, his protégé. Hadn't been able to stop them from revoking my medical license for good measure.

Four years later, forced to work with me again in Russia, Damian had revealed that he considered his peoples' blood to be on his hands, not mine. He'd ordered them to their deaths to save me. He'd ended my career not to punish me, but to stop me before I killed myself. Or worse. He'd been right. I'd been high on fanatic fervor and newfound abilities. I'd needed stopping.

Not that I'd stopped. Just found my brakes. I hoped. Damian's actions had triggered the chain reaction that led to my becoming who I was now. Still, my demons writhed constantly at the end of their throttling leash. The damn things lived for nights like this—to be let loose. I sure was my father's daughter.

Must be in my genes, taking the law into my hands when vermin gnawed holes in it to scamper free, spreading sickness and madness. I exterminated them, just like my father had before me. Just like he still did. From prison…

"Juan's BP is ninety over fifty." Lucia's statement jogged me back to our current crisis.

Better. But not enough. Had to keep the gap between arterial and intracranial pressure above seventy. I checked his urine output. Adequate. No danger of overloading his system then. "Hang two more bags. Normal saline this time. Open as wide as you can."

"You think he—th-*they* stand a chance?" Lucia drove at me with another version of the question consuming her.

I listened to Mercedes's chest before answering. "Air entry

better on the right side. Not so much on the left. Heartbeat not at all. I don't know, Lucia." Lucia's puffed-out face showed no traces of her unusual beauty. Now it crumpled, a mask shriveling in the flames of desperation and dread. If only I could lie. Comfort her. I couldn't. "We can only do our best and wait."

So we did. Our best. Then waited, helpless.

I'd done that, been that, too many times. I'd hung around, futility trampling me, as my baby sister died needlessly feet away on an operating table. As my father was dragged out of my grasp and locked away forever. As my mother slipped through my fingers and disappeared.

But Mercedes with her punctured chest…she echoed the horror and despair of another time.

Four months ago on a crisp October day. In a cave in the Caucasus Mountains on the Russian border. In the ghastly epilogue to the hostage-retrieval mission that had turned out to be anything but. Stumbling in on the only two men I'd ever loved, to find one torturing the other to death.

I'd stopped Damian, protected Jake, demanded answers from both at gunpoint. Got more mental blows with every accusation they'd hurled at each other. Then the final shock—when Jake had shot Damian. In cold blood. Through the heart.

It had become clear then. Both were consummate liars. But one of them—Jake—was a megalomaniac with a genocidal agenda.

And I'd had to let him escape. Damian had lain at my feet, his heart suffocating on its own blood, every beat sweeping him away from me forever.

God. I'd thought that Damian was beyond me. Beyond anything. Had to admit though, handling Mercedes' injury felt nothing like handling Damian's. I wouldn't want to die if she did. Guess it was only human—read primitive and unreasoning—to feel desperation chomping holes in my heart, to feel my will to live fading when my lover was dying.

Well, he *wasn't* my lover. My mentor, sure. My nemesis for quite a while, certainly. My unwilling ally and indispensable partner when circumstances dictated, yeah. But not my lover.

So I loved him, but what's that got to do with anything? So I had slept with him, but it was only one time…. Okay, so it was one *night,* one endless, transfiguring, sex-fest of a night, but…

Okay. Fine. Let's call him my lover, just for simplification's sake.

But the situation had been more desperate then for other reasons, too. Hemopneumothorax had nothing on cardiac tamponade. *That* topped the list of rapidly fatal injuries.

One of his heart's great vessels had been ripped, strangling it in its own leaking blood. I was in a cave, alone, with minimal equipment. Going mad, going to pieces and going numb hadn't been helping either. I'd had to stick a needle into his pericardium, siphon off the strangulating blood. Over and over. I'd prayed and wept and begged for him to hang on.

And he had. We'd sawed open his chest and sewed up his injuries. He'd given up a couple of times—his heart had stopped in my hands. But I'd pumped it back to life.

Then I'd gone after Jake and pumped his full of poison.

I hadn't stuck around for Jake's last heartbeat. I'd run. But not before he'd had his final revenge on me. He'd left me with a festering curse. His last look of reproach—and absolute love.

"Her pressure's going up." Lucia's hoarse words knocked down the constricting walls of memories. I let go, let tremors engulf me. It always felt like a stay of execution when a critical patient responded.

"You're doing great, Mercedes." As we worked around our patients, I always talked to them, hoped they could feel me fighting for them, tiding them over the worst. "Just hold on a little longer and I'll fix you up." *If* she could be fixed.

Chapter 2

Matt got us to the Sanctuary in one piece. Our patients were hanging on. Just.

Lucia and I snapped the bullet-riddled doors open and were jumping out before the van came to a screeching stop, kicking up mold-infested sludge in the Sanctuary's back alley entrance.

Ayesha ran out to meet us, her long, powerful ebony body swathed in black, looking nothing like the angel of mercy that she was. Our trauma team was right behind, part of the forty-two medical personnel that now made up the Sanctuary staff. They swooped en masse, fluidly practiced, überefficient, transporting our casualties inside, with every care taken, in under a minute.

I ran next to Fadel and Ishmael. "Get me head CTs on Juan, stat. Use the 64-slice-per-second machine."

They shot me surprised glances. Ishmael articulated his skepticism. "You reported possible intracranial hemorrhage. Shouldn't we go for craniotomy at once?"

I shook my head. "Controlling ICP is more important to

preventing brain herniation and to prognosis than prompt hematoma evacuation. And CT isn't a luxury here. It's a crucial emergency measure, *especially* if we operate. If hemorrhage is collecting inside there somewhere, knowing exactly *where* will mean a precise approach during surgery. Anyway, our new CT will wrap up the whole thing in seconds. If he deteriorates he'll be on the table in a heartbeat. Just watch out to keep both his systolic pressure and O2 sats above ninety."

Ishmael nodded, accepting my decision. My heart fired. Dread never went away, never lessened. Every time, with each injection and procedure and diagnosis, every wielding-power-over-life decision, everything inside me quivered, went queasy with fear. What if I was wrong?

God, where was Matt now? He should be handling this, taking over, taking responsibility.

My gaze and thoughts followed Ishmael and Fadel as they directed their team, wheeling Juan to the CT suite, a synchronized machine I knew would do the job in minimal time.

They were another two of my core eight. An ultimate example of what we were all about. Could any two people be more different? Each came from a different world, poles apart in every way. Age, race, background, character. Yet they were the same. On top of their game, dedicated and not a little wacky. At least by this world's definition, a world that glorified conformity and the pursuit of personal safety and gain. Our Sanctuary was a miniature United Nations of the unorthodox and intrepid, an asylum for misfits who'd decided there had to be another way and were trying as hard as they could to find it. Just knowing they existed made this planet habitable. Yeah. They were reason enough.

Too bad they weren't the dominant species. But we'd banded together, our numbers were growing. We'd get there. One day.

Ayesha's prompting touch dragged my focus back. "Let's get you ready for surgery."

Ready? How could I ever be when I stuck myself between

health and handicap, life and death, taking the responsibility of minimizing damage and warding off mortality? When I invaded a person's fate with my scalpel and imperfect knowledge?

I ran to Scrubbing and Gowning. The preoperative rituals helped. Swathed me in the illusion of control, preparedness. "You got Al and Savvy?" I yanked off wet, blood-splattered clothes.

She nodded. "They're on their way any second now."

"I'm leaving them the cardiothoracic case."

She blinked. "Thought you'd leave them the head injury. You hate head injuries."

"Yeah, and they love me. Personally and professionally." I snapped up the soap, worked a furious lather. "I promised Lucia." Her trembling hand and eloquent tears had bound me, inextricable as a blood oath. *If he dies, I want him to die with you fighting for him,* they'd said.

A cold fist unfurled in my chest. Times like this made me want to renege on all my vows, go hide somewhere responsibility free. Made me wonder why I wasn't hanging up my drugs and guns, tracking down Mom and joining her in whatever reclusive serenity she'd found.

Times like this I was also grateful I'd trained to do something about life's atrocities, was equipped to fight back, on so many levels now. Whether I made a difference or not remained to be seen. Which was never the issue. Trying was.

I finished scrubbing, held my hands up to dry, for Ayesha to snap gloves on them. What would I do without her? My left hand—she called herself that. To me, she was my back. She *got* my back, made it all possible. She anchored my resolve, shared my quirks, amplified my strength. She understood.

Too much sometimes. Like now. Her interrogating gaze asked first. Then she made it vocal. "How many did you lose?"

I exhaled, severed eye contact, jumped into scrubs. The confession was still wrung from me. "Of Juan's party alone, four. Three already lost. One, I left."

She gritted her teeth, ran ahead, put her back to the OR's swinging door. "How many did you take out?"

I ignored the question, rushed inside, took in the scene. Mercedes being cleaned up and prepped, Ishmael and Fadel wheeling Juan in, others wrapping up pre-op routines, getting all necessary supplies and blood works. My eyes snapped back to Ayesha. She was waiting for her answer, patiently. Imperatively. I shrugged.

"I didn't count. I *lost* count."

"Good." Ayesha's rich voice was even. Calm. Ruthless.

Good thing she was on our side.

Al and Savannah burst into the OR right behind us.

"What have you got for us?" Savvy, already gowned and masked, asked without even looking at me, her eyes where they should be, scanning for the patient she'd come to fight for.

"Close-range, high-caliber bullet, lower left chest. Massive hemopneumothorax, collapsed left lung. Chest tube in place, which evacuated over a liter of blood with more still coming. On aggressive fluid replacement. No transfusion. She'll just bleed it back through the injuries. She needs a thoracostomy stat to plug the holes."

With Savvy's deep scarlet hair and stunning face smothered in cap and mask, only her angelic blue eyes displayed her reaction. She was a new recruit and a damn good surgeon. A little weird, too. Had to be, to choose wading in blood and waging endless battles on the side of outnumbered good guys for a living. *Welcome to the club,* I'd said the day she'd hooked up with us two months ago.

She'd heard stories of a probably mythical task force that dispensed aid outside every public and private system. An outfit that didn't only save victims but went after aggressors, that didn't only rehabilitate drug addicts but wiped out drug lords and made use of their spoils to finance more cleanup and aid operations, and to stock up on a unique arsenal of drug-based weapons and a full range of both improvised and conventional ones.

She'd searched for us for a long time. *We'd* found *her*, taken her in.

Poor kid was still in over her head. Kid? Sure. At thirty-two, she was more than two years my senior, but she still seemed so much younger. Or I felt way older. Had to be my insane life, the weight of experience accelerating my psychological aging.

Savannah nodded now, past the first jolt, and joined Al, who'd made his assessment and was barking his preparatory measures. They started their surgery.

I couldn't move so fast with Juan. A head injury was a totally different animal. No use opening his skull up to relieve building pressure if his cerebral perfusion pressure wasn't under control. He'd only end up brain dead, even if I got him picture-perfect surgically. I had to give him the chance to stabilize before I resorted to the most hazardous procedure.

Doug rushed in with CT printouts and 3-D reconstructions. I pounced on him at the door, snatched them from his hands, calling out to Haiku at the same time. As the only anesthetist we could round up tonight, she'd handle both cases.

"How's Juan?"

Haiku raised her head from finishing Mercedes's anesthesia, tossed me the relevant stuff. "BP eighty over fifty."

No good. I needed his BP over ninety to keep his cerebral perfusion pressure up, the real factor in keeping the brain oxygenated. Time to play hardball.

I snapped the CT films on the backlit screen, called out measures. "Lucia, rapid norepinephrine infusion, 4 mg in 250 mL saline. Repeat until Juan's pressure stabilizes at a 100 mean arterial. Haiku, hyperventilate, mannitol 1 mg per kg bolus, and raise his head to get his intracranial pressure down. Get me a jugular oximeter for O2 sats. Ayesha—get me a transcranial Doppler and let's place an intracranial pressure monitor. We'll drain cerebrospinal fluid through it if needed. Be ready to initiate barbiturate coma, too. And for God's sake—where's Matt?"

I needed him with me on this. I needed him to do this, if we operated. Intracranial procedures weren't my forte. They were definitely his. I hoped he'd calmed down by now.

"I'm here. I'll take care of it."

Matt, his voice a shower of gravel pelting my bruised back. Wincing, I turned around. Winced again.

Matt was gowned but maskless, his rugged, handsome face sallow, pinched. But it was his eyes that worried me. The sea-green, perpetually alert probes were turbid, spaced out.

Nope. He hadn't calmed down. Man. Like I needed this. My best surgeon tripping on stress hormones. Riding the adrenaline breakers while extracting our casualties had been one thing, hadn't been bad. Had been good even. His berserker violence had gotten us out in one piece.

Yeah, then had almost smashed us to pieces. Behind the wheel he'd sure put a new spin on the phrase *narrow escape*. I still couldn't believe we weren't all lying here battered and comatose on the OR tables beside Juan and Merecedes.

But the adrenaline theory was fast losing favor. This looked like a harder trip—a real drug? Matt? Nah. Never.

Maybe it was the antihistamines he'd been gobbling down for his rhinitis. I'd seen people go from agitated to depressed to disoriented under their effect. No wonder the drugs came with dire warnings not to drive or operate machinery while under their influence. Last time I popped a tablet I had become almost suicidal.

But Matt was a hay fever and antihistamines veteran. He'd never had adverse reactions to them. So—maybe he was trying out a new generation or a combination that was knocking him for six?

Whatever. Didn't matter. Time to count our blessings and our in-one-piece bones and tell him to sit this one out. No way was he performing brain surgery in this shape. I hated to do it, but better me than him handling this operation right now.

I sighed as he passed behind me. "We're fine here. Juan's BP's going up and so's his cerebral perfusion pressure. We'll get him stabilized, then we'll review his CTs, decide how to proceed…."

Had he just ignored me? Yep. Still upset over my criticism of his demolition-derby driving? Probably. Goody.

He picked up a pin, ran it on the insides of Juan's arms, conducting another neuro exam. Good idea—if he wasn't scraping Juan's skin. Even from here, I saw livid scratches forming. On the last sweep across Juan's inner thigh, he drew blood. The hairs on my nape stood on end.

Matt didn't make mistakes like that!

It took the others swinging what-the-hell gazes from him to me to make me believe he just had. His pin was going deeper when I swooped down and snatched it away. "What are you doing?"

He just murmured, to himself it seemed, "Abnormal flexion, unilateral posturing. Must drill him open."

I snorted. "Yeah, sure. Why stabilize him and consult CTs when we can just drill him blind and finish him off right away? Okay, Matt, you've had it for tonight. Go sleep it off."

That came out harsher than I had intended. Guess I'd reached my limit for the night, too.

Matt did more than ignore me this time. His green gaze swung up, slammed into me. Everything inside me cringed. Never thought I'd be on the receiving end of his wrath. I opened my lips, something confused and concerned forming there.

He rammed it down my throat.

The shock hit first. Then, like a hurtling missile, the bone-cracking force of his blow registered.

My brain knocked against my skull. Reality wavered. Jagged pain burst, more behind my ribs than in my shoulder and jaw. I clung to his arm instinctively, my mind crashing, refusing to process the situation, his actions. *Not Matt.*

He shook me off, his massive body seeming to expand, an appalling sound spilling from him. I staggered back and he charged after me, snatched me up by the arms and hurled me away. I sailed back in the air, too enervated to twist into a safe landing. I slammed to the polished OR floor, right hip bone first, skidded, a headfirst collision into the autoclave aborting my momentum.

My consciousness flickered on images of Fadel and Ishmael jumping Matt. A wheeze wouldn't make it past my lips. *Not that way, you fools! He'll pulverize you!*

He did. The sickening sound of colliding flesh and bone reverberated in mine. Fadel was launched back with the force of the blow, already unconscious. Ishmael was flung into the horrified team deep in the middle of Mercedes's cardiothoracic surgery. The chain reaction took them down one after the other. Along with the anesthesia station—and Mercedes.

Time stuttered as she slumped off the table, slammed to the floor, disconnected from the heart-lung and anesthesia machines, her chest gaping wide, her heart exposed, her blood everywhere.

Okay, Calista St. James. You've cracked up.

This had to be all in my mind. It made sense. Nightmares crowded my waking and sleeping existence. Could I no longer turn them off, differentiate them from reality?

And here was my ultimate phobia—another of my loved ones turning into a madman I had to stop. At any cost.

What was I thinking? Matt had lost it, but his blind rage and aggression were nothing like Jake's long-calculated, ghoulish evil and genocidal intentions. I'd contain Matt—defuse him....

Somebody else do it this time—please!

There was nobody else. The others were struggling to restore Mercedes to the table, to straighten the upturned machines and replace the destroyed ones. Leaving Matt to me.

Matt, and the burr-hole perforator he'd reached for.

It was plugged in. He turned it on.

No.

Denial, suffocating, paralyzing—couldn't rationalize, couldn't process... *What was going on?*

Doesn't matter. Go to pieces later. Stop him—now!

A scenario played in my mind. Skirting him, knocking the perforator away and... No. In his condition, engaging him would only earn us more injuries—or worse. No way could I subdue him without inflicting serious damage on him. Without maximum force...

No way. Never. Had to find another way. Had to.

I staggered to my feet, injecting every scorching move with ease, forced to raise my voice over the burr's marrow-drilling whine. "C'mon, Matt, don't be so angry at me. I'm sorry I snapped."

"I'm in charge," he rasped. Was that directed at me?

Didn't think so. I ventured another step toward him as he stared at the perforator wobbling furiously in his hand. "Sure, Matt. I was waiting for you to decide to take over."

He looked up, through me, his words a deluge of passion. "I'll never let you out of my sight. No one will ever touch you." He suddenly roared a hair-raising laugh. "I ripped them apart alive, made them watch and wait their turns. I do it again, every day. I dance over their severed parts."

God. This was definitely not directed at me. He was halluci-nating. About his wife? And the vermin who'd kidnapped and raped her to death? He'd caught up with them, gotten—even. I hadn't asked how. So that was how. Was it why he'd snapped now? Having lived that atrocity, reciprocated in kind?

But I'd been there for him all through. He'd never lost co-herence. Never turned on his friends. On me. Going psychotic wasn't in his makeup. *Like it hadn't been in Jake's?*

No. Matt was different. This wasn't a breakdown. His pupils were dilated; he was pale and sweating rivers. He was under the influence. Of what, I had to restrain him to find out, to counteract it. And he hadn't done this to himself. No freaking way. He'd been poisoned. How, who and what, I'd find out later.

Maybe I could still reach him. "Let me help, please."

He shook his head, his voice a bleeding cry. "None of it matters. I can't kill enough of them to bring you back, to say I'm sorry. *To make your screams stop.*"

Oh God. Oh, *Matt...*

He raised the perforator. "But I've found the way. I have to drill it out of my brain."

He turned to Juan's limp, tube-infested body. "See how sick I look? Once it's drilled out of my brain, I'll be whole again." He nodded to himself, approached Juan with slow, determined steps.

A collective cry echoed. Lucia screamed. My hand chopped a silencing motion. *Don't antagonize him.*

I took three careful steps closer. "Let me help you, Matt. Give me the burr and I'll remove all your pain."

He kept on going. Lucia screamed again, begged. I shouted, too, a desperate last resort.

"*Matt!* Turn that burr off. And step away from Juan. *Now,* Matt!"

He touched the perforator to Juan's head. We all exploded.

I reached him first, got folded over his foot and almost broke in two, slammed to the floor again. Lucia threw herself at the electric cord, got a vicious kick to her head and crumpled, blood seeping from her mouth. Ishmael fell, bellowing, the drill in Matt's hand spattering tissue gouged out of his shoulder.

It was happening all over again.

Like Jake. My first lover. He'd forced me to execute him. Now Matt.

Something corrosive scorched down my middle, my cheeks.

"Take him down." Ayesha's voice, coming from another dimension. Frantic. The tug of her cold hand opening my spastic fist, pressing colder steel there. One of my special dart guns, loaded with enough tranquilizer to fell two men.

Matt's foot rammed into Doug's face. He'd disposed of everyone now. Then he bellowed and advanced on Juan again.

I raised the dart gun, pointed it straight at his carotid.

Chapter 3

All I had to do was shoot him.

He'd go down in seconds.

I couldn't. I'd die before I hurt him, and I could do more than hurt him now. No telling what he was high on. Couldn't risk adding such a chemical blow to the explosive mix tampering with his physiology. That was why I'd struck drugs off my list of options to subdue him—I could do him irreversible damage. Or kill him.

My urgent gesture brought Ayesha immediately behind me, close enough to be the only one to hear me. "Air Taser," I hissed. "I distract him, you shoot him. Set on minimum. No idea what more electricity will do to his fried synapses."

She streaked out of OR and I shouted to Matt, trying to drag his focus away from Juan. Didn't work.

Had to do this the hardest way.

As I snatched my scrubs off, my throat split on a curdling scream of his name. The perforator snagged in Juan's hair. I gave a desperate running start, launched into a *yoko tobi geri*.

The force of the flying side kick impacted the hand holding the perforator. Matt staggered back but didn't drop it. *Damn.* He crouched on the floor, preparing to heave himself up to his feet. *Now. Your only chance.* I swiveled into a minor *mawashi geri,* a roundhouse kick targeting his screeching weapon, connected again. Nothing. Was it welded to his hand or what?

On expending my momentum, my other leg landed in his large hand. He snatched at it. I yelled as my leg disappeared from under me, the other still not on the ground. I slammed on my back, new pain accumulating on old, deluging me.

The others tried to jump him then, to disconnect the perforator. Got slammed back one after another. Then I was looking the drilling end of the madly rotating perforator right in the eye.

I gripped his forearm, pushed it away with both of mine, with all I had. That was nothing compared to his power. I'd lose this arm-wrestling contest in seconds.

Where is Ayesha?

Matt suddenly stiffened, convulsed.

Bless you. The Taser.

Bad news was I got a secondary taste of the electro-muscular disruption. The current shrieked up my nervous pathways with jolting pain and loss of control. And the perforator was falling out of Matt's enervated hand, heading for my belly, like a malevolent sentient machine, bent on puncturing me. I used the last of my volition, caught it and groped for the off switch. It jerked and bucked in my spastic hands, grazing me across the abdomen. Then it went dead.

Ayesha had yanked out the power cord. But it wasn't over.

Like an unstoppable monster in an urban legend, Matt had overcome the jolt's effects, was pushing to his legs. I was, too. Nerves still discharging, I threw myself at his legs in a pincer tackle. He wasn't going anywhere.

The massive force of his violent kick would have pulverized my face had it connected. It didn't. I twisted out of range and his foot connected with my breast. I went blind, buried under an avalanche of agony.

I fought my way out of it just in time to see Ayesha going after him with another stun gun, the first one's hooks still deep in his skin. He tore them out, punched her in the jaw. Blood spattered from her lip in a wide arc, hit my cheek. Then she fell on me.

He stood in the middle of the carnage for a second, bellowing like an enraged, wounded lion. Then he burst out of OR.

I struggled from beneath the moaning Ayesha, got to my feet after him, horror and anguish almost eating through me.

Couldn't stop. Couldn't let him out of my sight.

He ran outside, ramming our security guards left and right, his explosive violence and superior strength bringing them down one after another. He snatched a weapon from the last one before he raced out of the Sanctuary.

He was making it impossible. Impossible to bring him down without hurting him. Without killing him. No—*no!*

"Listen to me!" I shouted at the security guards who were struggling to their feet, more shocked at their boss's rampage than injured. "We go after him. I'll charge him. Even if he shoots me, don't stop and don't hurt him. Just jump him, all together. Don't let go before you disarm him and restrain—"

Haiku's shout over the com-system had the words backlashing in my throat. "Cali! Juan has a unilaterally dilated pupil! His ICP has shot up to sixty!"

Damn, damn, *damn!* An impending transtentorial herniation. In the time he'd been deprived of medications during the fight, intracranial pressure had increased so much that his brain was trying to squeeze out of the base of his skull. Had to stop it.

Had to stop Matt.

Couldn't do both.

Couldn't trust anyone but me to stop Matt. The police would probably shoot him to subdue him. Maybe on sight. At best, they'd give him the dangerous-lunatic drill and bring him down with a heavy tranquilizer. Couldn't have that.

I grabbed one of our gofers. "Listen carefully. Go to OR, tell them to shave our patient and initiate barbiturate coma. And to repeat the interrupted drug protocol. If either Al or Savvy can be spared, tell them to proceed with a craniotomy."

I let him go after he'd repeated my message word for word. Then I ran to get me some silent, incapacitating weapons. Just as I stacked my bag of tricks, the com-system crackled again. Al.

"Cali, Mercedes is slipping, we're barely holding on to her. You come take care of Juan."

I couldn't leave Matt to his fate. To rampage out there, to kill or get killed. I could trust only one other person to bring him back safe. Damian.

He'd recovered from that bullet through the heart, thanks to his supreme physical fitness. And he was more than a match for Matt at his worst. He cared for Matt, too. Considered him a sort of brother-in-arms. I knew exactly what lengths Damian would go to, in the name of love and friendship, firsthand.

And I hated him for it.

Right now, it made him my only chance.

Problem was, he'd said he was no longer having me watched and followed. He'd promised never to do it again. That would make him of no use to me now. By the time he came over from wherever he was, Matt's trail would be cold. Only if he had his sentries somewhere nearby could he intervene quickly enough.

I groped for my cell phone, speed-dialed his number. He picked up before the first ring was over. Had it been on auto-answer?

"Calista." There was no surprise in his tone. No curiosity. This wasn't a probing greeting. It was an acknowledgment laced with a fathoms-deep welcome. Relief even. I hadn't returned his calls in over a month.

I wondered why he took it from me. Would have figured he'd consign me to the hell where alpha men believed capricious women belonged, and gotten on with his life. He hadn't.

"Damian, I need you."

"I'm listening."

He'd caught on that I wasn't inviting him to all-out sex, his voice no longer washing over me with that encompassing passion that messed with logic and priorities. He had his ultimate black-ops operative component back in the control room.

I panted out the situation, feeling the seconds taking Matt farther away from hope of retrieval—like quicksand, sucking what was left of my sanity.

It was only then that I realized Damian was driving, fast. In some other pursuit? Then he put me on hold. By the time he came back, I was screaming for him to talk to me.

"I was conferring with my team. Consider him caught."

"Don't hurt him…."

A beat, stern and bleak. Then he exhaled. "You're calling me because you know I'm the only one who won't."

Yes, I knew. It was insulting that I should even hint he would. I began to say this and he cut me off.

"You stay put."

I clamped up on a ball of resentment. Why did he have to go and spoil the incomparable favor he was doing me?

I bristled. "I'll be there to help the minute I'm not needed here. I'm only calling you because, with a brain surgery and a pursuit-and-retrieval situation on the menu, I figured you can only handle the latter."

"Tend your patient, Calista. I'll bring Matt in."

"Damian, if the police get him in their sights first—"

"They won't. My team will contain the situation. And don't worry, they won't engage him, just keep him occupied until I arrive. I should make it to his location in three minutes."

"Three minutes? Where are you? Matt couldn't have run far.

That makes you a few streets away from here. If even that. What are you doing in this neighborhood?"

I heard a car door slam, then his breath, slow, regular. He had to be running if it was audible. He finally talked as if he wasn't.

"I was coming to see you. Great timing, huh? I'll call when it's done."

The line went dead.

Something inside me almost followed.

Great timing, he'd said. A minute ago, frantic to have him respond quickly, I'd wished he hadn't kept his promise, that he did still have me under surveillance. Had I gotten my wish?

No. Damian would never break a promise.

I moved the suction probe to and fro over the subdural hematoma clot. A tremor broke through my control. My hand shook. Once. Couldn't afford a second time.

I snapped a look at the second operating station. I needed help. Needed out of here. *Please, Al, Savvy!*

Nope. No help. They had their hands deep in Mercedes's chest, fixing the additional injuries our fight with Matt had inflicted. I was on my own. Trapped here while Matt...oh, Matt!

I felt Ayesha's eyes on me, prompting, bolstering, sponging off agitation. I wasn't on my own. And we'd come a long way. Juan was still alive. *Keep at it. Don't think. Don't feel.*

"More irrigation here, Ayesha. Just a bit," I murmured.

Ayesha complied, gently irrigating in conjunction with my suction to develop a plane between the clot and the brain's innermost covering, lifting the clot away from its surface.

This was my third craniotomy. She'd assisted in dozens. I'd needed her all through scalp division and retraction, to bone perforation and cutting, to epidural hematoma evacuation. We'd reached the most delicate part, the subdural hematoma evacuation, removing the blood clots between inner and outer coverings of the brain, then delving deeper to remove more.

"Craniotomy has to be the worst surgery in existence," Ayesha muttered.

I agreed. I hated them. For the past four years I'd had tons of experience, opened chests and abdomens and backs, amputated limbs and put amputated ones back in place. Somehow opening the skull and exposing the brain took the cake.

And the *way* he'd been injured. Fury and uselessness pierced me like the drill had Juan's skull. All that rage couldn't be contributing to my healing abilities.

Healing? Did I really think we had a shot at healing Juan? I had no idea what kind of life we were salvaging. Wondered what Juan would say, if given the chance to go now and be spared a possible existence as a brain-damaged cripple.

Images bombarded me. Exuberant Juan wasting away, crumpled or spastic or incoherent. Another salvo discharged in my chest. My jaw hurt, my nerves tightened, snapped.

"We have to be satisfied with doing the best job we can." I always said that. Tried to mean it. To accept it. No other option was available. Not now, not ever.

It took all I had to turn off my aggression, to turn all my energies back to my task. Nothing more to be done about the brain tissue lacerations. Time to close up.

Both teams, bruised and exhausted, concluded our tasks, our patients still alive. Barely. Our nurses took them to Recovery while the rest of the team shuffled to the soiled room. I picked up empathic transmissions from each one, felt shock crushing down now that they could afford to give in to it. Saw them avoiding one another's eyes. Each of them wanted to be alone, to surrender control, to let it all hit bottom.

I streaked out of the soiled room dressed, my cell phone's wireless headset transmitting the interminable ringing of Damian's phone. *Pick up. Pick up, damn you.*

I called four times till the line disconnected. I dialed again, and again. Just before my heart burst on the fifth try, he answered.

"I said I'd call you," he hissed.

I hissed right back. "And you didn't!"

"I thought you had an emergency surgery."

"It's done. Tell me where you are. I'm coming in."

"I said stay put, Calista."

"Tell me where you are!"

"Why don't you calm the hell down and let me do my job?"

"Your job is liquidating terrorists. Matt has been poisoned."

"Still insisting I'm some programmed machine set on Kill?"

"No, it's just…"

"Trust me, then."

Trust him. Ha. But then—I did. With my life for starters. With Matt's, for sure. Weird, this selective faith.

"I've cornered him where he can't hurt himself or anyone else. I'll bring him over. That's the deal."

"No deal. He's my friend. My best friend."

"And I'm taking care of him as if he were mine. And hell, yes, he is my friend, too."

Tears erupted under pressure. My knees wobbled. I must have sobbed. He must have heard. His voice dipped, darkened, spread a soothing caress that showed me I was raw inside more than out.

"Spare yourself, Calista. Let me do this for you."

"He may need medical attention. I have to be there." *Please* went uncried. He must have heard it, too. He sighed. Hating it, he told me where to find them. They were only ten minutes away by car.

Ten minutes. It felt like wading in a morass of slowed-down time as worst-case scenarios hammered at me. Then I arrived.

They'd herded him to an abandoned factory, got him cornered. His rampage had been curbed, had gone unnoticed by authorities. All good news. Bad news was, he was on the roof, four levels up.

On the ledge.

Chapter 4

A geyser of pain erupted in one knee turning the graying night blotched crimson. I must have crashed down on it. I felt the frigid air all around, couldn't get any into my lungs. They were shriveled. And my heart was growing spikes, piercing out of my chest. Tremors robbed me of all volition.

So this was a panic attack.

The sight of Matt, teetering on the edge like that, made the final confrontation with Jake on the Georgian Military Highway over a mile-deep abyss less nightmarish by comparison.

Jake had been the first man to arouse my mind and body. Then for eight years I'd resigned myself to his loss. Finding him again had been a miracle. But no matter how I ached for him or dreamed of saving him, the time apart had dulled my feelings into distant memories. Had made it easier, marginally, to stand knowing how beyond redemption he'd become. Had made shooting that poisoned dart into his carotid possible. Survivable.

But Matt. Matt! The man who'd supported me when no one

had, who'd kept me together, held my hand and scalpel—my crutch and shield in this mad existence. My Calista-first, all-supportive rock. The big brother I never had. I couldn't lose him.

My grit-stuffed, streaming eyes registered Damian's team, rather the huge safety nets they had ready right below Matt. When did they get all that? Must be nice to have bottomless resources.

Still—a fall from this height—what if they couldn't catch him? If he fell on one of them, or—or—? Was Matt suicidal now? Or was he too out of it to know the danger he'd placed himself in, reacting instinctively to being pursued? How would the stalemate break? Did Damian have a plan? What? Was he up there? Would he try to catch him? Or just push him over, confident in his team's abilities, knowing it would end the situation? No! He couldn't be thinking that, couldn't risk it unnecessarily....

Get moving. Get up there. Find Damian. Get close to Matt.

I limped, a pain in my knee informing me I was climbing stairs. Then I was on the roof. Massive structures blocked my field of vision. Matt, Damian—where were they?

I pinpointed Matt's location from a new litany of butchered-sounding howls. The alien sound quaked through me, almost drove me to my knees again.

Fighting up a black well of nausea, I pushed forward, came around a chimney. Saw Matt, illuminated by incipient dawn, in stark relief against the still gloomy sky at his back. But it was no longer him. I was looking at a deranged, emptied shell, the man I knew and loved gone. Forever? *God, please!*

God upped the ante. A few more steps showed me Matt was not alone in danger of falling off to possible crippling or death. A dozen feet away, Damian crouched on the less-than-a-foot-wide ledge. And what was that shapeless mass in his arms?

"Don't come any closer. And shut up."

Damian's terse words froze me. I cursed myself for making him speak them. Matt suddenly swung toward him, remnant awareness registering Damian, for the first time it seemed, and as a threat. He charged. His bellow uprooted my heart.

Damian. Jump out of his way. I can't lose you both.

The scream suffocated in my bursting lungs. I couldn't risk compromising the precise balance that could mean his life.

But I can't do this. Stand aside again, futility corroding me, my loved ones in terminal danger. Damian. Matt. *Please.*

Dancing back out of the charging Matt's reach, Damian hurled out the mass in his arms.

No! You'll fall!

The next second panic was extinguished under a sledgehammer of relief. Damian was jumping onto the roof. And that mass, once it had left his arms, arced against the indigo dawn, and swooped down on Matt like a falling piece of sky.

A net. Made of some material that had a mind of its own, the ability to change weight and velocity. It engulfed Matt on that first cast. Then Damian tugged, tightening the snare as he sprinted away, bringing Matt down.

The deafening wrath that sprang from Matt had me revising my disbelieving stance on demonic possession. What other thing than a trapped demon could sound so terrible?

But he was caught. Safe. Now I'd examine him, and if it was a demon riding his body, I'd exorcise it.

Damian fell to his knees beside Matt, the first to reach him. He freed Matt's head from the net and Matt's howls suddenly stopped. Was he coming out of it? *Please, please…*

I saw Damian's head snap up in the bleak light, his face urgent, his call booming.

"Calista! He's convulsing."

I crashed to my knees, reached for Matt, my hands flailing on his bucking body. A grand mal seizure. He'd bitten his tongue, and his body was bucking in violent, full-body heaves, as if trying to break his spine and sever the aberrant nervous transmissions frying his brain. Or to expel the demon necrotizing it alive.

Had to stop the convulsions. Had to. But I was blind. Lost. The world blurred, then disappeared.

Something warm, gentle pressed my lids, smoothed them and my cheeks, wiping the moist barrier I was lost behind. Damian, cupping my face, urging.

"Tell me what you need."

"God, Damian, I can't give him a powerful sedative—I have no idea what's in his system—the drug interactions—his brain's already been battered enough. What if he never wakes up?"

He gave me one hard shake. "The convulsions are only getting stronger, and it doesn't look like they'll stop on their own. If you don't, he won't have much of a brain to wake up with."

If he woke up at all. *Status epilepticus,* the sustained convulsions that now possessed his body, lead either to death or to permanent brain damage if left untreated. I had a choice between two possibilities. Leave him to die or probably kill him myself.

Knowing Matt, he'd rather I did the latter.

Damian's arm came around me, opened the emergency bag I'd lost the ability to handle.

"Tell me what you need."

I pushed away, bit down on my tongue, the self-inflicted jolt beating back the crashing breakers of numbness and dread. "I'm on it. But you can help."

Please understand, Matt, if I do the wrong thing. Please help me. Hang on.

"Get me IV access." I shoved a cannula, a syringe and a dextrose bag into Damian's hands. "Administer fifty cc in one push."

I rummaged through my bag, the creeping dawn of a weirdly clear February day doing nothing to help its battery-powered illumination. Ingrained practice tided me over as I found the necessary anticonvulsant and loaded a 0.15-mg/kg dose into a syringe. I loaded another with the follow-up drug. I thought I heard weeping.

"I'm done." Damian shifted aside for me as I fumbled for

Matt's thrashing arm, put the syringe to the cannula and started pushing the drug in. "It has to go in over five minutes, followed by the fosphenytoin, 15 to 20 mg/kg," I muttered. My hands shook, dislodging the syringe.

Damian pushed me away, gentle, final, took over the injection. "See what else you have to do."

I allowed myself a moment, subsiding beside him as Matt began to calm. Then I began assembling my intubation kit. I removed the last of the inescapable net off Matt, took his still-rigid head on my lap, tilted it to open his mouth. His throat was clogged by secretions. I suctioned them, clearing his airway as Damian finished the injection. I felt Matt loosening by degrees until he went flaccid.

"Help me," I said. Without a word, Damian arranged Matt's now-limp head in position for me to slip the endotracheal tube in and start one hundred percent oxygen. "He's hyperthermic—usual with convulsions. Let's remove his clothes. Can your team get us cold packs?"

He stood up. "Continue your measures at the Sanctuary."

"I need to make sure he's stabilized."

"He is, for now. To do more you'll need more equipment, more help than I can give you."

I knew that. It made no difference to the phobia howling down my nerves, shrieking for me not to move him.

Damian drew me to my feet, replacing my fear's inescapable grip with his own. "For once, Calista, do as you're told."

Weren't nightmares supposed to end at some point? When you woke up screaming? I'd done my share of screaming tonight. I'd scream again, I wouldn't stop, if that would end it.

This nightmare seemed to be here to stay. It was getting more creative. More cruel. It gave hope, waited until we doubled over, gulping air, twitching in relief and expectation, then smashed our faces in again.

Right now, it seemed over. Again. But was it?

I leaned my forehead on the glass window of IC, acid in my eyes and veins, gazing at Matt. He lay there absent and subdued, hooked to a dozen monitors and drug-delivery systems.

Are you still there, Matt? Is it over? Or over?

Hands on my shoulders jerked me out of the mire of unanswered, unanswerable questions. Damian.

It was his first time in one of our Sanctuaries. I'd never invited him. He'd invited himself this time. I couldn't even have thought of objecting. He'd just saved Matt. And it wasn't as if this Sanctuary's location was a secret to him.

Oh, why don't you face it, St. James? You want *him here. Want him, period.*

Yeah. I wasn't so stupid I'd try to deny how much. Didn't mean a thing to the issues left hanging between us, though.

Just let him touch you and I bet you won't even remember afterward what they are.

Yeah. Exactly what I was afraid of.

"How is he?" His eyes swept their golden warmth and worry over me, asked another question. *How are you?*

I ignored the rush of comfort his concern, his presence, cloaked me in. Being in his debt forever, over Matt among other things, wouldn't change a thing. So I'd pay him back with my very life, on demand, anytime. I would defend him with it anyway, debt or not, but that was it. A second crack at my faith didn't figure into what I owed him.

Oh, it didn't? Strange, since your faith, and everything else you feel for him seem mighty healthy and back in control.

Shut up! I swore one day I'd find this exasperating voice inside my head and take a gamma knife to it!

Had to take one thing at a time. Right now I was all tangled up inside, not knowing what to feel or where to go from here. One thing I knew. I owed him an answer. As pathetic and uncertain as it was. It was all I had anyway.

I gave it to him. "I don't know." His magnificent head inclined. He turned me fully around, smoothing the bangs out of my inflamed eyes. The gesture, the gentleness and intention behind it slammed into me. My head almost flopped to his chest.

I stepped back, plastered my back to the IC wall, glanced up the foot difference in our heights and winced. How could he look like that in the fluorescent lights that made blue-tinged zombies of everyone? I didn't dare think how it mutilated me right now. On him, the light only struck more power and beauty off masterpiece bone structure, a jade twinkle off golden eyes and Prussian shimmers off raven hair. And how weird was it that I noticed this now? *Moron.*

I exhaled. "We used every intensive supportive measure. His vitals and monitors all indicate he's sleeping peacefully. Even his EEGs." Which was a surprise. I'd expected the electroencephalogram to reveal some abnormal brain activity. "No surprises in the past two hours with minor sedation. Lab's busy with the most comprehensive blood work we've done since forever, trying to figure out what's coursing in his system."

"So he'll be okay?"

The sigh was so deep it almost expelled my life force before I inhaled it back in. "I don't know. It looks that way, but I can't tell for sure. He surprised us one too many times today—I can't even begin to form a diagnosis, let alone a prognosis."

"What happened after you disappeared with him in ER?"

"For a while, nothing, even after he shook off the tranquilizer. He seemed stable if zonked out, as expected. Then suddenly he shot off on a rapid decline. With a *new* set of symptoms. I rushed with a desperate diagnostic treatment—that's when the clinical picture strongly suggests poisoning with a certain agent and we administer its antidote without proof, and if it works, it proves the provisional diagnosis is right—"

He waved his hand, stopping further explanations. He knew already, huh? Okay.

"Bottom line is, I have no idea if his stabilization indicates

that the physostygmine did work or if he beat this on his own—
if there isn't permanent damage already."

He let a beat pass, didn't contradict that last bit. Smart.
Wouldn't be wise to ply me with unsupported assurances. Then
one of his winged eyebrows rose. "Physostygmine? Atropine antidote?"

Both of mine came up, too. It never ceased to startle me, the
level of his medical expertise. Though it shouldn't. As a black-
ops agent, he had to be versed in emergency medicine for field
emergency measures. As an assassin, he had thorough knowledge of every drug and poison this sick world had to offer.

He pursed those luscious lips, unconvinced. "But his condition didn't resemble an anticholinergic toxidrome."

My shoulders rose in a damned-if-I've-figured-out-that-par-
adox-yet gesture, and wouldn't fall again. They'd cramped. I
was really beyond finished. I groaned, tensed, trapped in the
spasm. An urgent step had his body touching me down the
length of mine, his hands homing in on the foci of agony,
pouring comfort into them. My senses leapt, me almost after
them, closing the circuit of gnawing longing.

Not on your life, De Luna. Or yours, St. James. Move away.

I did, rotated miraculously relaxed muscles. The man had
some serious mojo at his fingertips. *Say something.*

Wasn't easy, with a raw larynx and a yearning, battered heart.
I swallowed. "You're right. I formed this theory that Matt's condition had two phases. You've gotten a good show of what I'm
naming 'phase one,' the pre-convulsive phase. That was the
sympathomimetic toxidrome. The hallucinations, the acute psychosis, the extreme violence and agitation, ending in the seizure.
Then came 'phase two' post-convulsion. That was the anticholinergic toxidrome."

"How could he have two totally different toxic syndromes?"

I sighed. "We combed through every database of drugs and
poisons for drug interaction, side effects, overdoses, idiosyn-

cratic and allergic reactions—the works—to look for something
that may develop both clinical pictures in different stages—and
nada. Of course. We didn't really expect to find one. No drug
ever changes its mode of action in midstride that way."

He stuffed his hands in his back pockets, spreading his legs
wider. Seemed he was wrestling with the inconsistencies and
finding no convincing way out, too. "Hmm. Could it have been
an anticholinergic drug overdose all along? Most hallucinogens
and incapacitating agents have atropine-like manifestations—
anxiety, disorientation, hallucinations, convulsions, even coma."

Yup. Sure had his assassin business down pat. I shook my
head. "All poisonings end up in those, in the terminal stages. It's
the starting symptoms that differentiate the agents. And he didn't
have anticholinergic symptoms to start with."

"Could you have been too agitated to notice?"

"Four words, Damian. Pale and sweaty before convulsions,
flushed and bone-dry after." Okay, so more than four. I
meant two diagnostic symptoms per syndrome. Pale sweaty.
Flushed dry.

He nodded. "I did notice how pale and sweaty he was, in this
cold, too. Even crossed my mind that it was a bad case of adrenaline rush. That is the original sympathomimetic syndrome. But
no one overdoses on their natural adrenaline. So—he went
flushed and dry on you later. Hmm. Could it have been two
drugs, then? An immediate if short-acting one kicking in first,
then, after he convulsed, the delayed-action drug taking over?"

Damian's ordered deductive process focused my own short-
circuiting one. "That may be the only answer to explain the
switch in symptoms. Yet two things don't gel. First, for one of
the known sympathomimetics, like methamphetamine or Ecstasy, to produce such violent mental symptoms to the extent that
he no longer recognized us, it must have been an overdose and
should have distorted his other perceptions, too. Not so. He had
perfect coordination on a ledge four floors up, for God's sake."

Damian nodded. "Yeah, someone on such a bad trip would have been physically incapacitated by the warping of all his other senses. And the second?"

"The time frame. Any of the agents capable of producing his symptoms have a short onset of action. From minutes to at most a few hours. So even if I consider that onset of symptoms to have started with his driving stint from hell or even during his ultra-violence during our blitz on the white-slavery auction, his exposure would still have to have occurred in the hours prior to our receiving Juan's call. And that's still out. Me and Lucia were with him at least six hours before any of that took place."

We'd been playing Scrabble and Trivial Pursuit all night. And he'd been calm, collected, beating the crap out of us and in the best mood I'd seen him in ages. *Oh, Matt...*

"Is it a possibility it was self-inflicted?"

Damian's question jolted through me. "You mean suicide?"

He let a second pass, then shrugged. "An experiment. An attempt to make his load easier to bear. Matt lives with a kind of pain I can't even imagine." His lids lowered, obscuring his expression. Then he raised them, catching me in a blast of fear. And aggression. "Or I can. It makes me contemplate massacres."

I jerked away. He wouldn't let me, pinning me to the wall, dragging me into a ride through his tormented imagination where I was in Matt's wife's place, suffering her gruesome fate, then deeper in hell to experience what he'd feel, do....

Get out of my mind! I can't handle more heartache. Not now.

He must have felt the unvoiced plea, decided to spare me. He let me go, lowering fists to his side. "Matt must be a far stronger man than me. I would have lost it a lot sooner."

"No! He didn't lose it. No *freaking* way would he pollute his system with anything that would tamper with his reason and control. You wouldn't even think it if you saw his murderous hatred of all drugs and their manufacturers and peddlers. Even without that, he'd never do this to himself. To us."

"Even if he'd reached his limit."

"No!"

Damian just nodded. Accepting my inarguable knowledge of my friend and his limits and reactions? Seemed so. Was *I* so sure?

Yes, you are. This is Matt.

Damian stabbed his hand into his luxuriant hair, the longest I'd ever seen it, lying thick on his collar, the action expending the last of his agitation. "So self-inflicted is out," he said, cool once more. "And accidental exposure is too much of a stretch. Then it has to have been intentional exposure. Any enemy you can think of who had access to him?"

"We're a deeply covert operation. Our enemies don't exactly have our names and addresses."

"You'd be surprised."

My next scheduled breath never made it.

Was this just a hypothetical, you-never-know-so-never-feel-safe kind of comment? Or did he mean that since both he and Sir Ashton had breached our shields, that anyone else could? Had? That we could already be in someone's bull's-eye?

But we'd gone to extremes to tighten our security ever since our return from Russia, pouring too many resources into maintaining our invisibility. We'd changed our L.A. Sanctuary's location three times in the past four months.

So was it not working? Did he know something I didn't? Would he keep something that critical from me if he did? Critical my foot! It would be *catastrophic*. It would be the end.

Damian, seemingly unaware of the chaos his remark had caused, went on pursuing his deduction process. "Let's start breaking down your movements recently, stressing Matt's. It's probably payback from one of the drug cartels you're so fond of decimating."

"How could they have reached him?"

"The only valid answer is an inside job."

"No!"

"Think, Calista. Who but a mole could have had access to him, to poison him while he sat in the Sanctuary's doctors' room eating pizza and playing Scrabble and Trivial Pursuit with you?"

He stopped, winced. Then his formidable shoulders rose in resignation, dropped, his golden gaze growing turbid, leveling on me. *What now?* it asked.

What now? He meant now that he'd let slip that he'd been monitoring our every breath inside our Sanctuary, that he had broken his promise, had he never meant to keep it? What did he figure? That I'd say, *Oh, well, at least he's not an enemy?*

Like hell!

Chapter 5

"You look like hell, Cali."

Sure I did. I was wrecked. Literally and figuratively. The simple motion of reaching for the set of preliminary investigations Ayesha handed me hurt. The very effort to think, to be, even more.

My sight and mind blurred over the printouts. *Dammit. Read them.* Making sense of them would be a real plus, too.

I did, I guess. Normal. Everything. Good. Or was it? I didn't know. And that summed up my reality. I knew nothing anymore. Ayesha's gentle hand slid down my back. Even that hurt.

"Cali. You're in bad shape."

Anxiety in Ayesha's ever-serene voice rubbed some more salt into my inflamed nerves.

I waved it away. "You don't look so hot yourself, Ayesha." The whole left side of her face was swollen, her lower lid pressing up on her eye. Matt's blow.

"I look a sight better than you, and that on its own is cause for extreme alarm."

I smirked at her. "See why I envy you your beautiful, dark skin? Your bruises are almost invisible. With my damn vampire complexion, I look like a crazy experiment in subdermal ink injections gone awry."

"Cali, I'm serious. You look real bad."

I moved out of range of her concern. "I started getting slammed about far earlier in the night that you did." I pointed to various beacons of throbbing pain around my face. "This is a gang member's fist. This is Lucia's cheekbone. The rest you know."

"Yeah, I know." We grimaced in tandem, remembering. "But that's not what I meant. You look—extinguished."

I'd just finished going through every scrap of Matt's belongings and directing an upside-down search of the Sanctuary. The others, the ones I trusted probably more than I did myself, were still searching. We were trying to disprove once and for all Damian's suggestion that it had been an inside job. That possibility alone was enough to drag me into despair. I had no idea what I'd do if it turned out to be true.

I headed to IC. Ayesha followed—hovered more like. I sighed. "It's been a hell of a night and a half, Ayesha. And the suspicion that it isn't over isn't contributing to my state of health, mental or physical."

"That's why you snapped? Yelled at Damian that way?"

"You heard, huh?" I paused beside Matt. He still looked to be fathoms deep in sleep. I brushed a now-dry blond lock off his leonine forehead. *Come back, please. I can't lose you.*

Ayesha reached out, did the same, then transferred her hand to mine, stilled it, gentle, inescapable. "I bet everyone in greater L.A. heard, Cali. What was that about?"

I started to shrug, remembered the cramp that had hit me when I last tried that trick, stopped. "Same old stuff. I yelled at him since I was too drained to kill him."

Ayesha's eyes bored into me, tried to read more than I was volunteering. Seemed she decided nothing else was forthcoming, decided to concentrate on more important matters for now. Wise woman.

She busied herself with the periodic adjustment of Matt's measures, following my murmured directions, further lowering his sedation, replenishing his fluids, handing me more tracings.

Again normal. And Matt looked better. His tan was overcoming the lividness, his breathing and heartbeat deep, slow, rhythmic. He even opened his eyes and recognized Ishmael at one point. That of all signs spoke volumes for no lasting brain damage. We had no news yet on what had plunged him into that psychotic-convulsive attack to begin with. But medically speaking, it was as if it had never happened.

But was he going to make it back, whole?

The digital clock on the wall said ten a.m. That made it more than thirty minutes we'd been going over and over Matt, conducting one neuro exam after another and checking and rechecking him down to his hair roots. There was nothing more to be done. He'd wake up when his body decided, not in response to anything we did.

Walking out of IC still gave me a sick feeling. Knowing he was in the hands of capable intensivists didn't lessen the waves of nausea each step away from him spread inside me.

Ayesha kept her hand on my arm. Knew I was starting to wobble? Bet she did. She kept it there all the way back to our "hub," the room in which the core team relaxed and held meetings.

I paused on the threshold. Last night I'd stood right here, bogged down in pizzas. Matt had been sitting in that chair over there, his blond head thrown back, eyes closed. God, he'd looked so strong and whole and stable. That perpetual thrill of thankfulness for having him had hit its usual spot behind my sternum. Stronger than usual. I'd announced the saving arrival of pizza and he'd jumped to his feet to take my load.

Ayesha towed me to an armchair, supported me down into it. Propping her lean hip on the table, she picked up where her line of interrogation had been aborted. Must have seen me wandering and decided to drag me back. Must be burning with curiosity, too.

She raised one eyebrow. "So—why yell at Damian tonight of all nights, right after he earned our undying gratitude by saving Matt? What happened to kick up the old grievances?"

I threw my head back on the battered leather headrest. "Oh, these are spanking new ones. It's the end result that's old. You know—him being a double-crossing, lying bastard."

Ayesha sighed. "He had a good reason to hide the truth from you back in Russia, Cali."

"Hide the truth? That's the new commercial name for lying through his teeth?" I rolled my eyes. They nearly didn't make it back to their original position. Boy, I was beyond done in. "Oh, yeah, I forgot. You're the president and probably the only member of the Damian De Luna Can Do No Wrong Fan Club."

"One day you'll push him away once too often, Cali."

"And may that day be today!"

The look she gave me transmitted all her sage thoughts. *Moron* was foremost among them. I exhaled, shook my head. "You're not the one to talk to here, Ayesha. Why tell you his latest transgression when you'd only excuse it, rationalize it and make it look like the only thing he could have done? You took one look at him and hopped on his side for the duration."

Ayesha's chocolate-brown eyes grew even more placating. *Help—she's in mom mode.*

"I'm on his side because he's on yours."

I snorted. It didn't come out as effectively as intended. "He says he is. Talk is cheap. And though before Russia I never would have believed it, Damian can bury you—hell, he can flood California off the map—in talk. And all the while he lies to me. At every turn. Out of caring, of course."

"He doesn't *care* for you, he *loves* you."

"Love doesn't give you the right to interfere in your loved

ones' lives!" Betrayal and indignation had me sitting up. They were no match for my muscles, which rebelled against the effort and gravity. I flopped back. "Your first husband loved you, didn't he, Ayesha? Wanted what was best for you, right? But of course you were too young to know your own best, so he beat you up to discipline you, imprisoned you in your own home to protect you from the big bad world and alienated all your family and friends, then decided what you should do every second of your life so you wouldn't be exposed to harmful influences."

Two long strides brought Ayesha before me, her lithe, whip-cord body tense, her feet spread apart. "Damian is nothin' like Jordie! Jordie was an insecure, vicious fool who couldn't hold the respect of a woman with identity or experience, who picked a sheltered, ignorant girl to marry so he could feel like somebody holding her strings. Damian is a powerful man, secure in his worth, so much so that he went and picked the toughest woman to fall in love with. But you being tough don't make worrying about you no easier. In fact, he has every reason to worry more. And it doesn't make him a sick monster like Jordie if he wants to make sure you're safe, Cali."

Yeah, like that was the reason he was keeping tabs on me and—

It suddenly hit me, full in the face. "You *knew* he was spying on us! Man—have you been supplying him with info, too?"

She began, "I only wanted to help—"

"Well, next time wait until you're asked."

She straightened to her five-inches-taller-than-me height, looked down on me like a stern headmistress. "You yelling at me, too?"

I was too raw, didn't know how to stop. "*Yes.* You're as yell-worthy. Dammit, Ayesha, he batted his long lashes, gave you a steamy golden look and made you his accomplice."

She folded her arms, wrinkling her blue scrubs. "He didn't make me do anything. I volunteered."

I threw my hands up. Wrong move. I groaned. "Fine. Whatever. I hope the two of you will be very happy together!"

Ayesha actually chuckled now. I turned away before my head burst with an overload of argh-factor.

"If the boy was available I'd snap him up."

"Boy?" I snorted again and it came out good this time. Sure. An all-out-male, overridingly virile, thirty-seven-year-old boy.

"He *is* ten years younger than me. But then, I have a thing for younger men. In fact, one particular younger man."

What? Curiosity ripped my eyes wide open. I groaned, with pain—and realization. "Fiendess! I don't want to know, that's how angry I am. I'm plugging my ears and slapping on the sleep mask so I won't see or hear you anymore. I'll set my cell phone's alarm an hour from now. Wake me up if Matt—"

"You'll go home and sleep till I tell you to come back."

"I can't and I won't. Matt—"

"Is stable and you won't be any good to him if you collapse. If you do, we'll be minus both our leaders and I'm not looking forward to being promoted to the position anytime soon."

"I can't be twenty minutes away if anything happens."

"He's been stable for the past four hours. He'll be okay."

Why had her face tilted at that odd angle? Had my eyes crossed or what? I sure was decimated. "If you promise to call me if he so much as mumbles in his sleep…" I stopped, glared, my focus back. "What am I doing asking for your promise? You'd only break it—for my own good! Too bad I can't break up with you, too."

"Save all that energy for the deserving, Cali. Matt may be okay and the crisis may be over, but the investigation into the reason behind it has only just begun."

"Yeah. You're right." My heat rose again. "I *hate* people who are right all the time."

"Like Damian?"

"Damian isn't right, he's…"

"A double-crossing, lying bastard. Yeah, I got that down pat. Now look me in the eye and tell me there can ever be someone else for you, someone else who can fit you or measure up to you like he does. Someone who can keep up— *put up*—with you."

"Who knows? There are two billion men I haven't met yet!"

"Sure. And you'd burn out, scare, alienate or end up killing each and every one of them."

My very same estimation. Didn't mean having it corroborated didn't smart. "Why, thanks!"

"Pleasure." Suddenly her eyes sharpened. "*Can* you love someone else, Cali? If you think you can, I'll shut up about this forever."

"Who says I have to love anyone at all?"

She exhaled her exasperation.

"Really," I insisted. "What's so hot about love? What's there to look forward to, in my particular case? No home, no family, and I'll probably wind up crippled or dead. The best there is to expect in all this is sex, for erratic periods of time till disaster strikes." I turned, walked away. "*That's* no reason to put up with the emotional and psychological hassle."

At the door, at Ayesha's eloquent "Oh, yeah?" I whirled around and hissed, "And he doesn't have the market cornered on sex."

Her serene smile looked crooked in her unilaterally swollen face. "He has *your* market cornered."

I tried to squeeze my bloated lids shut. They didn't cooperate. "Ayesha, how much is he paying you?"

"Offering to top it?" She handed me my bag of tricks and the keys to the beat-up Suzuki. "I'm holding down the fort. You go rest, store up all the stamina you can. I have a feeling resolving this riddle is going to be an even tougher ride."

I got a ride home. A smooth one as far as I remembered. I dozed all the way.

I had been standing in the garage unable to remember which

car I had keys to. Someone had taken pity on me. Right now, as I fumbled for my condo's keys, I no longer remembered who.

I ached. Inside and out and on all levels and layers in between.

And someone was behind me!

I knew who when the skewer in my heart twisted. *Damian.*

I forgot how to fit a key in its slot. Didn't object when he took it from my useless fingers and did the job. I wanted inside even at the cost of his help.

I staggered when the door's support receded, spilled inside my condo. I clung to the door, tried to turn, to slam it in his face. Would have managed if I wasn't already in the air. In his arms.

"Put me down or lose a—a…" Damn. What a time to draw a blank.

Dark satin, that mind-altering stuff that passed for his voice, poured out of his mouth. "I am not taking threats from a woman who can't even come up with one."

I could tell he was looking down at me. Not that I could see his face in my dark-as-a-crypt great room. Didn't need to see him to tell his mood. I'd yelled him out of the Sanctuary, and supposedly my life, a few hours ago. Seemed he hadn't registered my tirade, judging by the fact that he was here. And by the tone of that hormone-messing voice. Condescending, unperturbed and, damn his soul, indulgent, too.

"You're—you—"

"Save it, Calista. Even you can't come up with anything to top what you already called me back in the Sanctuary."

"You said you were leaving me alone."

And he had. He'd taken my barrage in silence, then responded with a simple "You want me to leave you alone? Done."

I'd watched him turn and walk away and had really believed him this time. It had felt like the end. Of everything. For me.

When would I ever learn?

As he carried me to my bedroom the faint daylight seeping

from the shoddy shutters illuminated his face. It had none of his voice's lightness. His face was forbidding, tear-your-heart-out-and-mash-it-to-mince beautiful. He laid me down on my king-size, shabby, unmade bed.

"So I lied—again. What else do you expect from a bastard? Which I literally am, by the way."

He—he...! I—ack! I never, ever insulted anyone that way. No excuses. *Fix this.* I tried, made an incoherent mess of it. "I never thought—or I'd have made the connection, sorta, technically speaking, and never would have... But I never meant it *that* way—just in a behavioral sense—a generic insult—oh, you *know* what I meant...."

His lips clamped mine, not in a kiss, in a vise whose sole purpose was to shut me up. The darkness of my tiny, bed-dominated room deepened. Figured. Exhaustion. Injuries setting in. A mild concussion. Oxygen deprivation.

Damian deprivation, that hedonistic inner voice sighed, sank into his feel, feeding, replenishing.

I growled at it. At him. Should bite mouthfuls out of him, hand him a few choice body parts. I bet I still could if I expended the last of my reserves.

Nah. Got to pick my battles. Ayesha had been right. I needed all my strength for what was coming. Let him play caveman.

A memory flickered beneath my lids. The night five months ago. Before Russia. When he'd come to lay ground rules for the mission. Our reunion, so to speak. Right here in my bedroom.

I hadn't seen him in four years, not since that day he'd gotten me kicked out of GCA and medicine in one fell swoop. I'd figured the chances of seeing him again in this lifetime were one in seven billion, and those of finding him in my bedroom were up there with those of finding the genie of the lamp.

Not that I'd seen him. Or heard him. I hadn't paid the electricity bill. I'd been wearing earplugs. Blind and deaf, thinking him an intruder, I'd erupted in all-out attack mode, shot him up with the first drug I'd grabbed. Truth serum, as it had turned out to be.

He'd kissed me then, under its effect. Our first kiss.

Now his mouth clamp was turning into just that, a luxuriant, life-draining-and-infusing kiss as he came down beside me on the bed, flowed around me.

Did he have to be so soothing, so giving? Why not try to show me who was boss, as he had during the two years he'd molded me into a fighting-killing machine as efficient as he was? Why not give me an excuse to knee him? All I needed really, to compound my aches and heartaches—a tender Damian.

I moaned in protest. At least I thought it was protest. It should be—should…

Mental debris and shrapnel ricocheted in a dimming, expanding void, and a disembodied lament echoed somewhere far, unreachable….

So tired. Tired. Of it all. Hate it. Hate you. Hate lies, never knowing for certain—hate *not trusting you, totally and unquestioningly again…. Do you have any idea what it means, how deep it goes, how irreparable it feels…?*

I was plummeting through the mattress, my brain seeping from my skull. A *shh, shh* sound absorbed the oppression, a warm bulk of soft steel replaced my bed, beneath me, around me, stroked well-being in places that had never known it. The scent of safety and strength shrouded me. Something welled from inside me and dissolved itself on the taste of life….

I sank.

Chapter 6

"Is it genetic?" The question came out of nowhere, the first thing that flashed in my mind the second I opened my eyes.

Damian didn't say anything for a moment, a huge looming shadow in the dark, flickering on and off with the bar neon lights that penetrated my shutters even from five levels down. Then he whispered, so soft and bone deep, "Are you awake?"

I didn't answer him. He'd get his answer anyway with my next question. "Or is it against your religion or something?"

"You're awake." His statement was the epitome of resigned sarcasm. He moved now, sitting up on one elbow, making me realize he had a leg thrown over both of mine.

I kicked, making him remove it, began to sit up. "I mean, are you incapable of telling the truth? Any truth? Would you be compelled to lie even if you were asked the time?"

For answer he flattened me to the bed again. I started to struggle, then realized. He was only reaching over me to flick on my bedside lamp. He leaned back again, flicked a look at his watch. "It's six fifty-six—fifty-*seven* p.m."

"*P.M.!* You let me sleep for *seven hours?*"

He consulted his watch again. "Seven, and eleven minutes."

"Oh, shut up! How could you? Matt—"

"I called Ayesha several times and Matt is doing fine. He even woke up at one point and asked if he'd been in an accident. Ayesha just told him yes, and he went back to sleep. So why don't you? I'll resume guard duty."

My sullen gaze swept over him. The side light detailed his spectacular face—and a no-less-so laceration below his left cheekbone. My hand, in league with my rogue inner voice, shot up, fingers whispering over the abused flesh. Matt's doing?

Damian pressed his cheek harder to my hand, turned his lips into it, catching my fingers in gentle teeth. Longing slammed into me, impacting my body and senses last. *Oh, no, you don't!*

Jumping out of bed and out of his field of influence was the only sane thing to do. I did, stood testing my balance and power. Whoa. Last night had really done a number on me.

And there he was, reclining in the same position, vital, mesmerizing, as if he hadn't taken a bullet near the heart just four months ago, golden eyes fixed on me, translucent in the lamp light, yet opaque, unfathomable. Dammit. What was he thinking? I'd lost my ability to read him.

Hah. I'd never had it. Just thought I did. For a while. Another lie he'd led me to believe. He had that way of lying by omission, by suggestion, by spewing multiple-choice jargon, letting me pick what I liked to believe. And self-deluding, besotted dolt that I was, I invariably latched onto the best interpretation. Made the situation even more argh-and-tear-my-hair-out worthy.

Right now, he wasn't volunteering any insights into the workings of his mind. It would go against everything he was, I guessed, anathema to his nature, to his ingrained conditioning as a chameleon black-ops operative, to expose his true self. Was there such a thing?

I mean really, how many convoluted agendas would it take before one's personality disintegrated? Had his? Or was it just so deeply buried it would take a few lifetimes to dig it out? And would I still love the man I dug up then?

How could I still love him now?

Just end this. "Listen, Damian. I owe you for Matt, and I'll pay you back in kind. Anytime, anywhere. You can count on me, always, in critical situations and anything professional. Personally, I already told you I don't want anything to do with you again. So, just go now and save us both the nastiness."

He sat there, bearing my anger, making no attempt to ward it off. To defend himself. To soothe my bitterness.

Then he shook his head, sat up. I wouldn't have imagined he'd give up that easily. Or at all, if it was important enough. Maybe it wasn't. Maybe *I* wasn't. Maybe he was sick of me.

Fine. Let him be. Let him take his gorgeous, treacherous butt out of my bed and his disruptive, addictive presence out of my life. Save me a world of hassle and heartache.

Seemed he felt me reaching critical mass. He sighed, decided to give me something before I had a seizure. "Calista, do you want me to answer? Or will it just make you angrier?"

I could swear I saw purple and blue comets shoot across my vision. Was this how people had cerebrovascular accidents?

A spastic finger jutted out at him. "Use that indulgent tone and lose your most valued anatomy part, buster. You never *answer* me, you just give me excuses. And promises. Well, news flash! I'm not legally bound to accept your excuses and I'm sure as hell done guzzling empty promises."

"What I gave you were reasons, not excuses. Which——" he rushed to add before I exploded "——you're not obliged to sanction, just to understand, to...tolerate."

"I'm supposed to tolerate the empty promises, too? I'm

supposed to say, *Poor man, it's a glitch in his DNA, he just isn't capable of making a promise he intends to keep?* I'm supposed to feel like a hard-hearted harpy for not sweeping this under the rug and jumping back in your arms?"

"Under the rug is where all this crap belongs. And in my arms is where *you* do."

My senses leapt. All they ever wanted was to smother themselves in his nearness, his pleasures. Damn them. And damn him. Pulling my strings, dangling himself, reminding me how it had felt to be mingled with his flesh, riding his need, drenched in pleasure, inundated with satisfaction.

Emotions and flesh swelled, surplus tension spilling out on a shaky exhalation. "You and Satan are closely related, right?"

He smiled. And why not? He felt me buckling.

No. I was damned if I did, probably literally, too, if I let the hormone-operated female into the control room. "I don't belong with anyone who can look me in the eye and lie."

He shrugged. *Shrugged.* I thundered over, slammed that shrug down, my hand stinging with the collision into his steel mass, his face an inch from mine.

He snatched me on top of him, my head in his large hand, my legs straddling his hard hips. Both his hands pressed me harder, sinking my lips into his, my core onto his erection. He rocked against me, promising me, deluging me in readiness and intimacy. Coherence and reason and outrage dissolved on his invading tongue, drowned in his maddened, maddening groans.

Remember what he did. What he made you do. What he may have cost you. The havoc that may still be coming.

I wrenched free. Felt like I'd left a couple of skin layers on his hands and lips.

Get to the point. "How about we drop the seduction scene and count the lies? First lie—the whole point of the mission in Russia. I risk everything to save kidnapped GCA doctors when all along there is no one to save, and my GCA medical mission is just the cover for **PATS**'s search-and-destroy mission to take out militants and biochemical weapons scientists. Do you know how I still feel about that?"

His lips twisted. "You updated me a month ago. Reserved about voicing your grievances is something you sure aren't."

"Hello—ever heard of rhetorical questions? No interruptions or wisecracks when I'm counting lies." I sucked in a burning stream of air and aggravation. "Second lie—misleading me about Jake. When I think about how you knew he was involved with the militants, that you left me in the dark even after you made sure he was their mastermind, afraid of my irrational reactions, I want to bash heads.

"*Third* lie—saying you walked away after getting me kicked out of GCA, intending to forget me, when you had me on the other end of a zoom lens all those years. And you never confessed. It was Dad who stumbled on your surveillance equipment when his people were helping me install my latest smoke screens."

He opened his mouth, closed it when I raised my voice. "*But,* after I blew up when he told me, I was coming to sort of accept why you didn't come clean. Before Russia, we were at odds. After Russia, you claimed you'd decided to stop it, so why bring up something that was over? See, I excused you."

"Oh, that's why you haven't talked to me ever since? That's excusing me? What would you have done if you'd condemned me?"

"I'd have hit you with one of my drug cocktails and sent you to a nice vacation in hell."

"You sent me there anyway. In fact, give me the chemically induced hell anytime. At least that ends."

Oh, no, he wasn't strumming my gullible strings. "*Fourth* lie—you *promised* to stop spying on me. You didn't. *That's* inexcusable."

"I tried. I couldn't."

So simple. So stymieing. Tell me again, why didn't I just hate him and get done with it?

He stood up. Air disappeared. "Calista, I can't apologize for keeping tabs on you. You lead a hell of a dangerous life—"

"Says Preemptive Anti-Terrorist Squad's commander!"

He cut me off, a ragged edge to his voice. "Suz reported in last night saying you were having a quiet night in. So I went off to a job outside L.A. Then she called back, frantic, saying you'd exploded out to answer some emergency and she had lost visual in the rain, then had lost signal when you got out of range of her tracking device. I *was* coming back when you called me. Do you know how I felt, driving back like a maniac, not knowing if you were in some dirty alley bleeding to death?"

I stared at him.

"It's bigger than me, Calista. Needing to know you're safe rules me. I'd rather have you by my side, but since I can't, I want to at least know where you are and what you're doing, that I can intervene within minutes if you need me."

This wasn't the reason he'd given for his past surveillance. He'd made it sound like he'd been making sure I didn't make too big a mess, or interfere in his jurisdiction. But Ayesha knew.

I was the last to know. Again.

But now that he put it that way, it reminded me of Sir Ashton, of the reasons *he'd* given for keeping tabs on me, for helping me covertly. God! How stupid could I be?

"You're in it with Sir Ashton!" Realization burst out, a cry under pressure. "Or is he in it with you?"

No reaction. Bingo. Right the first time. Was there no limit to their duplicity? "I can't *believe* the two of you! But watching me is not all you do, is it. You *interfere* in my work, you *manipulate* me and everyone and everything around me, don't you. And you pretend to be at odds!"

"We see eye to eye only where you're concerned. And we *help,* wherever we can. You can't blame us for that. To Sir

Ashton you're like the daughter he lost. And you're the woman I—"

"Don't. Say. It."

He plowed on harder. "I can't stop saying it or feeling it. I tried, remember? For years. It's no good. It's here to stay."

"Let me tell you what else is here to stay. My team. My work. And you're jeopardizing it all in your Big Brother need to have control over me. Or should I say Big Lover?"

His lips twitched. "Glad to hear you admit I am your lover."

"You're *not*. Having sex once doesn't qualify you for that."

He shrugged one shoulder. "Maybe, but your wanting me so bad you can't see or stand straight does."

That he knew, that he was teasing me with it! I stamped my foot. The room shook. Didn't take much to shake it, though. I could do that just by turning over in bed. With him and me there, we'd shake the building. We'd shaken existence itself four months ago....

Stop it, moron. You're playing into his hands.

"Why so indignant? It's only fair when you do this to me—" He dipped a glance downward. I wouldn't look. *I wouldn't.* "Even spitting mad. And you know what else makes me your lover? Loving you does."

"I told you before and I'll tell you again. Love doesn't excuse everything. Or anything."

He came over, held me by the shoulders. It was his tone that riveted me in his grasp. "Then don't excuse. Just understand. In the past, I felt like the dumbest fool on earth, unable to stop following you around when you seemed to have totally forgotten me. I didn't know I mattered at all to you until I almost died. You said you loved me only then."

An urge swelled, vindictive, cruel. *I said it as a therapeutic measure. Because I thought you'd die and I wanted to send you off into the great brouhaha happy.*

I shook my head. Nope. No way. I wasn't lying to get my own

back. Not in personal stuff. Not with him. He couldn't make me adopt his methods.

He pressed closer, wound a persuasive, cherishing arm that could crush men twice my size around my waist. I soaked up the feeling for a moment, then pushed away.

He didn't press me this time. He shoved his hands in his pockets, exhaled. "After being exposed to your hurt anger when the truth came out about Russia, I couldn't risk disclosing another secret. What we had was too new, too undefined. Then your father told you and I wished I'd done it myself. I promised to stop, hoping you'd let me in, let me know what I needed to know without resorting to these methods. Instead, you cut me off."

"So it's *my* fault now! Big bad Calista made you do it!"

"Yes, dammit. Big bad Calista makes me do things I'd give anything not to do. You can't even guess what it costs, time and resources, keeping an eye on you, protecting your back."

"*Ooh la la!* You're making it sound like a great favor now?"

"You stubborn, exasperating woman. I help you, I want you safe, and instead of at least appreciating the effort and the intention, you make me sound like a sick monster!"

"There's a fine line between helping and manipulating. One is asked for, the other is imposed."

"Then why don't you *ask?*" he growled, the hands digging in his hair the equivalent of a roar of frustration. "Why don't you accept my help and protection? Do you think I want to skulk behind your back? If you let me in, if you tell me your moves and plans, if you let me help you, like you do with your father—"

"Okay, stop right there. You're demanding the same treatment I give my father?"

"No. I demand more. I'm your man."

I snorted. He tutted.

"Prickly. I said I'm 'your' man."

Yeah. I heard. And it sounded so—so—everything. Not good at all, this moronic fluttering.

"Are you? Everything you say now is suspect." I could swear the air above him shimmered. His heat shooting off the scale. Just like mine, then. "Bound to happen, after all these lies. Your first ones ended in me killing Jake."

No need to guess what he felt now. No substitutes for roars, either. I bet this was his first good one in four months.

"Oh, no. Not that! I'm damned if I'm paying for a sin I didn't commit. You're *not* throwing Jake in my lap. I didn't make you kill Jake. *He* did. It's time you accepted *his* responsibility for his death. He would have killed you if you hadn't killed him first. And you confronted him in the first place because you knew if you let him go, you'd be his accomplice in the genocides he was planning. You did what you had to do. Just like I did."

The jagged memory of ending Jake's life struck again, stuck in my chest, shredding. Damian reached for me, contained me. Just a second, I promised myself, till the wave passed.

"I know it hurts," he whispered, his lips smoothing my bangs out of my misting vision. "No matter what he'd done. I wish to God every day you hadn't stopped me from killing him myself."

"I wouldn't have if you hadn't *lied* to me, making me misread the whole situation." I shoved him away, severing the soothing trickle of kisses cascading down my face. "But your other lies are far worse. You stripped me of secrecy and autonomy, and you may have doomed me and my operation."

Something jolted in his eyes before his whole face hardened around it. "You think I'd jeopardize you?"

"Not intentionally. Maybe." He growled but I went on. "But those who do your dirty work, who have access to my secrets can."

"*No one* but my core team, people who care about you, who've fought beside you and defended you with their lives, know about you. I'd stake my life on their integrity. I do every day."

"You're free to stake yourself. And if it was only me, I wouldn't mind much. It's my team I'm worried about."

"I follow only you. I ran checks on your team only to confirm their fitness to be around you. It's all about your safety."

"You have any idea how creepy this is? You're stalking me!"

He bore down on me, getting bigger in his anger. "You're not only the woman I love, you're the warrior I created. It's my damn *responsibility* to do everything I can to help you, to keep you functioning at top performance. To keep you alive."

That silenced me. *He has a point here, a claim,* a conceding voice insisted, taking his side.

And my answer? The consensus of my wounded heart and enraged mind? To the voice, a deafening *shut up.* To him, like I said before, "Like hell!"

I spun around, a whimper punching out of me at the pain tearing in my back and knee and right hip. "You and Sir Ashton said PATS and GCA were never involved, that your spying-on-Calista racket was a personal pet project. But is that even realistic? You breached us, probably have us documented down to our genetic maps. What's to stop someone from tapping you? What if double agents have infiltrated both organizations? Jake told me as much. By spying on me you may have sentenced us all to death."

"If so, why are you all still in one piece?"

"Maybe it's the calm before the storm. And anyway, Matt isn't, remember? Maybe some leak has already occurred and his condition is some enemy rattling the bag first, making sure the little mice are too confused, too busy hanging on to prepare for a big strike, to fight back or even run."

It was his turn to be silenced. I got out fresh clothes, almost hearing him replaying my words in his mind, cross-referencing everything surrounding the situation. Seemed he came up with a verdict. He announced it.

"Sounds like a fun theory, but totally unsubstantiated and implausible. A leak is not possible."

I shook my head and he came around me and caught it in his hands, stilled it, pressed one hard kiss to my compressed mouth. "It isn't. I recheck every move I make around you a hundred times. Matt's condition isn't a leak, not from my side."

"Still trying to convince me it's on mine? Maybe. If Ayesha can be made to betray me, anything's possible."

He snatched a look heavenward, rasped, "She helped me, put me out of my misery. She loves you, almost as much as I do."

Yeah, and I loved her. And him. God help me. "I trust you with my life but not to be aboveboard with me, to respect me! I can't live trying to guess when the next lie is going to come or what it's going to be. I can't keep rationalizing that your actions were concealed out of fear of my neurotic reactions, and taken with the best of intentions. You know where those lead."

"Calista, I'll never—"

"Don't you dare say you'll never lie to me again! You said it after your surgery and again last month. Both times I said I didn't believe you. But it turns out, I did. I believed you. *In* you. Deep down I always thought of you as—as Captain America or something—someone with black and white values. This disillusion is what hurts so much. It's what I can't forget."

"You're blowing this out of all proportion, entering a vicious cycle where everything I ever said or did is suspect."

"And whose fault is that? I've seen you act, Damian, and it felt as sincere as what you're saying now."

"You talk as if you don't act, too! You act every day on the job, to gain your ends—good, noble ends!"

"But I don't con my friends or my allies. I never lied to you, Damian. And you know what? After seeing how far you go to get the job done, I'm wondering what you'll do if one day your assignment is to liquidate me."

He reached for me, the arms convulsing around me eloquent with outrage and horror. "Stop! Stop it! You'll talk yourself into losing track of everything we ever had. You *know* me. You know how I feel, what I did, what I'd do for you. So I made mistakes, but they all stemmed from being unable to come to terms with how much you mean to me, being unable to contemplate losing you. I'm new to needing, to fearing for someone far beyond life and duty. So I made mistakes. Don't make me pay for them by losing you."

And I can't lose you. And I can't love you so much that losing you would end my world. And it seems I'm too late, on all counts.

I staggered away, flung my hands up, venting frustration, conceding vulnerability, limped to the bathroom. I paused on the threshold, my heart crumpling. "Be gone when I'm out."

His brooding gaze fixed me in place. Then he marched up to me, hauled me up into his arms. "Not without a shower goodbye."

Chapter 7

I couldn't believe I was doing this.

How self-sabotaging and counterproductive could I get?

Right now, as the bathroom steamed over and Damian's hands, lips and teeth caressed my clothes off me, slow, sensuous, hungry and careful, not only couldn't I give a damn, I couldn't wait.

There was only so much temptation a woman could withstand.

He got me naked as if by magic. His eyes roamed over me with blazing lust, making me feel all-feminine, all-desirable. Still fully clothed, he plastered me to him, his breath hotter than the steam as he whispered, thick and sexy, "Calista—you look like hell."

What?

I opened my mouth to hurl some in-your-face retaliation. I closed it. The infuriating and unfair thing was, no similar slur was anywhere near the truth. *He* looked heart wrenching. Every nerve down to my teeth roots was tingling, itching to sink into him.

But give me a break. Ayesha making that statement and my

knowing it was one thing. Him saying it as I stood naked for his inspection was another. This must be how a stained rag feels.

I turned to the mirror, glowered at my reflection, at him. "Thanks for the rave review. I'll sure use it in my ad campaign. Say, let me order you a stand-in. Any preferences or is anything okay as long as she doesn't look like a punching bag?"

He leaned one shoulder on the wall, crossed his arms over his expansive chest. Lust swept me unabated. "Five foot five, a thousand-shades, hip-long hair she keeps imprisoned in a braid to mess me up, obsidian eyes that drive me to extremes that make her mad at me, a mind I gladly cut myself to shreds on, a heart overflowing with addictive passion and a body that has me literally by the balls. Can you find me another one like that?"

Oh, come *on*. Was preemptive seduction part of his PATS training? Was this one of his duties as an undercover agent? Seducing women into selling out their men, countries, children and souls? He could bring down whole world orders that way.

It really wasn't conductive to my current confidence levels, imagining all the women who'd kill for a word of the sonnet-like phrases he was lavishing on me. Made me wonder again what made me so special, what made him say the words, feel them.

Made me wonder if they could possibly be true.

A new suspicion hit—hard. Could there be a reason he was pursuing me apart from his declared ones? Would I one day discover it? Discover that he didn't love me, never had…?

I was doing what he had predicted. And paranoia sure didn't become me. Better watch out before I found myself pacing and pondering, To be or not to be!

Take it easy. Go light. I smirked at him. "The only one resembling that extravagant description, if only in the bare outlines, doesn't only look like hell, she's hell to be around."

"Deal. Take me to hell."

He moved. More like flowed. Incredible. Nature was such a grossly unfair system, endowing one being with so much. Not even massive injury and dying a couple of times had left their marks. Wouldn't surprise me if he had paranormal healing power, like that mutant guy, Wolverine.

"This won't change a thing, Damian."

He caught my bottom lip, suckled and soothed, breathed his answer with his hunger into my lungs. "I'll take my chances."

I groped for his lips, needing a grinding kiss. He escaped me, rubbed his face over my neck and breasts, capturing each nipple and repeating the ritual. I crushed his head to me, cupped my breasts for a better offering. He just chuckled and moved away. The tormenting bas—uh, better find some other insult where he was concerned. Would *swine* do? *Scoundrel?* Nah.

He snapped off his sweatshirt and I turned away. Couldn't look at his chest. I relived sawing it open and bathing in his blood in 3-D horror clear enough without the visual stimulation.

Gentle, inexorable fingers brought my face around, others taking my hand to his fervent kiss before placing it on the ten-inch, almost-faded scar. "I'm fine. I'm better than fine."

My hand jerked over his satin skin, dug in the formidable muscles I'd sliced open. My heart and body liquefied. Pathetic. I hoped in the shower he'd think the puddle gathering around me was water and not drool—and other things.

But even if I was forgetting the past for now, was I really up to this? Had to warn him. "Well, *I'm* not fine. A mass of bruises and aches won't be too much fun for you—or me."

He gave me an are-you-out-of-your-mind smile. "Let me worry about me. And when I'm done, you won't have any worries, either."

Then he undid his pants and stepped out of them.

Mama! "Uh, another thing. We *can't.* I—have no protection."

Protection, in the plural, materialized out of his jeans' back pocket. "No problem."

Oh, yeah? "Came confidently prepared, huh?"

"I knew you'd see the not-to-be-missed opportunity."

My body's throbbing was escalating to pounding. I yelled it down. "Just for that crack, buddy, you get to miss it." I pushed him away. I doubt I could have if he hadn't ridden my shove. He ended up back to the door, an abrupt laugh escaping him.

I looked back. Not very wise, taking another look at that hard, long, thick promise of endless pleasure beckoning to me to come ride it. The pressure rose to critical. I snapped.

"What?"

He closed his eyes. "I'm wondering why I do this to myself. Why I don't walk out this door and save myself the grief."

I wondered myself. But then, Damian never gave up. Was that it? My attraction? That he couldn't be sure of me?

God, paranoia was an insidious poison once it hit your bloodstream, wasn't it? I was lucid enough to know I *wasn't* lucid enough. Better not let any ideas take hold right now.

Still, I turned on him, snarling, "Beats me! There's the door, beckoning. Go right through. Send a postcard sometime. Or don't."

He straightened, the eyes that had been teasing and seducing a minute ago, dark, troubled. "I'll need to hear one thing first. So let me hear it. Set me free. Say 'I don't care, Damian. It won't kill me to lose you. I'll just get another man.' Say this, Calista, and you'll be rid of me."

Say it, Calista, self-preservation urged. *Set him free. And yourself.* Was it kidding? I'd die before I lied to him that way. Even if he was lying to me. "You're one hell of a blackmailer, Damian. You know I could never say that."

His eyes lowered, then squeezed shut. Finally he spoke, deep, deep and hushed. "I *know* no such thing, Calista."

He didn't? Had he voiced his insecurities and asked me to validate them and end his torment? Or was this another act?

As soon as the thought hit me, I wanted to hit him and scream, *See what you've done to me? To us?*

He slowly approached me again, animation surging back into his gaze, his voice. "But you're a tormenting imp, aren't you. Giving me just enough to deny the extreme scenario I painted, but nothing really positive, either."

"Oh, you want an undying declaration of love?"

He bent, carried me into the shower. Feeling his hard, cool flesh against mine sent my head lolling on his shoulder. "That would be a start. Make it as frequent as you can manage it."

The hot water hit my wailing nerve endings. Arousal and aches swept into an indecipherable mess. I clung, moaning, when he set me down. "Why? Because you're a control freak? A conquest-fixated, chest-thumping Tarzan whose self-esteem would shrivel without constant fixes of female adoration?"

"*My* female's adoration."

I bit him. His taste, his chuckling groan, flooded me. A finger traced the canines embedded in his flesh.

"Retract these feminist fangs. I'm *your* male, too."

Really? How could I pick what to believe in what he said? I—I—aah...Another wave of sensation crashed, swamping all doubts. He was undoing my braid, his fingers and mouth working on the loosened mass, working me from head to hips. My legs buckled.

He went down with me, took me on his lap as he folded six foot five worth of muscle on the cramped shower floor. I panicked for a second. I had cleaned it yesterday, hadn't I?

He started shampooing my hair. The bolts of pleasure became a constant high-voltage current. "I dreamed of this for over six years, us like this, your one-of-a-kind hair shrouding us. The past four months, it's become an obsession. Owing you my life has sort of compounded the damage."

That dragged me back. "I can stop you feeling indebted, De Luna. I can push you off a cliff and cancel out my good deed."

"Very thoughtful of you. But if you insist, we can agree it was your actions, as usual, that almost got me killed in the first place, taking care of any gratitude." He winked as he turned the water off, started splashing globs of shower gel on me. Another salvo of desire detonated, imagining him…ohh…

His hands left no inch untended to. I bit into him again, pressing whichever part of me he was tormenting into his palms, asking for harder, more. Anything.

He gave me everything, his groans pained whenever he encountered a gash or a bruise. "But even if you hadn't held my heart in your hands and brought me back to life, you'd still have your grip inescapably there. What I feel for you sure as hell is enough on its own. More than I can handle most times."

My fingers dove into wet silk tresses, glided all over smooth toughness, his Native American legacy, lathering, kneading, lost in tactile nirvana. "Sounds like a debilitating disease."

"It sure is. It's invigorating and incapacitating. It's liberating and enslaving. It's every contradictory emotion I never thought I was equipped to feel. It *is* hell."

A hell I knew very well. Dammit. Why was it never easy? Why couldn't I just take him, let him take me and not think? "So why not do yourself a great service and just unfeel for me?"

He turned the shower on again, letting the jets bombard us and rinse away our mutual cleansing efforts. "You got an unfeeling-for-you medication? I'd need a lethal dose. Maybe some radical surgery."

"Mmm, how radical are we talking here?"

"Let's see. You'll have to remove my gray matter, my senses, my skin, and—" He looked down. I looked. Whoa. "That…"

That had to hurt. Bad. Good! I shouldn't be the only one with rivers of hormones swelling my tissues to bursting. And he was taking it so slow. Should I just attack him?

I almost had, that first time together. Back in Russia, in the refugee camp. There'd come a moment when I'd had enough. I'd lost too many people, in too many ways. I'd wanted him too long, too deeply. Then he'd protected me from the talons shredding my sanity, offered solace, laid back and let me devour him.

I wanted a repeat performance. Perpetually.

But *had* that been real? Oh no, I was losing it. I groaned. "Why don't you forget about me, Damian? Make things easier?"

He scooped me up, pressed me to the tile wall, slid up my body. "I don't want easy." He undulated his chest against my bursting breasts. I gasped, arched. "I want hard. I want tempestuous and dangerous and borderline fatal. I want *you.*"

Suited me. I wanted the same, and only he would ever answer the criteria. I took the words from his lips. He tasted like life and power and need and ecstasy, his words like everything worth having. I opened for his tongue, a sigh of immense relief pouring as I murmured around it, "I meant easier for me."

A profound sound escaped him, like he was a starving man welcoming the first bite. "Would you forget me if I stopped? Coming, trying?"

"Yeah. Soon as I unburn your brand from my brain." There. The appalling depth of my involvement. Let him use it as he would.

The need to mingle with his flesh stabbed me. I ground myself into his hardness, soothing the soreness. I hated that I needed him this way, that he was irreplaceable. Hated that I couldn't forget what he'd done and drown in him. Hated it even more that I was doing just that.

No more. Fear, doubt, responsibility, love... I heard echoes of what sounded like my voice vibrating the shower stall. Had I raved that out loud?

Of all times to have a breakdown.

"Shh, Calista, shh, *mi amor.*" Mi amor? Spanish? He coos to me in Spanish in my condition? Was he out to kill me? I bucked in his arms, pushing, pulling, wanting, needing—now!

"Let me—let me. I'll make it all right." His power cherished, flexed, plastering me to slick, hard flesh.

"You're making it worse." This was a definite sob now. I scratched him, sank my teeth in his pectoralis, beside his scar, opened my mouth on his heart, shook with every slow, booming heartbeat, relief, grief, arousal, sending me berserk.

Growls of pain, of voracity rumbled from his chest. He hauled me up, poured them into my lips. "Just let go, let go, *querida.*"

I sagged in his hold. He held me up, slid down my body, buried his face in me, murmured enjoyment. I pressed myself against him and he gently bit me. I screamed.

He cupped my buttocks, kneaded, spread, his voice scorching my flesh. "Open for me, *amor*—give me all you have…."

He hauled my thighs onto his shoulders, sliding my flaming, streaming back up against the cold tiles, opening me up, where all agony poured. And then he lapped it all dry.

A scream welled from my depths, too frenzied to form. I had to make him understand. My voice wouldn't come. I managed a word, the one that mattered. "You…"

The hand kneading my buttocks convulsed in my flesh, opening me wider. He gave me one more lap. I think I blacked out, blinked back to his raised eyes—gold gems housing his intellect and virility. "*Sí, amor.* Me, every way you want me. Take this now."

It was his words. All desperation detonated, each convulsion wringing me tighter, drier of sensation.

I sagged, my hands gripping his head as he sucked in my quivering flesh, making sure I had nothing more to want, to feel. He stopped when there was no more, leaned his cheek on my thigh, rubbed his forming beard into it, heightening the intimacy.

Man, but he was magnanimous. My heart clenched an obsessive fist around the memory. Whatever happened, I'd never forget this.

I melted off his shoulders into arms that cascaded relaxing strokes all over me. I groaned. "You promised yourself. What was it? Another insubstantial promise?"

He rose, powerful, beautiful—alive. "That's insubstantial?"

Nope. Incomparable. I staggered to my knees, grabbed him

between trembling hands and lips. His surprise at the role reversal was short-lived, his surrender to my worshiping even shorter. He stopped me, hauled me up, dried me, then swept me back to bed. Had I bought a king-size bed with him in mind? Only glitch here was—he didn't join me on it.

He picked up something from the floor. A black bag. His. He opened it, produced bottles, opened them, lined them on my bedside table. His lips pressed my forehead. "Close your eyes, *amor.*"

I obeyed at once, my heart galloping and stumbling.

The glug of thick liquid pouring brushed my straining ears, then a rich, honey-like scent with a fruity tea undertone hit my other senses, soaked them through. My tongue tingled. I moaned, swallowed. Would he paint me with something and lick it off?

Sure enough, he spread the substance around my blackened eyes, my cheekbones, my jaw. Then powerful, tender fingers began rubbing it in. Slow. Hypnotic. The scent got stronger, my senses expanded. Comfort seeped with the oil through skin to bruised tissues. One hand remained diligent on my face, the other melted down my body. My eyes snapped open, saw his face, savage arousal stamping his stark beauty, his lips parted, swollen. I cried out.

He groaned, "Close your eyes, *mi vida.*" His life. He called me that....

His tongue plunged in my mouth, his fingers in my core, in total carnal invasion. I convulsed on his third stroke. He didn't stop, his thumb joining in, rubbing, light, patient, then harder, relentless, just right. I splintered in another orgasm.

"*Sí, belleza, sí.*"

His encouragements singed my lips, peaked the waves of release to pain. I burned out my cries, my all.

I know I fainted. Then awareness seeped back, to him caressing healing into other injuries, to an alien feeling shrouding me. Supreme well-being. My blood ran a heavy, luxuriant potion, my limbs hummed to a score of bliss.

He watched my face, intent, polished skin taut over bones jutting with hunger. It was still supreme satisfaction that poured over me as he admired his handiwork, the puddle of fulfillment I must present. I spread arms begging to be filled. He only snapped up another bottle. This time he held it above my breasts, let the thick liquid pour, the golden trickle winking tiny stars against the background darkness. It smelled different, like ginger, with something spicy and warm, and a hint of something like sandalwood.

"What is it?" I moaned deep and long as he began to massage it into my aching shoulders and ribs and breasts.

"Ginger, celery seed and amyris essential oils. For easing muscle pain and reducing swelling, helping with fatigue and releasing tension and stress. Said to be an aphrodisiac, too."

I bucked up from the bed when he circled both nipples, subsided, heaved again, gasped, "Around you I need a dampener."

He bit and suckled the fingers trying to grab him to me. "No dampening. Only thorough and repeated satisfaction."

"And how." I arched up, noticed his sustained erection. Oh, no. I'd been getting it all myself, giving nothing! I never saw anything so engorged before, not even him. I stroked him, mouth watering, insides clenching. "Come let me give it to you."

His erection jumped in my grip, his whole body quivering with suppressed tension. "Just lie back and enjoy, *mi amor.* I want you feeling no pain when I make love to you."

"I feel no pain now! That stuff you used at first must be a miracle. What is it?"

"Immortelle." Okay. Aptly named. I felt reborn, limitless. "Or helichrysum. Boosts healing and contains powerful anti-bruising agents. Soothing, antidepressant—helpful in exhaustion."

Everything I needed. "Oh, Damian. Thank you. I never thought you'd be one for aromatherapy. You came prepared for that, too."

"You were battered, in and out. I wanted to comfort you."

"You did. More than I can describe. But you've been aroused for—how long has it been?"

"What's an hour to six and a half years?"

"Oh, stop showing off. I have firsthand experience with your legendary stamina. Make love to me. Don't you dare hold back."

The look he gave me had a new gush flooding me. "I'll hold *your* back. Turn over, *querida*. And around, head to feet."

I'd never flopped over and on my axis that fast, not even with bullets whizzing over my head. He came behind me, readying himself. My anticipation frothed, going mad guessing his intention.

The next second oil poured on my back. My fist slammed the mattress. Enough. He rumbled something as fierce. I rammed my hips back at him, my insides scrunched, crazy for a relentless ride.

He leaned over, sank his teeth in my buttock. "Rise on your elbows, Calista. I want you to watch this."

I obeyed him, found myself looking in my full-length mirror a few feet from the bed. My heart sputtered to a standstill.

In caressing light and shadow, bodies of gold and bronze melded. A woman I didn't recognize, a face of blatant arousal and a body inviting anything and everything, lush and small against dominant virility chiseled by gods and a face befitting a higher being, tender, tempestuous, out of control and totally in it....

Why wasn't this on tape so I could see it for all eternity?

I watched his hands flowing down my back, thumbs pressing, gliding into my muscles, melting around my hips, positioning me. He turned me to the side so I could watch him push his erection against my entrance. I lunged back, tried to force him inside me. He held me off, teased me with shallow strokes.

"Just watch, *mi amor*. Do you see how magnificent you look, how voluptuous, how wild? And your hair—*Dios*, it's blazing silver and bronze, flowing toward me like it would engulf me. Do you see how ready for me you are? How we fit? Do you see *me*?"

Now what kind of a question was that, when all I ever saw was him? The only man I could ever love. Was he that man for real?

His eyes closed, then opened on a new determination, his mass and might flexing around me. Everything in me opened, accepted.

The power of his massaging deepened as it started. At last. Damian. Invading me, completing me, holding my eyes in the mirror as he eased his girth inside me, letting me open for him, letting me see the emotions transfiguring his magnificent face.

I lost sight of the incredible sequence when pleasure slashed me. My eyes rotated inside their sockets. I swear. Like a slot machine. Clinked in a jackpot position—position… This was our best one yet. Or maybe each time he touched me it got better.

My body wept more for him and he thrust, sought my depths. Found them. Then farther, filling me beyond capacity. Beyond description. The searing fullness, the idea. His hands caressed my back to the intensity of his thrusts, creating new pleasure receptors inside and out. Moans sharpened to keens. Then his hands took my neck. Alarm flashed. I never let myself be this vulnerable. Never.

But this is Damian. Yes… I melted in his grip, moaned my trust and his fingers moved, poured healing into ten-year tension and pain. I opened my eyes, saw him smile, bitter and resigned. The involuntary doubt. It had hurt him. I had.

"Damian…"

He stopped my explanation, apology—whatever, started the jarring thrusts I was mindless for. All nerves fired. *No.* I wanted it to last. Forever. If it ended, I'd have to *think* again.

He gave me no chance to hold back. Detonations started from the point he was buried deepest, rippled out in shock waves, each building where the last diminished. He rode me through every one.

Then he left my body, turned me on my back, dragged me open over his thighs, then rammed back inside me. His oil-slick hands unraveled me nerve by nerve, massaging to the rhythm of thrusts that impaled me to my heart. His generosity, the enormity of passion on his face had me cresting and crashing again.

This time he joined me, shouted, *"Te amo, Calista!"* and let his orgasm rip through him. I opened for him to take of me as hard, as fully as he needed. I felt his every spasm of release, his convulsions feeding mine, feeling his seed filling me even through the barrier, tears erupting at the sight, feel, concept.

Barely breathing hard, he reversed our position, the raggedness in his voice all the more moving for being emotion induced. "Come fill my arms, *mi corazón.*"

I dove into them, clung, put my lips to his scar and gave thanks. Tomorrow this could end. Or my life. Or the world. Now was all we ever had. I took now, drowned. Replete, complete.

I think I dreamed. Of Damian, turning on me. Of all my friends disappearing. I clung to Damian, trying to stop him from metamorphosing into a monster and he shook me away as familiar music played a maddeningly comic parody in the background....

"Calista, I'm just going to get your cell phone."

Consciousness descended like a hammer. I jackknifed up, my head warping under its blow, sagged down again with dread. Matt!

No. Not Matt. When did it ever turn out to be what I feared most? Had to be Ayesha, recalling me to duty.

Damian pressed the phone into my limp hand. I punched the answer button. Ayesha's sob punched back.

"Matt? Did he deteriorate?" I rasped.

Another harsh sob answered me. "It's worse than that!"

The room reeled.

Worse than that was dead.

Chapter 8

Matt's huge body was folded in a tight fetal ball.

The frozen area behind my sternum expanded, my heart pumping ice in my veins. I shuddered.

I had no time for going to pieces. Everything was prepared. The minor surgery room had been turned into a quarantine zone. Everyone was on full safety protocols. We had to assume this was infectious. Whatever "this" was. Just hoped our measures made a difference. That we weren't too late.

I hiked up my mask, placed my goggles over my eyes—and was instantly blinded. Dammit. So much for antifog coating.

Snapping them down, letting them clear, my gaze panned to Matt, faltered, blurred. I inhaled. *Steady.*

First I had to understand what was wrong with Matt.

Haiku finished injecting the infiltration anesthesia, and daubed Matt's lumbar area with povidine. She raised her eyes. "Done. Want me to do it, Cali?"

As our anesthetist, Haiku was qualified to perform a lumbar

puncture. I should let her do it. I couldn't. Matt was my responsibility. He wouldn't let anyone else touch me, either.

I shook my head. "You record the opening pressure when I enter the spinal canal. And be ready for any developments."

For *developments* read disastrous complications. At the drop in pressure in his spinal canal when my needle pierced it and released cerebrospinal fluid, his brain stem could jam through his skull outlet, leading to catastrophic or even fatal consequences.

There was no way around this. All ICP lowering measures had failed and we could no longer wait. A sample of CSF and a diagnosis were our only hope of pulling him out of the vicious cycle he'd entered. It was a choice between waiting or intervening. The first would surely kill him. The second might. *Might* sounded far better.

Ishmael had left one of Matt's hands outside the surgical drapes. I reached for it. All power gone, limp and dry and hot. Measures to control his fever had failed to bring his temperature to the baseline. We had also had to sedate him again for the procedure. Not that he'd been violent, just disoriented—heartbreaking.

Matt, help us. I need time to find out what's wrong with you. Please, please hang on.

I covered his hand, came around the table. "Ayesha, spinal guiding needle, twenty gauge, three-quarter inch and Tuohy catheter." Had to make allowance for Matt's muscle mass. Most people warranted half an inch only. The catheter was for leaving in after taking my sample, to inject analgesics for his severe back pain, blind antibiotics, and to drain more CSF to lower his ICP. Neither was in our stock lumbar puncture tray. She was ready with them. I picked them up. "Ready fifteen tubes. Ishmael, Haiku, flex him a bit more."

They held him knee to chest. I palpated for the fourth lumbar vertebra, introduced my needle, perpendicular, just below it, advanced upward, giving myself another chance to try above this spot if I failed. My breath bled out when I felt the pop. I'd pierced his dura mater, the outer covering of his spinal cord. I was in.

I withdrew the stylet of the needle, advanced the catheter, and the cerebrospinal fluid flowed out under pressure. My own pressure shot up, my breath clogging my lungs. *Come on, Matt.*

Haiku, ready with the manometer, measured the opening pressure. "Five hundred and twenty mm/Hg," she murmured, removed it, moved away.

God. Normal opening pressures ranged from eighty to one-eighty!

Thirty seconds passed as we monitored his unassisted breathing, his heart rate, his pupillary reflexes. Nothing changed. He wasn't herniating. *Oh, God, thank you.*

"Tubes." I forced the word out. Ayesha handed me one after another, opened. I filled each with two cc's of spinal fluid. Usually we filled five tubes. I was sending a set each to two more labs. Time I yelled for all the help I could get.

I withdrew the needle and Ayesha followed through, dressing the puncture site. We removed the drapes, unfolded Matt, turned him on his back. In minutes we'd hooked him back to his monitors, made sure his supportive measures were in place and replenished.

Another neuro and fundoscopic exam showed that CSF withdrawal had relieved the ICP. Not that it had improved his condition. Raised ICP was just the by-product of the underlying disorder.

At first glance, when I'd stormed back into IC, he'd seemed to be having another convulsion. And he had been. It had been his other symptoms that told me this was something totally new. Neck rigidity, raised ICP, many focal manifestations. One of his eyes had rolled inward, indicating abducent nerve paralysis, the cranial nerve moving extraocular muscles outward. Then the facial nerve followed, with facial paralysis developing.

All our internists and surgeons had been rushed in for a consultation and they'd all had one opinion.

Matt had all signs of acute, fulminating encephalitis.

So we had a diagnosis. At least, they called it that. I called it just a name for his condition. A diagnosis told me causes and their theories sure as hell weren't providing those. What that name did provide was one thing: the verdict that Matt had changed afflictions in midstride again.

His first manifestations clearly had been chemically induced, then they had changed from one class of drugs to another. Now he seemed to be suffering from a brain inflammation caused by a biological agent, a bacteria or a virus. Somehow, in the space of thirty-six hours he'd gone through two poisonings and one infection.

And it sure as hell didn't make sense!

But it had to, if we were to find a way to cure him. We had to be missing something. We just had to be.

Which was what my fellow doctors insisted was the only explanation. That I'd misdiagnosed him from the beginning and he'd been suffering from encephalitis all along.

My answer? No freaking way. I knew my poisonings and drug-altered statuses like nothing they'd ever imagine. And that was what Matt had suffered from at the outset.

Now to find out what was causing this bizarre sequence of events and progression of symptoms. At all costs.

I turned. "Lucia, Damian's in our den." I handed her the multi-tube holder. "Give him five, after you label them. And draw five bloods, too. Tell him I expect him to find out all he can."

Yeah, what better time for me to make use of his carte blanche? It was also time to get Sir Ashton to make good on his.

Ayesha followed me out of our new quarantine. Her agitation raked along my back. God I had no time for her. I picked up speed.

"I'd only been that scared before when Fatima disappeared."

Her words almost tripped me. *Ignore this!*

I couldn't. My eyes jerked back to hers. No doubt mine were as abused. Almost everyone in my team had lost loved ones in horrific circumstances. I'd lost my sister Clara to a surgeon's—or was it an anesthetist's?—mistake. Matt had lost his wife to a gang rape. But it had to be Ayesha who'd suffered the most mutilating loss. Her daughter had been kidnapped by an organ-harvesting mafia. For her to feel as scared and helpless about Matt as she had been about Fatima said—too much.

I turned, no fitting words or gesture coming to my rescue.

She went on. "He was coming out of it, then he started getting agitated again. I was calling you to ask if re-sedation was in order when he started shouting, 'My head is bursting—do something.' I was afraid to give him morphine in case it depressed his central nervous system more. Then he was yelling about his back and his muscles and screaming for us to turn the lights down. God, Cali, I thought he was having a psychotic episode, that that was what was wrong with him all along. All the time he was in agony…."

Okay. Enough. I took her by the shoulders. "Don't blame yourself. There was no way you could have guessed what was wrong with him. Hell, we have tons of investigations on our hands and ten doctors around and we still don't know a thing."

She closed her eyes. Her agony splashed on the backs of my hands. "What do you make of the investigations?" she whispered.

I withdrew my hands, tempted to wipe the scalding emotion off. "What's to make? Perfect CTs and the most extensive toxicology tests came up with only traces of his anti-allergic medication and not even the most distant metabolite of any drug causing his first or second toxidromes. No elevated enzymes indicating poisoning or white blood cells or immunoglobulins or antibodies indicating any inflammation or infection.

"The positive findings are only to be expected. The elevated myoglobin in his urine and potassium and phosphate in his blood are only normal after his violent exertion. The elevated lactate is agitation induced alone. Clotting factors are also abnormal but they are consistent with his violence, convulsions and hyperthermia. So nothing specific. No answers, no pointers, no leads. For all these results show, this is a bursting-with-health, clean-living man after a grueling squash match who should be on his feet and out there smashing bad guys."

"Maybe this round of CSFs will be more revealing?"

"We can only hope. But I'm not holding my breath and waiting. We could be dealing with a new drug that marries many existing ones successfully, manifesting all their effects."

"But wouldn't we still find traces of something even if we didn't know what it was?

"I don't know, Ayesha. Maybe it's a new formula that leaves behind no metabolites for detection with current testing kits. Maybe a hundred different things. Only way to find out is to retrace Matt's steps during the past week or so. Find out who could have gotten to him, poisoned him. We have to find out if there is such a new agent on the streets and get our hands on an antidote. Or at least sample, to make our own."

She chewed her lip. "But what if the tests come back with results that make all this unnecessary?"

I exhaled. "The only tests left out are ultra-specific serologic tests that can take days to weeks to come out. I don't think we have that long, Ayesha. I have a gut feeling this is a message, and I intend to find out who sent it."

A giggle escaped Ayesha, a weird sound, her warped smile an even weirder sight in her current agitation. "And we all know how reliable your gut feelings are."

"Oh, shut up. Take care of Matt. Don't hesitate to call all of us back if anything happens."

This time, I walked away. Right into Damian.

In my mind's eye, I completed the collision, surged into him and sought refuge. In this realm, I pulled back, hands on hips. "You're still here? Don't you have something to do?"

His eyes swept over me, gauging my state. His compressed lips detailed the ugly truth. "Yeah, Lucia gave me my assignment."

I started walking, headed for the room in which I took rest breaks at Sanctuary. "So?"

Longer strides kept him ahead. "It's been taken care of."

"Meaning you saddled one of your people with the job."

"One of the perks of being the leader."

I turned on him, a barrage on my lips, about how important those samples were, that I expected him to do it himself.

He dispersed it. "Suz was going out of her mind worrying over Matt and dying to be of use. Anyway, she's better than me in handling fragile stuff. Not that it's fragile. With Lucia's packaging it would take a bomb to mess the samples up. Suz is already halfway across the city to our best PATS-affiliated labs. There'll be no questions and twenty-four-hour, full-facilities dedication to Matt's samples. I had to stay here. For you."

Had to have the last word, huh? I had nothing to say to that. I wanted him here. I needed him. There, I'd admitted it.

He followed me into my room. Well, I didn't need help changing. "And where do you think you're going?"

His reply was nonchalant. "I don't know. I'm just following you."

"You're taking that to new heights, huh? I want to change."

He nodded, reached for my jeans' buttons.

I jumped back, my nerves jangling. "I do remember how to take off my own clothes."

One eyebrow arched his opinion of my prudishness. "Go ahead then. I wanted to help. But watching is as much fun."

I shook my head, turned to my zipped plastic closet. Striking while the iron was still molten, huh? Entrenching his "lover" status into status quo. Not if I had anything to say about it.

But I wasn't saying anything now. Matt's crisis was *the* thing on my plate. Resolving my ambiguous state of affairs, pun intended, with my Machiavellian lover didn't feature right now.

Yeah, *lover*. He could keep the title if he so wanted it. I sure wasn't endowing anyone else with it. Not in this lifetime. If he didn't use it, it would just rust and fade into nonexistence.

I undressed in less then my usual minute, not once looking back to see Damian's reaction. He wanted to watch? He was welcome. He'd seen—and done—it all by now. I shouldn't even think of being uncomfortable having him around.

Weird thing was, I was. Blotched-red-down-to-my-toes uncomfortable. If I didn't know better I'd even say—shy.

I rummaged for my disguise for today. I kept about a dozen identities to keep my true identity a secret from the dangerous world we worked in. Staying anonymous meant staying alive. I pulled out a black Lycra micro-dress and coat, thick flesh-tinted hose, six-inch platform shoes. Completing the picture were jade contact lenses, purple lipstick and a black shoulder-length wig.

I sat down in the only chair in the tiny room, started putting the hose on. Damian's eyes scorched a path to my core. Good thing I was too messed up over Matt to respond in full power. He moved his gaze away. Suddenly I felt bereft.

He swooped down on the dress. One good look, then he stated, "You're not wearing this. Not if you want to leave this room."

I snatched it from his grip, hiked it on in two motions. "I thought you were only watching. Commentary isn't in the bargain." I shoved my feet into the shoes, stood up.

He took a step away, appraised the result. "If it's for my benefit, I prefer you in fatigues. Or naked. Take it off."

For answer, I turned my back on him, started the complicated ritual of wrapping masses of hair flat around my head. Once done, I flopped the wig on, popped the lenses in. Then it was on to applying another face. I needed mortuary-strength makeup to cover up my bruises. Good thing about them was they were almost identical. Contributed to making me unrecognizable.

He came behind me, capturing my eyes in the mirror, his simmering even in the cold reflection. "So where do you think you're going dressed like that?"

Absurd-answer-to-stupid-question time. "To pick up men, of course. I worked up an appetite last night."

For a split second, a spurt of danger leapt off him. Couldn't even be teased about it, huh? Possessiveness red alert! Then he switched it off, just like that, turned oh-my-goodness-I'll-die-if-I-don't-get-me-some-of-that seductive. "Then you should wait until you get a taste of the encore I had planned for you. I'd still be serving it if I hadn't been interrupted."

And of that I was certain. If not for Matt, I would have been back in my bed, over and under him, trying my darnedest to get him out of my system through overload therapy.

"Damian, we'll resume this set of our verbal match sometime in the distant future. I have work to do."

All seduction left his face, another ultra-convincing mood and mask slipping on seamlessly. "What's your plan?"

Nice save. Nicer performance. Superlative actually. If they held Academy Awards at PATS, he'd rack in every one. I shrugged. "I'm going to retrace Matt's steps, pay a visit to a couple of stoolies, check out a new designer drug racket. I found a memo about it in Matt's stuff. It's my best lead in all this."

He frowned. "But you said his new symptoms look like brain inflammation and not poisoning or overdose."

"Yeah, but he started off hallucinating. Maybe his condition now is a coincidence. Aseptic encephalitis with no infective agent is rare, but not unheard of. Or maybe it'll turn out to be a known side effect of the unknown drug I'll investigate. Matt's notes say the designer drug allegedly about to hit the streets is being hailed as the biggest thing since Ecstasy. Maybe someone recognized Matt, gave him an advance sample of it—revenge, or a warning. Maybe when I get a sample, study its composition, it will explain all the discrepancies in timing and symptoms."

He looked as convinced as I felt. He didn't voice his opinion, though. Weird. I would have thought he'd be the first to tell me to wake up and smell the formalin. What was that confounding man up to?

"You have names? Pseudonyms? Possible locations? Connections?" he asked.

"Drug dealers are up my alley, not yours, Damian."

"Says who? They sleep with terrorists all the time."

Yeah. I knew that. I just wanted him off my back. Or maybe I didn't. "If you're offering to help, just say so."

His smile poured right into my battered insides. "So."

Oh God. I needed this, his support, his caring. I leaned into him. He perched his hip on the dresser, pulled me into his large frame, surrounded me, hid me. "Give me anything you have."

"I will, on the way. Let's go."

He pressed my head to his heart, kissed the top of my wig, gave a grunt of disgust. "*I'll* go. You stay here and take care of Matt. And get that dead synthetic dog off your head."

I pulled out of his embrace. "No, Damian. You're not taking over. This is my operation. I need to get names and facts and samples. This is not a PATS search-and-destroy sweep."

"You'll get your samples, if they are there to be had!"

"You promise you won't get carried away, follow your programming and wipe out every hive you find?" What was I doing, asking him to *promise?* Did idiots ever get past their idiocies?

My raised hand closed his mouth, no doubt on the promise-her-anything reflex. "Don't. I already have a matching set of fake promises. And I changed my mind. You've done your bit for Matt. So thanks and please get me any info on his samples, but in any other way, stay out of it. I won't ask you to promise that you will."

He straightened. The room shrank. "Don't bother. You want me to stay out of it? You got it. Seems I have limits, Calista. You just pushed me to them. And this time, I'm staying pushed."

Chapter 9

"Yo, bitch, wazza rate?"

The nasty, guttural voice I'd been itching to hear all night called out to me over the pounding beat.

According to my freshly acquired info, this leering mass of DNA waste was Richard White, going by the badass street name of Filthy Rich. He had the filthy part down. I wanted him. And I'd succeeded in making him want me.

About time. I was beginning to get tired. Of being stuffed in that dress, of acting under twenty, of pretending to dig the rave scene. Of beating back the wandering hands and lewd offers.

Filthy was number three in the operation I was looking for. I'd had him tagged, had listened in on an afternoon's worth of a thoroughly disgusting life. I got my details.

There *was* a new designer drug. Very hard to manufacture, a top-secret formula, making this slimeball's operation confident of cornering the market, one they expected to be heroin-huge. The boasted effect of the new drug was unpredictable. Much like

LSD in its user-related differences but far more potent. Couldn't be clear what those effects were among the steady stream of lowlife lingo that spilled out of this creep's lax mouth.

At least my stoolie's info had been exact, first time out. Seems he'd realized I wouldn't just have him arrested with an anonymous tip to the LAPD with evidence of his latest felony. *This* time, he'd realized, my pressure methods would be harsher.

I swaggered over to Filthy, yelled over the grinding techno music quaking the warehouse-turned-rave-center. "You talkin' to me? Wassat? A lady can' dress up and get some respec', too?"

Thick lips spread. "Come'ere. I give you some real respec'."

And there shouldn't be any question what that dickhead meant. I smirked at him. "Wow, man. How generous. You fer real?"

Eyes black as mine, sans lenses, but dead matte with that nauseating mix of viciousness, cunning and stupidity, widened. His interest levels were shooting up. I'd done my homework. One sheet of paper had told me all there was to know about Filthy.

He liked his "bitches" fit and white. Very. And he had a sentimental streak, too. He fell hard. Hit harder when women tried to walk away. And he was in between "love interests." It was why I'd come after him rather than number one or two. I fit his bill. And he was following his programming with all the predictability expected from an amoeba-level life-form.

I needed a sample of his poison. A list of his sub-dealers, distributors and major pushers would come in handy, too. Then I'd walk away. If not before I broke every bone in his body as a collective overdue payment, courtesy of all those women he'd crippled or snuffed playing Othello. That and the life sentence I'd make sure he got. Maybe in my father's prison. The idea made me feel almost sorry for the scumbag.

Now his eyes were defiling their way up my muscled thighs. "You wanna drink? Or aren't ya old enough yet?"

Good old age-deceptive looks. Another thing that made me his kind of catch. He liked 'em young. Very. Yeah, his bill was a long one indeed. I stood before him, hands on hips. "I'm legal. And I'm buying. Move over. My feet are killin' me." I knocked his foot off his knee with mine.

That got him good. He was used to women sucking up to him and/or being scared out of their wits. He spouted off about needing a bitch who wouldn't buckle under his "strength of character." He had himself some of that coming, right down his throat.

My unblinking role breaking had him instinctively scooting over the couch, letting me flop down, his slanting eyes widening more, his lips getting fuller, wetter, the flare of interest taking on a glazed tinge. The bastard was falling in love.

"So—you someone?" I looked up and down his gym-pumped body. Thirty-four, kept in shape, a P. Diddy wannabe. Would pull it off, too, if he'd only bathe. "A rapper or somethin'?"

"I'm way better, girl. *Way* better. I make 'em. Or break 'em." He leaned over, one big hand snaking under my buttocks.

I made room, then sat on it, bending two fingers backward, hard. He yelped, withdrew his hand. I hit him with a harder look. "You a producer, then? Quit wastin' m'time!"

He rubbed his fingers, his grin malicious and soppy all at once. "Ya got a tight ass, girl." I started to rise. A hand on my forearm stopped me. I glared it off. "I'm a candyman."

I curled my lip. "A pusher? Hah. You and every pseudo-male I met tonight. I talk only to men worth talkin' to. Here, thass for the drinks." I tossed ten bucks on the table, jumped up.

He half rose after me. "You wait here, girl. I'm someone. I ain't no pusher. I'm the big man, the travel agent."

Would he stop it already with the street synonyms for drug supplier? And how come he was admitting it to a five-minute non-acquaintance, one who could be a cop? Felt secure, did he?

He had reason to. I'd counted seven underlings among the ravers, the all-brawn variety. And in a crowded place like this, getting rid of one female would go unnoticed, cop or no cop. There was no way any recordings could be made in this pandemonium. As for verbal evidence, he probably had his ass legally covered, too.

He had two hundred and five bones in his body. I wondered how many I'd break before I was through. Times like this I loved being a surgeon.

I looked down on him. Time to play him some more, move into the next phase. "You crazy, man? What if I wuz a cop?"

"You ain't no cop. I smell 'em a hundred yards away."

Like they'd smell you! But he had a good nose, I gave him that. A miracle he retained any olfactory powers with his aroma.

"I ain't no raspberry, dude." That was a female who traded sex for drugs or the money to buy them, since we were talking lowlife. "I don't do drugs, so if thass what you're sellin' me…"

"I don't do drugs, either. And I like my women clean. I smell those, too. Thass why I called ya. I'm selling…" He paused, lost for words. His frown detailed his chagrin at the unprecedented occurrence. He made a quick recovery. "What do you wan' me to sell ya? Anythin' you want, I'm sellin' it."

I braced one knee on the couch, brushed his thigh, dropped my lips to his ear, gagging inwardly on his stench. He quivered in anticipation. Males! "I'm a businesswoman. I deal in opportunity. Ya got one to sell me?"

His face brightened. *Bingo* all but flashed on his forehead. "Is yer lucky day, girl."

Bingo flashed in my mind, too.

"You got yerself a nice setup, dude," I drawled, still fuming at the frisking his men had given me before letting me into his office-pad. It was at the far end of the warehouse, on a split-level overlooking the rave. If not overhearing. The soundproofing here rivaled a spaceship's. Maybe I could ask for his contractor's number for my own noise-infested condo.

I walked away, went to the wall-to-wall window. Psychedelic lights, club drugs, young people throwing their health and lives away in the so-called pursuit of a good time and recognition as one of the hip new world. And freedom, of course.

Wondered when it would hit them, that they'd indentured their fates to a far more destructive form of conformity, belonging to the self-serving and abusing herd? That in running from societal control they had surrendered themselves to a malignant and inescapable form of dictatorship? Pathetic. Sad. Not to mention enraging.

Him, he was just nauseating. And obvious. The way he kept touching the painting beside the door told me he couldn't wait for me to notice, to comment on his good taste. The nouveau riche son of a bitch was "doing art," hungry for an upgrade in class and a coating of off-the-shelf refinement. He had the money and now wanted to rewrite his history, launder his image.

Time to throw him more off balance. "Hey, izzat a Marsden Hartley original? Man, I can' believe it. You into art?"

He obviously couldn't believe his luck, either, that he'd gotten hold of someone who understood the significance of his pride and joy, along with her other attributes. He could brag to his heart's content to someone who'd appreciate it.

He stroked it, imitating the way he would me, his newest acquisition. "Yeah. Ain't it a beaut?"

"Where'd you lift it from?"

That hit a nerve. He straightened. "I bought it, girl! Three months ago in a freakin' o-thentic art auction."

"Whatever you say." He bristled at my impudence. I ignored him, inspected the glass. An inch thick, probably bulletproof and one-way mirrored. No escape route this way if needed. Only visible way out was back through that door. Okay. Got it. I turned to him, smirking. "Business must be boomin'."

He strutted around, then toward me. "It ain't boomin' yet,

girl. This is regular earnings from unprofitable stuff like 151 and La Chiva."

Crack cocaine and heroin, unprofitable? That was whistle worthy. It sure spoke of the magnitude of his profit projections for the new drug.

"Once we start peddling the 'opportunity,' I'm buyin' me an estate. Wanna share it?"

He slipped my coat from my shoulders. What a gentleman. My act was working a spell on him. So much so that my stomach was starting to cramp. This was too smooth.

I was prepared for rough. His goons had missed my arsenal. My six-inch platform shoes, my trinket-filled bag, beneath my wig and in my bra support. And then, he was carrying—I could always borrow his piece. I'd still be glad if I didn't need any of that.

I slipped from the hands encircling my waist, heard him groan. "And what do the 'opportunity' have that others don't?"

"Exclusivity fer one."

I was impressed. He could pronounce a five-syllable word?

"Concentration fer two. One kilo gets you three thousand on the streets. Then there's the addictiveness. One hit an' they keep coming back fo' more, or they go ta hell."

Was that what happened to Matt? What was still happening…?

Time to wrap this up before I was tempted to wrap up his sick life. I cocked my head at him. "So what are ya selling me? I came up here to get samples and talk business."

His vicious eyes narrowed. "Ain't no good thinkin' you get away with a sample to make yer own, girl. It ain't happenin'."

As in, I couldn't if I tried? If he believed it impossible to replicate, it should make volunteering a sample easier. He kept a stash here, for cutting deals. I'd rather not waste time searching for it. Or beating him up for it. *That* would be my farewell.

He must really have his ass covered, to have the stuff lying around in a police-monitored rave center. Must also have a surefire escape route in case of crackdowns. Maybe I could persuade him to share it. Would prefer not to leave the same way I came in.

I shrugged. "Why should I go to the trouble if yer supplyin'? I wanna sample for my connoisseur to see if it's worth the hype."

He whistled. "You got yerself a taster? You mean business fer sure, girl. How come I never seen you before?"

"I'm new to the City of Angels. All the way from the Apple. Got too hot for me there. Nicer weather here."

"Yeah." He moved in the direction of the painting, stopped, turned. "So, I give ya yer sample, what ya sellin' in return?"

I turned to him. "Said I'm no raspberry!"

The door burst open on two gun-first goons. One of them snarled, "She's a damn mole, boss."

Uh-oh! They'd found me out somehow. Okay. *Here we go.*

I was already behind Filthy's massive oak desk as his gaping reaction started to form. My heartbeat slowed, the extra speed pouring into my reflexes, the engrained protocols firing up my nervous pathways, my awareness splitting wide open, taking everything in and acting out my plan simultaneously.

The two thugs weren't followed by more. I had three to contend with. Had to bring them down, at once. And for all.

One hollow heel snapped open under pressure in certain sequence, three cyanide blow-darts spilling into my grip, my fingers weaving around them. My other hand retrieved the *bo shuriken* darts from the other heel, brought them to my lips and then went after the *hira shuriken* throwing-blades in my makeup kit's hidden level.

All the time a volley of enraged questions and answers popped in the sound-smothering room, followed by shouts. His, calling to me to come out on my own or else, calling me names. Theirs, asking his permission to deal with me. But no shots.

I doubted Filthy would want me killed right off. I could feel the realization of his own stupidity hitting him, coming off him in primitive, humiliated fury, radiating his filthy aura, filling the room. If he caught me, he'd have too much of a good time getting even for my stringing him along.

Getting caught didn't figure in my plan.

I called out, buying time. "What're you crazy dudes doing?"

"Come out, bitch!" Filthy roared.

Then I almost heard his mind click, reaching the conclusion that I was unarmed and helpless, cowering behind his desk. He must have given his cronies a silent signal to go drag me out. Good boy.

They came at me, one from above the desk, one around it. Heart-snatching and healthy fear burst—the catalyst I needed. One of my hands hurled a *bo shuriken,* the other brought the cyanide blow-dart to my lips. I blew.

I got the first in his left eye, perforating it right down to its boney bed. I got the second in the neck.

The first one screamed, once, before neurogenic shock hit. Never heard anything like the already dead shriek, aborted in the echoless environment. The second one stared, hyperventilating, his gun right in my face, his finger on the trigger. One lurch and his last action could be blowing a hole in my forehead and a bigger opening out the back of my head. Didn't think so.

In another burst of repugnance and dread, I knocked his hand away with one fist, my leg ripping both of his from under him. He fell, in shock, with what cyanide victims suffer before they succumb physically—sure in the knowledge that a poison is already riding the rapids of their bloodstream, too swift for hope of an antidote, that their very heartbeats will deliver it to their cells, beating faster to bring a quicker end.

He'd stop breathing within three minutes, and living in under eight. Two were out of my way. One remained. Filthy.

His stampeding feet vibrated the heavily carpeted floor. I saw their shadow streaking beneath the desk. Had to deal with him before rage and macho stupidity dissipated and he wised up and ran for backup. There was also this matter of saving me the trouble and the time of opening his safe, of providing the rest of my needed info items. Of pointing out his contingency escape route.

Problem was, he was breaking out of character. He didn't come after me with threats and fists and feet, but with bullets. The muffled shots slammed into my hideaway. One ripped through two thinner panels of wood, whizzed out beside my head. I flattened to the ground, every nerve jumping, expecting one missile among the hail to explode its way into my flesh.

Breathe. Stay down. He was smarter than I gave him credit for. Or maybe the sight of his two behemoths dead in under a minute had boosted his intelligence fast. He must know now that he had no time to mess with me.

One way out of this. To lunge up, already firing a cyanide dart, hope he didn't get a bead on me in the seconds I needed, duck back down again. I could probably do it.

Problem here was, I needed him alive.

So it was either he killed me or I killed him and got out of here empty-handed.

Or maybe there was a third way….

I grabbed the dustbin, threw it in an arc designed to pass over his head. He reacted instinctively, lashing out at the perceived threat with a burst of bullets. I popped out, a *bo shuriken* launching from my hand, lodging in his wrist. He didn't let go of the gun, panning in disbelief from his wrist to me. His pain threshold was high—got to give him that. He didn't even shout. I was already crouching on the desk, taking my weight on my hands, lashing out at his bloody hand with a two-footed kick. He dropped the gun. Then he charged, bellowing like a warthog, and tackled me to the floor. He fell on me with his considerable mass.

My flesh ground into my bones. My lungs emptied. Bad mistake. Could only get leverage, power if I could breathe. *Get him off.*

I was on auto now, my ingrained training grabbing at fear and aggression, funneling them where they'd do the most good, the most damage. I rammed my forehead into his nose. He lurched backward, his blood spattering my face and neck. Air rushed into my lungs under pressure. For just the duration of one lungful. His hands were swooping for my neck, clamping, his thumbs fumbling for my larynx. *Don't let him get a lock.*

My *bo shuriken!* It was still lodged deep in his wrist. I grabbed it, twisted. That got me the scream he wouldn't let me have the first time. He still wouldn't let go. I thrust deeper. Then I snatched it out, corkscrew fashion. More blood sprayed me, a geyser now. I'd severed his radial artery.

The abused hand lurched away now, breaking his vise. Problem was, his other fisted simultaneously, hurtling for my nose. If it connected, he could drive my bones into my brain.

I jerked my face away, my open palm blocking his blow with nothing to spare, his fist still impacting my ear. I was covered in his blood now, nausea and pain still unregistering. One thing reverberated inside me. *Matt. Get what you need to save him.*

Filthy hit me again, his knee plowing into my pelvis. Jagged sensations shattered out, sweeping me.

End this. Claw his eyes out. He goes spastic with shock and pain, you drive your knee in his middle, throw him over your head….

No—that was out—I needed him to see, to get me what I needed. Needed another maneuver. *Go for the obvious—hope it'll be enough.*

I stabbed my thumb into his wound, hooked. Then I shredded down with all my strength. That got him howling. And off me.

I snapped to my feet in a hands-free elastic rebound, landed in position, launched into a *tobi geri* jump-kick, my platform-heeled foot ramming his face before he got off his knees. Micro-dresses—the next best thing to stretch pants in a fight.

He staggered backward, lost his balance. Just for a second. Then all his gym training kicked in and he rebounded to his feet, a wounded bull coming after me. No danger here anymore. Not from him. But anyone could still walk in, and then this would get sticky. Maybe more than I could handle. *Get what you need and get out.*

I jumped over one of the fallen men, swooped down on the Beretta I'd kicked out of his hand. Still had four rounds in it. Having it waved in his face didn't stop his mindless attack.

I shook my head, leapt out of his reach, tsking. "You don't realize yet that I just slashed your wrist, do you. That you'll bleed out in minutes and you're just shortening your time exerting yourself so much. Work it out, Einstein. The harder and faster your heart beats, the quicker it pumps your blood out of you."

He grunted, eyes widening in horror. And murderous hatred. "Bitch! Whore! Ya ain't walkin' outta here. Gonna skin you alive." He tried to stagger to the door. Asking for help at this late hour? Didn't think so. I rammed the butt of the gun into his neck.

He stumbled back, sagged on the couch. He looked up at me, read in my lens-covered eyes that he wasn't doing anything or going anywhere without my say-so. But I saw desperation, too. Hmm. The dead goons could have thought I didn't warrant more backup than them. But maybe they'd kept the news of my real agenda to themselves to be alone in their boss's good graces. Seemed Filthy believed no one else was going to crash this party. Which changed everything.

This might yet turn into a very fruitful night.

Filthy fumbled his jacket off, tried to shred it for a pressure bandage, failed. He tried to wrap the sleeve. It didn't work. He wrapped his other hand on his wrist, looking around in desperation for something he could use to stem his hemorrhage. He let go of his hand to undo his shirt. I kept kicking his hands down. Wondered how many times he had played with helpless women. What it felt like to be on the receiving end of a sadistic game.

His pig-like whimpers were an open window into his feelings right now. As well as feeling rage and frustration, he was getting shitting-himself scared. Lovely.

"I can save you." I produced an elastic pressure bandage from my bag of tricks, waved it at him. He lunged for it and I stepped aside like a *torero*, let his momentum crash him into the wall. "I have a price. All you have of your 'opportunity,' a list of your affiliates, scientists, sub-dealers—everyone who has or could have had access to it. And your special way out of here."

"Go ta hell, bitch."

"Want to join your men real bad, don't you. But it won't be as quick for you. No one will come to save you. They know you're expecting some action and won't dream of interrupting you. Not with that temper on you. Face it, the only two who knew anything's wrong are dead. I have you to myself till morning. And I'm good. You saw how good I am. I can make you last all night. And I can do a lot of bad stuff to you meanwhile, too. So what do you say?"

He was gasping now. "I said go ta hell…."

Holding out, was he? Gutsier and stupider than I had bargained for. Time for harsher lines of persuasion.

I looked down on him, smirked. "Say, how about I send you there?"

Chapter 10

"He's gone!" Fadel's indistinct words whistled through teeth clenched by swollen lips and a fractured jaw.

In the past twenty-four hours, since I'd taken care of Filthy and returned to Sanctuary, I'd gotten used to deciphering them. Did he just say—gone?

Words and numbers, values and verdicts on the investigations printouts in my hand merged, melted. My mind blipped as I swung around, my stare slamming into the monitor, only then registering the import of the endless *beep*.

"Crash-cart!" I yelled, flinging the investigations down. Hell. *Hell!* He hadn't even fibrillated, had just taken a shortcut and flatlined! "Fadel, initiate cardiac compressions. Lucia, ep-inephrine, 2mg IV."

Neither moved, just gave me "what the hell for?" looks. I cried out, "Dammit, we have to try."

Fadel shrugged, more words hissing between his teeth. "You saw the CTs, Cali. He wasn't coming back from that. I never saw such massive intracranial hemorrhage and cerebral infarctions. He was already brain-dead before his heart gave out."

"No, dammit." Bile rose up to my eyes, my body tightening on anger, futility—and guilt. This was my fault. "God, I killed him."

Fadel shook his head, disconnected our patient from the electrodes. "He killed himself and you know it. He's been trying his damnedest for years and the only reason he hasn't died a dozen times over is we pulled him from the brink every time."

I squeezed my eyes. "And then we went and gave him the poison that did manage to kill him."

Fadel cocked one eyebrow, the only thing in his swollen face that moved. At least he hadn't suffered a lasting injury from Matt's assault. "He volunteered to test drive the Mutant, Cali, for a thick stack of cash. He did it for a living anyway."

I exhaled. I guessed Fadel was right. I knew he was. Josh "Taster" Dickinson was the ultimate test-subject in uncontrolled, high-risk, not-so-clinical trials of illicit drugs. His name at the top of lists used by underground drug-producing labs, he'd turned his addiction into a job that supplied him with the cash to maintain his habit and the side benefit of new highs and more potent addictions.

Still it was a fact that Mutant, the drug I'd gotten off Filthy and into Josh's system, was what had done him in. Whichever way I looked at it, I had had a hand in his death. A big one.

My eyes panned to Josh's body. Weird. He looked at peace, almost good-looking dead, when he'd always been sickly and vacant alive. Seemed the face he'd worn in life hadn't been his, but his addiction demon's. Seemed death had exorcised it.

Haiku extubated him, threw the ET tube in the bin, sighed. "I guess we have the ultimate result for Mutant's clinical trial."

Yeah, we sure did. We'd observed and examined to our hearts' content as Josh had taken one dose after another, snorting the stuff, ingesting it, shooting it up. We'd documented every finding and observation, we'd drawn blood and CSF and urine, conducted tests before and after each dose, recorded values and reactions, peak action and half-life and excretion method. We had gotten all we could have hoped for on every dose-related clinical picture.

The minimal dose, even with his drug-infested nervous pathways, had him manifesting clear sympathomimetic effects, the same as Matt's first symptoms: the dilated pupils, the cold, clammy skin, a rush like that of methamphetamine and Ecstasy, but far more powerful, and a real good vibe. So we gradually upped the dose to a "regular" one, then above regular. With every increase in dosage, feelings of invincibility, of being "metamorphosed" as he'd kept saying, had shot up exponentially. Guess that was what the label *Mutant* was all about. He had intense hallucinations, too, but their nature had been very different from Matt's. That hadn't been surprising. Hallucinogens' effects were totally dependent on the user's expectations and their basic character. Josh, being a veteran of dealing with chemically induced phantasms, had just sat there babbling, not moving a muscle. Weeping.

But he hadn't convulsed. Even with the highest dose. Not that I'd hoped he would. I'd hoped his symptoms would switch without the convulsive crisis. They hadn't. That had been where our tests ended. I hadn't been about to overdose him in hopes of duplicating Matt's reactions. Even when he'd offered to go for an overdose. After all, with us in his condo, stacked to the teeth for every emergency, he'd been among the pillars of emergency medicine. He had insisted we'd pull him through anything. As we always had.

And no. I hadn't succumbed to the temptation. That overdose he'd taken on his own!

Filthy hadn't exaggerated Mutant's instant addictiveness. Just a few hours after his last dose, Josh had been crashing, no doubt into the hell Filthy had bragged his poison sent users.

I couldn't decide if Josh as a confirmed addict had been

more susceptible, or if his drug tolerance should have been higher and his reaction to Mutant less. Whatever—he'd lifted one of the powder vials from my bag before we left his apartment. We were already down the street when he opened his window and screamed. And screamed.

We'd run back up, broke down his door and found him unconscious. We'd rushed him to the Sanctuary, and on the way I'd made an inventory of my samples and realized what he'd done.

Before the CTs, we'd thought he'd been having a reaction like Matt's last and continuing symptoms, but his brutal headache and instant collapse had had a totally different etiology. And as Haiku said, we got the final stage in our clinical trial.

Overdose didn't produce convulsions. Or the encephalitis-like syndrome Matt was suffering from now. It led to an explosive form of hypertension, generalized rupture of cerebral vessels, catastrophic intracerebral hemorrhage and rapid death.

"I guess this brings us back to square one, huh?" Lucia covered Josh, looked at me.

I gulped the acid filling my throat. "At least we know Mutant isn't what Matt's been poisoned with."

"Not necessarily," Haiku interjected. "Maybe there *is* that fast release–slow release combination with another drug. Non-overdose symptoms elicited were similar to Matt's first ones."

I shook my head, rattling my thoughts back into order. They were looking at me, expecting me to wrap this up. *You did land yourself with the leader job. Get off your butt and do it.*

I stood up, nauseated, desperate, oppressed. I hid it well. "Fadel, Lab said they're close to cracking the formula. Tell them to concentrate on finding out if tampering with the compound can produce another derivative molecule, if it's possible to combine it in a stable compound with an opioid or an atropine-like compound, and if so, to test for the possibility of integrating both into fast-slow-release phases. And, if they succeed in that, to work on possible rapid-acting antidotes."

Fadel stared at me. What was that weird expression on his face? Was he in pain? *Of course he is, idiot.* Before I could say anything more, he turned, walked away, leaving us to handle disposing of Josh. Leaving me to do it. I felt Haiku's and Lucia's eyes on me. *Make the decision.* As if there was more than one to be made. No use pretending there was a choice here. We couldn't afford to have this traced back to us.

"Get a disposal team together. Have them drop him near his place. Then tip off the police, report his screaming incident and the people who took him. Make up specific descriptions. I doubt they'll investigate his death much. Not with his history."

My words pulsed inside my head long after Haiku and Lucia had wheeled Josh's body out, played over and over on echoes of my steady, emotionless voice. Even my friends who knew it had to be done had been unsettled by the way I sounded. They'd made no comment. Hadn't needed to. But it had settled them, too, having me assume the responsibility of the gruesome plan of action. It absolved them, eased their burden, solved their moral dilemmas. *We can just do our jobs, do as we're told. Cali's picking up the tab.*

What had Damian said? *You act every day on the job, to gain your ends.* Riding my moral high horse, I'd claimed that I didn't con my friends or my allies. Seemed there were endless forms of doing just that. For their own good. Damian's argument. Was I any better—any different? Or was I the same only plain worse?

No use debating my morality. Matt was still in a coma, we still had no diagnosis, and with the failure of Mutant's "clinical trial," and until proven otherwise, my only lead was cut. Dead end.

Everyone was dead. I was alive, alone. *I can't be alone.*

Invisible tentacles pulled me down, slow, almost gentle. Inescapable. I sank into a river of blood, gushing along convoluted folds of a brain. The tentacles spread into sheaths, encapsulating me, dragging me into caverns between tissues. My head was the last thing unsubmerged. Couldn't fight what I couldn't understand. Desperation had long since burst my heart and I lay vacant, drained. Useless.

They were gone. Why fight? Give up and rest. Die…

"Cali!"

No. Didn't want to hear. Didn't want to know. Just let go….

"*Cali!* Oh my God, Cali—*help!*"

The capsule suffocating me quivered, unraveled. No! Wanted it to end—and the screams were dragging me back.

"Cali, for God's sake, *open up!*"

I was out of my bed at Sanctuary and on my feet, wobbling and stumbling. I opened the rattling door. My eyes were open, too, my brain refusing to translate the images forming on their retinas. Something somewhere crashed. Then I crashed into my body and my mind into this world. Into another nightmare. A waking one. *Lucia!*

Drenched in blood. A gash slashed across her clothes and flesh, gouged a deep cleft from her shoulder to just above her clavicle. An inch higher would have slit her throat. "Lucia! How did this happen? Who did this?"

Her body shook, her chest wheezed. Her fingers sank between my muscles, transmitting her quakes and terror, shaking me down to my nerve roots. "Ayesha—God, Cali, Ayesha—just like Matt—then Ishmael and Fadel and Haiku and Doug—all of them went nuts!"

Had they? Or had I?

"Lucia—where are they? Did they hurt anybody else? Themselves? Each other?"

"I tried to stop Ayesha. She had the electric saw—wanted to hack Josh's body—kept saying that he did it, that she'd extract his kidneys and heart and liver and reconstruct Fatima…" Her gasps stopped, accumulated for a second as my mind churned, then burst into a wail. "What's going on, Cali?"

Frustration frothed. *You expect me to have an answer? Why the hell ask me?*

I knew less than nothing. Which had below-zero significance right now. It didn't take knowing a thing to stop it. At least now I knew I wouldn't be causing them more damage when I did. That was the single objective. Anything else could wait. Would wait.

I ran to my weapons' closet. A combination-number lock. I had one? Concentrate, you fool. The code, the code... It hovered just out of reach, leaping away every time mnemonic pathways made a grab for it. God—I can't remember when it was Clara died!

I leaned my forehead on the cold steel, rammed it, once, twice. The wavering memory crashed back, boring back into its home in the deepest scar in my mind.

My fingers slipped twice, messing the entry. I slammed my palm into steel, the sting numbing my fingers steady. The right sequence poured from them. I snatched the closet open, pounced on my disaster bag. And the dart rifle. Non-stealth, maximum range and precision. Saved for desperate measures. It came ready with five megadose diazepam dart-syringes. Five. Not four, not six. Five. As if made for them. Oh God...

Focus. Retrieve your training, Damian's conditioning and the long hard years in every sort of battleground. Let it take you over. Detach yourself. You're an instrument, first-and-only-time faultless. No hesitation. No other options. Get it done!

I ran out of the room, towing Lucia. "Where did they go?"

"I don't know. Last I saw Ayesha was when I locked Josh's body in the morgue and left her trying to break down the door. Ishmael and Fadel were in ER—they ran after me—then—I don't know!"

Had to hope they'd dispersed, weren't in each other's sights. But my first priority was our critical patients—Matt, Juan, Mercedes. "Did any of them reach IC?"

I thought Lucia gasped, "I don't know—don't think so."

"Who's on shift there?"

"Savannah and Al."

Good. Good! Now that those two weren't trapped in the middle of a surgery, they were only second to our core eight in defending patients. Our core eight—we were down to two now....

Not now. Get info. "And the rest of the Sanctuary?"

She rattled off the names. Those she knew. There were about thirty more people, patients and their kin. "I think most of them were in ER. When—when Ayesha slashed me, I knew Ishmael and Fadel were on rotation there—I ran for help and—oh God, Cali! They were tearing at each other, blocking the door. I barely shoved them out of the way so the others could run out."

We turned a corner. Alien noises funneled from the corridor. Desolation and derangement curdling into sound. Ayesha. *Oh God.*

Something acrid flooded my mouth. Blood. Answering anguish. My teeth in my tongue barely stopping an answering howl.

Focus, dammit! "Did you get the patients out of here?"

"Couldn't!" Lucia panted. "Doug was at the exit. I took them back to my room. I have no idea if I got everyone."

One way to make sure that wasn't an issue. Remove the threat. "Listen to me, Lucia. I want you all in one place. Get them all and run to IC, barricade it."

She stamped her foot. "No! I came for you because you're the leader, so you can decide what to do. Now you have a plan, we can all help, get your back."

"Lucia, you're the only fighter among them. The others know nothing about defending themselves against a berserk attacker. They'd only become more victims and get in my way. I can't worry about them while trying to contain the others. I need you to protect them and Matt and Juan and Mercedes."

She growled her objection. My grip on her arm tightened to silence her. "You're bleeding profusely. Get Savvy or Al to patch you up, start you on fluid replacement."

She shook her head, her stubborn selflessness acting up. "It's superficial. I can last until we take care of the others."

"For God's sake, Lucia. Do as you're told." Damian's same words to me, so many times. Did I frustrate him like this? No wonder I drove him to extremes. Weird to think that now. I shoved her ahead. "Get patched up, Lucci. When this is over I'll need you more than ever. If they're gone like Matt, and we're the only two left standing, you'll be all I have left!"

She shuddered, tears turning the hazel-brown of her eyes muddy black. Then she nodded. Ayesha's ranting was coming nearer. Lucia's room was through the other way. From there to IC, it took her out of Ayesha's path. No telling if it would keep her out of the others'. No telling how many more of us would fall before it was over. Victims to either the phantom affliction, or its earlier victims.

I grabbed Lucia's arm as she turned away, snatched open my front-pack, shoved two dart guns in her hands. "If anyone else starts acting up, just shoot them. If you feel anything weird, call Damian first, then do it to yourself."

"What about you? What if you succumb, too?"

"I don't plan on going crazy until I take care of the others. If you're the one left standing, you know what to do."

Then I went to hunt down my friends.

Six. My limbs and heart and backbone.

I'd gone after each of them. Ayesha had been even worse than Matt. Ishmael—I still retched to remember how vacant and violent he'd been. And the others... Beyond endurable, seeing them that way.

I shot them down on sight, each one on the first try. Until I shot Fadel, and Doug descended on me from nowhere, as calm as ever—and almost gouged my neck out with his teeth. I broke his arm in the struggle when he wouldn't let go, emptied of soul and coherence, bound on his macabre zombie objective.

They lay sedated in a row in IC. Absent, sabotaged. No clue as to how or who or why. No reason to hope they'd ever be back.

The first twenty-four hours, we'd struggled to stabilize them, as we had Matt. Nothing had registered but the need to stop them from plunging into a vicious cycle of complications that would damage their vital systems beyond repair.

Others around me had been perceived only as tools to extend my functions, other sets of needed arms and eyes. Mental processes beyond those concerned with medical methods and intervention had hovered at the periphery of my mind, in stasis.

I'd gone through more than I was equipped to feel, the responsibility of fighting for them, the possibility of making a mistake that would only kill them faster depleting my sanity and stamina. We'd expended all measures, done all we could.

Then investigations started coming in. With more dead ends.

Mutant was unalterable. Further reactions just destroyed its structure and deactivated it. The drug hadn't been the answer.

Sir Ashton's reports on Matt's CSF and blood samples were the first to come. Then Damian's. Our lab joined their opinions almost down to the last decimal in all values. No poisons, no infectious agents. Matt should be awake and active. I doubted the others' samples would be any different. I still took one sample after another.

Then numbness came.

Numbness was good. General anesthesia for the soul, for the love and need and fear and all that weakened. Once I was cold and no longer felt the bludgeoning emotions, processing power surged back.

Their collective affliction was a catastrophe. It was also my first solid clue.

All I had to do was ask the right questions, follow the thread back to its origin. Why did Matt fall first? Why did the others follow simultaneously? And why only them?

If this wasn't the beginning and we'd all succumb one after

another, if this illness hadn't been infectious all the time and we weren't already too late, there was one answer to each question.

To answer why Matt first, assuming they'd been exposed to whatever it was at the same time, I could only theorize that his phenomenal exertion during our white-slavery bust was what had led to his accelerated manifestation.

As to why them and only them, I had to take exposure to Matt out of the equation, since we'd all been exposed. No, those six had one thing in common. Something they shared that none of the rest of us did. Their covert vaccination mission in the *tugurios*, the refugee camps for internally displaced people on the outskirts of Bogotá, Colombia.

Since then, they hadn't been all together, not once. I'd double-checked. So the opportunity for them to get infected or poisoned en masse had been absent since Colombia. The idea of someone picking them off one by one didn't gel, either. From the way five of them had developed symptoms simultaneously, they had to have been infected at the same time.

Problem here was, they'd been in Colombia two months ago.

So even if we solved the opportunity and the method angles, what would take so long to manifest?

I had theories. Well thought out, detailed, logical. Insubstantial. And the only ones I had.

It was time to reach out to all my resources. Starting with the one who'd helped us set up the Colombian mission, who had gotten us all the supplies we'd needed through his extensive influence in black markets and smuggling rackets.

Dad.

Chapter 11

"**Y**ou gotta be kiddin' me!"

There he went again, that existing link between boar and hippo—with heartfelt apologies to both species for the unfair metaphor—snorting his fat-encrusted heart out.

Stained teeth chomped at a sticky, misshapen doughnut to the rhythm of his snorts, jelly oozing out and glopping on his blue prison-guard shirt. Lucky thing I'd barfed earlier. At least now I was immune.

I injected more schoolgirl primness in my stance, my expression. "I assure you, sir, I do have an appointment, if you'll please check it out."

"I ain't checkin' nothin', sweetcakes. That nut's in solitary." *Again?* "He ain't coming out anytime this winter. And he sure ain't receiving no visitors where he is."

As if visits were in abundance when he wasn't locked up in solitary confinement.

Seven years since he'd been taken from me and caged. For

the first two years, I'd been there every visiting day, palm-to-palm across the communicating glass, heart breaking at being unable to bury myself in his arms, feverishly checking him for the injuries I feared a convicted cop would sustain on the inside. Then he'd set up his operation and I'd set up mine. I started missing visits, and he was in solitary more often than not.

Then, in an effort to break up his control over the network of vigilantes he'd formed on the inside, he'd been bounced to three different maximum-security prisons. Then came the last two years—and the last warden.

He'd stormed into the prison crying reform, holding press conferences, pledging that the wave of unprecedented prison violence and soaring mortality rates was at an end. He'd cracked down on Dad, limiting his contact with other prisoners to nil, taking away his activities and cutting off his communications with the outside world. Dad had managed to thwart all these efforts, to expand his operation. What he hadn't been able to get around yet was the rescinding of his visitation rights. *My* visitation rights.

Two years. I hadn't seen him even once, had heard his voice only six times. It made me mad. Made me ache. A constant, permeating ache that stained my existence.

He'd told me he'd been working on a solution through his most trusted contacts on the outside, men he'd saved in prison from fates far worse than death, who now would die for him. Last night, his top aide on the outside, Rafael, had told me the plan was in place, had given me the props I needed. But, hell, this gem about Dad being in solitary again hadn't come up. What had he done this time? Had to have been something terminal. Again.

Couldn't wait to find out.

First I had to see him. Had to get around this lowlife.

Malicious pleasure quivered on the guard's corpulent cheeks. But it was his leer that almost persuaded my empty stomach to another uprising. "So, you say you're here to *interview* that bruiser, huh? I'm new, just this week, but I did hear how he manages to get special treatment around here. Wouldn't mind getting me some myself."

Down, Calista. Got to reign in my vicious vibes. Slugs like him turned vicious when exposed to female disgust. It held up the mirror they lived to avoid and they would go to any lengths to punish those who shoved it in their faces. Small-fry or not, he was the one stationed in the prison's visitation appointment office right now. I had no idea how long he'd be here. Antagonize him and he might mess up my chances of seeing Dad today. Or for two more years.

Not an option. For my friends. Or my mental health.

I leaned closer, giving him a good look at the press ID Dad had arranged for me. Just another of the dozens of identities his far-reaching connections had manufactured for me and my team on demand. Putting on my best unwitting expression, I toyed with the auburn wig's bangs, breathed, "You want to have a biography written, too, sir? I'm sure your experiences here would be worth telling. Once you've been here longer, of course. Maybe we can discuss particulars, with your warden's permission of course, after I'm done with Mr. St. James's story."

His inanimate blue eyes jerked. "You an author?"

Got him on that one, huh? I shook my head. "Just a ghostwriter. I put the facts together into an exciting read."

Still wondered how Dad knew they'd let his autobiographer in when they wouldn't allow his daughter. The daughter who blinked out of existence the moment she stepped out of the prison walls.

Maybe he'd promised the warden a piece of the action. And to only reveal his exploits up until he'd been convicted of forty murder-one charges, murders of psychotic criminals who'd slipped through cracks in the justice system, from child rapists to serial killers. No doubt he'd promised to leave out his post-conviction activities. The scope of which even I had no full knowledge.

So, according to Rafael, this was going to be the first of sev-

eral regular meetings. Whatever regular meant. I hated that I was
going in as a professional who'd be forced to sit across from him
pretending detachment and taking notes, and not the daughter
who had the right to let my love and longing show.

I hated the two years without Dad far more. Sure was in no
position to have a preference. Shades of beggars and choosers!

My artificially golden gaze now poured more innocent en-
treaty over the slimeball who was stopping me from having
even that much of my dad. "So, sir, you will check?"

Uncertainty wavered in his eyes as his opinion of me shifted
from possible lay to possible gain. He slurped at his sticky
fingers, wiped the surplus on his bursting trousers, picked up the
phone and reported my presence.

My lenses almost popped out at the metamorphosis. Slimeball heaved up to his feet, hobbling ahead of me at maximum
plodding speed, conciliatory smiles and apologies slopping off
his over-fleshed lips all the considerable way to my destination.

The waiting room to the warden's office, no less.

Dad must have talked big business with the guy. Sure hoped
he had the plan fleshed out. The first clue to the publishing
world and writing books didn't feature among my tricks.

The guard's shambling footsteps receded outside as he returned to his station. Then silence. Weird.

The warden's office was segregated in a separate building,
but we hadn't met anyone on the way. His assistant's desk was
empty. The guard hadn't even taken my ID in to him for verifi-
cation.

I heard a door open inside the office. Voices buzzed inside.
Male. Deep, calm. Impatience mushroomed inside me.

Cool it. Conjure up some good behavior.

Good behavior. Yeah. Nice pun, in a prison.

There was no chance even the best behavior could get Dad
out any earlier than the fourth decade of the 21st century. Not
that he knew the meaning of the term. Even as a cop, he'd

always gone for bad behavior. The worst, with the deserving. And boy, had he been effective.

Fact remained I couldn't antagonize the people holding the key to his cell, his home for the duration, and to our link.

Slow, powerful footsteps counted down the last seconds before the confrontation with his keeper. I forced my features into a whatever-you-want-me-to-be-I'm-it expression, my body language into I'm-harmless mode.

The door snapped open, and everything inside me sat up.

The blast of recognition hit first. Silence filled my ears, a brutal compression of vacuum, emptying my heart, stopping my vital functions.

Dad.

His form crowded my awareness. As he did the door frame. Vigor leapt off him, slamming into me. It was all there. The overwhelming presence, the enveloping charisma. The out-and-out connection. *Dad.* The one who'd infused me with my essence, the only one who shared it, on more levels that I'd ever fathom.

The force of him, the sheer magnitude of his love and focus kept me upright. Couldn't understand—couldn't believe he was here, not behind bars or behind a glass wall—here! Nothing but air and a few steps between us.

He opened his arms.

And I was there. Buried deep and safe and uncaring of what I was revealing. Crushed, carried, cradled. *Burrow deeper, hide in his embrace forever. Hide him, spirit him away, never let him out of your reach again. Dad...*

Moistness filled my mouth, contact permeating me. I'd withered without it, gone mad with the futility and the injustice.

I haven't touched you in seven years.

"Calista—my baby..." His voice resounded in my head, flooding me with everything unrestrained and unconquerable.

I'd thought I knew weeping. When Clara died, when Dad was taken away, when Mom left, when Jake was lost, then found, then murdered by my hands, then Damian and Matt and the others…

I never knew it was possible to lose all these fluids and remain conscious!

"So where are you hiding the tear tanks?"

Had he said…? He sure had. And I burst out laughing. "Oh, Dad…" I bit back the word. *Yeah, sure,* do *be discreet now.* After my tear-duct clearing marathon, anyone listening in had to be brain-dead not to know who I was.

But Dad didn't seem worried. I took my cues from him. Always had. Always would.

I wobbled after him to a black chesterfield couch. He sat down and I leaped onto his lap, curled up. He made that deep sound that always made me feel invincible in his protection. He seemed as big now as he'd seemed to me as a child. I took after my mother in size and looks. Not in character or tendencies. Not an ounce. Beneath the skin she'd bequeathed on me, I belonged to him, mind and soul. And between us, we'd almost broken her.

Did he ever wish things had been different?

Oh God. My friends. The reason I was here. I couldn't afford to wallow in being with him. Not now. Even if there would be no later. I spilled off his lap. "Dad—how long do we have?"

He smiled down at me. Something inside me burst into song. "As much as we need. Relax, sweetheart."

"Really? In that case…" I dove back into his embrace.

He chuckled and I reached out and skimmed his face and head and shoulders, absorbing his feel, storing up his closeness. He hadn't changed one bit in the past seven years. The same juggernaut who'd made me the proudest girl in existence to have him for a father. A fearless warrior like those inhabiting the legends I grew up devouring. Unique, noble, mesmerizing—lethal.

And boy, did he look the part! Apart from the silver that had replaced most of the raven shock of hair he kept mowed, the deepening grooves that made him even harder hitting, he didn't look anywhere near fifty-seven.

No doubt about it. Perfect nutrition and exercise regimen. And a hell of a healthy mental condition, too. Offing criminals sure agreed with him. I sighed.

"You look fantastic, Dad."

He contained my heavily made-up cheek in his large palm, eyed my bruises. Even their healing state and my disguise couldn't hide them from his knowledge of me. And of violence. His eyes blazed on the one I'd gotten saving Juan and Mercedes. The obsidian-colored eyes he'd passed down to me, our only physical resemblance, bore into me.

"You don't. Who did this?"

The memory flashed. My arm lashing out in a sure, final arc. A blade flash in the alley's dim light. Blood spraying my neck, already cooling. I shrugged. "I don't know. Someone dead."

"Good." He smiled. If smiles could kill, that one had. Then he smiled for real. The transition from feral to fatherly clogged up my insides again. He took my head to his chest, my sob right into his heart. "I didn't know missing like that was possible."

My nod was frantic. "And it hurts—even more than Clara, more than Mom…" I bit my tongue. Couldn't believe I'd said that. Guess it came out because it was true. Clara was at peace. So was Mom. Knowing that made the pain only mine. I could handle myself. But him—his pain I couldn't deal with.

"Yeah. The dead and the gone have no problems."

So it was the same with him!

"You have nothing but. Missing you all so much that it messes with my sanity is one thing. Even the rage and futility are survivable. Not sure worrying clear out of my mind over you is."

"Says the Terminator! God, Dad, you sound like Damian!"

His all-seeing eyes turned my mind inside out, spread out the pieces for inspection. "So—you're on those terms now."

Yeah. *Now* I remembered I hadn't disclosed the change in

Damian's and my standing. Not that I'd had the chance to in our last twenty-minute call, which he'd spent informing me of the depth of Damian's duplicity. If I'd told him anything then, it would have been that I was on my way to split Damian's head open!

I nodded, then shook my head. "I don't know what terms we're on. Or should be on." He made no comment. Probably none to be made. And I blurted out, "Have you heard from Mom?"

Silence boomed. *Great going, Calista, rub it in.* Remind the man that the woman he loved with every last spark of his tempestuous soul couldn't bear the burden of loving him. Went in search for peace of mind and left him behind.

"Yeah. I did."

My heart rammed against my throat. Then he said two more words, and it crashed back. "I do."

She contacted him. She still did. Oh, Mom—why not me, too? She knew where to find me if she wanted to. So she must not want to.

His exhalation was heavy. "She—sends letters. Didn't want me to tell you. She can't face you."

"She faces you!"

"I left her, in a way. She left you. She doesn't think it's forgivable."

"Tell her it is. It's me who needs forgiveness, for disappointing her. Please, Dad. Tell her I just want to hear from her, maybe see her sometime, hold her. I won't drag her in or scare her."

He turned my face with a gentle finger that had clawed men's eyes out, examining my concealed injuries, making his point. "Just being who we are scares her beyond endurance, sweetheart. In my case, she seems to have accepted it. In yours, I don't know if she ever will. Or can."

The world turned watery again. Dammit. I wasn't shedding more tears. Served no purpose. Wouldn't change her mind. Or mine. I spilled off his lap, looked around the swimming office. "So how come they're letting me see you? In the warden's office no less?"

He leaned formidable forearms on his knees, bent forward in a relaxed pose. "The new warden is Newt Kawolski."

Uncle Newt? Dad's partner from his days as a beat cop? Wow. "How and when did that happen?"

"As for how, he got a degree in criminal psychology, got involved in penitentiary system reform, became a warden about the time I was convicted. Seems he'd been trying to get a hold of a prison I was in for a while. He succeeded just a month ago."

"So why didn't I see you before? And why are you in solitary? The Uncle Newt I know would have let you get away with murder!"

"He does. There was this con who was in for attempted child molestation. My investigations turned up four raped, dead kids. But he had a good lawyer, appealed and was about to walk out. They kept him guarded so we couldn't get to him. The piece of shit teased me about it the one time I saw him, told me to lie in bed sweating what he'd be doing out there. Couldn't take the chance he'd slip through my net once he was out. So I took care of him on the spot. Smashed his head open, as he had all those little boys'."

Fury, fierce pride. Fear. All ran down my tangled nerves. The system punished Dad for acting as judge and executioner. To me, he hadn't only been justified, he'd been compelled. For two decades he'd watched the system letting monsters slip by, or catching them only to let them go, more rabid. But what if he—we—ever made wrong decisions? Executed the undeserving? That was where fear came in.

The child killer wasn't undeserving. I inhaled, nodded. "So Uncle Newt had to lock you up, for appearances' sake?"

"Yeah. The DA was enraged but everyone, the guards included, testified that it was a fight he instigated, that he fell.

Since I can't get more than life, it all died down. As usual. So—solitary for me. Where I want to be, really. It's where I take breaks to plan stuff, conduct business in peace. The only drawback about that in the past years was being unable to see you. In this past month I was preparing the autobiographer business with Newt."

"But why? Why am I not here as me again?"

"I have too many enemies now. You're safer this way."

Okay. Didn't matter how I got to see him. This was better than any arrangement I could have dreamed of. "What about when no book materializes? What will the grapevine make of me?"

"Says who there'll be no book? I *am* writing one. A series. I will include everything up to the time I got convicted."

A whistle escaped me. "It'll be a bestseller! Aren't you afraid of the high profile?"

"Why? I can't have more enemies than I have now. And it's all public knowledge already. I'll just put it in my own words."

He was really going to do this! I shook my ringing head as his eyes cleaved into me, searching for the focus of my agitation.

"But you're not here just to see your dad. Tell me, Calista."

I told him. He listened, as he always did. It took a while to give him a precise account of the past three days. Couldn't give him the watered-down version of my own imperfect views.

"You're sure Colombia is their common factor, huh?" He scratched the silver growth on his jaw. "I can't see how, after all our precautions. We sent them in one at a time, and their stuff even later. But there are rumors of an operation in Colombia that's sponsored by an unannounced terrorist organization. They blend in among the guerrillas in the area. They're researching a new agent designed to incapacitate then kill. It's said to be almost or completely impossible to counteract. My intel says it's revolutionary, could do most of what you described."

I blinked. "Could?"

"No updates suggest the beginning of production. But there are too many correlations for it not to be a possibility."

"Without the two months' delay, I'd say it is. But this time frame—it just makes no sense."

He nodded. "Maybe that's what makes it so dangerous. It resembles nothing we ever heard about or encountered before."

"Shaky, but I'll buy that—for now. Okay, so I got my new lead. Now to roll up the ball of twine to the origin!"

"I'll get you the info you need. Still—another coincidence I'm unwilling to buy is all of them being your deputies."

"You think it's a personal attack?"

He inclined his head in answer. "Dad, that also makes no sense. If it is, why not go for *me?*"

He didn't answer for a moment. Then he turned in that Dad's-got-something-to-tell-you way I knew and dreaded. "Maybe whoever it is, is toying with you. Or maybe it's the first wave in something far bigger. Or maybe it's something else completely. Whatever, it reeks of a serious, if not terminal, breach in your security. It's time to review all your methods and moves and relationships, Calista. Time to find your hidden enemy."

Chapter 12

Damn you, Damian De Luna. Where are you hiding?

Every ring scraped louder, screwing me tighter. Then the *click*. I jerked. Again. Disconnected for the sixteenth time.

The creep was lying low. More like laying it thick. The offended, upstanding man who'd had it with his woman's suspicious, capricious ways. Letting me accumulate missed calls in atonement. Showing me he'd keep his word this time?

Would he? Had I pushed him away once and for all, like Ayesha warned me I would one day?

Yeah. Sure. And I was a two-headed Venusian!

Not that I figured my irresistibility was responsible for that. Damian was just incapable of giving up. I bet his surveillance-interference machine was in uninterruptible mode. The "woman he loved" had him pissed. He'd leave that one alone. "The warrior he created" was another matter, would just have to abide his guardianship. Tough for me if I came as two-for-one.

I rang him again and—nothing. So maybe he *had* had

enough. Had to factor in this possibility. I could be pretty aggravating. I had been. I'd had every right—but that would be in my own humble opinion. Great. I needed—not guardianship mind you, just his help. My deputies, as Dad had called them, had fallen. I stood alone, and I couldn't afford pride or disillusion or doubts or the thousand misgivings I had about Damian's methods. Let alone his organization's.

Dad had offered me Rafael's services, plus muscle and resources. I'd take the last two. But when it came to taking turns at the helm steering through this mess, there was no contest. I had to have the best. It had to be Damian.

If he'd pick up the damn phone!

Didn't seem that was happening. Okay. The hoops were hovering right there, snickering at me. Wanted me to hop through them, did he? Fine. I'd hop. He'd better not take it personally!

Time to ferret him out of hiding.

An hour later on the outskirts of Bel Air I stepped out of the taxi. I took a minute to come to terms with where I was, what I was looking at. Again. I got the same whack of amazement as the first time I'd been here.

Shaking my head, my thick braid wagging like a confused tail, I went down the cobblestone passage winding through manicured lawn and lush shrubs, the magnificent two-story brick and stucco house's real size manifesting with every step nearer. It looked even more imposing as the last glimmer of twilight gave way to the eerie, strategic grounds lights.

Who would have associated a house like this with Damian? Not me, for sure. No wonder he called my dump a dump.

Not that it was his. This address was listed in the white pages under Desideria Henderson. Sounded like a porn star's name. And I *wasn't* wondering who she was!

This was where he laid down his weapons. Yeah, I'd tracked him down the last time he resurfaced. Two can play the under-a-microscope game.

It was me at the end of a telescope right now. A sniper's night-vision rifle scope. I could almost feel the crosshairs tickling my back. PATS troops guarding their commander. I hoped they either knew me, or would check with Damian before shooting me down. Hoped he'd answer them!

I reached his front door unpunctured. Light burst behind the French windows on the extensive patio a dozen feet from the door. So they'd sounded the alarm. Then the door opened.

And again, in the space of five hours, I found myself staring at a huge man, senses on a spiraling nosedive. Radically different glands at work here, though. Instead of the father I'd craved the sight of, there stood the man I craved, period.

And he was naked.

All right. Breathe. And let's not exaggerate. He wasn't naked. He did have a tiny towel around his hips.

"You called?" Harsh-velvet baritone poured over me, the intimate lights at his back sifting golden overtones over his work-of-art outline. Bet he was posing for maximum effect!

"You always answer the door naked?" Heat rushed to my head, the geyser holding its breath before flooding down my body.

One of his hands secured his towel knot, the other leaned on the door frame. Another pose. I knew it!

"When I'm dragged from bed in response to a situation, yes."

"I'm not a 'situation.' Yet. And who goes to bed at six p.m.?" And he went to bed like that, draped only in silk skin and steel muscles? He had when he'd slept with me, but I'd assumed it was because we were making love….

Maybe he'd been making love now. With Desideria Henderson…

Had they just shot me in the back? That ripping in my gut felt like a high-caliber gunshot penetrating my colon. Only worse. *You told him you didn't want anything to do with him. You set him free.* Fool!

Stop it. None of my business. He *was* free; he owed me nothing. *But he didn't have to say he loved me!*

So—sue him later. He had, and now he'd stopped. A man's prerogative. Get on with business.

"Will you answer your phone?"

He took yet another pose, indolent, insolent. Arousal punched through me, no longer acceptable, a stamp of weakness, a taunt of humiliation. I wanted to punch *him.* Sardonic eyebrows rose.

"You came up to my door to tell me to answer the phone?"

"Any other method you'd like to recommend when someone insists on ignoring you?"

"You told me to stay away from you."

"Hel-*lo? I* was calling *you!*"

"You called me last time, too. You needed help and once you had it, I was scum of the earth again. Thanks, but I don't feel like an encore."

And who was offering one? I hiked all the extra height I could into my body. "You said you want to offer assistance where you can. If you still mean it, just answer your damn phone!"

I turned around, walked away. It was what I wanted. What should be. The confusion over, the heartache silenced. The reason and feeling and life extinguished... Oh, shut *up!*

"You sure elevate aggravation to art status, St. James."

His words hit me in the spinal cord. I jumped. Hell! The man was just strolling after me for all to see, barefoot, lights and shadows slithering erotic fantasies over his shifting muscles, tiny towel dislodging with each powerful stride. He could save it for Ms. Desideria!

"Nothing like the aggravation you'll feel when the pneumonia you're courting hits." That was all I had? What a time for my doctor ingredient to break the surface. But since it had... "Do you have any idea what the windchill factor is tonight?"

"Couldn't be higher than yours."

A growl rumbled. From inside me? "Get the hell back inside,

Damian." I turned, walked on. This time I'd keep on walking. And this time, he let me. That was it, then. Good. Hell…

A minute later, my phone rang. I answered without checking the caller ID. *"Yes?"*

"Come back on your own two legs, St. James. Thirty seconds, then I'm hauling your butt in here."

My knees knocked once, my heart fired. I shouldn't allow him that much power over me.

I wouldn't. I'd deal with this later. Much later. When my friends were out of danger. Time to talk business now.

In the allotted thirty seconds I was brushing past him into a foyer out of an interior-design-for-budgets-above-a-million-dollars magazine, walking straight through to a vault-ceiling living room with an even bigger spending margin, his body heat radiating at my back even through my layers of thermal clothes.

Good thing there were distractions aplenty. That Desideria sure knew how to pull together a color-coordinated, all-luxuries dream. I reached one of the plush, cream couches, hesitated. When had I last washed my hands? Hell, I'd keep them on my lap.

My descent onto it was aborted by Damian's harsh "Don't."

I bounded back up. So this was to be a standing up meeting. Say my piece, then get the hell out. Suited me.

"Okay—this is the deal…" I started. The rest, whatever it would have been, went down Damian's throat.

My lips had been open. His pressed them back and plunged, aggressive, carnal. I tried to step back. I didn't find my feet. They were lifted, now dangling over Damian's arm. Then the world moved, in hard, hurried thuds. Strides. Each hitting my inner ear, spreading vertigo. The press of my head into his shoulder, the thrust of his tongue in my mouth pinned my gyrating existence. He was doing all the work—why was *I* gasping?

At some point, ground found my feet again, and his image,

wild and hungry, impacted my dimming retinal receptors. Then he pushed me. I fell.

Something solid and soft broke my fall. Then my body broke his. Just like that time back in my condo when I'd thought him an intruder, when I'd hit him with Pentothal.

Felt as if I'd been hit with something even stronger now. Sure I was. The hallucinogenic compound of his hunger, my own. I gulped it, washed it down with his taste and hot, ragged Spanish. Shock waves hit in succession, cumulative, each yanking a tangled nerve out of my screeching flesh. I shook.

His hands and teeth tapped my quakes, fed them, his massive body between my legs—when had they opened for him? His doing? Sure. He got them around his hips in a vise. He was doing the rest, though—undulating against me to the rhythm of his tongue-thrusts, each murmur and stroke and lunge pulling me deeper, into him, into blind arousal, hard and deep and irrevocable, screeching for completion. *Just take me now.*

Now. The word went off like a gong. I'd taken two "nows" with him. The laters should be enough of a deterrent. Not counting everything else. And Desideria. God, was this her bed?

That jammed the cascade of arousal. Now if only my voice would produce more than ravenous grunts. I gave it a try. It worked. Still grunts, but coherent.

"Get off me, Damian!"

No response. Figured. He must think I was kidding. My legs were still trying to integrate his hips into mine. Willing them to unclasp him, I heaved beneath him. Not that I thought it would dislodge him. He wouldn't budge if he didn't want to.

He budged, took his upper body off mine, looked down at me. Warm light from a black, ultramodern bedside lamp whispered on his tempestuous features. I almost pulled him down.

Good thing he got up, one impossible move taking him from between my legs and upright two feet away. One thing guaranteed about Damian. No matter how far gone he was, he was never gone beyond his unbreakable control. If he ever was, he'd never force himself where he wasn't panted for. Like any woman with breath left in her wouldn't expend the last of it panting over him!

Trying my damnedest not to moan with the gnawing in every hollow organ, I sat up. And got me an eye-level-full of his towel-less erection. "Put something on—now, Damian!" I croaked.

"Calista St. James, the Prude. Nah, doesn't suit you."

"I can't talk business with you like that."

He gave his erection a mocking nod. "Imagine my inability."

"Damian, stuff—that—into something or I'm out of here."

He bent and reached for a dark scrap of fabric…. "I got it already that you're not here starving for me."

He had to be kidding, right? He had to know I was blowing my ovaries over him!

"So—does business include saying thank you?"

Said ovaries were sputtering, going out of commission. "Let's cut the witty double-talk…." I gulped, watching him struggle on the scrap—black-silk boxers—and noticed I was sitting on a gigantic circular bed, spread with the same material and color. We'd almost made love on that? He made love to Desideria here…?

I bounced off, staggering to my feet, and almost fell back when he advanced on me, his arms going around me again. My jacket was gone, my blouse undone—and my bra's front clasp. I only realized that when his hard pecs pressed into my spilled, engorged breasts.

"Let's not be witty, Calista. I don't want to talk business or hear thanks. I want to talk savage passion and sex and satisfaction and hear your cries for more."

The damage spread. I panted. "I swear I'll knee you."

This got his hands off me. He stepped away, raised them in disgust. "I'll pass. I'm still smarting from the last times."

Yeah. Once in Darfur, to force him to let me go execute my kamikaze trick. Then in my condo that night he'd crashed back into my life. He'd accused me of having an emasculating agenda.

He stood, his boxers tented, eyes sweeping me with brooding lust, waiting for me to find my lost speech.

I blurted the first thing that slithered from my mind to my tongue. Okay the second. The first was *Are you sleeping with this Desideria?* and I was damned if I'd ask that! "And what the hell do you mean, thank you? What for?"

He shrugged. "For contributing to your standing here before me in one piece. One glorious piece, let me add."

I whacked his muscle-padded shoulder. "Meaning?"

This time he scowled. "That time in Filthy Rich's. Your stoolie tipped his thugs off."

I knew that. Figured he'd thought to get rid of me. I'd gone back for him and he'd disappeared. So he'd tipped off Damian, too. Should have known Damian knew my stoolie. Way better than I did, I bet.

"They were going up after you and we picked off five. Suz and Shad made it to Filthy's door only to find you'd taken care of the two who slipped our net and were playing cat-and-mouse with him, getting all you needed."

So that was why only two had made it. Seemed they hadn't noticed their pals' demise. Only problem here was... "You weren't there. I would have *felt* you. Would have recognized the others."

"I wasn't there. I didn't want to distract you and spoil your hunt. And you never saw Suz and Shad in heavy-metal getup and makeup. Their mothers wouldn't have recognized them."

I bet. "So, you didn't keep your word."

"Aren't you glad I didn't?"

Was I? Sure, to be in one piece, if only because he'd protected me from my own rashness. But that he'd lied—again! He could have just told me to live with his surveillance. That would have been honest at least.

He took my slack body to his again, holding my buttocks, letting me feel what I was missing. I *knew* what I was missing, thank you. And *what* was missing. On so many levels. Most of all I missed trusting him implicitly—like I'd miss a severed limb. He took my lips, passion no longer frantic and savage, profound, luxuriant, revitalizing—wiping all else out. Then he brought it all back, smeared it black.

"You didn't believe I'd pull my guards?"

"I actually considered believing you. A bit more time and I would have. I must be the ultimate moron." He grimaced at the hurt I heard vibrating in my voice. I slipped from his loosened grip. "What did you do with my stoolie?"

"He—had an accident."

"You killed him!"

"I wasn't there." My spitting fit had him backing away, placating. "They caught up with him and he got frantic thinking they'd take him back to you. He ran off and got hit by a trash compactor. Very poetic. So—we can say *you* scared him to death."

A countdown banged in my head. Would it burst when it hit zero? "There's no getting around you. You're *impossible!*"

"Yeah. So are you. Impossible, impetuous—irresistible…"

"And you can't help yourself yada yada. Enough. Business." I inhaled what felt like half the air in the room. I'd need it wrestling with this breath-depleting man. "Since you've never stopped your surveillance, you know what happened."

His hands on my shoulders pushed me down on the bed. He straightened, crossed the enormous room, went to a beverage stand. "Yeah, your generals have fallen."

Deputies, and now generals. Dad and then Damian, each with his own career-related metaphor.

He came back with a laden tray, sat with his back to the headboard, legs stretched, then hauled me onto his body. He prepared my mug with one hand. Almost-all-milk latte, four spoons of sugar. He remembered. Funny. Never thought he knew in the first place. He bit down on my lower lip, gave it a lingering suckle, then handed me my mug, started making his.

I somehow managed to fill him in about the specifics, ending with the Colombian factor and Dad's intel.

"So I'm going to retrace my friends' footsteps. We need to get samples of the agent. If Dad's intel is correct, much more than their lives may be at stake, and we must know what we're dealing with and how to counteract it."

He cupped my cheek, stroked my lower lip. "Okay. I'll go in, find that operation, get you your samples."

That easy, huh? Business as usual for him. But not for me. I bit down on the finger seesawing between my lips. "You're not going anywhere. Not on your own. This has to be my operation."

He fed me more of his finger, his face a mask of pleasured pain when I bit harder. "With all due respect, what operation? Your team is down."

"And your team is *out!* No way am I going on another PATS-maneuvered operation, now that I know…"

That got him rising to his knees, too. The eight-foot bed shrank. "You know nothing! All that bullshit Jake filled your mind with about me and PATS is unsubstantiated. And you can't afford to let that, or anything personal, stand in the way when your friends' lives, and who knows how many others', are at stake. Hell, Calista, for all we know we may all be next in line, infected with what the others fell victim to!"

He made sense. He always did. Damn it. And him.

Did the lout get how much I missed trusting him? How it had been preying on me? I *wanted* to trust him. I *did*. But I didn't. I needed his help, but not as a PATS agent. Could he separate Damian from Agent De Luna? Could he ever be aboveboard with me? Or would he still deceive me if he thought it necessary?

As for his organization—no dilemma there. No trust. Nada.

No matter what Damian said, that distrust didn't stem from Jake's revelations that he'd manipulated our mission and reached his ends with many a helping hand from rotten apples in TOP—the Order for Peace, PATS's parent organization. Their own refusal to initiate investigations into my allegations substantiated my doubts, all right.

Warm hands enveloped my head, warmer eyes delving in, probing, gauging. "That mind of yours shouldn't be left to its own devices in there. The havoc it can cause left unattended is like a precocious kid with superpowers."

The image of my mind as a nosy, cheeky, reckless kid zooming around sowing unwitting destruction was too much. I burst out laughing. He laughed, too. Ah...could anything sound so vital? In all meanings of the word?

Then I was putting down my mug and tumbling all over this vitality. He ended up on top. Not a problem right now. Not when he was undoing my clothes-rearranging efforts, freeing me from my shackles, devouring me from head to core, forcing open my floodgates. I tore at his boxers, the last thing between us, dragged them down. Had to have him inside me. Doubts be damned. He sprang in my grip, hard, heavy, thick. Then he jerked away. And off the bed.

What the—? What'd I do? Yank him too hard?

"Dios—Madre de Dios!"

That was all I understood among the rush of ragged and clearly incensed Spanish. Him and me both!

"Dios, Calista—I can't believe I didn't think of that—*lo siento..."* What *that? What?* "I have no protection here."

No protection in his own home? Or was it his love nest?

I'd forgotten about Desideria—whoever she was!

"What am I thinking?" He strode back to bed. Next second I was beneath him and his lips and hands were all over me. "Who needs protection when there's a hundred routes to pleasure."

Oh. Okay. *No, not okay!* I pushed at him. He probably

thought it another contradictory motion in my frenzy to get him closer.

"Let me pleasure you, *corazón*. Not what we need but…"

"Why don't you have protection?" This I had to know!

He groaned his answers in my mouth, my breasts. "Even without my mother around on occasion, I don't pack condoms if you're not around. I haven't had any use for them since Mel."

"Your mother? Desideria? And you mean…"

"Yes, my mother, and *I mean*. What did you think?"

Plenty. And all wrong. But one set of realizations set off a chain reaction.

I collapsed under my newest realization, something I should have guessed, knowing the extent of Damian's network. "God—you knew all along—about the Colombian operation!"

Chapter 13

It was that impenetrable look he gave me. This time I didn't push out of his arms, I knocked them down. Then him.

At least I would have if he hadn't parried. Too incensed for finesse, I launched at him. "You knew. Of course you did. No way would Dad know about this and you wouldn't. This is right up your alley, mister endless-agendas terrorist hunter. And you let me—let me…" The flow choked, tears' struggling to replace it. No way in hell. "You left me in the dark, going mad over my friends. You wasted time—*their* time—would have gone on wasting it until they…"

That did it. Tears came, dissolving my last punch.

He tried to contain me. I hissed, "I wouldn't advise it, Damian. Take your hands off. And keep them off."

His hands retracted. To press his point now, he'd have to put all he had into subduing me. Guess he thought things weren't as beyond retrieval as that. He guessed wrong.

I stormed into my clothes. He just reclined there, assessing. Thinking of ways to coax me back into gullible mode, no doubt.

Being the theatrical son of a bitch that he was, he had me at the door before he drawled, "Yes, I knew. What of it?"

Don't turn. Don't swallow his bait. Don't—just don't…!

Who was I kidding? Bait, hook and fishing rod were in all the way down to my toes. I swung back, images of ramming him headfirst filling my mind's eye. "And you want to die *how*, Damian?"

He unfolded, sprang to his feet in one of those uncanny movements, came to tower over me, his scowl impressive. *Try it on someone else, buddy!*

"So I knew," he snapped. "The question here is—why should I have told you? What possible connection could I have made between an early-research-stages biological-chemical agent project a continent away and your friends' conditions?"

What I'd give for a stomp-all-over-him-tear-him-to-pieces fight! "Because you were the only one who had all the pieces of the puzzle and must have put them together. Maybe not when Matt fell, but as soon as the others did. You knew they were in Colombia together. You don't make those kinds of oversights, don't miss that big a connection!"

He crossed his arms. "I only knew *they'd* been in Colombia when you told me, just minutes ago."

A harsh laugh hurt me on the way out. "You know every time any of us uses the bathroom!"

"I only know when *you* do" was his serene answer.

"I don't believe you."

I got a superb show of him wrestling with aggravation. The gall!

"I follow only you, Calista. With all due respect and appreciation to the others, I have no interest in their moves. If you'd been on that mission, I would have had a photomontage of it. You stayed here, and I didn't even bother to wonder where the others had disappeared to or noticed when they were back."

All right. Sounded very much like a truth. But when did anything spilling from his lips ever sound insincere? Still, if this was the truth, I had no reason whatsoever to die of an apoplectic stroke.

He took a step closer, his eyebrows rising with his hands, requesting a truce, offering solace. I shook my head, denying both request and offer, stepped away from temptation and overwhelming need. "Let's say I believe you had no reason to make a connection. But you did know of the operation. What are you doing about it?"

His hands fell to his sides as he turned away, went to pick up the jeans draped across the black leather chaise longue. He'd given up on any action for tonight, had he?

He answered only when he was doing up his fly buttons. "My job, what else? I have an operation under way in search of that alleged plant. Intel claimed many locales—the terrorists dividing focus, using decoys to protect the real installation. So far its location isn't known. Meanwhile, my team is bringing down as many as possible of the terrorists and their sponsors. I remained here, near you, while tending other sides of the job. Thought it as well to wait for them to locate the plant before leading the major attack." He struck "a do you have something to say to that?" pose. "Satisfied?"

"Delirious with satisfaction. On all fronts." He moved toward me, took the unbidden truce, and me in his arms. I stayed there, counting his scarily slow heartbeats. Thirty per minute, rose to a whopping sixty on extreme exertion. "What now?"

He stroked the hair he'd undone at one point during our aborted frenzy, spread longing and regret.

"Now if you can stop looking for hidden agendas in everything I do for a second, I can get on with business. The new evidence suggests production of the agent has started. I have to escalate efforts while the situation is still relatively contained."

Escalate efforts, huh? Was that as ominous as it sounded?

Probably far worse. I should have known. This time I pushed out of his arms intending to stay out of them. "You'll escalate nothing!"

"You can come to supervise my actions, if you insist."

"Oh, no. Never again. I sure as hell am not joining a whole slew of PATS operatives on a massive search-and-destroy mission. Get this, Damian—I need the agent to develop a cure for it and there'll be no chance of that if you and your people storm in and annihilate everyone and everything to 'contain' the situation. I know your methods and your margin of 'acceptable losses.' I know you'd consider those who are already affected, *my friends*, that!"

And he'd be right.

I cared nothing about "right." I was saving my friends at any cost. I wasn't sacrificing them for the bigger cause!

"Calista—listen to yourself. You'd really risk a major threat for a few people, no matter who they are to you?"

"Yes, Damian. I already did it once for you, put saving you before stopping Jake, chose your life over the hundreds of thousands he could have wiped out."

Memories flashed hard and thick on his face before it closed on them, final, adamant. "And you were wrong. I gladly would have died if the choice had been between me and others. *Any* other."

"But it didn't turn out to be that way, did it? I saved you *and* stopped him. We can do that again here."

He shook his head. "We have to consider that it might not be possible this time."

"I can't. And you know why? Because those hypothetical thousands are not in immediate danger. Either then or now. You were. My friends are. I will handle one danger at a time. And I'm giving priority to the clear and present one!"

"At least accept extreme measures as an alternative. A viable sample of something as potent can be what sustains the production, perpetuates the proliferation of the agent."

There. He'd said it. Admitted it at last. "That means you lied
again when you said you'd get it for me. You consider the agent's
existence in any quantity and in any hands to be as big a threat
as a steadily producing plant. So what are we talking about?
We're at cross-purposes, as I should have known we would be.
You're out to destroy it, I'm out to retrieve what I can of it. I
guess we're against each other on this one."

His gaze pinned me, more so than the hands that grabbed my
shoulders. "I'll never stand against you, Calista. Never."

"You did before. You will again if you believe I'm wrong.
And you do."

He let out a furious chuckle. "When have I ever believed you
were right, *amor?* And yeah, I stood against you, only to protect
you. But when the chips were down, I was on your side, no matter what you did, or what it cost. You remember the lengths I
went to. *Dios*—I'm every bit as crazy as you are."

"I can't count on that now. Can't discount the possibility
you'd decide to protect me against my will. Too much is at
stake. And anyway, you haven't pinpointed the plant's location.
The best bet is retracing my friends' steps to find the thread that
will lead us to the plant. Maybe even our samples. This means
going to the *tugurios.* So who do you think would look less suspicious going in there? A medical team or a black-ops one?"

"It can be like last time."

This was going nowhere. I turned to the door. This time I kept
on walking. "As if last time was all that great! God, maybe I'm
succumbing to the agent, too. I don't know what I thought I was
doing, coming to the cat to help me save the cream!"

Ocean-blue eyes regarded me across the room. Squaring my
aching shoulders, I regarded right back.

Yep. There it was. The forbearance that always reduced me
to the nineteen-year-old he'd first singled out to be his protégé.
Still wondered why he had. A med school dropout, with a lousy

record in my last year and a worse attitude. He should have taken one look at me and tossed me out and my application in the bin.

Instead Sir Howard Ashton had bent all rules to take me on, to enroll me in GCA's unorthodox medical licensing program. He'd gone above and beyond to give me the most intensive education and training. Then I'd been his groundbreaking Combat Doctors Program's prototype.

According to Damian, Sir Ashton had initiated it for *me*. He'd turned me over to Damian, to shape me into the entity Sir Ashton believed this world needed, a doctor commando.

Suave hands went to said eyes, thoughtful fingers pressing their hooded lids. A grave sign. He had no answer for me. Nothing definite. He had to come through for me!

The aristocratic head rose at the distraction I made fidgeting on his real-leather dark olive couch, the hands leaving his eyes to mine the depths of the immaculate iron-gray mane. An eloquent sigh completed the performance, stalling for more seconds than my suspense tolerance could handle. *Talk already!*

He did only after he started preparing tea, his British accent deepening. Another bad sign. "You ask nothing for years, you're incensed when you discover I offer you covert assistance, tell me you would never voluntarily accept any help from me, then suddenly your demands come fast and furious. First you had me putting whole avant-garde labs to work exclusively for you. Now this. When you do ask, you don't ask for much, do you, Calista."

I bet the smile I flashed him was hyena-like, matching the demented giggle that followed. "Only much is worth being asked of the legendary Sir Howard Ashton."

"Buttering me up?"

The phantom smile didn't fool me. I'd heard him guffawing belly deep once. The laughter software I'd thought missing in the six years I'd served under him was installed. He just ran it in extreme situations. Like when he'd contacted me about the

Russian mission after four years of silence and I'd four-letter-worded his pants off!

"Sure. Still it's true." And it was. Sir Howard Ashton was a living legend. Had been for over thirty-five years now. And he was only my father's age, give or take a couple of years. He was nowhere as pro-heavyweight-boxer built or inclined, but he was in perfect health and shape. Not to mention eternally *on*. Made my four-hour-a-day sleep pattern feel lethargic. Must be how he'd done what it took half a dozen mortals to achieve in as many lifetimes. Doctor, discoverer, adventurer, lobbyist, medical industrialist, billionaire philanthropist.

It was only true when I added, "If I needed something less than the impossible, I wouldn't have come to you."

"I would have hoped you'd come to me anyway, first, in anything, trivial or momentous."

Reproach. Would never get used to how Sir Ashton seemed put out by my preferring my father's help. Truth was, I was lousy at depending on others. Whoever they were.

I jumped to my feet, leaving misgivings on the couch. "I'm here now and it's momentous with a whopping capital *M*. So— was it worth the cab fare, or are you going to turn me down?"

He motioned me to resume my place. I did. He probably wouldn't continue otherwise.

"Ideally, I'd need more time...."

"Ideally my friends wouldn't be in a coma, or the tons of investigations would have hit on a diagnosis as to why they are. I have no more time because I don't know if *they* do. If any of us does."

"I thought they were stable."

"They are. But I have no way of knowing whether they'll take another spiraling dive. I don't know how much time whatever they have in their systems needs to overcome our intensive supportive measures and their own immunity and finish them off."

He gave the tea one last stir. "Your pessimism is probably

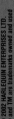

The Silhouette Reader Service™ — Here's how it works:

BUSINESS REPLY MAIL
FIRST-CLASS MAIL   PERMIT NO. 717-003   BUFFALO, NY

POSTAGE WILL BE PAID BY ADDRESSEE

SILHOUETTE READER SERVICE
3010 WALDEN AVE
PO BOX 1867
BUFFALO NY 14240-9952

NO POSTAGE
NECESSARY
IF MAILED
IN THE
UNITED STATES

well-deserved. Still, getting GCA to launch such a massive effort in twenty-four hours, or at all, with that objective…"

He brought me my cup, a graceful bend placing it on the solid mahogany side table. "GCA may prove intractable about putting their names on this mission. They've been panicking since being conned into sponsoring PATS's Russian mission, expecting the truth to come out, for the world to accuse them of using their humanitarian organization to cover paramilitary operations. They do know you were not to blame, but even under assumed identities, your actions under their flag will be attributed to them."

"You don't need to tell them what I'll be doing there, or that I'll be there at all! And anyway, any nonmedical actions I take won't be traced back to either my team or GCA. The ABCs of covert ops, actually. Damian taught me well. But that's another reason why we need to be there last week."

The still expression concealing his lightning processing powers came a true standstill, waiting for that reason.

It was hard to articulate it. To overcome the pain of knowing it was possible. "I have to beat Damian to it."

"You think it will come to that?"

So, that was how he looked when surprised. I shrugged. "Can't afford to put it to the test. His people are already there while we're wasting time haggling! They may be destroying every scrap of evidence I need to save my friends. To get to the bottom of this."

His lids slid down in acknowledgment. So he thought that scenario plausible. Could also be his readiness to believe the worst of Damian. He'd made it clear he considered PATS tarnished by the same terrorist mind-set of those they wiped out.

Weird, these two's relationship. Sir Ashton had been the one to pick Damian to train his Combat Doctors Program's prototypes. To train me. I'd discovered they'd been at each other's throats over me, when Damian was getting me kicked out of GCA and medicine. Then they'd joined forces, again over me, to forge their "help Calista in spite of her crazy self" act.

Still couldn't work out how Sir Ashton's due process, "fixing the law and not breaking or circumventing it" methods meshed with Damian's "just fulfill the damn objective" ones. Or was Sir Ashton only financing Damian's surveillance-assistance op? And where did they stand now?

"Speaking of friends," he said. "Even if I manage to secure you your needs, what would you be doing for human resources?"

"I'm taking my war-ready people, Dad's providing his IT specialist and some muscle, and I'm calling in a couple of whiz HazMat and anarchy science affiliates. All should be ready within twelve hours. Just get me my hands on GCA's Surgical Trailer Suite and Mobile Lab, and those legitimate permits and credentials."

He pursed his lips. "The STS and ML you used in Russia have been dismantled, to erase evidence of your using them as weapon-smuggling decoys. To put them back together without alerting GCA to the nature of your mission—the logistics alone are staggering."

I pulled a *well-duh* face at him. "Yeah. I know. So?"

This had to be his longest gaze ever. I waited it out breath free. He blinked first. *Gotcha.*

"Very well. You will get the STS and ML. I will personally finance the mission. But you may have to move without GCA's name. Or…" His gaze left mine for a second. Something "momentous" passed in his mind during it. No telling what. "Perhaps there is no 'or.' I will arrange it. Your mission to the *tugurios* in Soacha will be assembled in Bogotá in twenty-four hours."

Oh. Wow. Nice to wield that kind of power. Even nicer to have someone else wield it but have it at my disposal.

This could get addictive.

No, it wouldn't. This was a one-off. Anyway—got what I

wanted. I jumped up. "Thanks, Sir Ashton. Appreciate it. Wish me luck."

"Finish your tea, Calista."

Uh-oh. "Have to run…"

His arctic gaze's *Sit!* would have dropped a raging bull. Kept his psychic whip concealed under those extra-refined manners of his, didn't he? Had me forgetting about it, about how he had forged his recruits into whatever he wanted.

Not me, though. I'd been his greatest gamble. His greatest failure. Or—maybe he had wanted me to turn out this way? So I could remind him more of his daughter? The reckless adventurer who'd been infected with his zeal for discovery and none of his rationality, who'd gotten herself killed in a hostage situation after managing to save every one of her fellow hostages.

Always thought it weird he'd voluntarily relive his ordeal in perpetuity, picking a sort-of-surrogate daughter who was a far worse daredevil than the one spawned from his flesh. Not only that, but he'd gone ahead and given me the means to become a professional one.

Maybe it wasn't enough for him to see his daughter's substitute alive. Maybe what made a difference to his suffering was seeing me survive. Against all odds. And you know what? It made sense. There had to be something weird going on in that ultra-cerebral mind of his. No one could be that poised or perfect.

I dropped down to the couch and drank my tea.

Chapter 14

"Watch that baby drop its load!"

A thunderclap echoed in my chest. That voice. Rafael Menendez's suave, shrewd, barely accented drawl. Dad's second-in-command, the guy I had settled for instead of Damian. Being Argentinean-born he'd provide Spanish translations just as well. I stood a better chance of understanding said translations if my heart didn't bang in my head every time I heard his voice.

For over two years now, I'd equated it with hearing from Dad, with all the tagalong emotional mess. I'd gone Pavlovian.

Should pop some anticonditioning medication now that he was my mission partner. That voice wouldn't be delivering any coveted news of Dad for the duration. Or—maybe it would. Maybe he'd fill in the spaces Dad purposely left out. Who better to give me the lowdown on Dad's tangled business than the right hand who orchestrated his eyes, limbs and fists on the outside?

I turned from signing the last release form, handed it back to the airport official, faced Rafael. I found his awestruck eyes glued to the Surgical Trailer Suite and Mobile Lab disembarking from the cargo jet.

He had good reason for his fascination. The sheer size of the six-engined, An-225 Cossack Antonov cargo jumbo was humbling. That that bulk actually rode the winds was mindboggling. It hadn't been dubbed *Mriya*, or *Dream*, for no reason. The largest plane in the world, as high as a six-story building, with a wingspan of almost three hundred feet and a cargo capacity of two hundred and fifty tons, you could transport a house in it. It had easily accommodated both trailers.

The aircraft had just touched down at El Dorado International Airport, Bogotá's one and only, an hour after our charter plane had. Rafael and I had gone ahead to receive and release the STS and ML, leaving the others handling our luggage, customs and picking up the other vehicles Sir Ashton had provided for us. We needed to be on the road in an hour max.

I squinted against the steep slant of the six thirty a.m. sun. Glare, no heat. It had come as a surprise to most of my team to get out of the plane and breathe in the rarified, cool air. Seemed they'd assumed that Colombia, being equatorial, would be sweltering year-round. Seemed also that they hadn't heard our flight captain giving the usual info on our destination as we approached Bogotá, that it was the third-highest capital in South America and was located on a mountain-rimmed plateau known as the Sabana de Bogotá high in the Cordillera Oriental of the Andes Mountains, at an elevation of about nine thousand feet. He'd said we might even feel a bit dizzy coming from sea-level Los Angeles, and advised us not be too active for the first twenty-four to forty-eight hours until we adjusted to the higher altitude.

Yeah. Sure. Good luck with that.

"So what are we doing here?"

There we went again. He spoke, *wham*. Should tape his mouth shut for the rest of the mission. I turned. "You don't know?"

He shrugged. "How can I? I hooked up with your team half an hour before we boarded the plane, time you spent introducing me around, then you all zonked out on me the whole flight. Missing a meal of miraculous quality for plane food, I must add."

I blinked as if seeing him for the first time. And really, I was. In all our fleeting hookups, he'd just been the transparent messenger wielding the message I craved. Now I gave him my first good look, taking stock of my new co-leader.

Just a couple of years older than me, Rafael came in a solid, six-foot, in-shape package. The usual Latin coloring, black wavy mane, and teeth that had me blinking stars every time he flashed them against his tan complexion. But it was his vibe—that radiation of artless charm, that ease that overshadowed his considerable aesthetic attributes. Kind of laid-back and unassuming. Until you looked closely into those eyes. Then you could believe he was a world-class hacker, someone who'd had a three-year tenure in hell, who now dealt with hell spawn on a regular basis. Dad's foremost general in his war.

So had Dad thrown him in my lap blind? Or was the outgoing Rafael just being chatty? One way to find out. "Dad didn't fill you in? Were you having trouble securing communications?"

"Actually I'm untraceable and uninterceptable. Then there is always code if he wants. No, he just told me to gear up, to hightail my way to report to you."

Dad. Never let anyone know anything for certain, huh? "Left it up to me to fill you in, or leave you in the need-to-know dark, huh? Just cracked his whip and told you to hop to it?"

Those brown eyes joined a wide, easy-smiling mouth in a fond grin. "Youch. But hey, I go wherever he sends me."

I bet. Dad sure had himself one willing slave here.

He'd given me the basics on Rafael the first time he'd told me the man would be our go-between. Rafael had prospered in computer crimes since the impressionable age of thirteen. He'd been suspected, but no one could ever trace him, or prove anything. Until the day a planted girlfriend confirmed to her bosses, cyber-pirates whom he'd caused some heavy damage, that he'd been behind their losses. When she couldn't get any evidence, they'd framed him for something different and condemned him to three years hard labor in a maximum-security prison. He hadn't been supposed to survive his first week.

Dad, also on his first week there, had stepped in. But even after he'd foiled the first liquidation attempt, the young, good-looking geek amidst a repeat-offenders' swarm had been in constant jeopardy. Dad had kept him under his protection.

Along with his life, Rafael owed my Dad everything else, from dignity to sanity to humanity. He'd reciprocated by pledging himself to Dad's cause. And did it all with the flair of a selfless knight in the service of his worshiped liege-lord. And from what I heard, did it well indeed.

He now followed me as I went to inspect our rides. We reached the STS first. Didn't look like much on the outside, to avoid whetting appetites to commandeer us. Inside, it was a surgeon's and humanitarian operative's wildest fantasies come true, in glorious post–space-age alloys and gadgets.

I jumped ahead of Rafael through the entryway at the left side of the vehicle that had taken us through Russia and seen us through hundreds of surgeries. Damian's surgery…

Rafael whistled once. Then again. I turned to him, eyebrow cocked.

A sheepish smile curved up at me. Very effective. Would get anyone with a five-percent decency component to forgive him anything.

"Not that I understand what any of this is—but whoo-hoo, impressive."

I nodded. "Whoo-hoo is right. In the cutting-edge mobile surgery units arena, this is the equivalent of a massacre."

He guffawed. "Now I know I'll be very comfortable working

with you. With that sense of humor, it'll be just like being with the Boss again. You sure are your daddy's girl."

A whimsical twist to my mouth acknowledged his insight. "Uh-huh. Sure am. You'd be the first to like *that* about me."

I slid panels and inspected instruments and add-on facilities, my hands itching to use them on some patients. Rafael still stood at the threshold, looking around.

"But—uh, shouldn't it be, I don't know—bigger?" he asked.

"That fooled you, huh? Never fear. This is a much more compressible model than anything that came before it, to allow us to go on very narrow and rough roads up hills and through jungle areas if need be. The trailer alone now measures fifty-five by ten feet but expands to a full hundred and twenty by twenty feet, and also expands vertically, to a final height of ten feet." I pointed to the ingenious mechanisms where the trailer expanded. "I'll teach you how to operate the expansion controls once we're on the road."

He whistled again. "Is this made to your specifications?"

"Actually, I think the mechanics did use the notes me and Matt and Ayesha…" I hiccuped, memories punching out of tight containment. *Don't. Step back.* I shook my head, continued. "We offered suggestions after we put it to an extensive trial-by-fire in our last mission. Each of my—my team recommended changes to make the place more accessible and useful. Seems someone listened to the word of hands-on experience."

"Fascinating. There seem to be lots of computerized facilities here. Not that I see anything recognizable."

"You'll recognize plenty when the STS is expanded and all the hidden stuff comes out. Computers, OR tables, anesthesia stations, overhead operating lights, surgical microscope, CT and X-ray—the works. Let me give you a quick orientation."

I pointed beneath his feet as he crossed the threshold. "That's a stretcher lift for emergencies. And those—" I pointed at the identical stainless steel panels lining one side of the trailer "—are patient stations when expanded, accommodating up to twenty patients. Over there is the medical gas system, the fiber optic network. Here is the nurses' station, with systems monitoring and medication refrigerator. And that's the surface layer. Beneath it we have tons of—special supplies. And weapons."

I steered him onward. "That's the infrared scrub area, the really nifty soiled and clean utility rooms. The soiled room has ultrasonic cleaner, nitrogen blow gun, pass-through for biohazard storage and pick up…and, this is all going over your head."

He pretended to follow imaginary missiles zooming above his head, grinned. "Yep! But you sure know your specs."

"I'm just bursting with excitement over having my hands on this magnificent toy again. A case of brag or bust, really."

"I know the feeling. Gadgets, if computer related, fry my restraint, too. I use the same overpowering finesse when I drown someone in computer jargon."

I chuckled. He was one nice guy. So far.

His gaze arced around, landed on me. "So, from Lucia, the only one who actually spoke to me, I hear the medical aid mission is just a cover. Why all these facilities if it won't be for real?"

I sighed, regret pushing away the momentary lightness. "It will be, up to a point. We have to validate our presence there. The hell of it is we don't have time to help everyone who'll need it. And then, if we find what I hope is there, these facilities will provide the answers we need…." I paused at his inquisitive expression. Time to give him a rundown of the situation.

In two minutes flat I'd told him all my info. Which spoke volumes on how little I had. Then we jumped out of the STS and turned it over to those of our team who would take the first shift at the wheel during our drive to Bogotá.

It was the ML's turn for inspection. Already in residence there were Charlene Judd and Diana McPherson, our HazMat and anarchy science experts. Call them Char and Di. Yeah, they did intend the pun.

"Hey, Cali!" Char exclaimed as soon as she saw me.

I had to look up. Way up. As tall as Rafael and as fair as he was dark, she had another thing in common with him—a dominant bone structure. On a woman it was even more striking. Made her look openly predatory and intimidating. I envied her that. Though maybe I shouldn't. Looking like a maid from Valhalla wouldn't be effective in covert ops.

Char waved her hands around. "Where in this world did you manage to get this? I haven't seen anything so well equipped since my days with the CIA."

Di, Char's antithesis, brunette, five foot two max and truly endowed, came back from expanding a section of the lab, brown eyes elated, voluptuous body jiggling. "Where can I sign up to join GCA, Cali?"

I smiled at her. Of the two, I liked her best. Probably because of our history. But both were top-notch specialists. Beyond that even. In certain circles they were reputed to be the very best. A lot rode on their expertise in this venture if we found what we were looking for.

"Last I heard, Di," I said, "they signed us anarchist types only when they were scared witless."

Di snickered. "Should be all the time in today's world!"

Considering how easily Sir Ashton had managed to get GCA to cough up the goods and the creds, I'd say this was an accurate assessment. "Yeah. Anyway, as I was telling Rafael, with the STS and ML we're prepared for anything surgical, diagnostic or investigative. They will also give us the means and the excuse for maximum mobility. Our target is Soacha—that's a neighborhood on the southern outskirts of Bogotá. That's where my friends were two months ago in the *tugurios*—" I turned to Rafael. "That's the term they use here for areas filled with internally displaced people."

And what was I doing explaining a Spanish term to him?

He made no point of it. Gracious. I went on. "Anyway, since you're the ones who didn't catch my brilliant lecture summing up the local situation, let me give you a basic outline."

Now to sum up unending suffering and madness in ten sentences or less. I inhaled. "For the past forty years, Colombia has been in the grip of an armed conflict between guerrillas, paramilitary groups and the Colombian army. They all fight over control of land, natural resources, the drug trade and political power. In the middle are the civilians who suffer all forms of abuse and violence and are forced to flee their homes to survive. They gather on the outskirts of main cities, forming areas that are aptly called 'misery belts.' If anything, internally displaced people are worse off than refugees, since they're not protected by international human rights laws and don't have the same access to humanitarian aid, while every human rights violation against them flourishes in silence without any form of punishment."

Rafael's face lost its sunniness for the first time. "I've been away from my mother continent for a long time. But I've heard unofficial estimates claim over three million IDP."

"IDP?" Di blinked.

"Internally displaced people," Char answered. "Di, you still asleep, hon?" She brushed Di's bangs out of her eyes.

Uh-okay. Looked more than just friends to me. Had never thought of it, but they were probably a couple. Hoped it wouldn't interfere in their work. Or with their actions and decisions in case of danger.

Yeah. Listen to the ultimate "let your heart rule your head under fire" moron talking.

I exhaled a wave of futility before it dragged me under. "Anyway, isolated people are prey to diseases and chronic malnutrition. But of course they have no right to seek treatment. Rival factions control roads, and crossing checkpoints is dangerous since the controllers suspect anyone of supporting other factions. Threats against local hospitals make it impossible to organize medical teams. Enter unaffiliated efforts like GCA, which is among the few humanitarian organizations ever granted access to contested territories here. And that's why we're here under their flag.

"So—that's the general bleak picture. Soacha, where we're heading, is one of the main reception sites for IDP. Their number has mushroomed to almost four hundred thousand and growing, despite the precarious conditions. By that read almost nonexistent water, electricity and all other basic services."

"Ack! No water or electricity?" Di exclaimed.

Char frowned down on her, a fond sort of frown. "Expected room service, hon? It *is* a squatter settlement, a refugee camp!"

I cleared my throat. "We do have generators, water purification systems and septic tanks in tow. It won't be ideal, but when you feel like complaining, remember you're going home to all amenities, unlike these people who've lost them forever."

Char's hand descended on my shoulder. Good grip. Should recruit her for more than affiliate jobs. "You *are* here to do something about that."

"I wouldn't call a week's time doing much, Char," I huffed. "And we're not even here for them. But we have been getting supplies and medicines to segregated communities since the beginning of our operations. Still—nothing is ever enough."

Di gave me a bolstering thump on the back, too. "It's enough that you try! I think it's cool of you, Cali."

"Cool, huh? You're a pistol, Di." I turned to include the others. "We have an agreement with the paramilitary group controlling the *tugurios,* but we might meet others on the way, and since we're posing as foreign civilians…"

"We *are* foreign civilians. At least, we three here are!"

My lips twisted. "How many civilians do you who know dabble in terrorist brews every day after breakfast, Di?"

Di pouted. "I'm a civilian! And a scientist. It's my first time in the field, so excuse me for freaking out."

If Di in her line of business was unprepared for the fallout of violence, just what hope did the rest of humanity have? "Don't. Just sit in the *Enterprise*-level comfort of the ML and wait for me to bring you samples and do your magic."

I ran my fingers over the sputter coater, the cryogenic specimen system and the custom-crafted cryo-scanning electron microscope. Hoped the sci-fi equipment got us answers. "As I was saying, once we're out of Bogotá, there's always danger of being blocked or caught in the middle of an 'operation.' Though we have permits, flagrant contempt and violence toward medical facilities and personnel is common. Piracy is a fact of life. What I'm saying is, in case of attacks, lie low and let my team handle it."

"*Now* she tells us there's a chance of attacks!" Di moaned.

Char smirked at her. "It was the first thing she told us when she reeled us in. 'This may be terminally dangerous,' she said. *You* wanted to see the tropics. And the ML. You said you knew Cali would take care of anything, as she always does."

Yeah. Sure. Di did have that unrealistic-expectations problem where I was concerned, ever since we'd saved her from a life as an unconventional-weapons designer and sex slave in an underground "reform" movement. Matt and Ishmael had done most of the work, but she preferred to credit me, the woman, with it.

Di's solitary dimple flashed. "Hey—moaning is cathartic. Say, did you know there's a major city here called Cali?"

I snapped a look at my watch. The others should be done by now. "Yep. And no, we're not going there to avoid confusion. At least you're not. I don't know where investigations will take me. You'll do your parts, then head home. And speaking of that, it won't happen if we don't get this show on the road."

After deciding who'd take the wheel first, I turned and jumped out of the ML.

Right into Damian's arms.

Chapter 15

Delight hit first. The usual avalanche of sensations followed. Heat and intimacy and fitting together. Control slid with my body down his. My feet hit the floor, then his whisper hit me.

"Nice of you to drop by."

"You…!"

More gushed in my head, a babble of rage and shock and relief. *Relief?* Would I make up my mind and stick with emotions in column A or column B already?

It was just—having him near was like being in a bone-penetrating sandstorm. Craving lashed me. Then I saw it. The kiss forming in his mind. My knees wobbled. So I kneed him.

He was ready for me. My *hiza geri* connected with his left thigh instead. It still hurt, still emptied his eyes of that hypnotic passion. He grunted. "Sloppy first thing in the morning, *querida?* Never got the chance to find out for myself."

I salvaged my footing, my speech controls. My anger. "Just

stopping you from giving El Dorado airfield the idea we're shooting a cheap soap here."

"So you're giving them the impression we're shooting a cheap martial-arts flick instead?"

"What the hell are you doing here?"

Those painstakingly sculpted lips pouted in pure derision. "Oh, and you're asking because you just bought the country?"

According to our flight captain, it was fifty-seven degrees in Bogotá this morning. Not within feet of Damian, it wasn't. More like a hundred and fourteen! "You won't be able to dodge the next *mawashi geri* to your head that easily. Dammit, I thought we were done with all this crap."

He regarded my turmoil like a scientist observing a new, erratic species. "I'm not following you. I'm here to work."

"And your work happens to be in the same three square feet that I occupy of Colombian soil?"

"You're nowhere near that big. Except when horizontal and I—"

"Remember that gratitude thing you suffer from? How about I knock you out on the runway for a curative measure?"

His eyes only flared again. "*Dios*—I miss you."

And *God*, I missed him. Always. I'd been going crazy wondering where he was, what he was up to. Dreading a confrontation on opposite sides. Wishing to die before it ever came to pass. "Shows what a masochist pervert you are."

He gave a sage nod. "I've come to embrace this as fact." He raised both hands at my growl. "And before you vaporlock, I have this to say…." His eyes moved up. "What's *he* doing here?"

Huh? What…? I followed his line of vision, found it pouring hostility on the unwitting Rafael, who was hopping out of the ML.

I swung back to Damian. "You know him?" Rafael passed by us, smiling at me, giving Damian a nonchalant "Yo, man" before heading back to the rest of the team. "What am I asking? Sure you know him. So know this, too. He's invited. You're not."

"*Un*-invite him. You don't need him. You have me."

"I don't *want* you. I'm not letting you and PATS steer this. I've got my team, and I'm beating you to it, Damian."

Fury emptied from his gaze, a lethal softness cascading in. "You really think you can beat me at my game, *querida?*"

Don't you dare shudder! "Probably not. But I'm going to give it the best damn shot I've got. Or die trying."

"Watch it. That temper can slash the population in a mile's radius to pieces."

Red blotched my vision. I still saw his expression shift, turn grim. "And you think I'd let you die?"

"Godly delusions now, huh? Just don't stand in my way."

"I won't. With one condition. I come with you."

"I *can* run comprehensive hearing tests, Damian!" My voice rose an octave. "We're not joining forces. You and PATS—"

"You need those hearing acuity tests, too, it seems. I said *I* come with you—alone. Just me, Damian De Luna, your man."

That silenced me. Everything ceased to matter. This was everything. Doubts, questions, misgivings pushed aside. Eagerness, elation flooding in. I wanted him with me so much, so much...

"Think how useful I can be to you. This is my turf. I know the country, the people, the secrets, inside and out. I can be your mission guide, be another inconspicuous native."

That broke through the muteness. "Yeah, inconspicuous, sure. So you *did* manage to get one of those hologram disguise kits! You'd never pass as a guide, Damian."

"I did in Russia."

"You weren't a guide back then."

"So I'll be this mission's logistician again."

"Russia was different. There were no endless warring factions trying to recruit every able-bodied man. Here they snatch teens from their school benches. Convince them you're a native and they'll want to recruit all that muscle to their cause. Or else!"

"I know how to handle my own countrymen, Calista. Just say you want me with you."

I wanted to *yes-yes-yes* him to the ground. And I wanted to dig a hole where he'd never find me again. To knock him unconscious and keep him that way until I found my friends' cure. I wanted plenty more. I could only wail, "Why?"

He gave me four simple words. "Because you need me."

I did. And how. Beyond his extensive capabilities and knowledge of this land. Just him. But could I possibly believe that was his motive? His only motive? Could he sell out PATS and his own convictions for me? Would I want him to? And if I accepted, where would that lead? *To more heartache and destruction, idiot. Just say no.* I tried. "Listen, Damian, I won't have you doing anything against your better judgment here...."

"I've been doing nothing but, ever since I met you."

"Yeah, and every time you turn into a resentment time bomb. No more sacrifices of any sort for me, Damian. I can do this alone. Just please—please don't stand in my way."

I turned, and he did just that. I shoved at him. "Why aren't you with your men?"

He didn't budge. "They're fine on their own. And this is a multitasked operation. They'll find the plant, the origin. We'll investigate the end result and the cure for our people."

Our people. A fist trembled in my chest. "Why did you change your mind?"

He fell silent for a moment. Then he sighed. "I didn't. I just gave it more thought. Before you came to me I was operating under the conviction this was a containable situation. If they're conducting field experiments already, I must assume samples are dispersed and your investigation into the nature of the agent and its counteraction may prove even more important than eradicating its manufacturing plant and manufacturers. My resources and capabilities will serve better on your end of the fight now."

Sounded too good to believe. Was it? "What about your zero-tolerance, sacrifice-all-affected agenda."

He huffed a chuckle. "What? You think I'll storm into the *tugurios* and wipe out 400,000 people to contain the situation?"

He thought I could think with a brain sprouting roots?

"Think about it, Calista." There he went again with the think thing! "*You* may be affected. I can't jeopardize obtaining the diagnosis and treatment that would save you if you're infected."

Put that way—oh. Shall we say, moved beyond endurance? "As long…" Great, I was gulping now, what felt like acid around the boulder filling my chest. *For God's sake!* "As long as you don't have a conflict of interest."

"I do. I'm interested in helping you, saving our people and reaching a resolution. But I'm also interested in dragging you to the nearest hotel for an all-night, one-on-one orgy."

I jumped back out of his wandering hands' range. "There'll be no orgies if you come with us!"

"Why not?" At my glare he shrugged. "Guess I'll proposition you again when you're in a better mood. So did you take care of the hotel reservations or shall I do it?"

Okay. Had he just made a leap in logic or did I miss something? Like the whole point behind life on this planet? "What hotel reservations?"

"To spend the night, what else?"

"We're getting out of here and to Soacha at once."

"No, you're not. You're not going anywhere today."

"Now, listen here, Damian—"

"Today is Bogotá's car-free day, held the first Thursday in February. Only fire trucks and ambulances are allowed on the streets. Before you argue that you are a medical convoy and should be regarded in the same category, don't bother. Show one wheel in the streets today and you spend the rest of it in a traffic police station, negotiating the gross fine. See how beneficial my homegrown knowledge is going to be to you?"

A *thunk* echoed in my skull when caressing fingers closed my hanging-open mouth for me. "Welcome to my home, *mi amor.*"

We didn't have an orgy. But I did spend the night watching my mental stability ebbing in the gloom, going crazy for one.

Yeah, we spent the night in Bogotá. Damian hadn't been joking. The city was on foot. They chose one day in the whole damn year to conserve the environment and we arrived on it!

Our guards, Rafael's—or should I say, Dad's—men, stayed behind at the airport with the STS and ML. The rest headed to the hotel where Damian had secured us rooms. He insisted on handling the bill. I insisted right back. We ended up tossing for it. I won. I paid. Ouch.

I would have paid anything, though, to stop the gnawing, the whispering. *What are you fighting this for? Just cross that corridor and knock on his door, enter and enjoy.*

Enjoy. Right. I knew why I was fighting.

Accepting his help, his offering it at all, was complicating matters, expanding a dependence I couldn't foster, taking our relationship into depths I had no idea whether I could survive.

And then I had issues with single-mindedness, when I was its focus. Jake had made me his obsession, and the catastrophic domino effect had lead to the destruction of his life and so many others'. So Damian wasn't a psychotic megalomaniac, but still, his focus scared me, especially since it wrenched out mine in return. We were a foolproof formula for devastation.

And no, I wasn't forgetting his constant manipulation and lies. I had good reasons not to be with him. The best.

Good luck telling my body that.

And now the damn reason for my suffering was at it again. Right there at my door. Bringing another serving of temptation and torment, no doubt. I snatched the door open and almost fell to me knees.

He pushed past me, went to set down the tray in his hands, turned, came back to me, fresh, alert, mouthwatering.

"Calista the Idiosyncratic. It's a law of nature that freshly brewed *tinto*—that's our Colombian coffee—wakes anybody with a smile. Not a snarl." One long, knowing finger traced my canines when I gave him a real one. "Snarl is good. I like your snarl." His gaze glided to my mangled bed. "Rough night, huh? Good. On many levels. Revenge wise, end-result wise. Simmering all night will just make now all the more explosive."

"Okay, that's it. No way in hell is this going to work."

"It worked great in Russia."

"Russia worked only as far as you were still nursing your grudge, hating me and yourself, growling 'St. James' not *'mi amor'* and *'mi corazón'* and not touching me or messing with my hormones. And it's only hormones, Damian. Only sex. If I want relief, I'll get it. Your help is not needed or required."

His eyes froze. Felt like the time I got trapped in one of those huge slaughterhouse fridges. Oh, what the hell! *End this.* "Go catch up with your men and wreak havoc somewhere else, Damian."

He turned and walked to the door. "It's oh-six-hundred. We need to be on the road by oh-seven-hundred if we're to reach Soacha before nightfall."

And he'd expected to get stuff wrapped up here before that, huh? A quickie for the road? Though, his expectations were right on the money. In an hour it would have been several quickies.

At the door, he said over one intimidating shoulder, "Drink your coffee. And get some relief." Before I could throw something at his head the door clicked on his grim *"I will."*

"I won't be exaggerating if I say Santa Fe de Bogotá is not a city, but a maze. Of contrasts. Futuristic architecture, colonial churches, incredible museums, the latest in every luxury and technology, side by side with an abundance of beggars and shantytowns. First-time visitors are always shocked at the amazing mixture of prosperity and poverty, Maseratis and mules."

Damian, in maddening tour-guide-mode, drummed his fingers on the wheel, keeping perfect rhythm with the hot salsa number playing on the CD. What a time to discover his taste in music. And for it to be that! He even swayed slightly with the beat, almost rapping his words to it. Feeling mellow, huh? Or he was a better actor than I had thought he was. Probably both. Damn him.

And he was right. Bogotá, what I'd seen of it on the few fleeting times I'd been here, was breathtaking. Nothing like any metropolis I'd ever been to. Cool, dizzying, simmering—unfathomable. Its reputation as one of the world's most chaotic, seductive and aggressive cities was well earned.

Yeah. And all of the above adjectives fitted Damian. Now I'd seen him and Bogotá together, I might just have found out why he was what he was.

"No offense to your motherland pride, Damian." Lucia, who was sitting beside him, threw him a glance. "But all I want to know is—will we ever get the hell out of here?"

Valid question. We hadn't moved for fifteen minutes!

Damian shrugged. "Post car-free-day mania."

Tell me about it. Seemed the seven million populating Bogotá were taking revenge for being forced to relinquish their cars yesterday. We might just take all day—and night.

And to think I'd thought Damian's comment about making it to our destination before nightfall an exaggeration to frazzle me! I'd thought, *Like it'll take more than 12 hours to drive 20 miles back and forth from the airport then 60 to Soacha.*

So he'd known what he was talking about. Our local expert. A bottomless well of info, when he decided to share. Humph.

Lucia fidgeted, gulped another mouthful of that addictive

coffee, subsided against her door and went still. Damian started to hum softly and—what do you know?—he sounded like a cross between Elvis and the Gypsy Kings. Get relief, my ass!

Seemed he'd gotten his, though. Did I already say damn him?

I shifted in my seat, easing my cramping everything, resumed watching the avalanche of *busetas* on the opposite road, which for some reason was flowing. That got dizzying fast. I turned to the other side, scanned the extravagant stores and roadside stalls. Again. Anyone hand me a piece of paper so I could write down an inventory. The endless home-entertainment gadgets, the multitude of mouthwatering bakeries, the amazing collections of tropical plants and fruits—and that multi-colored evening dress... Hmm. Indecipherable material, could swear it was all hand embroidered—what there was of it.

Wondered what it felt like to dress up in something like that. Never would, probably. That was a disguise for a kind of racket I didn't frequent. As for wearing it in real life—ha.

I swung my eyes back. Damian's awesome presence caught me again—his head, what I could see of his profile—one day I had to find out which of his ancestors was a Native American shaman and which was a Spanish marauder. He was an amalgam of the best the two races had to offer, enhanced in every way....

"See anything you like?"

I jerked. Caught. So what? Huh. "Yeah. That dress!"

His eyes in the mirror called me liar. Well, him and me both! "You'd need your elders' approval for that one."

"Says the man who lives with his mommy." Oops. My eyes darted to Lucia. She was out. Whew. She needed a break after the night alternating on the phone checking up on our people and getting nothing but more doses of despondency.

The traffic moved. Damian put the Jeep in motion, kept devouring eyes on me. "And living with 'my mommy'—" he imitated my voice and sneer to perfection "—does what? Emasculates me?"

As if anything could. Still—it was an odd setup. The mother he'd once told me he hadn't known until he was sixteen. Then, twenty years later, big, bad and mass destructive, he went home to her. Didn't take his women there. Didn't keep condoms there.

According to him there were no women to take, no need for condoms. And that shouldn't make me all nauseous with relief. *Change the subject!*

"So what's a Desideria anyway?"

That's right. Shove your foot farther into your big mouth, Calista. Go ahead and slight the man's mother, why don't you?

A leisurely inspection of said foot-filled mouth later, his answer was monotone, matter-of-fact. Snickering heard loud and clear, thank you. "What's a Calista? Don't answer that, O Most Beautiful One."

He fell silent as he negotiated a bottleneck, then suddenly he was picking up speed, leading our convoy out of the city. I looked back. The trucks and trailers were right behind us. Maybe there was still hope of getting something done in the *tugurios* today.

After half a dozen traffic police and military police inspections and eons of mind-destroying humming, with the suburbs thinning and the roads worsening, he suddenly said, "Desire. Blinding. Enslaving. That's a Desideria."

Answer four hours later, why don't you?

"A name that served her well and describes what she was— still is—to so many men. All of them notorious."

"Just how many men did she go through?" Oh God! Somebody reel in that runaway tongue of mine.

Damian gave it more rope. "Nine. From my drug-lord father to her latest oil mogul. She's an unerring magnet for major league scum."

I took the rope and ran away with it. "Wow. But then again, what could your mother be other than a femme fatale?"

"Actually it was an *homme* fatal here. I got rid of six of them so far."

"You killed your mother's lovers? Shades of Oedipus!"

"Apart from my father—husbands, actually. And I eliminated them and decimated their operations."

Just like that, huh?

"Starting with my father. Oedipus had no idea who he was killing and ended up gouging his eyes out, poor guy. So I've got him beat."

So he killed his father. Or had him killed. Heavy stuff. What kind of baggage could he be dragging about?

He didn't let me wonder long. "If you're wondering if I fall into abysses of guilt over terminating my father, don't. He wasn't a Godfather-type goon with a soft family center. He was a soulless monster. My mother's Witness Protection Program wasn't tight enough and he got to me while my grandmother was babysitting. He killed her, abducted me for spite, then threw me to the poorest of the families he terrorized to raise among ten children.

"In that overcrowded, dirt-poor home, I was the straw that broke the camel's back, a resented burden and punching bag. Then when I was eight, my father decided it was time I earned my keep. He took his first good look at me and saw my eyes. They're neither my mother's color nor his. And even though I looked like a younger edition of him, he tortured me for it."

Oh God! "Oh, Damian."

"No sweat. I grew too big to beat up pretty fast. And I'm grateful that he put me to work. It was how and where I learned all there is to know about depravity—and how to bring people like him down. Then I found out who my mother was and I bailed to the States. It took some searching to locate her, and I still only went to her when I found out that she'd never stopped looking for me, had never given up. Meeting her for the first time when I was almost twenty was weird. She felt like an older sister rather than a mother." His eyes crinkled at me. "And I can assure you I have no perverted feelings for her. In fact, may she lure more and more villains for me to vanquish."

"You make it sound as if she entraps them for you."

He gave a fond chuckle. "I wouldn't put it past her."

"So she knows what you are?"

"What I *am*, not what I *do*, huh? Like I'm some demon?"

"You are." And I now had more insight into why he was. As if I needed more reasons to love him. Or to mistrust him. And just why was he telling me all this?

"I'll take that as a compliment."

Funny thing was, it was. Must be the demon in me wagging its tail in intensified appreciation of a kindred fiend.

A minute later, he leaned over Lucia to the glove compartment, opened it. "And by the way, see that makeshift checkpoint in the distance? They're really a death squad."

Chapter 16

"Death squad?"

Lucia's head jerked up when Damian slid open a secret panel in the glove compartment and dislodged half a dozen concealed semiautomatic pistols. He threw two in her lap. She got an instant grip on them, though from the dazed look she swung to me, not on the situation.

Damian slowed down, his voice unperturbed over the smooth whine of his Jeep's finely tuned motor. "They'll ask us all to step down, have a bit of fun first before they execute us."

"Are you sure about this, Damian?" My disaster bag was already unzipped, my weapons being assembled by touch, my eyes straight ahead at the straggly stop sign, the Jeep intercepting our path and the few gunmen loitering beside it.

"There are ten, two in the Jeep. Wind down your windows the moment we're in range and get them before they have a chance to retaliate. No place for your weapons here, Calista." He handed me two guns over his shoulder. "Head shots. Later we can add more elsewhere to make it look like whoever did it wasn't a marksman, that the head shots were posthumous vindictive overkill."

He considered that an answer? "You still haven't told me how you know they intend to kill us. What if they're with the paramilitaries controlling the *tugurios?* They've agreed that we can enter their territory, promised protection."

He slowed down more, stretching the remaining minutes before the confrontation. Whatever that would turn out to be. "Protection. Yeah. I pushed some buttons, uncovered some lids, made sure the paramilitaries meant it."

"And you still think it's okay to kill people who could turn out to be their vanguards just to be on the safe side?"

"With millions of dollars on wheels, you get one shot at the safe side, Calista."

Of course. I hadn't been in a medical convoy that hadn't been attacked with an eye to commandeer our hardware and supplies. Peace-loving bleeding hearts with pricey equipment were just too tempting for gun-toting cowards. But maybe it wasn't like that this time!

His growl stopped my inner debate. "If you need a reason to kill those vermin, how about that they abduct boys to add to their army first thing every morning after slaughtering their fathers and raping their mothers and sisters? That they picked us to provide their sport now not only to raid our resources but to stop aid from reaching those they terrorize and exploit?"

I poked him, protesting the polluting images, the infecting rage, demanding a situation-specific answer. He gave one, reluctant, grudging.

"They're not with *our* paramilitaries."

"You're sure? A direct answer would be appreciated!"

"As sure as you are of the ABCs of emergency measures. These men are not wearing the correct 'colors.'"

"They look like any other mercenaries I've ever seen."

"To me they're a clearly demarcated species. But the clincher is they're just outside our paramilitaries' territory. They're intercepting us, claiming the prize before we enter it. They wouldn't dare breach the limits when they're so few. And that's another clue. Our paras move in packs of a couple of dozen, minimum. This is a fringe job."

Okay. He was the terrorist-guerrilla-paramilitary-scum specialist. He could probably tell them apart in the dark. But... "Why not just ram through them, hightail it into our protected territory? Our vehicles are bulletproof. One-way, too, so we can fire from within if need be. Uh—your Jeep is, too, right?"

His eyes met mine in the rearview mirror. "See those M249 machine guns and their lovely ammo belts? How about that mounted Mark 19 grenade machine gun? How much do you think our armoring could take? And what if they shoot our tires right away and we're forced into an equal-opportunity confrontation with unpredictable results? We'd still wipe them out, but at what cost?"

None. I wasn't placing a single one of my people in danger.

Funny that, when you're dragging them right into it.

Stop it. You're the leader. Decide. Give the orders.

I couldn't risk contacting the others on the walkie-talkie, secure channel or not. Safe side. It was what it was all about.

"Damian, double-flash the others, three flashes, then two, then one. They'll know it's an attack. They'll be ready."

My grip tightened on cold hardness, the polished, painstaking instrument of death, my mind leaping over the ticking seconds to a point in time where it would come to explosive life in my grip, ending lives. We were now within three hundred feet of them. My other hand undid my braid.

"What are you *doing?*" Damian barked.

"If we're doing it, we're doing it right. I don't even want the paint job scratched. That means all fire comes from our side." I rolled down my window and tossed my hair out. It swirled and billowed in the cool afternoon wind. "If it distracts you, I bet it distracts any male."

His thundered *"Calista!"* drowned in the wind and blood whooshing in my head. Short of stopping to drag me in, he could do nothing but vibrate with fury. Though, maybe seeing my plan working might defuse him. The guerrillas were lowering their weapons, coming forward, even the couple manning the Jeep, intrigued, surprise clear in their body language. I could now see their faces. So they could mine. My gun-free hand tossed them an enthusiastic wave for a double whammy.

They started nudging one another now, laughing, exchanging merry obscenities and macabre plans, no doubt. *I* had no doubt anymore. I was in range. I could pick up a thug's intention to hack me to pieces after violating me in every way his sick mind could come up with, within a hundred feet. They were loud about it. I understood the vicious tone well enough.

"They're arguing, after they kill the men, who'll—go first with you," said Lucia. Always forgot she spoke Spanish.

All right. Good to know there was no ambiguity here. Unequivocal purpose was always appreciated. "They're all in plain sight now. All together…"

One—two—*three* hard-muffled pops went off, silencing me. Silencing everything. Nickel-sized crimson blossomed on three guerrillas' foreheads. Time hung still as the already dead men's filthy consciousness blinked out, as their bodies froze in that last snatch at life and corporeal volition, before going down like buildings in synchronized demolishing. Damian! Not leaving much for us, huh? Must have taken extra exception to the guerrillas' plans for us. Or for me?

Everything coexisted, all thought and movement and sound, actions and reactions. Damian hadn't braked to a standstill and the Jeep crept closer to our enemies, our victims, in drop-frame motion. His first three shots segued into mine, then Lucia's. Mine found two more foreheads, hers a shoulder and a thigh.

Damn. Shouldn't have included her in this. Damian and I could have done this alone. A mistake.

Now we paid for it.

Her victims fell, already firing back, bullets spraying. Right at her. She screamed.

She fell back inside the Jeep, agony pouring from her lips and blood gushing down her forearm. My fear for her gained our enemies a priceless second.

Machine-gun fire bombarded our windshield. The outer glass layer fissured, shattered, the radiating white overlapping networks obscuring visual. The middle polycarbonate laminate held under the barrage. No telling for how long. Three uninjured men remained, running for their Jeep—make that two. Damian got another one. Then I another.

The one remaining reached for his grenade machine-gun controls and fired.

Damian was ahead of him, wrenching the wheel in a ninety-degree swerve, the power of his foot on the accelerator surging into the engine, bringing it to thundering life, catapulting the Jeep into the air, veering us out of the grenades' trajectory—but—oh God! Savannah and Al's truck, right behind us, taking our place in the bull's-eye!

"Jump out. Run!" I screamed over the radio.

Too late—too late—oh God, oh God! They wouldn't have time to swerve. The grenades would explode on impact, piercing up to two-inch armoring. Even if they jumped out, shrapnel would kill personnel within twenty feet.

"The trailer's hit. They're clear." Damian's growl smashed into me as hard as his foot did the brakes.

Everything overlapped, merged again, training taking over, reactions on auto, no thought, no fear, no feeling. One objective. Wipe out the enemy. *Now.*

I felt it all, saw it, *was* it. Seven years ago, Damian had imprinted lightning-fast responses into my nervous pathways, eliminated hesitation, taught me to trap fear and nausea and pain into an unused corner of my mind, severing its connection with my body, my actions. It was happening again.

Our doors exploded back on their hinges as Damian and I hurtled out of the vehicle, hitting the ground within split seconds of each other, rolling, springing up, taking position. That bastard wasn't getting another shot.

He didn't. We both got him. Then Damian got the other two, the injured ones.

Then silence. Slow, expanding, enveloping.

It wasn't fooling me. I gave it three tripping heartbeats, rolled toward Damian as he did toward me, uninterrupted moves taking us both from knees to heels, then we huddled back to back, crouching low, arms extended, guns first. We swept around our axis, scanning for hidden enemies, a second wave. Our four guards had taken similar positions.

On one side tropical vegetation rustled and quivered. Just the wind running rampant in the jungle, wrenching dust devils off the unpaved road. On the other side, a gorge sloped steep and open and clear. No place to hide there, either. Seemed this really was a fringe job.

I swung around to face Damian. He heaved up to his feet, taking me with him, his gaze a feverish sweep, inspecting me for injuries, mine reciprocating.

Large hands constricted my arms like a blood-pressure cuff till my hands went numb, cold. His pupils were anxious pin-points leaving his eyes all-blazing amber. Then he squeezed them, swung on his heels, already running away. "I'll secure the perimeter and conduct the cleanup. You take care of the in-jured."

The injured. An image of Lucia burst into my head first, pro-pelling me to the Jeep. Midway through my sprint, my feet lost steam, faltered—God! Savannah, Al—did they need me more?

Damn, damn, *damn* triage! Dictating I prioritize those who

might be far more injured, unable to reach everyone, help everyone at the same time… Still, Damian had said they'd gotten clear. But how? They hadn't had time! What if he'd been saying that only to get me to concentrate on the battle? I'd kill him if he had. If I survived the new barrage of panic detonating in my gut. *Find them, help them.*

I turned and flew to their battered truck, feeling no ground beneath my feet. "Savannah! Al!"

Silence. No one came out, from the truck or the trailers. I screamed louder. Then it hit me.

They must be confused, unsure of what exactly had happened, if it was safe to emerge. Another shout built inside me—and I almost choked on it. Al appeared from behind the last vehicle in our convoy, the rear-guard truck. Then Savannah.

I don't remember running the last of the way. There was a cut in time, then I was hurling myself at them, hugging and sobbing.

"Hey, we're fine." Al patted me on the back and tried to unclamp my arm from his neck. "At least, we are for now." He pushed the muzzle of the gun still clutched in my hand up and away.

I stuffed the gun in my waistband, gave a distressed giggle, sniffed. "Don't be silly. Or *be* silly—be anything as long as you're okay. Oh God—oh, guys—how?"

"We jumped out the back of the truck long before you told us to. As soon as you flashed us." Savannah returned my hug, a tremor passing through her to me. "So is this is how it's going to be from now on?"

"Probably not, once we make it to Soacha and—*Lucia!*" I exploded, running back to the Jeep. They kept up with me, questions coming fast.

"They got her in the forearm," I panted. "But with the shower of grenades your truck got, I thought you were far worse. I'll initiate emergency measures, you grab a stretcher and we'll transfer her to the STS."

Without missing a step they swerved to their new purpose. I approached the Jeep, awareness wide-open once more, taking it all in.

The devastating scene, the dead enemies, Damian and the guards deep in the cleanup job, doing what needed to be done to draw suspicion away from us, to make it look like a regular guerrilla attack, emptying our damaged truck, stripping from it any sign of identification. We'd leave it behind. We wouldn't be able to drive into the paramilitaries' territory and explain just how we'd survived an attack of that caliber.

I swooped down on Lucia's door, snatched it open, found her heaped sideways onto the driver's seat, her injured arm beneath her, the other still clutching one of the guns.

I jumped on my disaster bag in the back, produced compression bandages. Stop hemorrhage first. Anything else came later. I slammed the door, returned to her. "Lucia, honey, I'm going to turn you over now."

She moaned, moved on her own, struggled to sit up, turned to me. "Is it over?"

I helped her, my eyes frantically seeking her wound. She'd already bandaged it. "Yes. It's okay now. I'll take care of you. Not that you seem to need me, huh?"

Her open face crumpled. "You won't say that when you see my arm. Oh, Cali, I'm sorry. I messed up. *I'm* messed up."

"Shut up, okay? You didn't mess up. This is all my fault. I knew you were exhausted and drained. I should have told you to duck and remain down until this was over. Hell—I should have insisted you stay back home beside Juan."

She shook her head. "I should have gotten better shots in. God knows you've trained me enough. I—hesitated. And I wasn't doing Juan any good back home. I was going crazy watching him lie there like that. Here I thought I would be of use, to you, to the others." A bitter laugh wheezed out of her. "Though I don't think I'll be useful any longer. Maybe ever."

"Remember that thing about shutting up?" I unwrapped her compression bandage, cautiously, slowly, ready to pounce with a fresh bandage. Tension leaked from my spastic muscles when no pulsating gush occurred, just a slow ooze. Boded well for no arterial injury then, only venous, muscular. Those were better, if they weren't extensive. If there was no compounding bone and nerve injury.

I could see two bullet entries in her slender forearm. A tangential one that had ripped out skin and muscles, and one through-and-through wound. I needed to surgically explore the wound, get Doppler studies and X-rays.

But first, to spare her the ordeal. I rummaged through my injections, grabbed for a ready-loaded morphine syringe. Rolling up her other sleeve, I looked into her eyes, smoothed a glossy black lock from her blotched face. "Don't worry, honey. I'll take care of you. We'll take care of you. You'll be fine." I located her vein, pierced it with the needle, poured the potent pain-eradicating, mood-altering drug into her bloodstream. Soon the euphoric effects would push aside her devastation, give her reprieve. "I'm sending you home when this is done, Lucci. Forgive me for dragging you into this."

"No. I wanted to come—I want to stay—help you—you know I'm ambidextrous. My left hand will do...I mean it...I'm staying..." Her protests weakened with every word, chemical influence blunting her awareness, releasing her grip on pain and worries.

The others had arrived with the stretcher and I helped her out of her seat and onto it. In a minute we had her in the STS. The others had already expanded an operating table, an anesthesia station and the needed diagnostic equipment.

I had just leaned down to her and murmured more reassurances, when the boom hit. A compression wave followed, rattling the STS and every bone inside my flesh.

The others stood, panting, eyes darting around at one another as they reeled with shock.

I had no time for shock, was already bursting into action, snatching guns, screaming "Get down, everybody!" I ran to the entryway and threw myself on the floor to open the door just a crack as yet another explosion went off. Then another.

Sounded like the world was ending outside.

Chapter 17

I lay facedown on the floor, panting, thinking we'd been too hasty assuming that it was over. Then I realized.

This was no attack. This was Damian!

He was demolishing our damaged vehicles beyond hope of recognition. Must have judged the radical measure needed to guard against identification.

He could have warned us first, the jerk!

Which was no issue to him. Scaring a few years off our life expectancy wouldn't be one of his concerns right now.

"St. James!"

I jerked to my feet and raced out, watched him striding toward me against the backdrop of flaming vehicles and scattered corpses, grim, intimidating, a warrior who'd just finished wiping his enemies off the face of the earth, aggression still emanating from him, spoiling for more.

One thing was wrong with this picture. Our Jeep was in one piece. He'd destroyed our enemies' Jeep instead.

He answered my unvoiced question. "Only the windshield was bullet-riddled. I removed it, so there's no need to destroy my Jeep. We'll say vandals shattered it. You done here, St. James?"

"We have to operate on Lucia right away."

"Can you do it while we're on the move?" His eyes flashed amber in the slanting sun, radiating his need for me to say yes.

Our operating tables were gyroscope mounted. I had no idea how stable it made them. Not on this kind of road. Wouldn't have considered finding out if it wasn't the lesser evil. I gave him a grudging nod.

His nod was as terse as he turned around. "Move out." He barked loud enough for all to hear. "And pour on some speed."

Two harrowing hours dragged by.

Lucia's injuries were bad. Shattered ulna and radius bones, an occult radial artery injury, incomplete radial nerve injury with transection of a few branches and veins. It took the three of us surgeons to put her forearm back together. Wouldn't have managed it without every microsurgery facility on board. We'd reconnected severed veins and nerves and muscles to put everything back in anatomical order. But functionally? I sure as hell had no idea. At best she wouldn't have the full use of her arm for the next few months. At worst—I wasn't thinking of that.

I was placing the last bandage around her wounds, the tears I'd frozen to get the job done melting down my cheeks again, when the STS stopped. *What now?*

I snapped off my scrubs, grabbed my gun, ran to the driver's compartment. We'd reached the paramilitary camp.

I ran back, hid my weapons before joining the others racing through removing evidence of the surgery, then rushed to help Savannah dress the sedated Lucia in a long-sleeved shirt and transfer her back to the emergency stretcher.

"Okay, guys," I panted once we had finished. "First one to come up with a plausible scenario when they come in to search gets first-shift sleep tonight and—" Too late! The paras were already climbing inside the STS, with Rafael and Damian following.

And just so my happiness would be complete, the unconscious Lucia was the first thing they asked about. At least from the sporadic Spanish words I got.

Medical knowledge evaporated in my overheating brain. Damn it! *Think!* A medical crisis causing loss of consciousness but not involving injury or sedation. What would that be...?

Al, who was actually Alvaro and another Spanish speaker, said something and they just nodded and moved on to their thorough search. Just like that? I was having a heart attack and they didn't even blink at his explanation? What had he told them?

Al took pity on me, dropped it right in my ear. "I told them she suffered an epileptic attack."

I wanted to kiss him! I settled for giving his hand a thankful squeeze as we followed the search party. They seemed to consider Rafael and Damian our spokesmen, and the two men translated back and forth. Rafael did it all with his tranquil flare. As for Damian—what could I say? I'd seen him submerging his demon before, witnessed his transformation to innocuous, genial pussycat, but it was no less startling and alarming this time around. An actor of monumental scope—no two ways about it!

The search went uneventfully, as always. No one could ever find our hidden weapons without taking the trailer apart panel by panel. And the rest, the poisons and material for explosives manufacturing, was hiding in plain sight in both our STS and ML, legitimate medicines and medical supplies that would turn deadly in the hands of those who knew how to tap their destructive potential. And among us, we had the best at that.

After the search we were taken to meet the leaders for an hour of questioning and detailing restrictions we had to comply with during our stay. The stay they limited to four days maximum.

That came as a blow, to be pondered and felt later. Now I took detailed inventory of their facilities, numbers and firepower.

Then we were on our way, escorted to our destination. At last. Walking in my friends' footsteps, tracing the actions that had led them down the path to their inexplicable affliction...

Clouds brushed across open tropical skies, lush hills undulated endlessly into the horizon and the breeze at over nine thousand feet above sea level blew cool and balmy. All the ingredients of heaven were here. It should have been a delightful sight, a peaceful site. It wasn't.

Among hills untouched since the dawn of time, the IDP community huddled, turning once verdant expanses into an eroded, crammed-to-capacity shantytown. Houses, hovels really, lay haphazard and discordant, clay-bricked, tin- or wooden-roofed, paperboard- or newspaper-windowed. Strips of green and a few trees struggled to survive among the chaotic growth of manmade misery. Low ground was flooded, even now in Colombia's dry season. Children played in the mud, sailing paper boats in the mini-lakes among a slapdash arrangement of electric poles.

For people to be forced to live like this! To be evicted, pursued, cornered, then held down in degradation and hopelessness, all for the mere chance to survive. Or not.

Simmering rage stripped away more layers of my control. I saw myself attacking their jailers, their oppressors, risking all to buy them a chance to escape. I'd probably do it again, like I had in Darfur all those years ago, if a similar result could be obtained. But it wasn't so simple here. This was not a village of a few hundred held hostage by a dozen monsters. This was a town. Worse, a State-perpetuated status quo. There'd be no kamikaze rescue here.

But at least there was something that helped defuse me, then deluge me, making me defocus, forget why I was here even. For a while. A reception party. And what a reception.

As soon as we disembarked from our vehicles, we were flooded by people, mostly Afro-Colombian women and youngsters, the ones who constituted most of the *tugurios'* inhabitants. They tugged at us, shaking our hands, introducing themselves, chattering, welcoming. I got lost in the smiling faces, my own smile so wide, so sustained that my muscles ached under its weight, an ache resonating with the ever-present one in my chest.

I looked around. Where was Damian in this instant translation emergency? Had he been anywhere in the open he would have stood out like a lighthouse. So where had he disappeared to? Still with the paras? I wondered what they made of him, what story he'd given them. Not that I needed to worry about him. *Worry about yourself now.*

I grabbed Rafael, kept him beside me throughout. His translation services left a lot to be desired, barely transmitting the essence, skipping all details.

Then four people, three women and one man, were forging their way through the milling crowd. From the way it parted for them, the way they carried themselves, it was unmistakable. They were the community leaders, people elected by the displaced to form an organizing committee that got the place running as smoothly as possible, based on their leadership qualities and skills. And they, thank the lord, spoke English— sort of.

Another thing distinguished them from the others. They were nowhere near as enthusiastic or welcoming.

Hmm. Scratch the Latin-American passion theory. Only one explanation for the poles-apart reaction here, the only one I could come up with. Those four, being in a place of authority and therefore of knowledge, knew stuff the others weren't privy to, stuff that made them unable to see our arrival as the boon the others thought it was. They were almost scared.

I got that just looking at them. Then we talked. And whoa,

these people *were* spooked. And it wasn't us. This just reeked of the Arabic proverb, "Scalded by soup, blowing in yogurt."

Which led to the next logical conclusion.

Maybe what they knew, what they were so afraid of, was directly linked to my friends' affliction!

It made sense. Or I desperately wanted it to. But really, why else wouldn't they be happy to receive aid? Unless a previous aid mission, or something parading as one, sanctioned by their jailors, as we seemed to be, had resulted in costly, irrevocable damage.

Ask them. Who came before us, who offered aid that turned out to be a curse? What happened? Where did it happen? Who got affected? Where are they now? Tell me, show me!

Down, girl. The paras hadn't even left the place yet. Even when they shoved off, I couldn't show my hand. Had to let things unfold naturally. Yeah, and go mad the same way.

Struggling with the corroding urge to find out now, *now,* I instead told them our mission goals. "We're here to take care of seriously ill people."

Yeah. This was the sum total of my investigative approach, betting I'd find those who shared my friends' conditions among the seriously, even terminally ill. It would be a legitimate diagnostic and treatment effort to dig as deeply into the origin of their affliction as needed. And get my answers.

Had to make sure they understood what I meant by "seriously ill." Couldn't afford to waste our allotted time with irrelevant cases.

"Seriously ill are those in danger of dying. Please, bring us only those. We have four days here and we only have three surgeons, two emergency doctors and six surgical and trauma nurses. We will be conducting exams around the clock and we want to make our stay here count."

One of the women, the oldest, the one transmitting the best vibes and the one I thought was in charge, came forward. "We get you sickest people in morning."

Morning? Was she kidding? I captured her wavering eyes, wouldn't let go. "I want them right now! Those people have no time to lose."

I was about to lose it. All. Dinner. Cool. Hope. Mind.

It was four a.m. and Savannah and I were the last ones standing. Even Al had taken that first-shift sleep offer two hours ago. Good thing, too, since he'd have to be on call here in three hours. We'd been receiving—or I should say drowning—in patients for the past eight hours. According to our accumulated numbers, we'd examined over four hundred people. And no sign of anyone with anything resembling my friends' condition.

Sure, there were serious cases, hordes of them, all urgent surgical intervention indications, from the potentially cata-strophic down to the chronically suffering. But no one had ever had explosive mood changes or convulsions. No one was in a coma—or had ever been in one.

God! What did that mean? Were we chasing the wrong lead after all? A mirage? This wasn't where my friends got infected? It was a coincidence, their being here together? If that was true, then—then what? Where to go from here?

"So what do you think?" Savannah looked over my shoulder at my patient.

I looked again, too, almost didn't see her. I was fading in and out. I'd examined her, taken X-rays, written notes—and hadn't connected any of my findings into a possible diagnosis. *Focus. Think.*

All right. Skin-on-bones, constant, crippling bowel pain, rectal bleeding. Terminal malignancy? Crohn's disease? No—she had arthritis, rashes, eye inflammation, liver disease. All that accompanied ulcerative colitis. Horrible, incapacitating and emaciating, but still much better than the first two choices. It at least had a surgical treatment.

I told Savannah so and she nodded. "I think you're right. But I actually meant the question in a more general sense."

I closed stinging eyes over grating sand. "You mean what do I think about not encountering any condition to prove a link to our peoples' conditions, to prove my theory?"

"Yeah." She helped the patient dress, patted her on the back as she escorted her out while I filled in her new file. Savannah came back, swaying with exhaustion where she stood. "If these *are* their sickest people…"

"You're suggesting they may be hiding the ones we need to see?"

Her shoulders rose, fell in one of those elegant movements of hers. "Maybe. I don't know. No. It wouldn't make sense. But then, what does? It just feels like a dead end."

Tell me about it. Would I find the origin to this phantom illness before it was too late? If it wasn't too late already, for my friends.

I sighed. "One thing I learned about dead ends, Savvy. You just smash your way through them and keep going, dig deeper and wider and hope to strike something."

"Someone tell me what we're doing here again."

I didn't remove my eyes from my task at Al's sighing comment, went on cutting through the grossly inflamed mesentery, the sheath covering the bowels, releasing them, then carefully dissecting their intricate network of blood vessels.

Each of us was at an operating station, deep in a surgery. This was my seventeenth today, Señora Perez with the ulcerative colitis. I'd had a mean time of forty minutes per surgery, with the rest of the sixteen-hour working day spent preparing for and wrapping up procedures. Al and Savannah had my record beat at twenty-one surgeries each. But they'd had simpler cases—until the ones they left for last. The others were dealing with minor surgical procedures and serious nonsurgical conditions. We were keeping only the most serious and fragile cases in our IC. The rest were outside in the field hospital we'd set up. Among us, we've had over one-thirty surgical and one-fifty nonsurgical serious cases today.

"We're presumably saving lives, Al." That was Lucia from another surgical station, helping Savvy with a bypass surgery. Yeah, single-handedly. The impossible girl had refused to budge, popping analgesics and trooping on with the rest of us.

I waited for my surgical nurse and part-time muscleman and guard, Ben Hennessey, to expose the arteries for me before I ligated them, tying them up to stop severe bleeding when we moved to the next step, removing the diseased colon.

Savannah murmured for a vascular clamp. Al sighed again after he asked for suction. "Yeah. We wake up two days ago to endless queues of patients and here we go. But much as I'd love to eradicate all disease and suffering in the *tugurios,* this isn't why we're here. So, Cali, is this a new plan or what?"

He had a point. A huge one. We'd strayed. For the past two days we hadn't even thought about our mission. Okay, we had, but I'd done nothing to further it, to get back on track. The track was obscured, lost in the IDPs' overwhelming need for us. We couldn't have ignored them if we tried.

So we'd taken care of business, doing what we'd originally signed on in this world to do, healing where we could.

Funny how things happened, though. I'd been thinking "gloomy end of the tunnel" when I'd seen a ray of hope. A flimsy, flickering one. But one nonetheless.

I started cutting out the colon after stapling it shut so the contents wouldn't fall into the peritoneum. "Probably is a new plan, just nothing I voluntarily did. Or yeah, sort of, all of us did it. Seems our performances for the past days have gained us what nothing else could—voluntary information!"

Every head in the STS snapped up.

I removed the colon, pulled on the ileum, the very end of the small bowel, using about twenty centimeters to form the J-pouch that would replace the colon in function. "Señora

Perez's daughter is one of the spooked community leaders. She was so thankful her mother's condition wasn't terminal cancer and that surgery would cure her, called us 'angels' and started talking. Uh—Ben, you can hold the intestines away for me anytime now."

He blinked, tore expectant eyes away and did it, clearing the surgical field as I communicated the insides of the segments to form a larger reservoir. "She confessed how afraid she was when we first arrived, how the last time people came here to vaccinate them was followed by a wave of violent illnesses."

"And they suspect our team of that?" Al exclaimed.

"Circumstantial evidence," I said. "She couldn't positively link it to our people, since most of those who succumbed weren't vaccinated. Still, they think our people's presence must have had something to do with the mysterious sickness."

"Anything resembling our cases?" Savannah asked.

I exhaled. "Wasn't clear on this one. Her English is dodgy and when I suggested getting one of you Spanish speakers, she panicked. But the interesting part? I understood that every previous community leader had been among those who got ill. She's one of their replacements. And those are the only ones scared of our presence because only they knew the nature of the sickness that killed their predecessors, having put a lid on it to avoid widespread panic."

"Great!" Al clapped his hands, reached for scissors. "We're going places here. So where are they hiding their sick?"

"Underground. Literally. They're all dead."

The noises of suction, the anesthesia and heart-lung machines took over the next minute.

I finally sighed. "They were all dead within three days."

Another minute, then Al said, "If it was the same thing—and it's too much of a coincidence for it not to be—their quick deaths aren't surprising, with their deteriorated health and nonexistent health care as opposed to our friends' superb physical condition and the superior supportive measures they're getting."

I shook my head. "Yeah. Neat and tidy explanation. *If* those people hadn't died only a week after Matt and the others left."

Another minute, then two and three of silence.

Savannah was the one to end it. "How could they have been infected or affected by the same thing at the same time and have an almost two-month difference in time of onset?"

"Could their deteriorated health and lack of immunity account for that, too?" Lucia put in. "Matt did manifest earlier than the others after severe exertion."

Ben spoke up for the first time. "Or maybe they weren't infected with the same thing."

"Two agents?" I chewed my lips under my mask. "At the same place, probably the same time? Guess anything's possible—but it just doesn't ring true. Still, it chimes better than my 'two possibilities' theory. First possibility being the agent is biological and they had already used up their incubation period when they infected our people. *But*, that would mean everyone exposed to them should have manifested by now, and since they haven't, it makes no sense. Second possibility is it's a chemical agent engineered to have a slow and rapid release form, explaining the delay. But then, how come two sets of people exposed at the same time end up with one and not the other so selectively?"

In answer to those theories, silence reigned—for the rest of the surgeries and beyond.

After transferring our patients to the appropriate recovery stations, I paid Constanza, Señora Perez's daughter, a visit. A gross euphemism for waking her up in terror thinking it was her turn to be "made an example of"!

After rivers of apologies and reassurances, I had a long, communication-challenged conversation with her. Scared her out of her wits while at it. But somehow I convinced her I wasn't crazy. I made a superlative show of masquerading as a sane and logical being. So much so, she ended up agreeing that my plans were the only thing to do in the situation, and thanking me for being here to do them. Madness was probably infectious.

I stepped out of her hut delirious with exhaustion. *Yeah, yeah. You and everyone else. Get over it.* The ticking clock wasn't slowing down for me to fit in recharging. We had two more days. The paras had been breathing down our necks. Had to go ahead and put plans in action now....

"What's up, Doc?"

I jerked with the jolt of perpetual chemistry. With the missing that never let up. Damian.

I hadn't seen him since we arrived, not really. While we'd been deluged by patients, he'd run circles around the three-times-a-day-patrolling paras, diverting them from us, from any suspicions of our link to the massacre outside their territory.

Rafael said he'd been helping him. When Damian hadn't received his input with a grin and a thank you, Rafael had told him the PR job would have been his if Damian hadn't crashed our party. Bet that made for cheery chats.

But not seeing Damian hadn't meant not feeling him, in my senses, in my blood, every second alone, or alone in my mind...

He straightened from the tree and our affinity engulfed me. As always. Then I was up against him, our mouths mating. My doing. And after I'd smacked his hands off in our last standoff. I deserved every bit of the mocking "Missed me that much?" that slid down my throat, washed down by his lust-laden groans.

I allowed myself one more plunge into our bond, gulping him down like a bolstering elixir. I needed all his life and vigor for what I was about to do. Then I pushed out of his crushing embrace, grabbed his hand, towed him behind me to our services trailer. He tried to follow inside. Thinking this was an invitation, huh? In the services trailer? Yeah. He had good cause to think anything. I stopped him, dodged inside, came out thirty seconds later with the tools we'd need for this specific type of surgery. I jumped down, shoved a shovel into his hands. He stared at it, then back at me, eyebrows raised.

I dragged him behind me. "Let's go dig up some bodies."

Chapter 18

"Autopsies are supposed to shed light, not more shadows, y'know?" I coughed again. And again. Trying to clear my lungs, my vision. Wasn't working. Everything remained stifling, distorted. The surgical mask felt welded to my flesh, sealing all outlets to a worldful of life-sustaining oxygen.

Man. What a time to discover I was a wimp.

"I don't know, Cali."

Char sounded—amused? Couldn't she have the decency to sound horrified-but-holding-it-in like the HazMat pro that she was? Sure she'd seen it all in her time, victims of every diabolical weapon ever spawned by sick minds. Must be tough as granite. Still, this—! Maybe I was imagining the amusement, hearing things. Probably. The whine of the bone saw was messing my gray matter.

"After vomiting three times, I think seeing shadows is just about natural."

I gaped at her as I helped her remove the vault of the cadaver's skull. "You vomited, too?"

"Talking about *you*, kiddo." She reached inside the open skull, removed the shriveled brain, our last autopsy item. "Would never have thought you had a touchy stomach, seeing how you blasted those mercenaries without turning a hair."

I shuddered again. "Oh, I turn hairs, every one I have. But then there was this we'll-all-die-if-I-don't stuff. Now, it's just… just…" Just a nightmarish dip into the future. My friends' future. They could be dying right now. I could return to perform a similar procedure on them— My stomach heaved again.

Char's glance saw it all, what made the grisly task unbearable. She cocked her head. "This your first autopsy?"

I hiccuped. "Nah. Just my first exhumation!"

She started dissecting the brain. "You get used to them."

Yeah. Sure. Like I'd want to! "Don't tell me—absence of any gross pathological findings."

That was gross pathology's verdict so far. Apart from the obvious injuries incurred by their violent attack before they were restrained, there was no gross tissue response to viral or bacterial infections or toxic substances in all organs. Absolutely no reason why those people, who looked to have been far healthier than the average refugee, should be dead.

"Actually," she murmured as she made another incision, "from your baffling clinical experience and with all those negative tests, I wasn't holding my breath for something grossly enlightening. But I'd say this is our first bingo moment."

I jumped, tried to get a look around her impressive frame.

"See this?" She pointed at paper-thin meninges, a corroded brain cortex. "Pathologic changes of severe encephalomyelitis galore, the severest I've ever seen. The meninges and brain are practically cooked. There's your cause of death."

It sure was. Oh God! "My friends are displaying signs of encephalomyelitis, too. But no investigations corroborate our clinical diagnosis." And their brains could be looking like that now! I subsided on my stool. "But what about the absence of systemic response? Something that potent had to cause multi-organ effects before reaching the brain. Enlarged lymph nodes, throat and joint inflammation and edema—I mean, what kind of infectious agent or toxin bypasses the blood and every organ and targets only the brain? And what about the prodrome of violence and hallucinations? Even the most acute inflammation doesn't result in such manic behavior. This still reeks of poisoning!"

She grabbed a slide box. "I won't have any answers for you before I see these tissues under a microscope. Time to put the ML's formidable forensic and biochemical facilities to use."

"Tell me you have something to tell me!"

At my storming entrance, Char and Di exchanged startled glances, a silent tug-of-war, then Char rolled her eyes. Oh, goody. They were haggling over who'd give me the bad news.

Char started. "Cali, it's only been six hours...."

"That's what you get. I don't have more to give you!"

She disregarded my outburst. "Even if highly specific tests were possible in that short time, immunologic and toxicologic studies, not to mention bacteriologic and viral isolation, are tricky, postmortemly speaking."

My hands clamped my head, pressing back against the mushrooming pressure. We'd done it all for nothing.

Di raised placating hands. "Uh, before you have a stroke, Cali, our forensic tests did get us our first facts."

"And those are?"

"Fact one," Di said, reasonable, methodical. "It's not CJD."

"You thought it a possibility this was Creutzfeldt-Jakob disease?" Mad cow disease? It had never even occurred to me. Because in this instance it was ridiculous! The "prion," the abnormal protein causing the disease, could only be transmitted through inheritance or direct tissue exposure like during brain surgery. Even vCJD, the variant form that is said to infect humans from diseased-cow-infected tissue or by-products, took years, sometimes decades, to manifest.

Di shrugged. "Well, good old spongiform encephalitis does lead to dementia, coma and death."

"And you thought what?" I gaped. "That they had a mad-cow pot roast a couple of months ago and got infected? You know that's not the way it works!"

Char cleared her throat. "Actually debate is still hot about vCJD and how early on it manifests—but that's for another day. We just don't know the infection method and had to take into account that maybe something diabolically new is making it possible. So we were happy to exclude CJD and its variants."

"Yeah. Happy." And put that way, happy wasn't a sarcastic comment. If a new method had been harnessed to actively infect humans with prions—God—there would be no limit to the devastation. CJD was one hundred percent fatal. "So you excluded the rare and untreatable. Anything more common and treatable on the radar?"

Char rose, leaned her hip against the electron microscope mount. "Yeah, we believe it's viral, leaning toward an arboviral infection. But to get a specific diagnosis about which arbovirus and how it made it to the brain without manifesting in any of the blood, serology and CSF tests, we need a live sample."

"You want brain biopsies?" Visions of holes drilled in heads, biopsy needles going in, harvesting tissue, flooded me. I almost retched again.

"It's justified here, Cali. This is the only way we're going to get a diagnosis now that we know it's encephalitis."

I groped for a way out. "What about the toxic symptoms?"

"We honestly have no idea. But the killer condition was encephalitis and we should go with it. So just get your whiz cyberspace guy to transmit our findings, photos and results to your homebound team, with the order for a brain-tissue sample from your teammates. Send them to those Level D labs you have access to with our specific list of tests attached to them."

My stomach quit heaving, settled into a slow, inexorable twisting. I snatched a lab chart. "What do you need?"

Di inhaled, fired away. "Okay. Virus isolation tests, viral antibody titers, VecTest antigen and Vero cell plaque assays— uh, you got that?"

I nodded and Char added, "Enzyme-linked immunosorbent assay to detect immunoglobulin M, since they've been sick a while and ELISA is for convalescent stages or prolonged courses. It may also detect antiarboviral IgG. Wouldn't hurt to have another go at serum hemagglutinin-inhibition and complement fixation titers and CSF protein concentration, red blood cells and WBC count. But most important is EEE-specific TaqMan reverse transcriptase polymerase chain reaction analysis."

I stopped writing. "We already did that in the first forty-eight hours, testing for Eastern equine encephalitis virus, since PCR has high accuracy for positive virus results. We did *all* those tests. Came out negative, slashing our encephalitis theory. It was why we didn't even think of brain biopsy."

"You did serology, blood and CSF studies, not cellular ones. And do the ones you did before again. The erratic course of illness warrants repeated walks down the same paths, and I bet some produce new results. And since you have the equivalent of a national effort at your fingertips, I say use 'em."

Di raised her hand. "Wait. We also need more imaging tests. Look for a predilection for thalamic nuclei and basal ganglia involvement. And cross-check with every viral panel known to cause encephalitis and that can be used in bioterrorist attacks. On our side, we'll keep on working on the samples we have."

My hands cramped as I finished taking everything down. I threw the pen down, looked up. "Okay. Got it. One more thing.

Say I disregard the earlier phase and regard this as a viral infection, it could only mean a bioterrorist field experiment that had to have been dispersed by either an infected vector or an aerosolized form. Do you have any idea how only those thirty-six people and my friends were infected? And how my friends got infected with what appears to be a different variant?"

Self-deprecating shrugs answered louder than words. For the time being, beyond putting us on the first steps toward identifying the causative agent, they had no more for me.

"Can I come in?" Damian asked from the STS's vestibule.

My eyes defocused, losing visual of the spinal nerves and arteries. I backed away from the surgical microscope, blinked a few times, adjusted my focus, went back to my task.

I called out to him. "Why don't you? And invite all the germs. We sterilize the surgery area for laughs!"

He gave me some, their warmth penetrating through the steel partition. "You can talk to me across the partition," he said.

"I'm wrapping up. Can it wait? Is it an emergency?"

"Nah. Just explanations of the selective deaths. It'll keep."

"Damian!" I screamed loud enough to wake the sedated. He didn't answer and I yelled again. My assistants groaned. But Damian had already exited the STS. Damn, *damn*. You didn't do that to a woman with her hands deep in someone's vertebrae! Sure, I was already halfway through putting in the half-buried vertical mattress sutures closing the wound, but still!

Ten interminable minutes later, I left Ben wrapping up and rushed out. I jumped out of the STS, hit the ground running, eyes swinging all around seeking Damian.

"Looking for something?" He appeared around the STS, all easy drawl and easier stroll. Argh!

"I *can* shoot you with something coercive, Damian."

"Like that time you hit me with truth serum?" So he finally mentioned it, huh? "I came volunteering information, remember?"

"Yeah, and your timing was impeccable."

He stopped an inch away. "What can a man do when his girl ditches him after he digs her up some ditches?"

My swaying obliterated even that. "We dug together. Am not your girl. *Or* a 'girl.' And I've been buried!" Okay, bad word choice, considering our recent activities. And what was that? Bantering? Now? My blood sugar levels must be dipping again.

I stepped back and he sighed.

"My point exactly. No time was a good time. You were face-down in surgery, or in fitful sleep. And I thought you'd want to know ASAP. My mistake."

Humph. Point taken. I hadn't surfaced in the past thirty-six hours. Been burying myself in work to stop the going-crazy process of waiting for my homebound team to come back to me with answers. I'd even been sleeping in the STS.

He took my hand, led me to a nearby hill, took his jacket off and spread it for me on the ground. My lips twitched. Like I was in that dress in that Bogotá shop and this was a park stroll by moonlight. I sank down, said moonlight illuminating a more comprehensive view of the depressing vista of the *tugurios*.

It was past three a.m. and we were the only people in the open. The ochre rays of a gibbous moon cast more shadows than light on his pure, hard beauty. I sighed. "Out with it, Damian!"

He came down next to me, didn't touch me. I'd never figure him out, would I? Now if I wanted the contact that would ground me, discharge the surplus of tension and anxiety, I'd have to go for it. Not a good idea.

He sighed, too. "I've been doing research—with Rafael— since the paras stopped breathing down our necks. Yeah, he's— useful."

"*Very* useful. Untraceable communications isn't any of my team's fortes and I'm not that computer savvy."

"I'd say no one is, not compared to him."

Now *that* comment was really big of him!

"Anyway—to avoid looking like an interrogation squad, we did it as surveys. We directed answers toward unusual activities during the past three months, and guess who the mysteriously dead turned out to be?"

That was it? Disappointment kicked up my heart rate before it plunged to its usual sluggish rhythm of despair. "I know. Most were community leaders."

"Not just leaders. *Everyone* important here—everyone with effect, voice or potential. And each one of them and only them went to the paras' camp in the month prior to their deaths. Nobody made the connection that they were all there at the same time. But we did. Want to bet they were taken there specifically to be exposed to the agent? That's why we don't have a widespread infection. They were targeted."

So that was it. "The paras. They have to be in league with your terrorists, conducting their field experiments for them using guinea pigs from the *tugurios*. Getting rid of headache inducers while at it. Still—those people returned to die here. That means the agent isn't infectious, that it is contracted only through direct exposure. The infected are terminal hosts."

He processed that, then cocked his head. "This only makes it harder to explain our people's infection—except if they'd gone with them. Did they mention a side trip to the paras' camp?"

Nope. Just one thing, though. "Matt only said the paras took over the territory, with the military's approval it seems, just as his team arrived. And since no one mentioned any interaction with the paras, I assume they were not as controlling then."

His lips twisted. "I know when the paras seized this territory." Of *course* he did. "But I also know what they do to bring the communities they blight to their knees and these targeted, silent eliminations are nothing like their usual MO."

"Probably because it isn't—just directives from above."

"Which explains it all." Leaning back on his elbows, he

extended endless legs. "Ever since they came here, I've been investigating the reasons why they did. This place has nothing to offer them. Armed groups want control over oil-rich land or coca plantations—or land they can resell to businesses, politicians or settlers, like those in the northern departments where most of the people here were chased out of and which is now in hot demand with the plans to construct an inter-oceanic canal between the Pacific and Atlantic. Now I have my answer. They're here conducting experiments for their financiers."

And that had to be the truth, just for being so gruesome.

A minute passed as we contemplated stars starting to shine now that the moon had made way for them. Then he said, "Is it possible Matt and the others were targeted, personally?"

"I don't see how. We prepared for this mission carefully. They didn't march in here like we did in a medical convoy. They trickled in one by one, incognito, with settlers, in disguise. Their supplies were smuggled in through reliable contacts, and once they were here, they didn't set up medical outposts. In fact, the vaccinations were done by the community leaders—the dead ones, I assume—under our team's tutelage, so the community didn't know who they were or what they were doing here. They stayed a couple of weeks, it went smoothly, then they went home."

His eyes narrowed, assimilating, deducing. "Then it's a possibility they happened to be with the community leaders when they got rounded up and taken to the camp, but since apparently nothing bad happened there, Matt and the others neglected to tell you about it."

My nod was slow, deductions hindering it. "Maybe they got picked up along with the known leaders just for being fit."

"An experiment to make sure no one was above succumbing to their agent, no matter how originally robust, huh?"

My eyes squeezed. Conjectures hurt now, maddened. I was close. Could have been light-years away for all the good it was doing my friends. Or anyone else those monsters were targeting. No good. Had to have answers *now*. The real ones. The truth.

At least now I knew where to get that.

I got up on my knees. "Time to visit the paras."

He threw back his head, his lips relaxing in anticipation. "Yeah, time to level the place." His smile spread at my growl, his fingers tracing my glower in sensuous patterns. "You object to my cleanup methods, huh? You have to be the first woman ever to complain of her man's tidiness. So what's your alternative? Storming them and forcing them to cough it all up?"

His warm flesh against my cool skin sent liquid flames through me. "We report to their camp on our way out, go beg their protection until we're in civilized areas, pretending to be alarmed at the massacre that occurred outside their territory. I poison their head honcho and they need us to save him. I'll give him a pseudo heart attack. I can draw out his improvement for as long as we need to search the place and get our samples. And this time, Damian, we do that *before* we level the place. Once we have our hands on the agent, we infect the hotshots. *Then* we get them to cough up any vaccine or antidote—any info."

He leaned closer, sucked me harder into his magnetic field, his hands running up my arms. Longing burst through my centers of coherence. "Gotta love a woman who knows what she wants and how to go get it. When?"

I took the moment, leaned into him. Closed my eyes and let him permeate me with power and passion. "Tomorrow."

"You're done here, then?"

I let out a tremulous exhalation. "We'll never be done here. There *is* no done here. You know that better than anyone."

The layered muscles beneath my fingers twitched, turned to vibrating rock, warding off the pang spearing through him. This was painful to him. Personal. His people, degraded, abused, massacred. No wonder he wanted to level the paras camp.

"Yeah, I know. Tomorrow we finish this."

* * *

For the next twelve hours, we returned our patients to their homes, gave them and their own all the detailed instructions and medications needed in their postoperative periods. We shook hands and hugged and chatted and laughed and shed tears and promised to be back. Then we moved out.

An hour later, we approached the paras' camp. Foreboding blasted like a furnace. Could be because we were nearing a showdown. Could be because it was already going awry, the visualized steps different, missing. Nothing was as it should be. There was no one manning the scouts' position. Then we arrived at the gate and no one was there, either.

Frustration blurred my vision. "Sons of bitches. They cleared out! So that's why we haven't seen them in the past two days!"

Lucia made a disbelieving sound. "Clear out and leave all those facilities? They're probably out spreading mayhem."

Good point. Their camp was a hundred-tents strong, with good accommodations. But to leave them unattended? And I could see their trucks, Jeeps—how would they spread mayhem without those?

Damian brought our Jeep to a halt, hopped out in silence. No speculations to add? Or did he know something we didn't?

Without volition, I was running out of the Jeep. I caught up with him fifty feet into the camp—then lost all momentum.

My legs trembled, my heart quivered in a mess of shock and nausea. For about ten seconds. Then other emotions pummeled their way through. Rage. Betrayal.

All around us, there were no more paras, just mangled masses on the ground. No survivors.

Chapter 19

"You did this!" My scream ripped the silence.

Damian turned to me, slow, grim. "As much as I'd like to take credit for this lovely sight, I'm sorry to say I had nothing to do with it."

"I'm supposed to believe you? God, I told you my plans and when I was going to implement them, and you beat me to it!"

"I didn't. I gave you my word."

"And we know what that's good for." The words were out. Heard by all who'd followed us. No use wanting to leap after them.

But hell, he'd put me here, in this place of debilitating mistrust. I wasn't apologizing. I wasn't railing at him, either. This wasn't important now. One thing was.

I stepped into his path. The deadened expression in his eyes was a slap of remorse. *Say it.* "The agent. Will I find a sample or shouldn't I bother looking?"

"Be paranoid, your prerogative. I'm done listening to your ranting. I have to find out what killed those people."

Could he be telling the truth?

He can. He is. He wouldn't betray you this way.

Oh, shut up! What a time for my Damian-forever voice to resume its unquestioning decrees. Distressing thing was, it was in agreement with all other voices, too. I believed him. Regret suffocated me for having jumped down his throat.

Which was irrelevant now. Our only source of info was no more. God—what a time for a rival faction to wipe them out. Couldn't they have waited until we were finished with them?

I approached the nearest three bodies, turned one over with my foot. Two things leapt at me. One, his stiffness. Rigor mortis was at its height. With the cold temperatures of the past couple of days and the exposure, this put time of death in the past twenty-four hours. Two, his injuries. Several, severe. The killer one had to be the neck's. No gunshots. This man had been shredded to pieces, tooth and nail. Literally.

"Your bodies ripped apart, too?" That was Savannah.

I turned. "Yeah. Wouldn't take blood and tissues all over their teeth and fingers to know how they died."

"Shades of *Dawn of the Living Dead*," Al groaned.

"The *dead* Dead. Thankfully. On all counts," Char retorted. "So the agent got them, too."

Damian walked back to us, not looking at me. Just as long as he didn't pout!

"Let's clear out, people."

My hands found my hips. "We're searching the place first."

He looked at me now, hard as a blow. "For what? A quick infection?"

"We may already be infected just standing this close to them—just being here." Savannah shuddered.

Char shook her head. "I don't think so. Don't even think

HazMat protocols are needed. If this is the same agent—and I bet it is—we have no reason to believe they're infectious."

I turned, walked away. "Spread out. Take inventory, check for survivors. Don't hesitate to shoot any perceived threat."

In twenty minutes, we reconvened where we'd started. We collated numbers from each checked area. Five hundred and ten. The exact number I'd counted on our first visit. Some had been shot, but most were ripped apart. But it was those who'd been found dead in hiding, without a mark on them, that confused me.

I looked at the others, hoping for insight. "So what have we here, folks—accidental exposure? I mean, we all assumed those thugs were the ones dispensing the agent. If so, what could have happened to make them get a taste of their own fatal medicine?"

"Maybe they were being used all along," Rafael said. "Maybe whoever was using them decided their roles were over."

Possible. "Still—stuff here doesn't add up. The earlier exposures were limited, slower. Now we have a hundred percent fatality rate over the considerable area of the camp. And brute-healthy men dead without a mark on them, in under forty-eight hours."

Char cleared her throat. "As for the scope, it's either airborne or waterborne. I favor water here. They get their supplies in tanks, everybody drinks and—voila. As for virulence, maybe it's an upgrade, or a bigger dose. Probably both."

"Still seems directly contractable and noninfective," Di added. "Since we all were in contact with them for their ultra-short incubation period and none of us even has a headache."

My fists pressed my temples. "I'm way beyond headache, Di."

Al gave an unsettled chuckle. "On the flip side, we could be all wrong and we'd start falling one after the other, or tearing at each other. All the more reason to rush!"

Char straightened from her slouching stance to her full height. "Okay. These are the questions we need answered. If it is not the same agent, how many agents are there, and are all produced by the same operation? Or are there many now, using the same technology but with their own twists? Most importantly, which one were our people exposed to?"

I turned to Damian. "Can you tap your sources on this?"

Damian's eyebrows shot up. "You talking to me? You rubbing my lamp?" His teasing hit right behind my sternum. He wasn't angry. *Oh, thank you.* "I'll get on it."

"Uh, people…" Rafael. Something in his voice. I swung around, found him standing by a Jeep. "Got a live one here. We may get answers after all."

"This one isn't participating in any Q&A anytime soon." Al finished gaining central venous access in our patient's neck.

Tell me about it. The boy—and he was only a boy, no more than fifteen—had been conscious, could talk when Rafael found him. He wasn't by the time we'd hauled him over to the STS to initiate resuscitation. And his coma was deepening. Fast.

His clinical picture and CTs were dismal. We'd intubated him, started him on antivirals, antibiotics, anticonvulsants and anti-inflammatories, implemented every ICP-reducing measure. I'd even installed an intraventricular catheter through a burr-hole but it wasn't making much of a difference to the malignant rise in ICP. Had to be the far more acute course of infection.

The others were hard at work analyzing his CSF, but what we really needed was a brain-tissue sample. Someone at the height of infection with a more virulent strain, or a more concentrated dose—that was what we needed to reach a diagnosis.

But if inflammation was so severe that subarachnoid hemorrhage was starting, an invasive procedure could finish him. Still, we had to go in with a craniotomy, to drain the hemorrhage, to try to stop it, or he was dead anyway. Yeah, but draining his hemorrhage and dipping into his brain for samples weren't the same, were they? I could be just talking myself into sacrificing him to get my hands on bits of his brain.

Everyone was waiting for my decision.

I snatched off my mask, ran out of the STS. Needed a minute. Air. Escape. All I found was Damian, leaning against his Jeep, waiting. He unfolded his arms, approached me.

"I got your info. It's one operation, the same one we're after." That was something. "It's one product—so far. Just one with variants. No signs of a stockpile here. Probably cleared after the massacre."

So all we had were dead bodies pumped full of the agent. And one live sample-provider, a boy who'd been snatched from his mother and forced into a life of debasement and atrocity. He lay waiting for me to decide to sacrifice him for the greater good. I snatched Damian's hand in mine, blurted it all out to him.

He gripped me back. "Just letting off steam or do you want my opinion?" I opened my mouth. He just pressed on. "Here it is anyway. You can't cure him. You can wait for him to die, *then* obtain your samples. But they won't be as sensitive. Do it now and your intervention *may* extend his life and provide answers."

Our eyes locked. Long and deep. He left me no place to hide. I ran for one, jumped back into the STS. Before I was out of his earshot, I hurled over my shoulder, "Have I told you lately how I hate people who make sense all the time?"

"Dammit—will you look at that!" Al exclaimed. "What did Char and Di say in their forensic report? That the brain looked cooked? This one looks like it's been dropped in boiling water."

"Takes a man who's never cooked to say that." Savannah adjusted the computer-assisted magnetic resonance imaging directing my stereotactic, three-dimensional probing needle inside the brain. "If it were, it would turn all pasty-colored and dull, not angry-looking and bloody like that."

I let out a trembling exhalation before it burst my lungs. "While it's fun to discuss cooking brains, I would appreciate more suction and a better focus, guys."

They complied in silence, didn't talk again until I'd obtained
the biopsy—and done a lot of damage while at it, although less
than I'd expected. I'd expected to kill him the moment my
needle penetrated his brain. Not that I was optimistic about his
prognosis now. *Please, let it be worth it.*

"Hot damn, guys, it's priceless!" Char swung around as our
team entered the ML en masse in answer to her and Di's
summons. Elation was splitting her face wide open. "No wonder
we've been stumbling over ourselves. This is just *ingenious!*"

She'd found it. The answer.

Hope and dread mixed inside me. I could only wheeze,
"Great to see you value evil genius so much, Char. Now spill!"

"You want to know why they had all those contradictory
symptoms? Because it is neither a biological nor a chemical
agent. It's *both!* Can you believe it? And you know *how* it's both
and *why* all that didn't show up in CSF, blood or urine?"

Unable to contain her excitement, too, Di blurted out, "I tell
you, the sheer malicious brilliance of it all. We never would have
found out in a hundred years, if not for all the obscure, underground research stuff Rafael unearthed for us. You know why?
Because the agents were delivered by biomatrix nano-capsules
designed in a small enough size to cross the blood-brain barrier…." She turned to Damian and Rafael, explaining the term.
"That's sort of a filter that protects the brain and spinal cord from
infiltration by molecules above a certain size."

Unable to wait, Char jumped in again. "Those capsules are
designed to chemically react only within the brain cells' environment. Once there—and here's the sheer bloody genius of the
design—they conglomerate, so it's impossible for them to pass
out again, therefore defying detection except by direct, **live**
brain biopsy. And even then, on first and second appraisal, **as it**
happened with us, looking very much like a normal polysaccha-
ride molecule… It took the highest suspicion index, and the ex-

tensive networked knowledge Rafael put at our fingertips, to suspect the innocent-looking Trojan horses!"

Di jumped back in, even more excited. "Once we broke that code, we found two types of biomatrix, one with traces of the chemical agent, one the biological. We even postulate they are further subdivided into slow-, intermediate- and fast-release subtypes, like in drug vehicles, explaining the discrepancy in onset of disease in people infected at the same time."

Savannah raised her hand to get a word in. "So it's designed to dissolve inside brain cells at predetermined speeds, chemical-agent-bearing ones first, producing attacks of violence and hallucinations, followed by the second line of attack when the virus is released directly into its target organ's cells?"

Di nodded. "Actually, the biological-agent-bearing biomatrix dissolves first, if we allow for incubation period."

Al whistled. "Twisted. But why don't the agents make it out into the blood and CSF once they're out of their biomatrix?"

"That's what the conglomeration does," Di said. "Blocks permeability from brain cells! And that's what makes the victims noninfectious. No transfer to bodily fluids, no chance of infection except by direct tissue transfer."

Silence. Long and loud. Everyone struggling to wrap his mind around the diabolical construct-concept.

Savannah finally exhaled. "I can barely imagine it."

Char spread her arms. "Then imagine the genius who not only designed it but made it work!"

Ben gave a harsh laugh. "You sound in love—both of you!"

"Well, you have to appreciate something of that complexity and ingenuity," Char said, defensive. "And if you're like us, and you think you know all there is to know in your field and then get hit by something like that—I mean, wowee!"

"What about dispersion?" I asked. "Why doesn't the agent linger in an infected area, like the 'persistent' anthrax?"

"No one said it *wouldn't,* Cali. That's what makes it so versatile. Put it in water or food and you'd have your basic surgical strike, affecting only those you target and not risking infecting others. Disperse it in air and infect everyone within breathing distance—probably until a designed dissolution time."

Lucia pressed her eyes. "So it's attack on all fronts, confound diagnosis and make treatment impossible."

Damian spoke for the first time. "Or just not feasible."

A moment of silence greeted his words. Seemed no one got what he meant. Starting with me. What *had* he meant?

Not important now. Had to convey our findings back home. The trio of Char, Di and Rafael probably surpassed even Damian's and Sir Ashton's fancy specialists put together. I turned to Rafael. He got my unspoken urging, gave my arm a tiny squeeze and rushed out. I watched him leave, something nagging at me.

Then it hit. I swung back to Char and Di. "Hey—you didn't tell us what the agents are!"

Di giggled. "Oops. Silly us. The chemical agent is a new and I'd say more potent cross between the incapacitating agents 3-quinuclidinyl benzilate—BZ—and Agent 15. I bet it's far more potent, therefore all the hallucinations and aggression. The biological agent looks like a vicious variant of Venezuelan equine encephalitis virus. At least the viciousness is explained by having it bypass all the body's defense mechanisms, reaching its optimum site of replication in huge concentrations. I'd say it raises the mortality rate from the usual twenty to one hundred percent."

That was it? What my friends had? The answer? That didn't explain the first sympathetic toxidrome. But something like BZ and Agent 15 accounted for the parasympathetic toxidrome. VEE explained the encephalitis—but, oh God—such a direct, focused invasion! Even if they survived, the possible catastrophic neurological sequels! I'd been fooling myself into thinking a diagnosis would make all the difference. And it probably *would*.

Just not to Matt—to Ayesha…

"Hey, Cali, won't you go to see what Rafael wants?"

Something on my shoulder shook me. Di's hand. My eyes refocused. On one of our guards. In the ML's vestibule. Looking expectant.

"Uh—you want me to tell Rafael you'll come later?"

Time was interrupted, clipping out the section when I must have answered the guard, made the trip to Rafael's truck.

I found myself panting, staring at him sitting at his workstation near the driver's compartment. His urgent gesture sped up my rush toward him.

"Your homebound team just came through. Just a sec, I'll print it all out for you."

A warping minute later, he handed me the first of many pages. Tears and tremors merged values and figures and tests. *Concentrate, dammit. Get a grip. Moment of truth.*

I subsided on one of the benches, smeared the offending moisture from my eyes, scrunched my brains. All tests validated Char's and Di's diagnosis. The biomatrix delivery system, the double whammy of chemical–biological affliction. One difference, though. A bonus agent, methamphetamine-like, explaining the first sympathetic toxidrome, making diagnosing Matt and the others even more impossible than the rest.

This had to have been engineered. The differences couldn't have been haphazard. Why only them? To what end?

Then I read the verdict of the reports. The first light.

Now they understood the agent's mechanism, experts were certain it was survivable. *If* the victim was maintained as vigorously as my friends had been in the first week…

After that period it seemed that the conglomeration of the biomatrix, having achieved its purpose of killing the victim, dissolved. If it happened while the victim was still alive, as it was beginning to happen in my friends' cases, it was released into the CSF. Not that it was clear sailing now. A brand-new problem had arisen, just an hour before this last contact. Impaired CSF circulation and excretion due to inflammation led to percolation of the agents where they continued to do damage.

But *that* they were handling. They said. Their game plan to stop the agents' vicious cycle was to both administer specific treatments and antidotes and drain the infected CSF, gradually letting freshly formed fluid replace it.

The report ended with the belief that our immediate, extensive intervention had ameliorated the pathological process, with hope for reversible or minor central nervous system damage.

More invasive procedures, more gambles. More uncertainty.

Oh, Matt—Ayesha...

At least they'd live. I had to hang on to that. Whatever damage they had, we'd get through it together. At least now we knew this was survivable....

Which didn't make much of a difference really. Not in case of a massive attack. No health-care system could sustain the level of critical care that had been given to my friends.

Just not feasible. Now I understood what Damian had said. Ever the logistician. He'd seen what none of us had, scrambling over scientific details. The big picture. The sheer logistical impossibility of counteracting such a disaster. Whoever designed this knew sustaining the victims long enough for the biomatrix to degrade, compounded by the intricate method of ridding them of the agent, would be a far more taxing catastrophe than the plague.

Evil genius didn't even begin to do it justice.

I knew of only one evil genius of this caliber.

Oh, wow. Logic meltdown here. Talk about hopping-to-another-galaxy far-fetched. Another realm even.

The realm of the dead.

But, oh God, was it any wonder it all reminded me of Jake?

The very ingenuity of the biomatrix design, combining a biological agent with a chemical agent or two, hiding all within a deadly, silent messenger, the very stealth compounding damage with chaos—it all had the hallmarks of Jake's clinical cruelty, the farsightedness of his convoluted mind.

Against the very possibility was one: the deaths he'd been responsible for in Russia had different presentations and were infective; two: he was dead!

Problem was, I had answers to these objections.

One: Russia could have been phase one of his projects. Two: his work might have outlived him.

I never found out what his deadly weapon was, only knew that it had scared even biochemical terror scientists stiff. It could well be the biomatrix itself. The answer to every terrorist's dreams.

The only reason the world wasn't overrun by biological and chemical terror strikes was that every potential lethal agent was limited in effectiveness and use by the monumental difficulties in harnessing it, protecting it from degradation by physical influences and dispersing it over large enough areas.

With the biomatrix, agents in any combination, limited only by availability and the attacker's plans, would overcome their shortcomings, would leave no one targeted unaffected, sitting inside their nano-fortresses, performing any level of damage.

Another point for the beyond-the-grave theory was that while Jake's base had been on the other side of the world, Russians had well-known dealings with Colombians, and he had said his work was coveted by more international outfits than I could imagine. He had bragged, just before I killed him, that destroying the Russian base had been part of his plan to get rid of his imprisoning allies, that he'd just turn to those willing to provide him with anything he needed so that he could produce an unbeatable weapon to use in their bid for chaos and power.

So had he perfected the method in his life? Had he sold it long ago, and was it now in more hands than we could imagine? Or had one of those outfits managed to obtain his research, perfect it? Was it now testing the method before a much bigger strike?

Straying, St. James. There was no proof Jake's weapons were the ones involved here. But it was just this gut feeling.

Yeah. Sure. We all know how reliable that was!

But dammit, it wasn't only churning guts and compressing heart talking here. Jake *had* constituted a potentially global threat to warrant the elaborate plan Damian had staged, even if according to Jake it had been Jake-manipulated all along. I might have failed to recognize his psychosis while he lived, but I shouldn't overlook his damage potential now.

Of course, I could also be hallucinating all this. Wouldn't be strange. We were dealing with the mind-boggling.

An hour later, we reentered the ML to find the discussion still in full swing. Char's voice was the loudest among the chaos. "For protection against a new attack," she was saying. "We must be ready with anticholinergic antidotes!"

"What about the VEE vaccine?" Ben asked.

Savannah chewed her lip. "Isn't that not licensed for public use? I heard it's only available to people at risk."

"And that would be us," Al exclaimed.

Char chuckled. "Chill, Al. We do have enough doses of the live attenuated TC-83 vaccine with us. Cali told us to come prepared for anything, so we did."

I joined in. "But in the event of a widespread attack, the world is not ready with the quantities needed for the population at large. Probably never will be."

Di shook her head. "Global panic to produce mass quantities of vaccine isn't the answer. The best thing to do is to stop the conglomeration of the biomatrix nano-capsules in the first place, so they'd be excreted within hours from the body, before they have a chance to release their load, no harm done. Executing that procedure will require far more equipped labs than what we have right now."

Savannah gaped. "You mean you know how to beat this thing?"

Di puffed out her sizable chest. "Yup. I have it all worked out, step by step, right here." She patted her laptop. "Anything can be taken apart, Savvy. Once you know how it was put together."

It took two hours to get our act together. Getting vaccinated, distributing "antidotes," updating the rest on the home-front news. Then I went after Damian. We had to talk.

He found me first. As usual. "Feeling better now?"

I turned to him. "Now that my friends are out of danger and hopefully undamaged, with measures of counteraction all mapped out? Yeah, sure. Still doesn't mean a thing to potential victims until we do secure those measures. We have to get those bastards before they launch any major attacks. And then there's this thing that keeps niggling at me…"

And I told him. Everything I suspected. Feared. From his grimness—or was that his fed-up face?—my theories weren't meeting with his unqualified approval. Still, when I let him have a word in he said, looking in the distance, "It no longer matters where it originated—or who created it. It's here and it's got to be wiped out. At any cost. And it will be. My team located the plant. Ed is sure this time. We're moving in."

I grabbed his arm. "We?"

"Do I really have to answer this? You've done all you came here to do, Calista. Now take your team and go home."

"Now I send my team home and join your team, Damian."

"I always liked the sound of 'no' with 'way,' Calista."

Distract him. For now. "Say, how about we get my team out of this mass graveyard first, then argue about it?"

He was on to me. "No arguing. Gather your team. I'll explain everything, shake hands and then you're gone."

I couldn't wait for my team to leave, too. I'd accompany them, and no doubt Damian would too, only until they were safe. So I did call them. This would be my goodbye speech.

Everyone gathered in minutes under the midday sun, in the

best mood since this harsh dip—or should I say drag-over-thorns—in Colombian reality began. They felt it. Their approaching release. Probably couldn't believe they were still in one piece. I wondered about the odds all the time myself.

My eyes, my chest itched. Had to get it done and send them off. Fast. "We began this show with me in the pits, thinking no one can ever stand by me like my core people, but you guys were beyond everything I could have hoped for. Every one of you is a hero a hundred times over. You should be very proud of yourselves. I am. I can never tell you how much."

"Aw, Cali." Di giggled. "It's been a fun challenge in a macabre way. You sure know how to give a gal the time of her..."

I saw the red blotching her lush breasts first, her shock, uncertainty—panic second. I heard the gun thunder last. *No! No!*

"Take cover!" ripped me, from me, gun materializing in my hand, body launching in the air, diving for cover, eyes panning in an arc, seeing everything. The coming-out-of-hiding hunters. Two of our guards, convulsing with the staccato of machinegun fire. Rafael scrambling for cover, jerking, keeping on, reaching it with others. And Damian—both hands wielding silent guns, firing, flying sideways, riding the airwaves, landing behind his Jeep. A nanosecond before he disappeared, the side of his head exploded.

Chapter 20

Crimson. Everything was crimson. Horror, rage, blood, carnage. Suffocating, deluging, crippling. Damian dead…

It's over. He's over. Just give up, die…

No. Not now. Now avenge him. Avenge Di. And the others.

I ran out of hiding, exposed, gun blazing, unerring shots finding the treacherous monsters' heads—

No! Banish these impulses. They would only get you killed. Die and you don't protect the others, don't avenge Damian…

I slithered below the ML, jutting rocks shredding my flesh unabated gunfire hacking at nerves long burnt, at a heart long burst. *Keep going. Get weapons. Destroy the sons of bitches.*

But oh, God—I didn't even see him die!

Stop it. Get inside the ML—now!

Couldn't access it through the opening on the other side. Had no guarantee they didn't have us surrounded by now. I'd last seen them pouring from the foliage-covered, cloud-shrouded mountain. Had no doubt their snipers hung back, protecting their charging team's frontal assault. Use the bottom entry. Matt had asked for one. They'd made one. I found it, slid the panel back, hauled myself in, rabid eyes slamming around. What to get—what?

Hadn't counted them, had to assume they were too many. Must get all I could, leave them no chance of retaliation. Think. What would do maximum damage? Without catching my team in the fallout?

We'd mixed gelatin explosive from antifreeze, baking flour and smokeless powder, plastique from aspirin, battery fluid and sodium nitrate. Both had explosive power rivaling nitroglycerine and TNT. But I must have those thugs together to get the needed result. Lure them inside, detonate them. I'd detonate me, too. Not an issue. I was dead anyway. This way, I might save some.

No—no kamikaze tricks. I'd get them in here, do something else. Greet them with a refreshing cloud of sarin gas. Char and Di had made the nerve agent from the insecticides we had with us, had it pressurized now, masquerading as the fire extinguisher. Once I unleashed it, it would storm the murdering bastards' bodies through skin and lungs with their next exerted breath. Then fun began. Drooling, tearing, cramps, vomiting, convulsions, respiratory paralysis. Agony, panic, then death. Way better than bullets. They didn't deserve the mercy of bullets.

I ran for bag-valve oxygen mask, goggles, gloves, atropine/cholinesterase re-activator auto-injector, the antidote in case of skin contamination or the volatile vapors getting past my mask. Now, for an invitation they couldn't refuse.

I retrieved my cyanide blow-darts from my heels, slid the door open just a crack, took aim at the man about to round a trailer's corner where my teammates were hiding, blew. I didn't watch him fall, turned to another, then another. Then opened the door and let them see me, see what I was doing. *Come and get me.*

They came. Throwing myself behind the central steel lab counter, I waited for boots to stop thudding up into the ML, all who'd attend the party. They didn't shoot. Didn't want to damage the pricey equipment, huh? They thought I'd gambled, lost, was now cowering, that they could always blow my head off if I showed it again to give my blow-darts another go.

Ready in goggle and gloves, nose and mouth clamped with the bag-valve mask, I let them have it.

I left the lethal nerve gas blowing full steam, rolled to the floor opening, tried to slither through. But my body was swelling—or the world was shrinking—mouth filling, eyes, too, chest tightening… The sarin—I'd absorbed some—*the antidote—God where is it?* I thudded to the ground, over something hard—my gun—nausea imploding me… *The antidote…*

Fingers were spastic around something—smooth, cylindrical—a syringe? Already hallucinating—*do it now before it all stops making sense!* Guess I did. A penetrating jolt—the three-inch needle into my thigh—pain—the hard rush of fluid between my muscle fibers. Would take time to work, time I didn't have—*get away*—nerve gas seeping through the opening…

I crawled, weighed down, spikes lodging into me, like a hundred times before, in training, with Damian in pursuit, pushing me to overcome my limits—Damian, oh God…

Anger erupted, a geyser of strength and focus. Got me to the ML's end, peeking out to assess the situation—and—*oh!*

Damian! Alive! Oh God—oh God—*alive*—running backward to the open STS, firing an automatic rifle, someone—Al—on his shoulder. Arms reached to receive his burden.

Yes, *yes.* He was almost safe. *Get in. Drive away. Run!*

He didn't, just rolled on the ground, exploding from one cover to another, roaring for me. *"Calista!"*

I tried to scream to him, whimpered instead. I staggered up from beneath the ML, expending the last of my bullets, buying him more cover, blowing my own.

The ground zoomed up into my face. He roared, stood up in plain sight. My scream made it this time. "Save the others…."

Shadows fell on me—felt solid enough, one kicking the gun, my hand with it, the other ramming me beneath my ribs, compacting my viscera into my spine. Blue-white nothingness flashed, went supernova, razing me. I stumbled over my enemies' arms into a black hole with a hurtling truck kicking up a blinding cloud in its middle. Still saw Damian, distorted, slowed down, blood covering his left shoulder, roaring my name, threats. I think I called out again.

"For me—save the others...."

Me—they had me. It was over.

Something hard and dry was impacted in my mouth, and a running motor sputtered in my chest. My tongue, my heart.

Antidote side effects. Plus the sarin's lingering effects. *Way* better than the alternative.

I tossed on my side, bound, overheating, dry mouthed and skinned in my captors' hurtling truck. The crashing waves of my physical symptoms were parting, a tide no less brutal rushing in. Relief. Damian. Alive. He hadn't charged after me. Thankfully. Only he could get the others to safety. Yet leaving me to my fate must have been as hard for him as treading water. Damian—my ultimate protector...

Then agony supplanted all. Di—her gaiety, vitality, genius—gone. Hadn't even been able to spare her a look as she died. The others—Rafael, Al, Savvy—how bad were they?

The answer I needed now was not who these masked men were, or why they had attacked us, but why they kept me alive. Did they want something from me? What? I'd find out. First I'd get more comfortable.

Feet tied, hands, too—in front. I curled on myself, pretended distress. They'd kept my boots on. Wouldn't have reason to suspect them. Fisk had designed them too well. No wonder he'd been the Magnificent Fisk, the greatest magician since Houdini. Should still be. I should just be thankful fate had let me find him in that alley he'd ended up living in four years ago, in time to save him from a perforated appendix, and that he had bestowed on me the magic that had saved my life and those of others a hundred times over.

I felt for the edges of my boots, pushed in the right places in the right sequence, extending the hidden blades. My hand ropes went easily. Had to remove the blade to do my feet. Took a while. Far longer than on Damian's restraints-escape watch. A whiff of nerve gas coursing in my system and atropine dousing its fires hadn't been a factor then.

Too long later, the rest of my weapons in hand, still curled, I prepared, ordered my senses, analyzed.

Those men were no local garden-variety mercenaries. They dressed the part, sure, but I knew high-end assassins when I saw them. So were they the ones who'd held the paras' strings, who'd cut them? Had they been back to check their handiwork and burn the place to the ground, stumbled on us, decided to leave no witnesses behind? If so, were they still pursuing my team to complete the cleanup? Damian had already wiped out a decent number. But what if they'd been too many? Would they overwhelm him, with him injured, losing blood…? *What will you fight for, go back to, if he's gone?*

Ice spread, numbing the fight, deadening my will—*no.*

He'd taught me about that, too. *Fuel your anger. Never let the enemy win. No reason needed beyond that. Now* think!

If they hadn't wanted witnesses, why take me? Their bosses liked to play with women hostages? Hmm, unconvincing, but what else was there? Time to ask.

I called out over the considerable truck noises. "Hey! *No hablo español,* okay? So just tell me, what do you want with me?"

Silence. Not encouraging. Had no time for coyness. Maybe some goading? "So how many of you have I killed? I counted five outside the ML, but didn't get the number inside it. Won't you be nice boys and tell me the real numbers—killer to killer?"

One exploded to his feet, charged, kicked me hard between my scapulas. The dim truck turned black. I think his colleagues dragged him off. I lay gasping, waiting out the breaker of pain.

So he spoke English. So I had gotten them ticked. But not talking. Well, no info, no reason to stay.

Keeping my untied hands between my knees, I took inventory. Three men—every one as big as Damian, guns held loosely, eyes on me. Had to wait until they looked away. Had two blow darts left, a few *bo shuriken*. No way would I get the three of them. Had no room to dodge gunfire here. If I could get two, in silence, with darts, engage the last one—or maybe wait until they'd taken me wherever—no. Finding me untied would buy me inescapable shackles and a real stripping of means of escape and weapons. *Do it now.*

The moment their eyes turned away, I blew the first dart.

And it all went wrong.

The damn guy cried out, they all turned on me, guns first, fingers already pulling triggers as I got another one, got the *bo shuriken* lodged in the last's throat. They were all as good as dead, just too far from dying, and I was too close. Explosions ripped into my eardrums, reverberated in my flesh…. Was this how dying felt?

But no—this jarring combo of sound and sensation was no bullets exploding my insides. This was a shock wave, a real explosion, close enough to rock our truck, blowing it on its side.

Damian.

I hurtled into one enemy with the heaving and crashing of the truck. Another hit me as we all slammed down on the sidewall. Damian had bought me a reprieve. No—he'd saved me, was outside my truck, bellowing in Spanish. Bet he was telling them to let me go or else. Problem was, the one on top of me couldn't comply, going spastic, starting to convulse, as was the one beneath me. I struggled, shoved my load off somehow, found the one with the throat injury on his feet still, facing the now sideways door. It was opening. He'd shoot Damian the moment he appeared.

I exploded into a run, rammed him in the back just as Damian opened the door and took our hurtling bodies right in his face. Or rather, on the point of his gun. He was ready for an attack, used our momentum, threw himself backward, hurled us over him in a huge arc—I doubted he realized my and the enemy's Siamese-twins state….

I cushioned the mercenary's landing, my bones pureeing into my flesh, the jarring impact paralyzing me. Still my mind was speeding, screaming, *move*. Before I could, Damian was on top of us, then blood gushed on my cheek. He'd finished my job, slashed the mercenary's throat, rolled him off me, dragged me up. Then he dragged me behind him to the vanguard trailer, an upright one—formerly Rafael's. Damian had already disposed of its new occupants. We climbed over their bodies, shoving them out. Damian took the wheel, threw me two guns and a remote control—more detonations?

His grim "Give 'em hell!" answered me. I did.

"You enjoy sending me to hell, don't you."

It was night. At least, I thought so. Hard to tell this deep in the Andean foothill jungles. And I'd just been congratulating myself that we'd shaken off our pursuers, the few who'd remained, and were now untraceable. Wanna bet this yell would change that fast?

I blinked with the force of Damian's up-close, sudden fury. "Steady that flashlight if you don't want your ear sewed into your scalp!" I grumbled. "Is this about suturing you without local?"

His answering growl dissolved on a hiss when my needle dipped another talon of pain into his ripped, inflamed scalp.

No wonder I'd thought his head had burst. With one of the body's richest blood supplies, scalp wounds were veritable fountains. His was bad. He'd lost a lot of blood before he stemmed the hemorrhage. Thank God every vehicle in our convoy was equipped for stand-alone survival, from extensive supplies to a complete emergency kit. Uh—not so complete. Lidocaine was inexplicably missing, therefore this unintentionally sadistic situation.

"You went kamikaze on me, *again*." A string of apoplectic Spanish through clamped teeth, then more hissed English. "*Dios*—you used the sarin gas on them, didn't you. On yourself!"

"It was a calculated risk. I'm fine, am I not? And cut me some slack—I offed enough for you to get away."

His tirade went on. "You incapacitated yourself, made me watch them take you, forced me to protect the others, to leave you behind. *Dios,* hell is probably a better place than the hours it took getting them to safety and on the way back home."

He'd told me everything. Uh—I'd wrung it from him. Al and Rafael had multiple injuries. Back, thigh, shoulder, abdomen. Nothing fatal. Only because they'd made their escape in the STS, had had access to top-flight doctors. Anyone else would have died.

They'd had another minor raid, which Damian had dealt with, with excessive force. But our enemies hadn't pursued them. Only because Damian had been with them, I was certain. They'd found out how lethal he was. Could be they'd taken me to keep him at bay. Stumbling on the one thing ensuring their fate was sealed, really.

"Then driving back, planning my attack, going insane wondering…" His hand shot out to mine, the one with the needle holder. "Did anyone lay a hand on you?"

I extricated my hand, placed the last suture, tied, cut, going through the motions, bandaging his wound, injecting him with antibiotic cover and tetanus toxoid, upping his fluid replacement. His hand convulsed around my arm, demanding an answer.

"And you're asking why? So you can kill them? You already did, if you remember. I did, too, by the way." And now that survival was no longer driving me, the memories, the lives I'd snuffed, no matter how deservedly, slashed at me. I turned from him, nausea dragging me under.

"*Madre de Dios,* they *did* touch you!"

A giggle choked me at the grotesque misinterpretation. "As if I'd let a man touch me—when he's not trying to kick me, or kill me—other than you—uhh… Hey!"

He ripped the cannula out of his vein with the fluid delivery line, reached for me. Then I was all over him. Yeah, me. I pounced first, straddled him. Hard. Then we were fighting together for a faster descent, a deeper surrender, a fuller invasion.

I could have lost you. An inch and you would have died. Again. All it'll take is an inch and I'll lose you—and I can't….

I cried out as his mouth collided into mine, feeding me his anger, his dread and sensuality—his life. My blood thickened, rolls of thunder propelling it in raging rapids in my arteries. Had to hide him, inside me, keep him from harm, forever. Had to burrow into his refuge, safe from anguish and fear and helplessness. No limits, no barriers.

I tore my lips away from our fusion, keened. Needed an outlet, unrestrained. He gave it to me, freeing me from clothes, shackles, doubts, savage hands closing on fistfuls of my flesh, silencing the screams. I squashed myself into his palms, tore at him, bore down onto his thrusts, felt him almost inside me through our clothes.

I struggled with him, offered him my body, snatching at his, panted it all to him, wept it. "Want you—inside me, Damian, always inside me—if I lose you, I don't want to live…."

It rose off him like a tidal wave, blasted through me, squeezing my eyes, jerking me away, the brunt of his reciprocated addiction. The mirror image of my messy, scary need.

Couldn't survive it. Couldn't survive without it.

I opened my eyes and let him flay me with that need, all the compartments of my being melting into one chaotic space.

This love business was torture. An abyss. Permeating, unremitting, endless. I hurled myself, no longer me, a giant need, a driving frenzy to shelter him, own him, cede all to him.

Yup, I'd made it. Gone nuts. And I'd called *him* crazy once, called those who chose to love fellow warriors so. It was sheer psychosis, inviting it, surrendering to it, living with the acrid taste of torment, of dread and incapacitating anxiety lacing every breath, tainting every thought, polluting every moment.

Welcome to the ranks, St. James.

His hands convulsed in my bruised flesh, his litany of adoration in my battered heart. Who was I kidding? I'd joined them long ago. There hadn't been a time when I didn't go insane thinking he might go where I'd never reach him.

My hair was free, flowing around us. He tugged and caressed the waves, drowning us both in stimulation, in frenzy, his hands and teeth savaging me with pleasure.

I rose, quaking, tearing at the last barrier, his pants, and he crushed me to him, filled his mouth with my breast, filled me with his fingers. Ignoring my "No—you!" he kept me still, suckling, probing me, knowing just how, where, how fast and hard, twisting the pleasure tighter. I struggled, a lost battle, every thrash another bolt of stimulation. Then his thumb whispered sure circles on the knot where all my nerves converged and I imploded on screeching torment, swell after swell of release buffeting me.

I collapsed around him, raw, jerking in aftershocks, lost, enervated. Mad. A wavering hiss finally escaped me. "If I locate my voluntary controls—you're dead meat."

He pressed me onto his erection, thrust at my flowing heat. "You're killing me just fine."

He was, too. Something was charring inside me. Relief didn't even slow the pangs. I hadn't needed release. I needed him, riding him as he filled me, pounded into me. It was the final invasion and captivation that I needed. The admission.

"I haven't done anything—yet!" I staggered off him, tore at his pants' fly, released him, captured him in shaking hands and mouth, groaned at his magnificence, at the intimacy, at touching and tasting him, having him throb and buck and writhe in my care, my power, my hunger. He pushed me away.

Trembling, stunned, I looked up, found his eyes squeezed, his teeth bared. Ouch. "*¿Está usted loco, hombre?*" He barked a laugh at my Spanish attempt. "I'm feeling and doing what you always say you want me to. Not to mention you're bursting out of your skin."

What was I talking for? I pounced on him again. He roared, his hips flexing, plunging him deeper into my mouth. Incredible. Experiencing him, all his power and lust and dependence made hard flesh, filling me in a no less profound way. And how I needed his surrender, his pleasure. This time, this way. Next time, the hard way. The hard ride. He'd better make it rough.

All I got was a rough heave spilling me off him. "I don't want relief…." He grunted.

Yeah, right.

"Okay—I do, and if it was any other time, I'd take it this way."

I punched his arm. "You never take it that way, never give it to me, not back in Russia, not before this mission."

"I want to be inside you, filling you, feeling the pleasure tearing through me impaling you, real-time. You arouse me too much for oral sex. And I don't want you returning the favor."

"Favor? You think driving me to orgasm was one? What exactly didn't you get in 'dead meat'?"

Before he could move, I mounted him again, wrapped both hands around his shaft, slid him along my slick, swollen flesh, absorbed his shudders, vibrated to their frequency. I rose to scale his length, rammed him at my entrance, cried out with the sensation. The concept. Never could get over the sheer brilliance of it. The dependence. The fusion.

He still kept us from having it all. His arms trembled as he stopped me sinking down on him.

He was panting now, the man who didn't even breathe hard after a ten-mile run. "I may be *loco*—but you think I'd stop for—any reason other than—your safety?"

What did he...oh! Protection. Never even occurred to me.

He slumped, his hands releasing me. "Local anesthesia isn't the only missing emergency article. I could kill myself for not carrying some condoms. Probably already did just that. Guess I despaired of anything happening...."

"You mean anything like this?" I rose, bore down on him, engulfed his shaft with my body on the next labored breath.

Pain at his abrupt, passive invasion ripped through me, a spiked cry shredding my throat. Like the first time. Was ready then, was readier now. Still not ready for him. *Him.* This time for real. No barriers. Beyond description. His bare flesh in mine. So this was how it felt. How could I ever have it another way?

He went mute, motionless, breathless. I bore down on him harder, pierced myself with him, all the way to my womb, my mind overloading. "Damian, do it—love me...."

His whole body buzzed, jerked, leashed tension going into critical mass. "*Misericordia, amor*—mercy..."

I slid up, my core wept its demand for him. I gave it, pumped him into me, wallowing in scalding pleasure. My mouth opened on his as fully as I did on his erection, my tongue maddening his into a duel, confessing in his mouth, "I'm safe." His hands dug into my scalp, my buttocks. I threw my head back, started riding hard. He still didn't meet my plunges. My hands shook, my heart flailed, I babbled, delirious now. "Not that time of month—and safe—every other way—trust me, I'm a doc...."

Something—in his eyes, like a roaring-by train. Regret? Did he want—wish...?

I stiffened under the onslaught of images, the never-can-be's—safe, ordered lives, babies... He misunderstood my hesitation, grunted, "Safe, too—never had sex without—heavy-duty protection."

I clung to his misinterpretation like a lifeline. "Me, neither. So—uh, it'll be—our first time...."

"It is. Every time with you *is*." He dragged me down into his mouth, onto his erection, thrust up, savage now, showing me I'd taken nothing of him. I screamed.

Never. Never before. Never knew. Real abandon, his full ferocity, mine. We tore and ground and bit and snatched. He took all, gave more than I could bear, what I couldn't bear not having. I took all he had, clear out of my mind, convulsing and shattering, pleasure pummeling me as I did him. He pounded me to the last abrading twitches of orgasm, then again to renewed clawing. I heard wails, for his release inside me, my tears filling his mouth. *Give me. Fill me.*

He did, in hard rams, long, roaring jets, triggering another paroxysm of release, one sustained seizure that frightened me, finished me. Fulfilled me. This. What was missing. True completion. My full feminine potential realized.

Then I was floating, in his arms, pleasure still an acute plateau, felt the cold, then the warmth again, then his mouth and body covering mine, plunging deep once more, many times more. And he bared more, confessed deeper. And he exploited me, and, boy, taught me, tons. Took lots of notes for future exploitation. Did some on the spot. Before I hurtled down a suspended animation chasm, I remembered thinking—*Have to have this, have* you *this way unfettered, primal, from now on...*

I had a suspicion I said it out loud. And an almost certainty that I heard him groan into my neck, "I know now how I'll die. Pleasure overdose. Inside you."

* * *

"Get this into your head. You're not coming!"

I ignored him, hopped over a dead body, slid a panel and hauled out more hidden weapons. I'd already put together an extensive disaster bag, replenished the weapons on my person.

Yeah, we'd made it back to the attack scene. No sentries left behind. Only the sarin-contaminated ML and their dead. I'd counted twelve my doing, eighteen, Damian's.

He snatched the guns I handed him, dragged me outside the ML, pressed me between its and his steel. "I'm taking you back."

I smirked at him. "And delay the now-or-never strike?"

We'd woken up to Ed's report. They'd located the plant. And the good part? Just in time for the escalation to a major strike. And the overprotective lug was worrying over me!

His lips compressed. "They'll have to start without me."

I snorted. "Yeah, jeopardize world peace for helpless me. You didn't train me, and I didn't spend all these years fighting to duck when the shit hit! So save it, Damian. And move it."

We ended the stalemate with me threatening to tranquilize him and haul him to his team. He didn't put it past me. Wise man.

We'd been on the move for over ten hours. Plus one more hour of rowing before that. Now a star-studded night enshrouded us as we followed Ed's GPS signal. We'd pinpointed their location almost to the exact square meter, stopped about three miles away, loaded up on weapons and continued on foot through the thickening jungle.

Suddenly swords of light slashed our night-goggled vision. We took them off, adjusted to the faint flickering lights, reached the edge of a clearance. And there it was. The plant of doom.

Huh. Kinda of an anticlimax. Just another prefab building. Ed had sent us layouts, vital areas, sentry stations. We had enough explosives to level ten buildings this size. Still wished for the feel of my hands on live scientists. To question, to settle my mind.

Damian stiffened. Incoming message. He read it, turned, transmitting—what? Uncertainty? Hesitation? His voice was tinged by neither when he talked. Must have imagined it.

"Ed needs to liaise with me at the eastern end of the plant. You stay put."

"You're going in without me!"

"No, I'm not. But if *anything* goes wrong, turn back and run, and keep running. Please, Calista." And leave him? Was he crazy? I shook my head at him and he dragged me into a fraught kiss mingled with one more *"Please"* that drenched me in dread.

Then he was gone, fading with inhuman speed and stealth into the gloom before I could cling to him.

Apart from yelling for him to show himself, or running after him, which wouldn't be conductive to the covertness of our operation, I could do nothing but what he said. Stay put.

Humph. Never been good at that. Cruel and inhuman punishment.

Two minutes passed. Getting itchy here. Five. Getting anxious. Ten. Getting mad. Fifteen—*going* mad!

Couldn't contact him. Might distract him at a crucial moment. My legs were on fire. I was. Waiting, worrying, watching the sentries doing nothing, all relaxed.

Something had better happen right now!

Uh—you ordered something to happen, moron?

Here it was. Something happening. Guards running out. Toward me!

Chapter 21

Panic hit first. Robbed me of five seconds.

Over three dozen charging mercenaries, three hundred feet and closing, high-powered, scoped, night-vision rifles targeting me warranted a five-second panic, I'd say.

Couldn't afford more. *Think. A counteroffensive.*

But—they weren't firing. So it was capture and interrogate. I could let it play, wait for Damian's incursion... Sure—and cripple him and end every possibility of winning this. *Blow them up, then, run for cover, pick the remaining off.*

Yeah. Blowing Damian's team's element of surprise right along, saving myself and endangering the whole thing—but— what element of surprise? Had no idea how, but our cover was blown. Still, they could be coming only for me. A blowup now would be a diversion, a heads-up, a distress call.

I waited until they were in throwing range and let them have it. I ran as the detonations went off, shock waves pummeling me like body-sized fists. Damian had said to keep on running. No way. I'd reach good foliage cover, climb a tree, pick them off, wait for Damian's backup or go back him up—

Something snagged at me, hauled me back. Damn—my disaster bag, caught on a branch. I fought the imbalance, my momentum lost. I slammed on my back, the bag taking a bit of the brunt before my head hit the ground sideways. The usual explosion of pain and disorientation followed.

In a minute, I was looking up at a dozen automatic rifle barrels. My heart fired. They didn't.

So they still wanted me in one piece, after I'd blown some of them to pieces? Okay. So they got me. I could still use this, help Damian from the inside. Wasn't much fun finding myself captive for the second time in less than thirty-six hours, though.

The guerrillas, or whatever they were, hauled me to my feet, all nice and helpful. One of them told me in mutilated English to please come with them as others carefully disentangled me from my disaster bag, frisked and disarmed me, as usual missing the important stuff. The unusual thing, the downright *weird* thing, was how courteous they were about it. Hell if I could find another way to describe their behavior…

I walked ahead of them, my head still ringing, my back throbbing with echoes of the mercenary's kick and this latest fall, getting a better view as we approached the plant. An installation made to be erected in days and dismantled in less. Probably one of many in their bid to confuse intelligence, and hop to another location at the drop of a pin.

Wondered what pin dropped and tipped them to me? Better surveillance of the perimeters than Ed reported? Had we been on camera all the time? If so, why wait until Damian—oh, no! Had they already captured his men, used them to lure him away? Was that why he hadn't come back?

My heart tried to pummel through my ribs, the urge to ask them what they'd done to him bursting it.

Yeah. Alert them to his presence if he is still free.

Had to go with the assumption that a sentry with night-vision goggles was vigilant, had seen me in a regular sweep after Damian left. Probably when my body heat shot through the stratosphere. Yes, yes. Keep thinking that. So where was Damian now, and why were they treating me so well?

We were inside the plant now, passing through inner security, the layout exactly as in Ed's intel—and one question was answered. The mollycoddling. It was their boss's orders.

Jake's.

Air disappeared. The floor. The world followed. Moist heat burst behind my eyes, inside me skull, a thousand screeching bats flapped in my ears, my chest...

God—it's starting. The agent. It's been infective all along. I'm starting to hallucinate. Jake. My worst nightmare, my greatest regret—my indelible pain. The man I loved, the man who loved me—so much he went to hell for it. The man I sent to hell.

Like with Matt, like Ayesha and all the others who'd been stricken, the hallucinogen must be accessing my trauma, caging me in a tunnel-vision world with mutilating memories made flesh. So convincing—and oh, so *real*...

My heart stampeded, thoughts screeched—but—but—wait a sec—I still *had* thoughts—could still think. Recognized where and what and who, not oblivious to place, circumstance and self, like the others had been. Drained, depleted, my aggression wiped, resistance spent— not manic-high on simulated strength and artificial stamina. This wasn't the agent!

What did it mean? That it was real—this was *him?*

Jake! It *was* him—had been him all along—I'd sensed it, couldn't credit it—and it had been him. Jake...

Tall, beautiful and, oh God, alive!

But I killed you!

Pain burst in my knees, sent bright crimson sparks into my vision. Like that time I'd watched Matt teetering on the ledge, I fell on them. Least I could do. Anyone with an ounce of feeling, confronted by the ex-lover they'd murdered, would have fainted.

He walked toward me now, slow, graceful, radiating authority, power. How? *How?* I'd killed him, shot him right in his carotid, pumped enough phenothiazine into him to kill three men. I'd seen him sag to his knees, flushed, trembling, losing control of his every muscle. I'd seem him gasping, known his heart was firing, erratic, ineffective. I hadn't been able to stick around and see it stop. I'd been certain it would in a minute.

How hadn't it? How had he survived? He hadn't been faking it. I hadn't missed—hadn't used the wrong thing. I was certain!

He stood above me now, the heavenly color of his eyes bright, like the last gaze we'd exchanged as he breathed his last breaths, his gaze filling with reproach, disappointment and, oh God— love... *So much love...*

They *hadn't* been his last breaths. But his eyes were still filled with the same emotions.

Please stop. Don't look at me as if you missed me, as if you love me. Not after I killed you.

The horror of it was I'd missed him, too. The Jake I loved. The man, not the monster. Looking up into his incandescent bronze beauty, the sheer poetry of his every feature and line, he bordered on angel. An angel of forgiveness, extending his soothing hand to me, raising me from my abject misery.

I clung to his hand, surged up.

And I hugged him.

And he was real. Solid, warm, alive. His masculine scent, his heat, his aura, the first ever to mingle with mine in passion, flooded me. *Oh, Jake—why did it have to be this way?*

He stiffened in my frantic hug, like in Russia, the scene replaying. Jake resurrected, shocked, elated, overwhelmed. This time his rigidity dissolved, his arms lifted around me, one hand pressing my head over his steady beating heart.

"Ah, Cali, you astound me. As usual." His tone lanced me. I hugged him tighter.

Lord, anytime now I'd be whimpering, *Sorry I killed you!*

A gentle, persuasive hand beneath my chin coaxed my head up. I let it, kept my eyes closed. That hand joined the other, brushing aside my bangs, teasing my lids open. I hiccuped on a stab of anguish as his eyes bore into me up close. His sensuous lips spread, his hands dropped to mine. He tugged me.

"Come."

I registered everything on the way to what turned out to be his quarters, quite the lavish setup for the utilitarian place. He'd always liked his creature comforts. Until he'd been kidnapped and tortured literally out of his mind. This Jake was the product of irreparable mental and psychological damage. Fatal damage. My Jake hadn't survived the abuse. A new persona had risen from his ashes. This Jake. Damian believed this Jake had been the real Jake all the time, just harnessed by an easy life, put in stasis by lack of incentive. I didn't know anymore.

He followed my eyes around the room, towed me to a burgundy leather couch, a gentle push lowering me down on it. "Noticing my foibles?" He chuckled, his elegant British accent back in full force. "I admit, I have developed a dependence on good interior decoration since my days in the dungeons."

He sat down beside me. I feasted on his sight. Whatever he was, he'd been my lover. I was still alive because he felt something for me still. And I was so sorry I'd killed him. It didn't matter that I'd been right to. I nestled into him again.

He gasped this time before his arms went around me. "Ah, Cali. I thought the first hug was shock. But I should give up trying to anticipate you. You never cease to exceed all my expectations when everyone else falls short. You're the only one who ever challenged and satisfied my jaded mind. Is it any wonder I loved you that long? Even after you killed me?"

I jerked away. He followed, his hands soothing down my back. I buried my face in my hands. *Just stop*.

He sighed, stood up, walked away, came back in minutes with hot drinks. I reached for the proffered cup, squinted at it. Exquisite Limoge china, golden trim and initials. A fist closed inside my chest. *CJ*. He'd had it monogrammed. To us, I knew it. My eyes stung. Something told me he remembered how I liked my tea. I gulped it, my eyes filled. Earl Grey, hot, sweet. Very. Yup. He did.

"You could have no concept of how I missed you, Cali." He sat down, body language at once deliberate and eager, a superior being entertaining the one guest he deemed worth admitting into his sanctum. "Of course I forgive you for killing me. I totally understand you thought it had to be done. In fact, I admire you for it beyond words. I of all people understand what it means to do anything, no matter how crippling, because it has to be done."

I put down my tea, found my voice. "Is this how you rationalize killing thousands? It has to be done?"

One bronze eyebrow rose, blue flames flaring in his eyes. *Careful. Don't antagonize him. You've never been at his mercy before.* He only smiled, that elusive, serene smile. "Hundreds of thousands. Millions. But it will bring war on the planet to an end. For a long time, at least, before the cycle restarts."

"You still think if you scare people enough they'll stop fighting each other, unite against a common, unseen enemy?"

"It has always been the case. After disasters, people come together. I stand by my original plan to end war by annihilating all sides. My weapons—you do know about those, they're why you are here, after all—are designed to be lethal yet noninfective, to wipe out only the exact populations I target—the chronic, debilitating septic foci of the world—so that the rest of humanity, scared and chastened, can start anew."

I opened my mouth to say we'd gone over that before. He pressed on. "*But* it's far more complicated than that. This is my bid to bring the most diabolical of all human inventions to an end—the war *industry*. You know that no one is trying to or will ever try to stop it. It's just too profitable for everyone. That's why conflicts are so chronic. The warmongers aren't only the politicians, the military, the business conglomerates or the weapons' makers and dealers. Their lower echelons spread down to the common, upstanding citizen on every street.

"Everyone needs to keep solvent and in business. Everybody has a vested interest in keeping wars alive, everyone in media, real estate, food industry, technology, law, finance, medicine and everything in between. To keep the current markets open and to open new ones, they need to *create* needs. Everyone needs lawless arenas to test diseases, ideologies, religions, gods, extremism, addictions and hatreds, to create hunger and conflict and injustice, then spread them. It's what makes their trades and existence indispensable. I'll deprive them of their playgrounds, exterminate all their puppets, their clientele and pushers—their mutations. It will take something even more atrocious than all they do to put an end to it, something that'll breach every fortress, make no discrimination and scare everyone equally."

And the scary thing was, *he made sense*. Gruesome, undeniable sense.

I'd felt that empathy with his cause and methods before. It had scared me shitless then, too. He'd sensed that potential in me, that more-than-my-share-of-extremism ingredient. He'd been confident he'd bring it to the fore, sway me to his cause. He'd had a right to think it. I did feel the tug. After years of dwelling amid disease, destitution and depravity, I sometimes felt the need to strike out at everything and everyone, the causes, the facilitators, even the victims, both the cowering ones and those who hit back in all the wrong places, perpetrating the atrocities and the madness.

Good news was—I'd never do it. Even if I sometimes played judge and executioner, I had no desire to play God.

So, Jake's plans had expanded. No place, no one was exempt. But now he had the time and the upper hand, he was again trying to convert me to his way of thinking. I should let him try. It was my best weapon, his obsession with me.

Give him a good argument, stimulate him, please him. You know just how. Oh God, yes, I did.

I raised to him a gaze injected with all my heartache. "I can—I *do* condone annihilating the warmongers. But why kill their victims? Why not give them a second chance? Maybe they won't turn out to be future oppressors as you stipulate. Maybe once better markets open they'll rush to them."

His gaze was all tolerance. "This remains your one flaw, Cali. You choose to be blind where so-called innocents are concerned. War, and profit, even basic self-interest, leave no innocents, only mutilated monsters, addicted wretches or eternal self-serving cowards, who aren't only beyond redemption but refuse it at any cost.

"My time in medicine, on front lines, then in the circles of high-powered politics and finance, taught me that. You know I once was a bleeding heart, risking my life to help the 'helpless.' But being among the 'victims' made me see them for what they are. Previous and future aggressors. The weak who both breed monsters, and who make it possible for the present ones to prosper. I heard only sickness from mothers' lips, fostering violence and preaching extermination. *Survive so you can kill and torture the enemy's people.* As for the rest, the *normal* people in the modern world, in their pursuit of comfort and safety, they are the greed and common evil that perpetuates war. That's why anyone touched by war has to be eradicated. They're all diseased beyond cure."

"But this leaves no one. We're all touched by war one way or another. Are you planning to end all life on the planet?"

"As if that would be a tragedy." He shrugged. "Don't worry, it won't be as radical as that. My targets are extensive, but what's a few hundred million in a planet of over seven billion? There will also be more surgical strikes. My list is long. Of course my financiers believe I'm ridding them of their competition. Until it's their turn."

Wow. And the wow-worthy part was I knew he could actually do it. Do anything his nihilistic mind could conjure up.

Okay, another try. "Why not start with surgical strikes? Get rid of the masterminds? See how things improve with them gone? Leave those who are innocent *today* alone."

"I know why it is so painful for you, Cali. You were always so prone to letting your heart rule your head. I love that about you. But then, who am I to take you to task over it? I let you rule my priorities, too." His hand brushed my cheek.

I shuddered.

Something flitted in his eyes. He sighed. "I'm only putting into effect the part of the Hippocratic oath that you've chosen as a way of life. I am 'effecting prevention, for prevention is better than the cure.' You're as radical as I am, Cali, but you still have that line you won't cross. And it's because of that line that we stand on opposite sides, when we should be hand in hand. You know that eliminating the festering ulcers of civil, religious and ethnic wars from the face of the earth is the only humane thing to do. And I—all I want is you—with me."

I opened my mouth and his hand caressed it shut. "You don't have to be a part of what I do and I won't interfere in what you have to do, even if it's against my work. But on the personal level, away from the mission each of us has embraced, man to woman, can't you accept that we were made for each other?"

Was this my cue to laugh? Or cry?

If I accepted too easily he'd see through it. And if I told him what I really thought, it wouldn't help any. Better play the resistant-wavering part to the hilt.

"Jake…" I sobbed for good measure. And it wasn't faked at all. "The years without you, thinking you were dead, the changes we both underwent—the heartaches and uncertainties and anger and if-onlys—I don't know anything anymore...."

He smoothed my hair, passion and sympathy blazing on his unique face. "I understand, especially when Damian has done everything he can to further confuse you. Too bad I couldn't put him in his place, couldn't play my hand, earlier. But how I wanted to, to let you know Damian is one of my lackeys."

What?

A rap on the door took him from me, left me hanging. His men. Speaking Spanish. Said everything was ready. What was? The strike? And just what the hell had he meant? Damian, his lackey? Through his alleged control of PATS? Or did he mean something else? Something more direct? More awful? And where *was* Damian? What could have happened? I hadn't felt any disturbance. Had he discovered my capture and was he now canceling the plant's invasion, changing tactics toward saving me? What was going on?

Ask Jake. He'd tell you. He loves to talk to you. To brag. Or did he only want me to think so? Giving me only what he wanted to give, reading me, playing me at the game I presumed to play on him? With a mind as convoluted as his, anything, even coming back from the dead, was possible.

And here he came, the ultimate maze. A thousand questions collided in my mind. The agent, the biomatrix, what he'd done, where he'd been, what he'd meant. What was that in his hand?

As if I didn't know. A syringe. No guesses whom it was for. Or why he was coming back with his men flanking him. Uh-oh.

Eight. Dammit. He valued me highly. He murmured to them, *"Suavemente."*

I got that. Gently. Wondered what he'd say when I crushed a couple of larynxes, jumped him and used him as shield.

"Don't, Cali."

He knew, huh? Was there no surprising him?

"I don't want to hurt you."

"You should know I'm just programmed to fight, as long as I can. Nothing to do with you, you understand?"

"I do." He nodded, so gently. "Your need to be in control rivals mine. I would have left you conscious if I could."

"That's what you have here? A sedative?"

Translucent azure turning dense cobalt. "Can you suspect me of using anything worse on you? You still doubt the extent of my emotions for you?"

Oh, spare me!

"But I can see you intend to fight. And I know how lethal you can be, and are." He said that with ultimate pride. Jeez. What was it about us violent, erratic women that appealed to these twisted men? "If you start crushing windpipes and cracking skulls, these vermin might disregard my orders, panic. They might hurt you. I can't let that happen."

He snapped his fingers, gave orders in Spanish. In a minute a man ran in with my disaster bag. I watched Jake sort through my hidden-in-plain-sight arsenal. He was probably the only one who could fathom what each item was for, who'd probably find more diabolical uses for each one, far more lethal combinations.

He picked the components of a dart gun, twirled them in his hands. Virtuoso hands. They'd initiated me into womanhood, into saving lives, performed miracles, snatching hundreds of lives from massive disability or death. Images shifted from memories to conjectures. Saw them performing the dark magic that brought the biomatrix into existence, the insidious killers that confounded and horrified first, turned the very victims into the ultimate threat. Had he known who my friends were when he'd had his men infect them? How could he have? How did he do it? Why?

Why all of it? Why couldn't it be different? Such massive potential, warped, wasted—such vast intellect…. Why had it survived when his soul had been consumed?

Ponder the unfairness of fate and alternative courses of

history later. Act now. He'd given orders not to hurt me, at least not to shoot me point-blank. My only chance. Had to take it. Would think about ticking him off later.

I hurled my saucer at the closest thug, catching him in the eye. His snapped into a protective ball and I charged him, using his huge body to ram two others off their feet. I jumped on the couch, springing off it to launch at the next closest, catching him in the throat with a flying *yoko tobi geri*. He dropped. I landed on the next, spinning him around, using him for shield, anchor and pivot, swinging, ramming the next two in the groin. The others roared, charged, the element of surprise and niceness depleted. If they caught me, it was over. I somersaulted behind the couch—had to reach hidden weapons... Uhh...

I didn't feel the sting, just a sickening expansion—the rush of fluid squeezing between my muscle fibers. I looked up. Jake had shot me with my tranquilizer. He looked down on me in regret.

"As much as I would have loved to see you finish them, I had to stop you. I'm sorry to sedate you, but I want you with me in this historic moment and I just don't have time to talk this through, to convince you that you don't have to fight me."

Two questions burned holes in my fogging mind. Damian. And how he'd survived, in Russia. I asked the second.

He stroked my cheek, bent to carry my going-limp body. "I survived by understanding you. I anticipated you'd try to stop me, even if you had to kill me. I expected you'd use the last poison you used on our common enemy. I was ready with the antidote. And a few others, in case you surprised me. I pretended I'd shoot to kill, forcing you to do the same. It was the only way to break the stalemate. But my gamble was very precarious. You really gave me a lethal dose and I was barely able to take the antidote before convulsions robbed me of voluntary movement and my heart stopped. I nearly died of exposure as I recovered. The whole ordeal left me with an even more intense appreciation of you."

I moaned. "Oh, Jake…" *Why did you have to be so hopelessly warped? Such a perfect devil? Try to kill me already! Give me cause for peace of mind when I kill you again….*

Absurdities frolicked at the periphery of my vision, my consciousness. Heralds of la-la land. Blotches of darkness replaced those, encroaching from all sides, vying for my center.

The last thing I felt was cool, soft sensations. His lips. Like that first time they'd ever touched me. Gentle, worshipful, at my pulse—my slowing pulse.

Chapter 22

I'd been awake for some time.

I'd seen no reason to let anybody else in on the fact. Unconscious people make their captors relax, talk, spill beans.

Not that I'd held much hope of gathering many spilled beans in Spanish. Or with all the noise. I'd gotten a surprise—a pleasant one for a change—when there'd been close-enough-to-be-heard and English beans spilled. Jake's multinational allies, no doubt.

One thing I didn't need telling was where we were. On a plane. Cargo, from the sound of the engines. From the peeks I got, probably an Ilyushin Il-76 "Candid" if we went by its NATO reporting name. From what I heard over the drone, we were on our way to a major aerial strike. Which meant this was probably an Il-76MP firefighter, able to dispense the agent from the two fire-retardant tanks. If so, and according to their capacity, major didn't begin to cover it. Did Jake really have fifty tons of agent?

Wouldn't put anything past him. Not that any less would be

less catastrophic. No use worrying about it. Doing something
about it seemed a better choice. The only one.

So I prepared and gathered info. I estimated over twenty fellow
passengers, commando types, armed to the teeth. For me? Even
after my performance back at the plant, I was flattered. Aside from
that, cargo planes had flight crews of from two to five—two pilots,
and possibly a flight engineer, a navigator and a radio operator.

We'd had three midflight refuelings. Our destination must be
farther than twice the three-thousand–mile maximum range of
a fully loaded Il-76. Hmm—over six thousand miles plus the
first leg in the return trip. So where could we be heading? Iraq?
Afghanistan? Korea?

Had a feeling I knew where. Had another feeling I wouldn't get
more info pretending sleep now. Time to put on a wake-up show.

I stretched my unbound limbs. Yeah, he hadn't had me
trussed up. Had me in a cot even, covered. Very considerate. And
convenient. I'd prepared undercover, so to speak.

I'd seen the coming-out-of-sedation grogginess times enough
to pull it off, watched him approaching through twitching lids. He
sat down beside me, taking my face in both hands. My heart
expanded, compacted again. Wondered when it would just give out.

The Jake I'd met back in Russia, after his eight-year impris-
onment, had had a Clint Eastwood–Steve McQueen harshness.
Now he was back to looking like my Jake, back to Paul Newman
sheer beauty and Errol Flynn flamboyance. Just so this could
hurt more. I turned my face in his palm and squeezed my eyes.

He fondled them open. "We've almost arrived, my love."

I blinked back the tears, steadied my gaze. "Where?"

He knew I was stalling, loved it. His beautiful eyes crinkled.
"You know where. The place that was my home for eight years.
I owe it to that region to put it out of its misery first. The spraying
tanks have enough aerosolized agent to kill everyone within four
hundred square miles, taking care of refugee camps, rebel
outposts, government and armed forces installations with all

civilian neighborhoods in between. This operation will be my calling card. Regretfully, I have to disappear for quite a while afterward, but then I will resurface to strike again."

Didn't seem there was any use stalling anymore. No time. Time to play my last card. "I'll never be yours if you go through with it, Jake. It won't be Damian who comes between us then, it'll be the people you kill."

He just smiled. And what a smile. Compassionate, all-knowing. Hypnotic. "Ah. Damian. The sod is my accomplice, even if he isn't bright enough to be so knowingly. It's time you learned Damian's mission in the Caucasus wasn't to search and destroy all, as he said, but to search and destroy the people and retrieve my weapon."

"No!"

He sat back, the very amalgam of understanding and irony. "Don't like the truth, darling? Or are you just angry that you let yourself be so thoroughly taken in and used? The objective of the attack on the paramilitary compound *was* to salvage my work. Even though they went against my set plan and tried to sacrifice you and your team. I'd planned his demise after he got me out, but you remember how things went wrong. Of course, being a stupid low-rank, Damian didn't know PATS sent him there by my orchestration. And he thought they'd use the weapon to their own ends. But being stupid doesn't make him less of a mercenary monster."

Wow. What did he need the agent for? He was mass destructive enough just talking. "You'd make anything sound plausible, Jake."

He laughed, rich, spine tingling. "That's true. But all I need here is the truth—that PATS themselves are the ultimate terrorists. But contrary to me, their and Damian's motives aren't ultimately altruistic. You suspected it. You *have* shunned Damian. But that only made him decide to force you to surrender to him. So he infected your friends, eliminating your support system.

And it worked. You're back to counting on him, back in his arms."

I sat up, tried to escape. What? Realization? The explanation of my distrust of PATS? Of Damian? No! No. Never Damian. Never *this*. "Quit trying to screw around with my mind, Jake. This isn't how you get me on your side."

Sensitive fingers ran up my back. I moaned.

"I'm just filling in the spaces for you, darling. Who else but Damian can come close enough to your friends to administer the agent? Who knew whom to target in particular, to cost you your security and strength and leave you flailing? You couldn't explain the delay in onset of symptoms in your friends because there was no delay. He infected them when you gave him his marching orders."

"Stop it, Jake!" That was snarled. "I mean it."

His hands went up in mock defense. "Don't kill the messenger, my love. If you have better explanations for what happened to your friends, how about the attack on your team in the paramilitary camp? Once you fathomed the agent and discovered a counteraction, he ordered his men to attack, to kill everyone but you. Starting with the one who posed the biggest danger to the agent's future."

Di.

"He already had her findings and proposed procedures on her laptop and couldn't risk having her disperse them. His marksmen gave him a scalp wound to make it look more convincing. During that attack and your so-called rescue, he only eliminated the guerrillas who work with his men. The ones due for elimination."

His impenetrable logic was jagged pieces hurtling into place, ripping right through my sanity.

Was it any wonder? With this superhuman insight and persuasion, he'd wrapped armies of monsters around his finger.

Well, he wasn't wrapping me.

No harm in hearing the rest of his convoluted masterpiece. Not more than the festering ugliness he'd already sowed. "You're saying it's all about me? Damian went to all that trouble for me?"

"He'd go longer. He's totally obsessed with you. I sympathize absolutely, even if it never ceases to astound me that a common, vicious mind like his can possess the acumen to appreciate a being of your caliber. Anyway, you weren't his only objective. His plan was manifold. Getting you, stopping you from finding out the game he's playing, *and* employing you and, through you, GCA, who would never have dealt with him again, in finding a counteraction for the agent so he'd have the whole package, weapon and antidote, to better bargain with, to better hold the world hostage with."

Incredible. The depth of pain even a lie could cause. And it had to be a lie. I rubbed both hands over my burning face. "So Damian never knew he was working for you. How come? A man whose whole life depends on digging up the unthinkable and connecting the implausible?"

He made himself more comfortable on the cot, crossed his legs. "Before Russia, he was an avaricious fool. You did see one of his mansions, didn't you? No doubt he told you it's his mother's. He keeps her there as a front, uses her to catch the men he eliminates. After Russia, when he found out I made pacts way above his head, it was thanks to your convincing him I was dead that he never suspected I continued to move the pieces. His bosses neglected to inform him of my resurrection, of course."

Okay. Next lie. "Didn't you start to worry that he was pursuing his own ends? Finding ways to counteract your weapon?"

He looked almost surprised. Silly question, huh? "Why should I? A method of counteraction was something I wanted, too, to perfect my weapon, to fix any shortcomings. That dead friend of yours had the kind of erratic genius it took to actually find out something I hadn't been able to."

An image of Di, bullets ripping her, her incredulity and terror... I couldn't even feel fury for her death now. Too confused, too battered to know where to direct it. Hated it. Hated Jake for doing it to me. *What if he's telling the truth?*

No. No way!

My hands wiped over my face again, came off wet. Dammit. I sniffed, cocked my head at him. "Okay, Jake. Here's another postulation, since we're playing fill-the-plot-holes. It was all *your* doing. Being dead in everybody's mind gave you all the edge you needed. You could have sneaked up on my friends. You're clever enough to leave all the crumbs to lead me into your trap. And then, just how do you know everything that happened as if you were there, if you aren't the one masterminding it all?"

His smile broadened. "Your boldness just goes to my head, Cali. There is a very simple answer, if you weren't too distraught to see it. I got everything I know through Damian, your monitor. But don't let me babble on, let me produce proof."

He looked up, gestured to one of the massive men and I noticed the folding partition for the first time. The man folded it back and—and—he was there. Battered, bound—but alive... *"Damian!"*

Jake stopped my explosive movement up, kept me sitting. "They'll bring him to you. Sit down, please, Cali."

And bring him they did. Four men hauled him up, thrust him forward, ramming him in the back with the butts of their rifles, every impact shattering my bones, squishing my heart.

I screamed. "Stop them!"

Jake gave me a considering sidelong glance, nodded, raised a hand. They stopped, but still hurled Damian at our feet. He slammed to the ground, the impact of his mass rattling the cot. He lay there unmoving, facedown. Seeing him this way...oh God...

"His men sold him out, as you can see." Jake's ultra-cultured drawl hammered in my ears.

Something chafed against my cheeks. A handkerchief. Drying my tears.

"Yes, these gentlemen are PATS's finest. They insisted on accompanying me on this trip. They're anxious to see the demise of this hotbed of headaches, too. Now, aren't you glad I brought you Damian, just so you can see the truth of my words in his eyes and put your mind to rest?"

I snatched Jake's hand off my face, crashed beside Damian. My hands flailed on his head and back, useless, ignorant, no longer capable of reading injuries or assessing damage.

I struggled to turn him on his back, couldn't, then other hands were helping me and I saw his face. One side of it pulped, his lower lip swollen, bleeding, his left eye almost closed. The right one—the right one—told me everything.

He has been lying to me. For how long? How much? How far? All the time? All the way?

It spread, the malignant decay, razing all, belief, reasons, reason. God, oh God. All a lie. All for nothing. All monsters…

No. Damian was no monster. Not like that. He'd never hurt me. *But he* has *hurt you, over and over, lying to you. What if the lies weren't to protect you, but to subjugate you? What if he is no less a monster than Jake, just pettier, smaller?*

Stop it. No time for thinking, for feeling—for me. Time to stop the real danger. Any guesses who that was?

My hand under Damian's chin brought his face up. "Damian, one thing. Did you salvage Jake's work back in Russia? Was that the whole objective behind our mission back then?"

His silence answered. His eyes—or eye—did. I waited for a verbal confirmation, a bass, almost inaudible "Yes."

Then I hit him.

The backhand blow to the unbludgeoned side of his face knocked him sideways. He didn't try to dodge it, to lessen the impact, and now lay motionless. My hand felt broken. I was.

A nasal string of Spanish crackled from above us. The pilot.

"I'm being paged, Cali. We're over the Caucasus Mountains where it restarted, and ended again, for us. Have I ever thanked you for rescuing me? Anyway, I have to excuse myself. Though I'd love to stay and watch you come to realizations and abuse Damian, I have to go take care of business."

I watched him leave. Going to begin his silent attack.

Now. I had to act *now*. Before the plane began its decent, losing me the only edge I had.

"You think you have a chance with him?" Damian. Every hair on my body erupted. Talking to "his" men. "Can you be so stupid? You think anything he's offering is worth a slow, agonizing death, the kind he rewards those who help him with?"

"This plane has a rear door?" I stood up, turned to the men giving Damian grim faces and deaf ears. Not that they weren't rattled. Betraying your superior officer didn't come at no price.

One of them nodded automatically at my question. I turned on Damian, kicked him in the back, hard. He took it in silence, his eyes squeezing. "Open your eyes, *bastard*." I stressed the word. That got his eyes open. Good. "I should toss you out of the plane—hell, I think I *will!*" That got him shifting away, his back to the cot. Better. "Leading me on, endangering me and my friends to get your hands on Jake's weapon. At least Jake is honest about his agenda." My monologue ended on another blow.

He spit out blood, raised a blank eye. I watched it turn lethal. Then he smiled, his distorted face turning the chilling grimace macabre. "Well, *bitch*, you want honest? It's all been an act, to stop you from joining Jake when I had uses for you. *All* of it." He made a vulgar sound, his explicit expression more offensive. "Yeah, I knew he was alive. You think all the time and resources I expended keeping an eye on you was for *you?* No woman is worth the trouble. You, *'amor,'* are worth nothing."

My facial muscles shuddered, my nostrils flared, an acrid scent burning through them, shriveling my lungs. I thought I was ready. I wasn't. God, hearing it *hurt*.

Damian wasn't finished, his tone slashing, his golden eye defiling. "I just played one card wrong. I didn't realize that PATS was that far gone down his pocket or that the guy actually cares for you and would want to kill me for fucking you. But no problem, I always play the winning side, and that's Jake now. After he realizes you were just business, he'll recognize my potential and accept my offer to work for him for real."

I kicked him in the head this time. He jerked away at the last second before I connected fully. Hands behind his back, he still made that elastic rebound movement, was on his feet snarling at me in two seconds.

"I'm done being nice to you, St. James. You don't get pulled punches anymore. I want to work out some of the disgust being with you caused me. Don't worry, I won't kill you. My new boss wouldn't like that. I'll just show him that—how can I put it?— I'm *really* not interested."

"Well, I'm interested, bastard. In crippling you." I struck out with a *yoko geri,* raising my knee, pivoting sideways, hips twisting out, ramming my heel into his knee. He jumped back, my ram just missing fracturing his knee backward, retaliated by a *mawashi geri.* His roundhouse kick connected, full on, the power of his formidable leg impacting my shoulder sideways, sending me flying. Two inches up and he would have snapped my neck. Blocking out pain, I completed the fall on a somersault, landed in a crouch on hands and heels, snapped my leg out, reaping his legs. He just twisted on his axis midfall, catching me full in the face with an *ushiro geri* back kick before landing on both feet again. I spit blood this time.

Enough. "Trying to show me you can beat me with your hands tied behind your back? Well, surprise, bastard. You can't." I charged him, ramming my head into his ribs. He fell backward in an *ushiro ukemi* break-fall technique. I latched on to him, didn't let him complete it, rammed his head into the floor. A hard haul brought me straddling his chest. Then I pummeled him.

A hand on my shoulder jerked through me. "Hey, the guy's out. The boss didn't say you could kill him. He may have a use for…" The man didn't complete his thought. My elbow ploughed into his hard gut with an *empi uchi*, emptying his lungs.

His instinctive defense gave me the excuse to jump off Damian and assault him. Abandoning all finesse, I was all over him, until he managed to restrain me back to front. I struggled until I felt the time was right, then suddenly rammed my head backward into his face. He fell like a butchered tree.

The others jumped me now. Suddenly one of those who wasn't all over me shouted, "Guys, these two are dying!"

Yes! I shoved at my restrainers. "Get off me, you louts. Let me go see them. I'm a doctor, or haven't you heard?"

The guy I'd almost bitten a chunk out of grimaced. "Better sit this one out, Doc. You're not exactly in healing mode."

I glared at him. Then shrugged. "Whatever. Good riddance."

After five more minutes of resuscitation efforts, they changed their minds. The same guy turned to me. "Uh, I'm not getting a pulse on Caleb, and I hear no heartbeats, just—noise."

I shrugged again. "It's ventricular fibrillation, moron. Heart flapping ineffectively, blood going nowhere, quick death."

Moron went on. "Damian's different. I'm barely getting fifteen beats a minute from him. What did you give him, brain damage?"

"Does it look like I care?" They stared at me. I snorted. "What the hell. Get me the external defibrillator." They stared again. "This type of aircraft is also used to transfer people in disasters. There must be one on board. And get my bag."

And what do you know? Jake *had* taken it with us. Things were looking up. In a couple of minutes I had my weapons ready, and the defibrillator charged. And I attacked.

I electrocuted two and, thanks to their road-accident-curious-mob huddling, three more through body contact.

Jumping behind the closest one, holding him up, not waiting for the others to drop, I shot two others with curare darts. Then gunfire blasted. Theirs. Boss's orders only went so far.

Bullets meant for me riddled their teammate, my shield. Too heavy. Heavier in death. Dammit. Couldn't hold him up much longer....

More bullets burst, from another direction. Down. Damian!

He got three, four, exploded up, ropes undone, the man I'd pumped full of arrhythmia-inducing digitoxin held as shield. I'd readied the drug beforehand, injected the man with it during our struggle. Damian had slowed his naturally slow heartbeats at will. I'd expected any heart arrhythmia from my victim. He'd obliged with the worst-case scenario. Now his teammates' retaliatory high-caliber rifle fire finished him. And breached the plane's hull.

A banshee scream battered me—depressurizing in progress!

The plane shuddered, dipped. We'd gotten thirteen, ten remained, five would recover. Had only a few seconds before they overwhelmed us—killed us. *Implement the real plan.*

My legs were giving out under my shield's weight. I screamed to Damian, "Oxygen! Bag!"

He snatched out my oxygen mini-tank out of the bag, tossed me the latter, hurled the oxygen tank at our adversaries. Depressurizing got it before his bullet. It exploded among them.

It didn't get them all. Still bought me the seconds needed to don the bag, use it for partial shield as I ran to the rear.

"Damian! Now!" Couldn't wait to see if he'd hung on, yanked the lever down, dropping the back door open.

Massive depressurizing was like a planet-size monster's inhalation at the opening of the plane, sucking out all who hadn't grabbed a hold. Everyone but me and Damian.

Make that Damian. I got sucked out, too, dangled by both clawing hands upward from the lever, flapping like a wet flag outside the plane. The falling plane.

Terror choked me—uncontrollable, alien, paralyzing. Annihilating. Far below-freezing temperature, far beyond hurricane-force wind, pummeling, inside and out, puncturing eardrums, ripping lips, stripping lids, awareness, survival instinct. Mass and momentum hurtled downward while my body sheared upward, the wind skinning me, drawing bones from flesh—flimsy grip slipping…

Damian—I hadn't said sorry for the ugliness—didn't matter that it wasn't real….

The door. Closing. My hand frozen on the lever. I screamed now—voiceless—consumed—*want to die in one piece…*

Not after you go splat from twelve miles up…

Something desperate yanked at the bag battering my back, me with it, against the overpowering pull. I spilt, came apart—then came down, slammed on something solid, solid, *solid*… Then roaring silence, heaving motionlessness. Over. Over.

I choked, wept, quaked, giggled, kissed the floor. *I never want to do that again.* I rammed a flailing, frozen body into my savior's. *Damian.* His hug crushed me back together, his face meeting mine, his gasps and shudders echoing mine.

Then he withdrew, spastic, spitting one word, "Jake."

He exploded to the cockpit. I staggered in tow.

His kick should have sent the door through the cockpit window. Cockpit doors were unlocked in cargo planes anyway. It opened a fraction, rammed closed again. Jake must be barring it. Damian gave another explosive shove and the man barring it went flying back, ramming into the copilot's seat occupant. Jake.

Jake only grabbed the man, hid behind him, his eyes a cool, deliberate sweep from Damian to me.

Then he shot the pilot. And the controls.

Chapter 23

"So, who has who in a corner now?"

I stared at the blown-out head that came in and out of view beyond Damian's heaving body, heard Jake's calm shout over the din, slammed about as the plane nose dived.

"My biomatrix is heat resistant. An explosion will serve to disperse the agent just as well. Not as extensively, but with the air currents in the region in this season, I have every hope."

Damian growled and pointed his rifle at Jake, and the man in Jake's grip—the copilot, no doubt—cried out a plea. I barely stayed on my feet, unable to stop shaking, my heart just starting to pump blood through my frozen system.

Jake stood, the bigger copilot covering him fully, his gun to the man's head, his balance somehow unaffected by our downward plunge. "Will you shoot me and risk more damage here? Or risk this fellow dying and reduce your chances of handling the plane to nil, not to mention all those who'll wind up dead if we crash? Let's call it stalemate for now, finish this another day."

Damian charged. I clung to him, for balance, for sanity. Jake made sick sense, as usual. This was another form of brutal triage. The man behind the impending disaster was low priority compared to the disaster itself. No use wanting to rip his jugular out with my teeth. I yelled over the chaos.

"Let him go, Damian. Where would he go anyway?" Jake? Ha. That had to be delirium talking. Jake would go anywhere, do anything he pleased.

Damian slammed against the door with another brutal pitch as Jake staggered past him with the copilot. The same pitch threw me over the dead pilot. I struggled to knock him from his seat. Stepping over him, I took his place, stared at the blasted controls. Flying all sorts of planes had been part of my training. Troubleshooting was, too. But not control shooting. I tried all the controls. Nothing. I yelled.

"Damian!"

"In a sec."

I swung around. Oh, no. Damian couldn't resist. Wasting unaffordable time on his vendetta. Getting the copilot shot. But he had Jake now, disarmed. Then I heard it. Even over the cacophony. Agony. Bones snapping. He'd broken Jake's arm in multiple places. The same arm he'd broken in Russia. Then his fist smashed into Jake's face. Jake went down like a sack of wet cement.

"*Now* will you come?" I yelled again.

Damian threw me his rifle and Jake's gun, dragged the shot copilot to his feet and threw him back in his chair, kneeled on the floor between us, said something in Spanish. In answer the man's whimpers rose. Damian smacked him on the head, barked again.

"How bad is his injury?" I yelled.

Damian ran a series of checks of the controls and shouted, "He won't die now."

Nothing more to say. The plane wasn't responding to any control inputs. This meant total loss of both the plane's hydraulic systems, which operated flight controls, brakes, landing gear and other key systems. As a final backup, the Il-76 had manual controls, which worked control of rudders, flaps and other control surfaces with mechanical cables and links. We turned to these. They were much stiffer, less responsive. Seemed damaged, too. The copilot gasped something. Damian translated.

"He says we must fix a few circuits. He'll guide us through it."

"You do it. I'll try to fix him." I escaped his glare. "Have to, even if we don't need him or anything else ever again."

I examined the man as he struggled to give directions to Damian. One bullet. Just right of his vertebral column, exiting his chest between the fifth and sixth ribs. In minutes I had a chest tube installed, draining the accumulating blood, and fluid replacement making up the blood volume deficit. He wouldn't die. This way at least. It seemed we wouldn't, either. Not from a crash. Damian had leveled the plane!

"Calista, take the controls. I have to organize emergency landing with the authorities." He barked at the copilot, who fell over himself vacating his seat for him.

I took the controls as Damian poured a stream of Russian over the radio, every tremor I'd held in check blurring the world out of focus once more. Was nothing not painful? Even relief?

"Son of a bitch!"

What now?

"Jake slithered out." Damian hauled the copilot up, rammed him back into his seat.

I grabbed at him. "Damian. Jake's more dangerous than you can imagine. *Don't* take any chances with him. Finish him quickly."

He squeezed my hand, critical emotions crowding his face, squeezing my heart. Then he ran out—leaving incoming transmissions bombarding me.

I struggled to make it out. To fathom directions, orders. Screamed for them to go slower, to repeat. In the end I shouted,

"Speak English. The man who speaks fluent Russian isn't here."
Yeah, both men who did just stepped out. To battle to the death.

Then I felt it. A blast of horror, my life's worst. His distress.
Damian. Then I heard his call. Was it in my head? It boomed,
expanding my skull, cracking it. *"Calista."*

With the copilot at the controls, I burst out of the cockpit,
found Jake struggling into a parachute and Damian on the floor.
Both men reached their hands out to me. This image would burn
on my retinas throughout this life and beyond.

I crashed beside Damian. What had Jake done to him? I
hadn't heard another shot, he didn't have another gun. *What did
he do?*

Damian hands grabbed mine. "Came through the door—
stabbed me in the leg—must be one of your poisons—feels like—
like…"

I snatched my hands away, scrambled on my knees, scouring.
A spent dart, a syringe—*found it.* Cyanide.

No time, not one second to waste—my bag—the antidote kit.
I spilled back into the cockpit…and the bag was gone!

I ran out, and Jake—Jake had it! I charged him, roaring, took
him down, slammed with him to the floor. I left him a grunting-
in-pain mass, ran back to Damian, barely conscious now. My
cyanide injections were overkills. Didn't know if even the
antidote would work. Oh God, oh God, please, *please*…

I fumbled for the antidote, both sodium nitrite and sodium
thiosulfate. Had to give him one after the other, IV. Nitrite first,
then thiosulfate, larger, 50 cc's, longer to inject and—

Gunshots ripped through my charred awareness. Coming
from the cockpit. Jake, finishing the job.

"Go…" Damian's faint plea, like an ax grinding my vitals.
"Not potential victims now—sure ones—all my mistake…"

He was right. And I didn't care. Only him…

*Don't be stupid. Let Jake sabotage the not-quite-fixed
controls and you* all *die, Damian included.*

"It's cyanide," I choked, thrust the ampoules and syringes in his hand. "Inject…"

He echoed my gasps. "I know—go!"

I went. Out of my mind. After Jake.

Of everything he'd done, I'd get him for this the most. For forcing this choice on me.

In the cockpit, I found him slumped, parachute to the sidewall, broken arm held at an awkward angle, the gun in his left hand completing his vandalism. My fury, before my kick, knocked the gun down. Then I grabbed his broken arm and twisted.

He roared, convulsed over me. His eyes, as clear and endearing as the first time I'd looked into them, beseeched me. "Don't, Cali," he rasped. "Come with me. Do you think I would have left you to die? The parachute will carry both of us."

I punched his broken nose. He fought me now, then made a grab for the gun. The plane, in league with him, pitched at just the right angle, making him reach it, throwing me off.

He half straightened, gun in hand. Moment of truth. He'd be a fool if he didn't shoot me now. Jake was no fool.

He fired. One of the cockpit windows shattered.

Had all this heaving made him miss?

Or was he forcing me to give up trying to salvage the plane, panic and join him?

I had no time to figure out which. Either way, he was a sick man.

He turned away and staggered out, leaving me another impossible choice. Watch him run over Damian and jump out to freedom? Or try to fly the plane and save millions?

Not so impossible. I no longer saw the big picture. He'd boiled me down to basics. That crazy bastard had to go!

I ran out as the rear door opened. No depressurizing now we'd descended so far. "Jake!" At my shout, he turned at the edge. "I loved my Jake. He died eight years ago. I never got to say good-bye. I say it to him now. And to *you*, I say good riddance."

Disappointment flooded his eyes as we both raised our hands with our weapons, mine a shard of glass, a momento of his latest scene of destruction. Yeah, him and me both.

I hurled the glass. It lodged in his neck. Only then did he fire, the shot going wide. I rolled on the floor, then sprang up as he stumbled backward. I secured a hold at the door's edge, snatched the gun out of his hand as he fell out of the plane. I watched blood spurting in undulating ropes from his neck in the downward draft.

Shoot him! Between the eyes this time!

God help me, I couldn't. Couldn't kill him again. He might have spared me, earlier….

His final look of love mutilated me, and I saw no more, tears blinding me, gut-heaves disemboweling me.

Somehow I managed not to plummet after him, closed the door, lurched back to Damian, found the empty ampoules but not the syringes—God please—was he…?

A sudden plunge launched me up into the air, weightless, hurled me to the floor. Voices bombarded me, cacophonous, sanity consuming. *Too late for Damian anyway if he hasn't managed to inject the antidote. Get up, get the controls. Try. Do it!*

Oh, Damian—sorry, so sorry…

I was back at the plane controls. Didn't remember making the trip—didn't feel, couldn't—*too much.* Not equipped to process all this. Dissociating, dissipating… Damian, Jake—millions…

Metallic screeching impinged on shut down senses, brought back with it the roaring din, the crushing wind. The radio!

Couldn't make anything of the garbled voices, English now, orders, explanations, directions, still alien, faraway, surreal.

Guess something inside me was on auto, receiving, processing, enough to make the coordinates, approach the landing strip. Couldn't work the brakes, couldn't get the wheels down. Land was a zooming up violent end, terror beyond registering.

Crash-land on the tanks and it'll still rupture them and disperse the agent.

No idea whose voice, whose thoughts these were. They made sense to whatever remained sentient, functioning inside me.

I forced the flying behemoth on its axis a couple of dozen feet from the ground. The wing scraped against the tarmac, then ploughed into it, snapped, sheared, the noise screeching like a million shrieking demons.

And then the crash.

A judgment day boom and brunt, razing from the outside in, disconnecting cells, teaching new levels of helplessness, of insignificance. So permeating it invaded unconsciousness, maybe even death... Didn't mind, as long as the plane didn't explode.

Wake me up only if Damian does.

Hands, voices, pain, burning stench, pain, nausea, oppression, dread—and did I mention pain?

Not exactly pain. Pain was defined by the very property of being localized. This was all-receptors, all-together-now misery. I no longer had skin, but a red-hot map of lacerations, no nervous system, but an exposed wires network, no organs, but a squelchy-mass mess.

All proved one thing. I was alive. Death couldn't feel so corporeal, could it? Or so noisy. Or so annoying!

It was annoyance that got to me. "Hey—quit poking me!"

My eyes opened, squinted at faces, recognized the universal manner that said medics. We were in the open air. So I made it? This was really happening? And if this was real, and that was the plane on its back like a gutted bird in the distance, then we'd crash-landed, hadn't gone kablooey and—Damian! The agent tanks!

I jackknifed up and a thousand hammers struck inside me. The octopoid caregivers tried to keep me down. I slapped hands right and left. Found one hand to do it with. The other was in a splint and sling. "Let me up. Anyone speak English here?" My Russian seemed to be another casualty of the accident.

A woman patted me on the back. "I'm Dr. Misha Voloskaya. You must have a concussion or worse. You've been out for two hours."

Just two hours? After all that? And in just two hours the crash site had became almost a town, filled with every emergency and state personnel Russia had to offer? I croaked, "I'm fine."

The blonde shook her head, adamant. "You're not. You had a dislocated shoulder, which we reduced, you've broken your right wrist and five ribs on the same side. You probably have lung contusion. You're only feeling good because of the morphine."

This was *good?* Sure it was. I could move, talk without keeling over, without howling. I *was* fine. I was alive when I shouldn't be. "You've done a great job putting me back together. I need to know about the man on board. And the plane's damage."

"Which man? There were two dead men…." Her face distorted, the world with it.

Damian, no—wait—not Damian, the *pilots*. The woman was going on.

"And there was a man with multiple injuries, who seemed to have been poisoned."

Was?

"He said he injected himself with an antidote."

Said? As in conscious? Talking? Alive?

"He spoke in Russian, too. He's being treated but is stable." I sagged. She tutted. "It's why I left him and came to you."

I shot up again, pain unfelt. Damian. Alive!

I was up and stumbling. The woman ran after me, answering my questions still, bless her.

"The plane's top came off like a sardine can, one wing broken, the rest is intact."

Thank God! But that didn't mean much. Couldn't let the

agent fall into the Russian government's hands. Into anybody's hands. Only one set of hands I trusted not to abuse it.

I saw parts of Damian among the wall of people. Parts that moved. Good enough. *Deal with the catastrophe in the making now.*

I turned to the woman. My age, taller, strong chords striking between us. I took her by the shoulder. "I had a bag. I need it."

"They emptied the plane, put all they found there." We passed the dead pilots on the way. Jake's last victims. "The distress call said hijackers commandeered your cargo plane intending to crash it into a government installation, that you overpowered them but not before they damaged the controls. Is this what happened?"

Damian. Always ready with convincing stories. I nodded, limped through the heaped articles with my newfound protectress warding off security personnel. My bag. Found it.

In five minutes I'd contacted Sir Ashton, told him the gist of what happened. And to do *whatever* it took to get us the hell out of here with the plane before someone unleashed Armageddon.

And what do you know! His "extraction" team was already on the way. Good to know the good guys also had their intel sources. Just hoped he had an abyss deep enough to bury the agent until we produced its counteraction or deleted it from time's records.

It took five hours for his Antonov to reach Vladikavkaz's airport, land and load the damaged Il-76. Five hours when constant interrogations and treatments kept me from Damian. Nothing would have if I hadn't seen him sitting under his own power.

Then we were on board Sir Ashton's private jet, with full medical facilities on board. They transferred Damian first. I entered the jet upright, my first demand for everyone to just disappear. Had to have time alone with him. Now.

I approached his stretcher. He kept his good eye closed. The other was shut involuntary. Another pretense, huh? Nope. No more. Buck stops here.

"You know, Damian, I'm up to here with Jake almost killing you and then me killing Jake."

He still didn't open his eye. Couldn't look me in mine, huh? "It's safe to say that particular scenario isn't playing ever again." His voice darkened, softened, the very sound of anguish and re- gret—and love. "How are you?"

Asking for a toll report? From our vicious scene, when he'd battered me inside and out? From having to kill Jake—again? From the ordeals of the past ten days? Or those still waiting for me into the no-end-in-sight future? *Go for the obvious.*

I tapped my finger over his eyebrow. That got that eye open. "Dislocated shoulder, broken wrist—goodbye to surgery and vigilantism for the duration—and ribs five through nine. Oh, and three thousand five hundred cuts, bruises and lacer- ations. You?"

His eye swept my nightmarish-looking self, a world of ouch filling it. He still took my cue. "Compound fracture femur, torn latissimus dorsi, a few hundred stitches, a few liters of blood spilled, concussion, post-cyanide toxicity funk, the rest pulped, thanks." A beat. "Alive and too damn well. Calista…"

I went down on my knees beside him, careful not to bend even a few degrees. Morphine was starting to ebb. "Sit up."

He obeyed, pain and hesitation impeding him, blasting off him in breakers. My left hand captured his head, dipping in ex- quisite contact. I completed it, gently pressing the lips he'd bruised into his, mingling blood and hurt and yearning, life flowing again with every restless shift, tongue exploring his injuries, soothing the tattered flesh, swallowing my reiterated name and the *"perdóneme"* seeking forgiveness. Then he took the kiss over, taking it from pain to passion. Uh-uh. Didn't think so.

I broke the kiss, rose in slow motion, headed for the seat opposite his stretcher. "That was to thank you for surviving."

His surge of animation drained. He still moved his cast,

hopped up on one foot, dropped beside me. Too long later he murmured, "You don't sound too glad I did."

"I'm delirious. In every sense of the word."

His short laugh was bleakness made audible. "Another way of telling me you'd certainly want to live if I died now?"

"You think I'd resort to sarcasm instead of telling you straight you're relegated to the category of 'good riddance'?"

His laugh this time was even bleaker. "Wouldn't blame you. I'm not worth it."

You, amor, *are worth nothing.*

An act. I'd made him do it. I'd given him cues in our code and he'd picked it up by the next heartbeat, played his part far beyond Academy Award performances. His men had bought it. Hell, *I* had. Even knowing, going in with eyes wide open. Made you wonder when he stopped acting. Made me wonder how my feelings remained constant when he was a chameleon. "Maybe. But you're *my* not worth it."

He raised a reddened eye, the gold eclipsed with so much emotion—God, so much. *Was it real?*

"Do I need to tell you that what he said I did to you, to Ayesha and the others, was a lie?"

That easy? Off the hook with one "about to weep for the first time in my ultra-macho life" look? Was I supposed to follow with an of course not to appease his agony?

Really didn't think so. "I once told you I can't pick and choose what to believe in what you say, Damian."

He slumped into his seat on a trembling exhalation. "Do I get a hearing? Or did I forfeit that, too?"

"Don't start talking if you don't intend to tell me the truth, the whole truth or even God won't help you if I later discover more juicy details that you left out."

"Fair enough." A moment of silence, then he began. "After Russia I dug into Jake's allegations that he was holding both TOP and PATS strings. He was a master manipulator, but he still built his lies around a core of truth, to make them harder hitting, more convincing. I found only evidence that my PATS team was uncorrupted. That's the PATS I've been defending to you. The core team I trusted with my life, the old-schoolers. That is, until the day before I came offering to go on the *tugurios* mission alone with you. I finally found out how PATS and I were duped into taking the mission to Russia."

I gave a disbelieving laugh. He exhaled. "Stranger things happen. You know we started out as a branch of The Order for Peace, but I've been moving us away, cutting the umbilical cord. I didn't appreciate some of TOP's directives and thought PATS would be well rid of their influence. I was planning Russia when TOP higher-ups added two conditions in return for not impeding the autonomy I was establishing. Taking you on, and bringing back the research."

I'd known he had lied, had read it all over him back in the plane. I'd still prayed I'd read him wrong, as usual. Self-deception *was* inexhaustible, wasn't it? Pain razed me all over again.

"So Jake told the truth. And you lied all along."

He turned, angry, supplicant. "He told a couple of truths among a hundred lies. To make them all sound like the truth."

"These are the only important truths—and lies. He asked for me, and you delivered. Then you gave them an apocalyptic weapon in return for funding, gadgets and a longer leash!"

"It wasn't like that. You *know* I tried to stop you from coming. Remember, it was you who thwarted me, insisted on coming, on staying every step of the way. But I would have chained you in a dungeon if I'd known why they insisted you come along, that they were delivering you to Jake. At the time I had no reason to doubt them. I've known these people for fifteen years, and though I disagreed with some of their policies, at the time they rationalized it all to my satisfaction. It was only just before Colombia that I discovered these TOP people haven't been in control, have been fronts and mouthpieces for a good while now, that a radical group of ex-intelligence moguls are holding their strings in diabolical ways. They're the ones implementing the new MO to work with terrorists like Jake to bring other terrorists of their choice down."

"I don't care who did what," I said, seething. "It all boils down to this—you're the reason all this happened!"

His despondent frown admitted it all. "Yeah, I salvaged Jake's research and it all followed. But even without knowing the real situation, I regretted it the moment my men turned it in while I lay in IC. I've been trying to fix my mistake ever since. But I was sure I had time to prevent any damage, believing the agent wasn't being produced."

I'd blacken his other eye any minute now! "Really? You believed those good people you knew for so long would just put the research in a safe and guard it from falling into the wrong hands? You, the world's leading hardened, ruthless cynic?"

He took my flaying, subdued, accepting. "It made sense when they said we needed it, to understand and counteract it, in case it was already dispersed. But afterward I decided destroying every trace of it was the only answer. And I believed there was no agent not because I'm a trusting soul, but because the research had missing parts that rendered it useless—parts Jake kept in his mind so he'd be indispensable. I still wasn't gambling on anyone filling the holes and deciding to use it, and was about to retrieve it from TOP when duplicate research surfaced in Colombia *with* the missing info. I still thought development was some time off, until you tied your friends' affliction to their being in Colombia. It's only now I realize Jake resurfaced there and struck a deal with those holding the bulk of his work. They spend and protect, he completes the job, everyone's a happy demon."

Yeah. And what a happy, exonerating explanation. Not! "So you found out the conspiracy and just went ahead and exposed me and my team to danger, while your team helped Jake!"

"I gave TOP and PATS every possible proof to believe your mission was purely humanitarian and that I was going with you for personal reasons. And those Judases aren't my team. You know my team. Those men were foisted on me to train while I recovered. I did train them for a while, until I got out of it. I had no reason to suspect them then, but my objection was that I didn't want a bigger team, didn't have time to train anyone. Needless to say, I didn't trust them with any important stuff."

Heat shot off me, shimmering the air around me, distorting his face even more. "Like following me around?"

"That—and the search for the Colombian plant."

"Funny how the team you didn't trust ended up with your original team there, then! God—to think you knew all that and kept me in the dark!"

"I didn't. I didn't suspect Jake was alive. I believe in your lethality too much. I only understand it all *now,* and how he got to your friends. Jake, with his far-reaching liaisons with Russian mobs and Colombian drug cartels and through his surveillance of you, must have found out about your friends' mission and sent the paramilitaries to the *tugurios* at the same time they arrived to strike two home runs. Road test his agent and send you a calling card, the crumbs as you said, to lead you into his grasp. The infected refugees were the community leaders, the only people who knew who your friends really were, and Jake must have had them infect Matt and the others with a different form of agent as a puzzle to further test the genius he was so proud of. You, and his need to recapture you, were the two predictable things about him. His fatal weaknesses."

Made sense. Added up. Didn't mean I couldn't be mean. "An easier explanation would be, you got rid of my friends to get your paws on me. You always said you'd do anything for me."

My jab struck. His pummeled face twisted. "*For* you. Not against you. I'd never coerce you, or hurt you, to control you. I don't want to control you. I want you only if you choose me, if I'm what makes you happy, what completes your already full life."

Ayesha's unshakable belief. He misread my wry huff, went on, impassioned now. "Even if I were such a monster, I couldn't have infected them because I didn't *have* the agent. No one had it but Jake. He even leveled the plant before we left. He was dedicated to making sure he never became redundant. I'll get you evidence to every word I'm saying, no matter what it takes."

"No way will you ever conclusively prove any of it, Damian."

Defeat, total and final, extinguished him before my eyes. He believed I actually suspected him, huh? And it had never even registered as a possibility. Weird thing, faith. Against all logic and evidence. Weirder coming from me.

He finally smiled, the smile of one who'd lost everything, cared no more. "And I went to all these lengths to hide what I did back in Russia, hoping to erase my mistake without having to confess it, so I wouldn't lose your trust. And I never had it."

In pain, the poor baby? Good. Maybe it'd teach him to stop lying to me. For a month or so. "So—if your corrupted superiors weren't on to you, how did we end up in Jake's hands?"

He fell silent. Until I thought he wouldn't talk again. It must have been half an hour before he whispered, "Ed."

The name hit me like a crippling blow to the spine. "No!"

He didn't answer. I couldn't talk. Couldn't breathe even. For almost an hour. It was only when the flight attendant placed a meal in front of us and actually shook us to make sure we hadn't died in our seats that I binged on an inhalation, moaning with the stabs in my rib cage and every other magnified ache.

"Are you sure?" Ed. In Russia, he'd been my ally in Damian's team. And he was Damian's right arm—his soul brother. The only one above all suspicion.

Damian gave a dejected nod.

So this was how Jake had all that knowledge about everything that had happened. I'd said it was like he'd been there. And he had been. Through Ed, who knew every move and word through Damian and the rest of his team.

Damian at last spoke, his voice hushed, thick. "He sold my life for Anna's."

Anna was another member of Damian's trusted team.

"We discovered coming back from Russia that she has a rare and progressive autoimmune disorder, that seemed to have been triggered by her latest injuries. It's invariably fatal. But there is an experimental treatment program that's been securing results, from slowing the disease's progress to actual cures, but which costs millions and which is conducted in top-secret research facilities that even the world's billionaires have no access to. Jake got to Ed, offered it. Ed asked me to understand as they overpowered me. And I do. I don't blame him for a second. I'd choose you, too."

I remembered now, how Ed felt for Anna, how gutted he'd been over a minor injury she'd gotten in Russia. Damian's acceptance of Ed's motive grated most of all. "Hell, Damian. It doesn't work that way. You don't sacrifice innocents for your loved ones. It makes you worse than the monsters we fight."

"I'm no innocent, *querida*. She is—at least, the baby she's carrying is. It's Ed's. But he did one mitigating thing. He sacrificed only me. At the last moment, he warned the rest of my team, told them to disappear before the new team arrived. I pray they and the ones back home weren't hunted down."

"But now Jake is gone, why hunt them down?"

"You're totaled, aren't you." He huffed. "My former bosses and their puppeteers know now that I wasn't on their side, that I cost them their precious new ally and ultimate weapon. Reason enough for anyone loyal to me to be hunted. Ad infinitum."

A moment's silence, then he blurted out, "Is this beyond repair? Is this the end? *Madre de Dios,* Calista, just tell me."

"And you'll what? Give up and blend into the background, Agent Chameleon? Leave me be to move on and love another man?"

He jerked as if with a close-range bullet. Amazing didn't

begin to describe it. The dizzying range of emotions the man could project. "My God, Damian. I can practically see jealousy taking a machete to your insides and despair an ax to your heart. Back on the plane you were as—"

He cut me off. "Faked rifts were part of our strategic and psychological warfare training. You acted, too. You were just as convincing!"

"*I* was genuinely pissed, yet I still didn't get half as creatively abusive as you did. I bet it was *your* performance they bought."

Both hands rose in a please-no-more gesture. "*Misericordia, amor.* It was your life and the lives of millions in the balance. Nothing less could have forced me to go that far. I had to say the worst—the absolute opposite of the truth—for it to work."

"Yet said 'absolute opposite' is indistinguishable from said alleged truth."

And here, I was treated to a completely new sight. Damian at his wits' end.

"You want the truth, Calista? I don't *want* to feel this way for you. Yet I can no longer live without feeling it. But I can't go on not knowing, either. So just *tell me!*"

I should have been angry. I should have been all sorts of things. I wasn't. We'd averted a disaster, won a battle, but mostly having him alive against all odds—what could I say? Plenty here to intoxicate a woman clear out of all judgment and reservations.

You'll regret it.

Ah, logic having a say at last. And getting the gag.

Was this the end? He could bet his gorgeous bod—not. What it was, was open to debate. A surge of unthinking kindness had me sharing my conclusions. "This isn't the end, Damian."

Relief and elated sensuality radiated off him like a furnace blast. Whoa. Why did I feel I'd just fallen into the slot he'd inched me toward? My splint in his ribs stopped any passionate displays. "Not so fast. You say you fear your team will be hunted. Didn't hear you mention yourself. Any reason you're exempt?"

One caress broke through my barricade.

"I died in that plane crash, remember? And so did you."

"Huh? We've been seen alive by tons of people."

"In Russia. The best place to crash-land in. All info is suppressed on a mandatory basis. Russian authorities didn't allow independent news investigators on the crash scene, they announced the total destruction of the plane and its occupants in a spectacular explosion. Under my advisement. They agreed they should make an accident out of it and not the militant act I convinced them it was. So—until PATS and TOP prove or even suspect otherwise, we're dead along with Jake and their men."

So he'd conducted deep-cover measures even as he recovered from cyanide poisoning. Got a foreign government to play it his way. Unbelievable. "What happens when no epidemic sweeps the area around the crash site? They'll know the agent wasn't dispersed."

He had no ready answer for that. At last he frowned. "Maybe they'll think it got destroyed in the explosion. Maybe they don't know it's heat resistant, or maybe Jake was lying about that to buy himself time to get away."

Too many maybes. Hated the critters. And then there was one more thing. "I know Sir Ashton cut a huge deal with the highest Russian authorities to return us and the plane, no questions asked. But their intelligence must be hard at work investigating the whole thing. They'll piece it together sooner or later."

"And you think they'll share their findings with their PATS and TOP counterparts?"

In about a million years, yeah. PATS and TOP would have to penetrate the maze of Russian intelligence before they got any intel. Still, they'd do it. And there was another thing. "What about all the people with us now?"

"I contacted Sir Ashton, made sure he realized the full measure of the danger."

So that was how Sir Ashton had already been on the job! Damian beat me to it.

"He said he was sending us his most discreet people. He gave them the manufactured story and the false identities I recommended for extra security."

So he'd made Sir Ashton his accomplice again, left him no choice but to get mired in convoluted, highest-risk black-ops stuff. Guess I had, too, the minute I threw the responsibility of spiriting the agent away in his lap. And if our enemies found out…*oh God—Sir Ashton, what have we done to you?*

But maybe they wouldn't. Not before we managed to clean up the mess. For now, we were dead, and the agent and its creator, gone. Even to Ed and the rest of Damian's team. There was no way for them to know what happened after we boarded that plane.

Damian didn't let me breathe the self-deceiving placations long. "Though I believe Jake didn't share the info about the counteraction method with his TOP and PATS allies, they'll find out about it, about everything, sooner or later. Then they'll do anything to get their weapon package. And us."

So we had a breather, nothing more. Others might not have even that. "How will you alert your team to retaliatory actions? They're probably confused about the whole thing now, not knowing what to do or who to trust."

"I have ways of contacting each of them, without the others knowing. Once they're clear on everything, they can take care of themselves. It's your team I'm worried about."

My blood stopped in my veins, congealed. "You think Ed will give my secrets, my people to them, too?"

His struggle with having to say it, to face it, thrashed on his face, in my chest. At last, he said, "He's a broken link now. Anything's possible."

My blood suddenly gushed with dread and denial. "What about your mother?" I whispered. "Do they know about her?"

He frowned. "They don't. But Ed does. I'll alert her." He gave a bitter laugh. "*Dios,* I almost wish they'd try something. Desideria would probably bring them down single-handedly. She once brought down a dictatorship. The snipers around the house are hers, not mine, by the way."

He talked tough. I could still see fear for her blossom in his mind, trickle down his battered features. I groped for a way out. "Maybe if we bury this deep enough…"

"Nothing can ever be buried deep enough, Calista."

And he'd know. I closed my eyes. A long time later I exhaled. "I'll have to take drastic action to protect my team. As for Dad, he has his army of ex-cons. PATS and TOP would probably lose in a war with him. Do you think Sir Ashton may be targeted, too?"

He gave this long consideration. Then he shook his head. "He is too valuable on many fronts to harm. Not on account of his involvement with you. As long as they don't know his role in all this, I think he's safe."

"But it will all come out, and it will be all-out war."

He raised one arrogant eyebrow. "Yes. I'll be ready for it."

"*You* will?" I turned my face to him. "What? I look like the running-and-hiding type to you?"

"The running-into-the-minefield type. That's what worries me. There'll be no room for confrontations here. This is stealth and preemptive strikes territory. We must go deep undercover." His eyes added, *in every sense.*

Seemed hormones really made the world go round. Battered and broken, my body still wagged its every cell in agreement.

"We must regroup, reassess, gather intel, plan counterstrikes, cleanups—"

"Hey, hey, wait a minute. Who's 'we'?"

"Me and you. Our teams."

"I have a team, buddy. On the last count, you don't."

"I bet I salvage one yet. But you're right, until I reroute my career, I'm out of a job."

His mock-mournful expression tickled me. I found myself smiling full at him. Bliss, to just have him to smile at. "Maybe I can offer you a job. I can use someone with your—skills. If it's okay with you to have me as absolute boss that is…"

You'd never think anything was wrong with him from the way he pounced. "Where do I sign for my first submission course?"

Ha. And I was born an hour and ten minutes ago. "On the dotted *lie,* where else?"

His eyes went dead. "You'll never forgive me." Statement.

"I'll never forget. Your actions cost me a lot, Damian. No idea how much they'll still cost my closest people."

His voice when he recovered enough to talk was monotone, tight. Determined. "I—understand. But let me make amends, offer all I have dealing with the fallout, and as we start over."

"You mean work-wise or you-and-me-wise?"

"Every way. Whatever it takes."

Start over. Seemed like a good idea.

And whom was I kidding? It was the *only* idea.

What else was there with my operation's cover most probably blown and my friends' futures, on every count, uncertain? With the world getting darker, crazier by the hour and *trust* becoming one of the dirtiest words around? Add a global-scale intrigue, and a man I loved, had faith in, but would never fully trust or fathom and you had your basic highest-stakes mess.

Called for a clean slate, no tracks, new rules, extreme measures.

Just what I needed. To make life interesting. To renew my resolve. To survive.

I turned to him, met his pledge with mine. "Let's wipe everything out then and start from scratch. Whatever it takes."

Action, romance, unforgettable heroines...they're all a part of Silhouette Bombshell and they're right at your fingertips! Turn the page for a sneak preview of one of next month's releases, SNEAK AND RESCUE by USA TODAY *best-selling author Shirl Henke.*
Available March 2006 at your favorite retail outlet.

"Sam Ballanger to see Mr. Winchester. I have an appointment."

Looking highly dubious, the blonde checked the computer screen at her side to confirm. "That was for four p.m. It's now—"

"Look, Blondie, I can tell time. I was unavoidably detained by a couple of bozos who tried to run me down, then shoot me in your parking deck. Next time that happens to you, let's see if that fancy 'do' of yours doesn't get a little messed up, okay?"

Ms. Chandler, as the nameplate on the desk indicated, glared disbelievingly before she caught herself and forced a smile as genuine as the mauve silk floral arrangement beside her computer. "I'll see if Mr. Winchester is still available. Please have a seat."

But only if I promise not to get grease on the upholstery. Sam walked over to the window and looked at the stunning vista, all blue skies, gold sand and green palm trees in the distance. Miami Beach with its art deco pastels beckoned from across the water, a faded diva ringed by garish new high-rise condos. Her kind of town. She'd known it since her first trip here when she was thirteen and stowed away in the sleeper of Uncle Dec's rig. He'd been mad enough to chew nails when he'd discovered her at a rest stop in North Carolina. Turned the air blue with his cussing, she recalled fondly. By that time it had been too far to turn back without sacrificing a big payload in Miami, so he'd called her frantic parents and reassured them he'd take good care of his favorite niece. She'd been grounded for the rest of her freshman year, but it had been worth it.

Her reminiscences were interrupted by Ms. Chandler. "Mr. Winchester will see you now," she said. "Please follow me."

The snotty receptionist looked like she was trying to digest a bamboo stalk from one of those urns out front and walked like another stalk was jammed where the Florida sun never shines. They moved down a long hall, footsteps muffled by two-inch thick Karastan carpeting in a shade Sam would've described as Attica gray. Winchester's nameplate was inscribed in polished brass on the door of the corner office. Of course. He was the senior partner, after all.

Chandler knocked deferentially and was bidden to enter. She stood with her back pressed to the door, careful not to let Sam touch her when she walked inside. A tall silver-haired man with the narrow face and long, straight nose of a blue blood stood behind an immense walnut desk devoid of anything but a leather blotter and a set of Mont Blanc pens.

"Ms. Ballanger?" He did not smile.

"Mr. Winchester?" she shot back, making her way into the room. "Pardon my appearance—and tardiness." She paused to glance back at the Chandler dame, who was slowly closing the door behind her. *Like to eavesdrop, don't you, honey.* When Sam heard the muffled sound of the latch click, she continued. "I was involved in an altercation in your parking deck. Can you think of any reason someone would try to stop me from taking your case?"

He blinked. "Certainly not. What do you mean by 'an altercation'?"

So much for manners. He still didn't offer her a seat. Even Chandler had done that much. She took one anyway, directly in front of him, and he reluctantly lowered himself into the custom leather chair behind the desk. She gave him a quick rundown on the attack in the downstairs garage, studying his response. Hard to tell if he believed her, or even cared.

"It could've been related to another investigation, but I'd appreciate it if you'd have the building security check their video cams at the exits between three fifty-five and four ten or so."

Winchester shook his head ever so slightly. "I'm afraid that's out of the question. If you report this…event to the authorities, I'll be dragged into something which has nothing to do with me. In fact—"

Sam put up her hand. "Okay, just a thought. The Olds is probably being fed into a compactor as we speak anyway." She'd dealt with uptight types like Winchester before and knew how to handle them. As for a couple of dozen wrecked cars in the bowels of the building, well, let their insurance companies handle that.

"Who do you want me to retrieve and why?" she asked straightforwardly.

He hesitated, then replied, "Jay did recommend you highly." Although he still appeared skeptical, he continued. "My son Farley is missing. The boy probably thinks he's on a secret mission for the Confederation of Planets, but my guess is that he's still somewhere on Earth—with my stolen Jaguar and his friend Elvis."

"Elvis?" Excuse me? Sam couldn't help the incredulous expression on her face.

"Elvis P. Scruggs. And don't ask what the *P* stands for," he snapped. "My son is only seventeen and has been under the care of Dr. Reese Reicht for the past five years."

Sam waited for him to give her the rest of the story. He drummed a set of well-manicured fingers on the desk, as if debating some more. "Dr. Reicht?" she prompted.

"He's a psychiatrist. My son sees flying saucers, spaceships, even imagines he's part of some kind of intergalactic war." His thin lips formed a tight line, then he scoffed angrily. "A secret agent for the Confederation of Planets." At her blank look, he explained, "Farley is a...a *Space Quest* fanatic. Has been ever since he was a boy."

"You mean he's a movie buff—loves sci-fi films and television shows?" Weird, but not as weird as a pal named Elvis P. Scruggs.

"I'm afraid Farley's situation isn't quite as simple as being an avid fan." Winchester grimaced. The drumming fingers stilled when he realized she had noticed the agitated movement.

Sam knew if he had any papers on his desk they'd be aligned in perfectly straight rows. She'd lay a lot better than even money that everything on his computer was organized in perfectly ordered folders and every single item could be pulled up in an instant. And that he had a double backup system.

"Farley has been known to use drugs—and I am not speaking of the medications Dr. Reicht prescribes."

"That could be serious. When did he disappear?"

Winchester gave a dismissive wave of his hand. "Sometime in the past two days. I was out of town on business since Monday. I returned late yesterday. The housekeeper informed me Farley hadn't slept in his bed for the past two nights."

A real concerned parent here. Doesn't want the cops. No idea how long his kid's been missing. "Does his mother have any idea when he took off?"

"I regret to say his mother passed away five years ago."

The loss of a pet guppy would elicit more reaction from most people, so she didn't waste time offering condolences. "Any idea where he went? Is this Scruggs with him?"

"Yes. Farley's been spending time with that illiterate cracker for weeks, perhaps longer." The vagueness again irritated her as he continued. "Scruggs is from somewhere in the panhandle.

Oh, I tried to put a stop to it, but my work requires me to be out of town frequently and my son has always been...difficult."

With a dad like you he oughta be impossible. "You think Scruggs is Farley's drug connection?"

"I don't know. Quite probably. I do know that he's a thief and I discovered quite recently that he may have spent some time in prison. In any case, Rogers, my chauffeur, informed me that Scruggs took my vintage Jaguar. Since Farley was in the passenger seat, he didn't question it. That was Monday afternoon. When I was going over my personal records this morning, I found twenty thousand dollars had been withdrawn from a savings account to which my son has access."

"You're sure Farley took it?"

"Yes, and I'm equally sure Scruggs encouraged him, but I won't press charges. I simply want you to recover my money, my car and my son. Quietly. No headlines. Do you think you can do that, Ms. Ballanger?" He glanced at his Rolex, indicating the interview was over.

"I'll do my best to bring back your son, Mr. Winchester. But I will need a few names and numbers—his doctor, your housekeeper and chauffeur, the registration info on the Jag."

He nodded, turning to the console at the side of his desk and pressing a button. "My personal assistant will be happy to furnish whatever you need."

Sam stood up. Winchester didn't bother. Neither did he offer to shake hands. "About my fee—"

"Ms. Ettinger will take care of that, as well. Send a bill." With that he swiveled his chair around and opened his computer to long columns of numbers spread across an oversize monitor.

She'd been dismissed like a chambermaid in an English melodrama! "Where do I find Ms. Ettinger?" Sam said to the back of his head.

He didn't turn around. "She'll be along."

As if on cue the door opened. A wraith-thin woman with gray

hair pulled into a painfully tight knot on top of her head and the worst overbite Sam had ever seen, said, "Please follow me, Ms. Ballanger." She didn't smile, either.

The kid may be into Space Quest, *but his old man and this staff could play in zombie movies.* She made a mental note to have Matt check out Dr. Reicht while she was searching for Farley.

The last thing Sam Ballanger ever intended to do was to deliver a client into a worse situation than the one she snatched him from.

USA TODAY
BESTSELLING AUTHOR

Shirl HENKE

BRINGS YOU

SNEAK AND RESCUE
March 2006

Rescuing a brainwashed rich kid
from the Space-Quest TV show
convention should have been a cinch
for retrieval specialist Sam Ballanger.
But when gun-toting thugs gave chase,
Sam found herself on the run with a truly
motley crew, including the spaced-out
teen, her flustered husband and one
very suspicious Elvis impersonator....

BOUNTY HUNTER.
HEIRESS.
CHANTAL WORTHINGTON WAS

HELL ON HEELS

by Carla CASSIDY

Chantal was on familiar terrain
when she went after a fellow blue blood
who'd skipped bail on a rape charge.
But teaming up with bounty hunter
Luke Coleman to give chase was a
new move in her playbook. Soon things
were heating up on—and off—the case....

Available March 2006

**From the author of the bestselling
COLBY AGENCY miniseries**

DEBRA WEBB

VOWS *of* SILENCE

A gripping new novel of romantic suspense.

A secret pact made long ago between best
friends Lacy, Melinda, Cassidy and Kira resurfaces
when a ten-year-old murder is uncovered. Chief
Rick Summers knows they're hiding something, but
isn't sure he can be objective...especially if his
old flame Lacy is guilty of murder.

**"Debra Webb's fast-paced thriller will
make you shiver in passion and fear."**
—*Romantic Times*

Vows of Silence...coming in March 2006.

Detective Maggie Skerritt is on the case again!

Maggie Skerritt is investigating a string of murders while trying to establish her new business with fiancé Bill Malcolm. Can she manage to solve the case while moving on with her life?

Spring*Break*

by *USA TODAY* bestselling author

CHARLOTTE DOUGLAS

Silhouette®
BOMBSHELL™
COMING NEXT MONTH

#81 SNEAK AND RESCUE by Shirl Henke

Samantha Ballanger had the golden touch when it came to extracting people from dangerous places; she'd even married one of her rescued clients. But retrieving a brainwashed fan from the *Space Quest* TV show convention was a stretch. Even in her sexy sci-fi disguise, Sam couldn't coax the wealthy teenaged boy back to reality—not when she was up against one *very* suspicious Elvis impersonator keen on keeping the kid spaced-out....

#82 HELL ON HEELS by Carla Cassidy

Heiress turned bounty hunter Chantal Worthington was on her home turf when she went after a fellow blue blood who'd skipped bail on a rape charge—and years ago had raped her own best friend. But Chantal wasn't the only one on his trail. Instead of butting heads, spitfire Chantal teamed up with bad boy Luke Coleman on the case...and soon, from Kansas City to Mexico, even if the leads got cold, their passion stayed red-hot!

#83 THE DIAMOND SECRET by Ruth Wind

Good girl and wild woman by turns, multifaceted gemologist Sylvie Montague had a knack for trouble. So when a bag switcheroo at a Scottish airport left her in possession of a stolen medieval diamond, she had to escape being the fall guy—fast. As she scoured Paris and Bucharest for the jewel's rightful owner, could Sylvie protect herself from another grand larceny—the theft of her heart by the wealthy Frenchman behind the heist?

#84 NEVER LOOK BACK by Sheri WhiteFeather

Painter Allie Whirlwind preferred the quiet life. But mysticism was in her blood, and she stirred up a tempest when her painting of Native American spirit warrior Raven literally came to life. Now, with a handsome activist's help, Allie sought the talisman that would release Raven from her great-grandmother's hundred-year-old shape-shifting curse. In the face of evil, Allie could never look back...until she righted her troubled family's wrongs.

SBCNM0206